W9-ALK-937

It All Comes Back to You

ALSO BY FARAH NAZ RISHI

I Hope You Get This Message

It All Comes Back to You

FARAH NAZ RISHI

Quill Tree Books
An Imprint of HarperCollinsPublishers

Quill Tree Books is an imprint of HarperCollins Publishers.

 For information address HarperCollins Children's Books, a division of HarperCollins Publishers, 195 Broadway, New York, NY 10007.
www.epicreads.com

Library of Congress Control Number: 2021937277
ISBN 978-0-06-274148-6

Typography by Torborg Davern
21 22 23 24 25 PC/LSCH 10 9 8 7 6 5 4 3 2 1

First Edition

To Kid Me, who spent most of Sunday school
daydreaming of love stories with Muslim characters . . .
and to God—sorry about that.

It All Comes Back to You

LOADING

[CAMBRIA: THE EVOLUTION EXPANSION PACK]
[ROANA GUILD CHAT ROOM]

Devynius Foxx: totally random but

Devynius Foxx: you ever think about how being on this game, playing together here, in a virtual world

Devynius Foxx: is basically equivalent to being a parallel universe?

Kasia Coribund: lol

Kasia Coribund: and here I thought we were staying away from revealing real-world details about ourselves

Kasia Coribund: but now I know the real-life Foxx is 420 friendly

Kasia Coribund: good to know

Devynius Foxx: ha ha.

Devynius Foxx: no but seriously

Devynius Foxx: In class the other day

Devynius Foxx: we were talking about parallel universes, alternate realities

Devynius Foxx: How scientists are trying to prove the theory of the multiverse and all that BS

Devynius Foxx: I dunno, I was barely paying attention in class tbh

Kasia Coribund: wait wait wait

Kasia Coribund: now I know you're a student!

Devynius Foxx: oh come on

Devynius Foxx: that doesn't tell you anything about me

Devynius Foxx: I could be a third grader for all you know

Kasia Coribund: true

Kasia Coribund: You definitely act like one sometimes

Devynius Foxx: damn Ms. Kasia, that's cold

Devynius Foxx: ANYWAY, it occurred to me

Devynius Foxx: What a waste of time, trying to prove parallel universes

Devynius Foxx: I got one right here, in Cambria

Devynius Foxx: Like, in real life, we lead vastly different lives, right

Devynius Foxx: Wholly separate from each other

Devynius Foxx: In real life, I could be a famous actor

Kasia Coribund: Or a third grader

Devynius Foxx: and in real life, you could be a hot nurse.

Kasia Coribund: or a hot doctor

Devynius Foxx: Two strangers who have no way of ever knowing who the other is, or ever meeting

Devynius Foxx: But here, we've made a parallel universe of our own

Devynius Foxx: Where I'm a level 50 rogue,

Devynius Foxx: who talks to you, a level 50 warrior, almost every night

Devynius Foxx: no frills, no bullshit, no weight of real-world obligations

Devynius Foxx: a place we can just throw open our trench coats and reveal the bare-naked truth of ourselves

Kasia Coribund: . . . okay but why did you have to make us sound like two flashers competing over territory

Devynius Foxx: and that, my dear Kasia

Devynius Foxx: is why I love this parallel universe so damn much.

CHAPTER 1

KIRAN

Friday, June 4

I FIND AMIRA SITTING ALONE at a table, huddled in the back corner of a Joe Coffee on the Upper West Side. Even with her head half-buried in a book—some brick of a fantasy novel—I can tell it's her: the familiar way her oversized glasses perch crookedly on her nose, the way her long, straight dark hair rests perfectly around her heart-shaped face. She's wearing an impeccably stylish floral shirt dress, and there are at least two different guys checking her out, including the barista, who keeps gazing longingly at the back of her head.

"Sorry I'm late!" I splutter, nearly tripping over my feet to reach her. "Dance practice went overtime." And I was up late playing Cambria, my favorite online role-playing game, with my friend Foxx—but I don't tell her that part.

Amira looks up from her book, round doe eyes blinking in surprise behind her glasses. I can only imagine how horrible I look.

I'm in my baggy Greenville School T-shirt and leggings (since it's too hot for my usual sweatpants) and I'm huffing loudly, dripping sweat from every orifice imaginable, made worse by the fact that I'm wearing a backpack.

I don't think Amira even *has* sweat glands.

I move to shove my damp bangs off my face when she leaps off her chair and envelops me in a hug. "I'm glad you made it," she says. I can barely hear her over the upbeat jazz in the background, and the clatter of forks and ceramic mugs. But I don't need to. Her hug says it all.

As much as I'm excited to see her—it's been weeks since we last saw each other—I always dread coming to visit my sister in New York. I hate leaving Philadelphia, for one thing. And the Chinatown Bus, the only method of transportation I can afford without a summer job, is a mobile metal monstrosity designed to torture its passengers for the entire three-hour trip with a two-pronged attack of mediocre leg room and fart inhalation. Then there's the city itself, currently swallowed by a shroud of sticky rain, all stony browns and metal grays and muted disinterest. Sometimes I imagine New York as a person: one who smokes lime-flavored vape, who wears an easy, shit-eating grin even though their coffee-and-sweat-stained shirt is on backward with the tag showing. As soon as the bus pokes its head out from the Lincoln Tunnel, I can feel this threatening energy humming beneath the streets, wild movement around me like erratic breathing. The city looking at me with a dare in its eyes. *I took your sister and there's nothing you can do about it.*

I hug Amira back tightly. Screw you, New York. Just a few more months, and I'll get her back.

"I think this is probably the first time I've *ever* seen you late for something," Amira asks, once we settle at the table. "How was the trip in?"

"Good. Great," I lie. I wave my arms a little to let my armpits breathe and gesture toward the spare cup of coffee in front of me. "This mine?"

Amira grins. "Yep. Latte, one sugar."

I hide my smile with my cup, and sip. It's lukewarm. "The subway system here is *so* bad. Did you know how bad it is?"

She snorts. "Yes. We all know. That's why whenever I have an appointment I have to give myself an extra half hour of travel time. And then another, to account for desi time."

I make a face. "More reason to hate it here, I guess."

I sound bitter, but three years without her hasn't been easy. Of course, I know it's not like she *wanted* to leave me alone with my parents. It was just that her idol, Dr. Margaret Kline—the foremost expert on teen incarceration—happened to teach at Columbia Law, and ran a superinfluential clinic there that worked directly with teens. Amira had always dreamed of working with her, ever since she turned fourteen and decided to become a lawyer. Between the two of us, Amira was always the sweeter, quieter one—but when Amira decides to do something, there's no stopping her. You're better off trying to wrangle gale-force winds with your bare fists.

But it's not like she could've known what would happen after she left.

Just a few more months.

Amira glances at the window, distracted.

"You okay?" I ask.

"Oh. Yeah, I'm fine," she says, waving dismissively. "So? Did you get what I asked?"

I sigh and pull out my phone. A couple of sweaty finger taps. I pull up a photo my best friend, Asher Santos, took of me and Dad, about a week ago, on graduation day. Dad is in a wrinkled button-down shirt that's two sizes too big, a faint hint of a smile tugging at his mouth. I'm standing next to him, grinning, and my wavy brown bobbed hair has the reddish hue of henna. Amira couldn't come because she was finishing her law school exams.

I pass her the screen. I can see the reflection on her glasses.

"So let me get this straight," she says, after a beat. "You wore pajamas at your own graduation?"

"They're not pajamas!" I reply, indignant. "They're *joggers*. They're *trendy*."

"I hate to break it to you, but I'm pretty sure those are pj's," she says, shaking her head solemnly. "Where did you get them?"

"Found them. In Mom's closet."

"Oh no, Kiran. Those are literally pajamas. Mom got them at Gap, like, two years ago." Before I can argue, she hands me back my phone, where the picture remains open. My black graduation robes do little to hide the offending outfit, and I realize she might just be right: even with the floral, silky top, my pants do look an awful lot like pajamas.

". . . Oh."

I feel my cheeks warm as I try not to think about the implications of the fact that I walked across the stage in front of the entire graduating class to receive my diploma in my mom's old pajamas. How did Dad not notice? Then again, he has virtually zero observation skills and probably doesn't even realize I wear the same sweatpants three times a week.

This is *precisely* why I need Amira to move back home.

Just as I'm yelling at Dad in my head, Amira laughs, a sound like the jangle of a tiny bell, or soft morning birdcalls before dawn. It's the sound of better times. Like when she lived at home with me and Dad in Philly, before she left for law school. Or before Mom died.

Sometimes when Dad isn't home, I stand in Mom's closet and take in the familiar scent of antibacterial Softsoap and jasmine oil, just to *remember*, just to reassure myself I still *can* remember. With Dad working his clinical research job all the time—trying *not* to remember, probably—and Amira living in New York, the silence gets unbearable, and I get scared that my memories of Mom will just keep scattering, beyond recognition, until the day they fade away for good.

But when Amira laughs, I swear I can feel a warmth between my broken memories, a sort of pulling-back-together.

"Well, speaking of you saving me from myself . . ." I shove my phone into my backpack, pull out a thick red folder, and drop it on the table with a dramatic splat. This folder represents the one thing I've been waiting for, the one thing I'd been holding on to for the past three years: the day Amira says goodbye to New York and we get our own place in Philly, together. The folder is stuffed with packets of paper. Some are wish lists of different household items I thought would be useful, like a Crock-Pot or a weighted blanket. Others are lists of our old favorite hangouts and restaurants that I know Amira misses, like Saad's Halal Restaurant and NuNu Sushi.

I hand her the first section, the fattest one by far. It's tabbed with my favorite cat stickers.

"What's this?" Amira begins flipping through the pages.

"Apartments," I reply proudly. "I've put them in order from closest to farthest from my campus. The ones with the orange tabby paw sticker are *slightly* above budget, but I think we can make it work if I get a part-time job." I could live in one of the dorms at Penn—staying on campus freshman year is encouraged, not required—but I'd far prefer living with my sister, while still being close enough to visit Dad at home.

"Wow, Kiran. This is . . ."

I beam.

"A lot." She puts down the packet on the table. Condensation from her iced coffee begins to soak through the pages.

"Well, yeah," I reply, deflating a little. "We gotta have options, right?"

"Of course, but . . . it's just *really* early to start looking. We still have three months before you start school."

"Less than three months, actually." Eleven weeks, to be more precise.

"Right . . . ," Amira says slowly, "but a lot can happen from now till then."

"Sure, but it's still good to start looking into it. . . . Right?"

She bites her lip. Her eyes slide to the window again. I don't see anything beyond a couple of passersby walking their dog against the darkening sky, but she's focused, like she can see something I can't.

"What is it?" I ask her.

Amira quickly throws on a stiff, plastic smile. "Nothing."

I narrow my eyes. "Then why do you look like you have something to tell me?"

"What? No." She shakes her head. "Just tired. Exams were killer."

I'm pretty sure that in addition to a lack of sweat glands, Amira also lacks the ability to lie. The girl is an open book with a worn, bent spine that won't even let it close properly. "*Amira?*" I press.

"I promise, there's nothing." She stirs her iced coffee again, though it's mostly just ice now. "But I am really happy. Happy to see you, happy to be done with school. Fulfilled, I guess."

"Okay . . ." I trail off, watching her.

"I really appreciate you doing all this research, though," she continues. "It's sweet and thoughtful. You're always so sweet and—"

"Stop," I say, slapping my hand on the folder. "Seriously, just tell me what's going on."

She takes a deep breath, then another. "Imetsomeone," she finally blurts, as if it's all one word.

"Wait, what?" I lean forward to better hear over the background noise.

"I met someone!" she says, louder. Almost too loud, because now the barista is looking forlorn.

"What the hell do you mean, you met someone?"

She glances at the window again. Then she looks right at me.

Her eyes are watering.

And it's not just that. Everything about her is coated in a sickly syrup-sweet happiness that's stickier than the humidity. Flushed cheeks. Warm glow. All the telltale signs of a person in love. Which means she's not messing with me.

Oh God.

My sister has actually met someone.

I blink. Swallow. "Wait. When? *How?*" The connection between my brain and my body has short-circuited, and I can feel the frantic pump of blood vessels coursing through me, can feel every cell of my being vibrating with confusion.

"I've been seeing him for the past three months. You know how I did my final paper with Professor Kline, at her clinic?" I nod. "I met him through the clinic. He's trying to start this nonprofit to help kids released from juvenile detention get life skills. It's amazing. The work he's doing"—she blows a puff of air—"*he's* amazing. I interviewed him for my paper, and then we kind of got to working together, and . . . I really, really like him, Kiran."

Amira closes her eyes, sinks deeper into her chair, and I shit you not, she *hugs* herself. Wraps her arms around herself like a lovesick Disney princess. I've never seen her like this before and it's like I can barely recognize her.

"God, it's the first time I've said it aloud, but I *really* like him. Really, really, really, really—"

"Okay, okay, I get it. But three *months*? Why haven't you said anything?"

"It was never a formal thing"—she starts blushing—"I mean, not *that* informal, either, until . . . recently. It just kind of happened. Plus, if I'd told you, you'd have told Dad. And you know what he's like—we can't talk about boys unless it's serious."

I bite my lip. It's true; dating in the casual sense is still frowned upon in many Muslim communities, and it's not something you can openly talk about unless you've practically made a formal Jane Austen–style declaration that you're in pursuit of a life partner.

It's partially why I never told Amira about my first and only boyfriend, either. But still.

My skull's buzzing like the inside of a hive. Amira meeting someone is . . . big. She's always been so focused on school and her career. I don't think she's ever even had the *time* to fall in love before, until now.

Silence settles in the space between us, and there's a sickening weight in my stomach that wasn't there before. In a matter of minutes, something has irrevocably changed between us—had already changed, without me even knowing. A change in the status quo where I might not be the first person Amira calls to rant about stuff at the office or update me on the latest books she's read. Or tell me her secrets.

Slowly, Amira pulls herself up. "Nothing is set in stone yet, but . . . he might be moving to California soon, so we're still trying to figure things out for us. There's an organization there that works with legal nonprofits and they're going to help fund him, get him up and running. Again, nothing's set. We just need to discuss our future a bit more. Make plans, maybe."

My throat aches too much to say anything.

"I know this all sounds like it's moving absurdly fast, but honestly, Kiran, I've never been more sure about anything in my life. And trust me, I've thought about it a lot. He was there for me.

When Mom died. The work we did gave me something to hold on to. *He* gave me something to hold on to. . . . Kiran?"

I'm squeezing the edge of my chair, digging my fingernails into the wood. The sound is gone: the jazz music, the clattering, the hiss of the espresso machine. Everything is just a dull ache in my ears as the room spins around me.

California? What about job searching in Philly? What about our new apartment, the Crock-Pot, the late nights, the macarons? What about visiting Mom's grave together and crying together to make up for the grieving I couldn't do because I was waiting for her? What about Dad, and living together as a family again, like Mom wanted—does that mean nothing to her?

What about me?

Touché, New York. You've bested me yet again, and now your buddy California's come to beat me with a flip-flop while I'm down.

I look past Amira, trying to focus on anything but her sitting across from me, looking at me rosy-cheeked and in love and worst of all, *conflicted*, waiting for me to end her life with a word. My eyes settle on a single light bulb on the iron chandelier hanging from the ceiling, and I stare until it burns.

"I'm happy for you," I eventually say, my voice grating through my throat. "I really am."

Amira lets out something that sounds like a sob. "Really? Because I'd love for you two to meet. I want you two to meet. I know you'll love him, too. Nothing is final unless you approve. I swear. And if I move to Cali—*if* I do—I'll visit you all the time, I promise."

She's talking a mile a minute—about us all meeting next

weekend, about not telling Dad yet, I think. I'm numb.

"So, who's the lucky guy?" I ask finally, shoving the folder back in my backpack. The papers crumple at the bottom.

"Faisal," she replies. "Faisal Malik."

For a moment, time stills.

"He has a little brother, too," Amira continues. "About your age, actually." A slow, conspiratorial grin breaks across her face. "His name's Deen."

I short-circuit. Shatter. And inwardly, I scream, and the whole world screams with me.

Because I know *exactly* who Deen Malik is.

Of *course* I know who he is.

As much as I want to—and trust me, I really do—I could *never* forget the name of my one and only ex.

THREE YEARS AGO

[UNKNOWN NUMBER]: hey

[UNKNOWN NUMBER]: are you going to the Eid dinner on Sunday?

KIRAN: ?? Who's this?

[UNKNOWN NUMBER]: oh sorry

[UNKNOWN NUMBER]: it's Deen Malik

[UNKNOWN NUMBER]: from Sunday school?

[UNKNOWN NUMBER]: I got your number from the six flags field trip a month ago

KIRAN: oh yeah lol

KIRAN: best Sunday school field trip e v e r

[UNKNOWN NUMBER]: unless you're me

[UNKNOWN NUMBER]: and you get lost in the arcade for like an hour

KIRAN: lolllll
KIRAN: "lost"
KIRAN: we all know that was your excuse to ditch us and play Mario Kart

[UNKNOWN NUMBER]: what can I say, I know how to live

KIRAN: an inspiration to us all
KIRAN: anyway yeah, I'm going
KIRAN: to the Eid dinner, I mean

[UNKNOWN NUMBER]: cool
[UNKNOWN NUMBER]: just wanted to know if there'd be anyone I knew there

KIRAN: are none of the other guys coming?
KIRAN: Imran? Hassan?

[UNKNOWN NUMBER]: Imran's visiting fam in Bangladesh
[UNKNOWN NUMBER]: and Hassan's celebrating Eid in Virginia
[UNKNOWN NUMBER]: I'm still kinda new here too, so
[UNKNOWN NUMBER]: don't really know a lot of people

KIRAN: ah
KIRAN: makes sense

[UNKNOWN NUMBER]: yeah

KIRAN: well fear not

KIRAN: I'll take you under my wing

KIRAN: unfortunately for us, the masjid is woefully unequipped for video games

[UNKNOWN NUMBER]: shocking

[UNKNOWN NUMBER]: and slightly blasphemous?

KIRAN: lollll

[UNKNOWN NUMBER]: but yeah, cool

[UNKNOWN NUMBER]: I'll see you there, then

KIRAN: yeah

KIRAN: See you there.

CHAPTER 2

DEEN

Friday, June 4

"DEEN, WHY DID YOU DECIDE to take summer classes?"

Professor Pryce stares at me from behind his desk. It's just the two of us in the classroom, Intro to Poli-Sci having ended five minutes ago. He's leaning back with his hands behind his neck, the posture of choice for all professors who seek to give off an air of casualness and calm—the whole *I'm not like other teachers because I'm like a friend* shtick. Except today, he's wearing a serious expression behind his perfectly round wire-framed spectacles.

"Deen?"

The only people I've seen pull off those kinds of glasses are Korean pop stars. Does Professor Pryce think he's more attractive than a Korean pop star? The nerve. He does have a nice jaw, admittedly. He's pretty young for a professor, too, but he's already got the beginnings of salt-and-pepper hair at his temples, which I'm pretty sure is one of those weird things that everyone agrees is a sign of Hotness. Like dimples or rolled-up sleeves.

Whatever. I fold up my sleeves to expose my brown, sinewy forearms. I'm not feeling insecure or anything. It's just warm in here.

"Deen?"

I sigh. "Professor—hey, can I call you Jeff?"

"No."

"Wait, didn't you say on the first day of class that we could call you Jeff?"

Professor Pryce's face remains stony.

"Got it." I clear my throat. "Not sure how it matters, but I'm taking summer classes because I wanted to get ahead. Get a head start on sophomore year. This is NYU, man—I mean, sir. So like any student who has thrown an exorbitant amount of cash into securing the privilege of entering our nation's wonderful capitalistic system of higher education, I wanted to take advantage of the incredible and diverse course load that's offered here."

I flash a smile. It's not entirely a lie as much as it is a conveniently flexible stretch of the truth. Taking summer classes was the easiest way for me to avoid being at home this summer. Living on campus, I told my parents, would ensure I'd stay focused on school. I could concentrate better here. And my parents bought it hook, line, and sinker. But who am I kidding? At the end of the day, they don't give a damn what I do, as long as I don't "*totally screw up like Faisal.*"

If only they knew.

"Uh-huh. Right." Professor Pryce folds his arms—arms that are definitely not beefier than mine—across his chest. "Well, it's my experience that students who claim they want to get ahead usually come to class on time."

"But consider this: I was in the library, studying before class, and lost track of time."

I had *actually* been in the rec room at Brittany Hall, playing wingman for Vinny, with his crush, Amy, and some hot junior bio major named Rachel, or Raquel, who was kicking my ass in pool. But damn. The way she was bending over the pool table, I'd let her kick my ass any day. And before that, I pulled an all-nighter on this MMO game called Cambria, which I've gotten pretty hooked on. But I keep that on the down low.

"I'm finding that a little tough to believe. I just don't get it, Deen. You know, I spoke with Professor Foster earlier. I think you might remember her from your writing seminar last semester? We got to talking, and funnily enough, you came up."

Uh-oh.

"She said you were a model student in her class. Thoughtful, mature, *on time*. I had to ask her if we were talking about the same Deen Malik."

Damn.

"That Deen Malik, *if* he were ever late, would slip quietly into his seat and actually pay attention to the lecture."

"That's what I did."

"You barged in through the doors, addressed me with 'sup,' and sat down in the center of the front row, knocking over another student's stack of books in the process. You then proceeded to take a nap, as if I couldn't see you *right there*. Deen, I don't know what to say at this point."

I sigh again.

College was supposed to be the place I'd *finally* be treated as an adult, in the sense that people would leave me the hell alone. Guess even here, though, I'm not fully free. "Just spitballing here," I say, "but you could always say nothing?"

Professor Pryce pinches the bridge of his nose. His perfectly round glasses now sit crookedly on his face. "Please take this seriously. I know you like to think of yourself as a funny guy, but I also know you're intelligent. You wouldn't be here if you weren't. Professor Foster showed me some of the papers you wrote. You're clearly better than this. If you just *applied* yourself, you could actually go places. So what I want to know is: What's the issue here? What's going on?"

Fuck if I know, bud.

Suddenly, my phone vibrates in the back pocket of my jeans. There's a long, awkward silence between us, a game of silent chicken. Finally, Professor Pryce lets out an exasperated breath. "Just answer it."

"That timing, huh?" I say, yanking out my phone.

I'm half hoping it's my friend Kasia, from Cambria—when we're not playing the game together, we talk on our guild's chat room on Discord.

But it's Vinny, shooting me an obnoxious amount of texts.

Yoooo D-MONEY get back here!

Raquel keeps asking for you. She's into you, fool!!!!

A REAL chick, not some online one you play with on that lame ass game

I can *hear* his thick Long Island accent, and stifle a laugh. Vinny means well, even if he's not-too-subtly shit-talking about Kasia.

"Sorry about that." I clear my throat and shove the phone back in my pocket. "You were saying?"

Professor Pryce grimaces. "Look, I just need you to understand that coming to class late, especially in this fashion, is a distraction to the other students. I've overlooked your tardiness several times this summer already. You know what they say about three strikes?"

"I don't watch basketball much, Profes—" My phone vibrates again. There's a vein popping out of Professor Pryce's left temple.

"Wow, thought I turned that off." I sheepishly pull out my phone once more. But when I see the name on the screen, I can feel the smile slip off my face.

Faisal.

My older brother.

I open the text, trying to ignore the painful gnawing in my stomach.

Professor Pryce must see the expression change on my face, because his knife-point glare softens. "Is everything all right?"

I don't answer.

Hey

You free soon?

I need to talk to you

The pit in my stomach has grown to a critical mass.

I hate when people say things like that. Nothing good ever comes from someone saying, "I need to talk to you." It's even worse when it's through text. I do not enjoy being at the mercy of my own impatience. Even the most innocent things sound ominous. Vinny's the worst at it—I think it has something to do with the fact that he's a music major, which means his understanding of *actual* language is nonexistent. Sometimes he'll text something like, Deen. Emergency. Then make me wait five minutes, writhing with a hundred violent imaginings of the worst possible scenarios, before saying, Never mind. Got the last slice of pizza at the dining hall. Almost didn't make it. Or False alarm. Girl gave me her number but it was just to get my notes! Life amirite, lmao. If I ever commit homicide, it will be because of him.

When Faisal, my brother, texts, it actually means something. He doesn't text very often, maybe once every couple of weeks. And I think even he knows something's a little . . . broken between us. So every message, every hesitant attempt to reach out, in a way, is a question for me: Do I reach back?

This time, the answer is yes. Faisal isn't the kind of person to say *we need to talk* out of the blue like that, unless . . .

What's up? I type back. My thumbs hover over the screen, and I can't tell if they're trembling or if I'm just dizzy from the heat and/or Professor Pryce's glower.

Three little gray dots pulse on my screen, and I wait for what feels like forever.

Then:

Would just be better to talk in person.

It's nothing bad, promise :)

But I don't believe him. Not for a second.

Meet you at M&D's tonight? I type back. *M&D* is short for Mom and Dad's. We've never called it home. It's never really felt like home. We weren't even allowed to decorate our own rooms growing up, which explains why mine looks straight out of an Italian summer villa in *Architectural Digest* instead of a nineteen-year-old guy's bedroom. To say my parents are controlling is putting it lightly.

Yes :), he responds. I don't put my phone away, instead clutching it tightly in my sweaty palm.

Professor Pryce is still looking at me. I clear my throat. "I have to run. Family emergency, if you can believe it. Rain check on the, uh, pep talk?"

"This isn't a pep—" Professor Pryce stops himself. His mouth hardens in a thin line, a look of defeat. "*Fine.* We'll finish this conversation next week after class. Where you will show up on time and do the reading and come prepared with the intelligent observations you keep buried within that head."

"Sounds like a plan!" I say, already halfway out the door.

I practically sprint to the train station.

A few hours later, I'm in Short Hills, New Jersey, and the lights are off at M&D's. It's six, and while most families are probably happily preparing dinner together, my parents are still at work at the nearby Rotterdam Hospital. Can't even remember the last time the four of us were in one room together. It's better that way.

The house is imposingly big, to the point of being threateningly tall and intimidatingly girthy. It's a gray stone Tudor—I know this because Mom wouldn't shut up about it when we first moved in—with blue-and-white timber frames and arched windows. It's cradled by a family of enormous oak trees that Faisal and I had to tearfully beg our parents not to chop down. We thought they'd be perfect for the epic tree house of our dreams. But in the end, Mom and Dad got the biggest tree removed, claiming it had grown too close to the house.

I clumsily jangle my key through the front door, tense with dread, and find a light peeking from the basement. That's where I go.

Faisal's been living in our parents' basement since he got back from college, but it's a walk-out, so he has some privacy, and he has a really sick office setup down there. Still, though. I hate that he still lives here. I hate that he has no choice. I don't know how he can stand being under the same roof as our parents.

I knock on the door to the office.

"Come on in," I hear him say.

As soon as I open the door, I'm greeted by a bear hug so huge that I'm lifted off the ground a couple of inches.

"Deen," my brother says, as if it's the most wonderful word in the world. "Deen, Deen, Deen."

"Hi, Faisal, you're cracking my rib cage," I choke out, and he finally lets me go.

"Sorry, sorry." Faisal grins as I fix my hair, showing off his several-thousand-dollar smile. The kid had godawful teeth when we were little, and it was a favor to us all when he got braces. He's also now sporting the beginnings of a beard, and though he was once the scrawniest excuse for a noodle growing up, not getting into law school had the unexpected side effect of doing wonders for his physique—these days, he's built like a tank.

He takes a seat at his desk by the window and spins to face me. Books and legal textbooks cover every spare inch of the desk's surface, creating a mountain range of paper around his open laptop where he has a website open: AFFEY: A Future for Exonerated Youth. It's Faisal's nonprofit, or at least, he hopes it will be. It's been his dream for the past two years. A dream quietly growing under our parents' oblivious feet.

I remain standing. "So? What was the emergency?"

"No emergency!" he replies. "Just . . ."

"What?" I try to keep my voice level, but I'm nervous.

Faisal leans forward, resting his elbows on his knees.

"You remember Amira, right?" he asks.

"Hell yeah."

I don't know much about her, but Amira is Faisal's business partner, of sorts. Or maybe *consultant* would be the better word. But she's also way, way more than that.

A couple of years ago, when every law school on Faisal's list rejected him, he became a shell of who he once was. It sounds overdramatic and it's definitely ridiculous, but for the desi families who can afford it, not going to grad school is an automatic minus fifty points on the report card of Life. And Faisal felt it; every ambition he'd ever had died that day. I remember when he got that final rejection letter and sat at the breakfast table, trying to eat a bowl of cornflakes, his movements mechanical, his eyes painfully focused on the wall in front of him. As if he was tensing his eyeballs to force the tears back.

It broke him.

We all feared this would happen. Law schools, ironically, aren't eager to accept students with hands-on experience of the criminal justice system, even though our parents paid plenty, despite Faisal's protests, for their lawyers to get his Class A-1 felony lowered to a misdemeanor.

That didn't matter. Nor did it matter that he was now forever doomed to be on our parents' shit list. For Faisal, getting that last rejection meant nothing mattered anymore.

Until Amira.

Faisal takes a long draw of water, and his cheeks bulge like a chipmunk. He can't stop smiling, the idiot. He always smiles like this whenever Amira comes up.

"I think . . . ," he says slowly, "I think I'm going to ask her to marry me. Inshallah."

"Holy shit. For real? For real?" I can feel my voice rising, but I can't help it.

"Yeah." And honest to God, he looks shy about it. He runs his hand through his hair and won't look at me, and he's got this goofy grin on his face I've never seen before.

"Shit, I—" I put my hand on his back, give him an awkward half hug. "I'm happy for you, big guy. Really. That's so good to hear."

Honestly, this is the greatest thing that could have happened to him. Ever since Faisal met Amira, he's had a fire in him I haven't seen in years. It wasn't that love healed him, or any cliché shit like that—Faisal had already started getting better on his own by then, despite our parents' constant quips. He'd even started seeing a therapist, which was good because M&D, in typical M&D fashion, were adamant that we never talk about what happened, ever, to anyone. They made us swear on our graves.

When Amira showed up, it was like after a thousand nights of fitful sleep, Faisal remembered how to *dream* again. Looked forward to dreaming again. He slept better, in every sense of the word—and when I first saw him without the giant purple bags beneath his eyes that I'd gotten used to, I almost didn't recognize him.

I can't imagine loving anyone so much. It's almost terrifying how much it's changed things for him.

Faisal lets out a breath. "So you're cool with it? One hundred percent?"

"You deserve the best." And I mean it. Faisal is honestly the best person I know. "Always have."

He grins again. "And she is the best. I can't wait for you to meet her."

"Man, my sister-in-law. She's going to be my *sister-in-law*."

"Inshallah. There's a lot of stuff we need to figure out—and I really want you to meet her—but . . . yeah. Yeah. Hopefully."

My mind's a whirlpool, but all I know is, I'm happy. Genuinely happy for him.

And relieved.

Like maybe, just maybe, things are finally looking up for him. If he's found a partner, someone he wants to start over with, that would give Faisal his own life back, in a way I never could. And maybe I could finally let go of a little guilt.

Especially since it's my fault he didn't get into law school.

It's quiet for a moment, until an alarm goes off on Faisal's phone.

"Prayer time," he mutters.

I stiffen, suddenly feeling awkward. Faisal's been a damn good Muslim for the past couple of years. A damn good everything, really. Whereas I . . .

"You wanna pray together?" he asks hesitantly. "We should hang out, after. Would love to celebrate with you. Play something, for old times' sake?" He nods over at a TV in the corner, where our old PlayStation sits, collecting dust.

I hate that he almost sounds hopeful. Like he's the one rehabilitating *me* now. Stepping on eggshells around *me*.

"I would, but . . ." I run my hand down the back of my stiff neck. "I gotta get back to campus, you know? Early class in the morning."

"Oh." Faisal's face dims, so briefly that I know he's trying his best not to show his disappointment. "Of course, yeah, sure."

I clench my fists. I'm sure he knows I'm lying—that I can't stand it here, can't stand seeing him stuck here in the basement like a shameful secret. Sometimes, I wish Faisal would actually say what he's thinking. But he's never once expressed disappointment, never once *not* forgiven me. I don't deserve kindness from him.

Sometimes, I wish he knew I didn't deserve anything.

I reach for the doorknob, but suddenly Faisal stands, stares at something on his desk like he's thinking hard about something.

"Hey, Deen?" he says finally, hesitating. He looks at me.

I swallow. "Yeah?"

"I know . . . things have been hard. For you. Because of me."

I grip the doorknob tight.

"But I want you to know that I'm okay now. I'm good. For the first time in a very long time, I feel really good. So . . ."

"I know," I reply. "You're going to be amazing. We share the same genes, after all."

Faisal laughs a bit.

And then there's silence again. My feet feel like lead, and there's a weight on my tongue, words I want to say. But I'm not even sure what they are.

I drum my knuckles on the doorway.

"Speaking of same genes, Amira has a sister." Faisal looks at me meaningfully. "I haven't met her yet, but I hear she's pretty great."

"Oh yeah?"

"Her name's Kiran, I think. She'll probably be there when you meet Amira."

Kiran.

Kiran.

"Kiran Noorani?" The name spills from my mouth.

Faisal's thick eyebrows furrow. "Yeah, exactly."

I put my hand on my stomach like I'm going to explode. I lean over, try to hold it in. But I can't.

Of *all* the people in the world. God must be punishing me.

"Deen?"

That's all it takes for me to come apart. I laugh so hard my entire body quakes and I have a coughing fit and Faisal's rubbing my back and asking what's wrong, which only makes me laugh harder.

But Kiran always could make me laugh harder than anyone.

LOADING

[CAMBRIA: THE EVOLUTION EXPANSION PACK]
[ROANA GUILD CHAT ROOM]

Kasia Coribund: Do you ever get the sense that the world is conspiring against you?

Kasia Coribund: Like no matter what you do or how good you try to be

Kasia Coribund: Bad things are going to happen?

Kasia Coribund: Not really sure where I'm going with this, but lately, I've been feeling kind of helpless

Kasia Coribund: And it doesn't help that every time I see something in the news, I get an ulcer

Devynius Foxx: Hooo boy

Devynius Foxx: Let me tell you

Devynius Foxx: I feel that every goddamn day.

Devynius Foxx: And I love it when people are like "just stay positive!"

Devynius Foxx: "good thoughts attract good things!"

Devynius Foxx: Okay NANCY, the problem is, things WERE good and now they're not—for no damn reason.

Kasia Coribund: Exactly.

Kasia Coribund: And it's not like I can do much about it

Kasia Coribund: I'm still just . . . a kid, you know?

Devynius Foxx: Err . . .

Devynius Foxx: How young we talkin?

Devynius Foxx: Asking for a friend

Kasia Coribund: Old enough, you ass

Devynius Foxx: In all seriousness though,

Devynius Foxx: I wish there was something I could say.

Devynius Foxx: I don't have any answers since I'm basically in the same boat, but that's just it:

Devynius Foxx: We're in the same boat.

Devynius Foxx: And at the end of the day, that kind of makes me feel better.

Devynius Foxx: /shrug

Kasia Coribund: Heh.

Kasia Coribund: Honestly

Kasia Coribund: That kind of makes me feel better, too.

CHAPTER 3
KIRAN

Friday, June 4

PLEASE TELL ME WHY I shouldn't be freaking out rn, I text Asher for what must be the hundredth time tonight, and it's not yet midnight. I just got home; the rain followed me from New York to Philly, and now crystalline rivulets dance across our windowpanes. From somewhere in the house, a clock ticks like an erratic heartbeat.

Dad's asleep across the hall, so I tread carefully until I'm safe in my bedroom. Thanks to Morning Kiran, it's a mess. My computer's still on from when I played Cambria for half the night, and I nearly trip over the dance bag that's puking the sweaty dance clothes all over my floor. I've been taking dance classes since I was twelve. It's why the only art I've got on my wall is this print of a Fabio Fabbi painting, a 100 percent offensive, Orientalist piece of work of an inappropriately pale woman dancing in a harem—a spontaneous gift from Dad, actually. *Note to self: get Dad a copy of*

Orientalism *by Edward Said for his birthday.* But it's totally ironic and somehow makes me feel powerful.

Mom was a dancer, too. I almost quit after the funeral; it was Asher who convinced me to keep going. *You actually have a way to honor her memory*, he said. *You'd be stupid to stop it.*

I shove my clothes into the hamper and try not to obsessively check my phone for Asher's reply.

Asher was our next-door neighbor growing up, and even though he's nearly four years older than me, we'd hang out a lot after school, mostly to play video games or hang by the waterfront and stuff our faces with homemade ensaymadas from his mom. He's always been a big brother to me, which is why when he moved to New York for college, two years after Amira, we had our first ever fight. It felt like a blow that he'd do the exact thing that would hurt me most.

I think secretly Mom hoped one of us would end up with him. That's not to say I haven't *thought* about us being something . . . more. It's just that whenever I do, my stomach threatens to jump ship and flee. And I have reason to believe Asher feels the very same way. Exhibit A: I'm 99 percent sure he used to have a crush on Amira.

Because Amira is allowed to have a life? Asher responds, finally. Anyway, are you even sure this is the same Faisal Malik?

I call him.

"Listen, smart-ass," I say as soon as he picks up, "she's had her own life for the past three years. And yes, I'm sure—how many Faisal Maliks do you think there are?"

There's a rustling on the other line, like Asher has his phone on a pillow. "The nerve of her." His voice is slightly muffled. "Please tell me everything, now that it's one a.m. and I have an eight a.m. lecture tomorrow. Can't you talk to your online boyfriend about this?"

"Foxx is *not* my boyfriend. And if I could, I would. We don't talk about real-world stuff." At first, it was a guild rule; the two leaders of our guild, Nilina and Solen (who I'm pretty sure are a married couple in real life), claimed that talking about reality ruined the immersion of the game. Cambria is a role-playing game, after all, and it feels wrong talking about magic and taming wyverns and then how your instant mac and cheese exploded in the microwave and now you have to go clean it up before your dad comes back. Not based on a true story.

But Foxx and I found that we preferred not getting bogged down in real-world details anyway. It makes Cambria feel like our own special place, a parallel universe where we can be ourselves. Learning about who we are in real life could ruin the magic.

"How convenient," says Asher.

I pace angrily around my bed. "I don't understand how this could have happened. Of all the people in the entire world she could have fallen in love with. This is injustice. This is a conspiracy."

"Yes. A conspiracy."

"That's what I said. Ugh, she should have told me about Faisal sooner. Then all of this could have been avoided."

"Not to sound like a smart-ass again, but you didn't exactly tell Amira about Deen, either."

"See, *that* doesn't make you sound like a smart-ass. That makes you sound like an ass," I retort. "Deen and I were a *secret*. We made a pact."

Asher sighs. "You and your pacts."

Deen and I started dating, if you can even call it that, when my mom first started getting sick. I kept it a secret back then because I didn't want to add to the stress my family was going through.

"God, what if they actually get married? That would make Deen my brother-in-law. Do you realize how messed up that is? My ex. Would be. *My brother-in-law.*"

Asher yawns. "Okay, so now that we've established that this is technically your fault—"

"Not my fault."

"Should we be worried about this Faisal guy?"

"I'm not really sure." I feel my chest tighten. I never told anyone about Deen—except Asher—because talking about it feels too much like acknowledging that it was a real thing that happened. I prefer to think of it as a particularly lucid nightmare, like the kind you get after scarfing down an entire box of frosted animal crackers and reading Archive of Our Own until you pass out on the couch. Not based on a true story.

I exhale. "I've never actually met Faisal. But I've heard about him. Through Deen, a little. And youth group."

"Really? *Youth group?*"

"Yeah, I know. It's lame. Anyway, Faisal was a lot older than us, so he was never there. Actually—wait, now I remember. Faisal Malik was *never* there, for *anything*. Not just youth group but *any* of the masjid events or dinner parties. It was like he didn't *exist*.

Everyone thought the Maliks only had one son until that aunty who must have known them from somewhere else blabbed about Faisal. So naturally, there were rumors, a lot of rumors—that their mysterious eldest son was cut off from the family; that he'd gotten in with a bad crowd. Even Deen wouldn't talk about him. That's weird, right? Tell me that's weird."

Asher is quiet for a beat. "Do you think Amira knows about the rumors?"

"Not sure." Amira was in college at the time, so she wasn't going to our masjid often, and it's not like I had reason to mention the rumors before. Do I tell her? God, how would that conversation even go, anyway? I don't think she'd care, though—she's better than me in that way. *Totally innocent until proven guilty!* she'd say.

"Well, if this were, say, three years ago, I'd say it's pretty freaking weird. But he *is* here, now, and obviously not in a bad crowd if Amira's in love with him, right?"

"She's never been in love before, so how would she know? You know how she is. Freaking Disney princess in a pantsuit."

"Have *you* been in love before?"

I hate that Deen runs through my mind. Deen and his easy, dimpled smile, glowing beneath a ginkgo tree. Deen and his late-night texts and promises of more to come.

Deen. The more I think about seeing him again, the more attractive throwing myself out the window seems.

"I thought I was. Once." *When I was fifteen and ridiculous.* "Let's just say I know what happens when you fall too fast."

I can practically feel Asher rolling his eyes on the other end of the line. "I think Amira probably knows what she's doing." His voice lowers. "I think you have trust issues, Kiran."

"Fine, maybe, but so does Amira—she's *too* trusting! Changing her entire life plans for this guy she's known for a couple months—it's naive."

"I'm not saying I don't agree they're moving unnecessarily fast. But wanting to see the best in people doesn't make her naive. Or stupid." The line crackles, like the phone is pressing against his bedsheets. "Good news is, you know Amira isn't going to marry him if you're against it. Just tell her the truth."

I lie down on my bed. I'm suddenly starting to feel tired.

"I *can't* tell her I'm against it," I say softly. "I can't be that person who stops my sister from marrying someone just because of something that happened to me three years ago. Even if there are shady rumors. Even if Faisal's younger brother is the devil."

"Jesus. How bad was he?"

"Bad, Ash. Would I be freaking out like this if it wasn't bad?"

"Well . . ."

"ASHER."

Asher laughs softly, and I sink deeper into the blue plush of my comforter. The patter of rain on the windowpanes feels soothing now, like fingers on my scalp. Even though talking about Deen hurts, it's almost a good hurt, like the easing and unraveling of a tight knot. I wanted to tell Amira about Deen years ago. There were so many things I wanted to ask her. She's never dated anyone till now—she was always so focused on school that I don't think she even had the time—but she always knew the right words to say.

Before I could tell Amira, though, Mom started to get sicker.

I clench the comforter beneath me. "All you need to know," I say, "is that three years ago, Deen just appeared, like a freaking magical fairy prince. I liked him a lot. And I think he liked me, too. He was the only person I could really open up to then."

I grit my teeth. The memories are still fresh, too fresh. "But one day, he became an absolute monster. A pig. A, a total—"

"Dick?" Asher offers.

"Yes! A total and complete dick! For *no* reason. And then to top it off, a couple weeks after going full jerk mode, he and his family moved away. He didn't even say goodbye. Never heard from him again, even after Mom died. And that, my friend, is the story of my first love."

"Woof."

I roll over on my bed. "Amira wants me to meet Faisal next weekend. But what if Deen's there, too? What am I supposed to say to him?"

"Kiran, it was three years ago. Obviously a lot has changed since then. You're older, wiser. You can be mature about this. It's for your sister. Let her be happy."

Let her be happy.

That's all well and good, I think, but what if she doesn't know what makes her happy? What if this is all just a dangerous coping mechanism for Mom's death? I don't think I've ever seen Amira really . . . get angry. Or upset. She bottles things up and tosses her feelings out to sea. I think I've seen her cry *once*, when Mom died, and the only reason I know that is because I found her hiding in

Mom's closet the morning we had to bury her. Alone. I wonder if that's why Mom told me to make sure we always stuck together.

On one of Mom's final nights in the hospital—I'd offered to take the night shift to let Amira and Dad get some sleep—I gave her a legal pad and pen so she could write. Mom's disease had made it hard for her to talk, but she had enough strength in her arm to write, at least.

"Amira and Dad will be here first thing in the morning, okay? We'll talk about next steps together," I'd said.

Slowly, Mom began to write: *That's the only thing that's getting me through this, Kiran. Knowing you're all together.*

Promise me you'll look after them.

Thinking about it, my chest contracts.

"Anyway, I gotta go," says Asher, yawning. "If you need a healthy distraction, there's always your online *boyfriend*."

I sit down at my computer and pop open the launcher for Cambria and the guild channel on Discord. But Devynius Foxx isn't online right now.

My heart sinks. "He's not around."

"Ah, right, busy doing *mysterious* things that you don't know about because you refuse to tell each other any real-life information."

"We don't need to know any real info. Foxx is one of my dearest friends, and we know each other's *hearts*." And as corny as it sounds, I'm not exactly kidding; Foxx has been my rock since the day I first started playing Cambria, my emotional dumping ground. It's hard to explain, but I can imagine his voice, clear as day against my ears. Warm and familiar.

"Uh-huh. Okay, weirdo. I'm out."

"Fine. I'm gonna go play some Cambria."

"Hey, just think: if you actually meet Foxx one day in real life, you could have group dates with Amira and Faisal."

I hang up.

THREE YEARS AGO

DEEN: I can't believe you

DEEN: who brings their Nintendo 3DS to the masjid

DEEN: ???

KIRAN: okay first of all

KIRAN: you were THRILLED

KIRAN: and second of all

KIRAN: literally every kid under the age of 10.

DEEN: And you, apparently

KIRAN: and me.

KIRAN: what can I say

KIRAN: I was inspired.

DEEN: you're the weirdest person I have ever met

DEEN: but that was probably the most fun I've had at an Eid dinner, ever

KIRAN: you're welcome
KIRAN: next time, I'll bring Mario Kart

DEEN: you sure you wanna do that? :/

KIRAN: ??

DEEN: I mean . . .
DEEN: I'm gonna kick your ass, so . . .
DEEN: Dunno if you really wanna risk the embarrassment

KIRAN: . . . oh my god
KIRAN: you trash talking me right now, Deen Malik?
KIRAN: are you actually trash talking me
KIRAN: on this holy day of Eid al-Fitr???
KIRAN: I'm gonna make you eat your words
KIRAN: eat em like a good Muslim during iftar

DEEN: wow Noorani, you are . . .

KIRAN: :)

DEEN: SO corny

KIRAN: :(

DEEN: But you know what

DEEN: it's on

DEEN: like Donkey Kong

KIRAN: HA

DEEN: see you next week?

KIRAN: more like beat you next week

DEEN: SO CORNY

CHAPTER 4

DEEN

Friday, June 11

"COME ON, I *NEVER* ASK you for anything," Vinny whines. "When was the last time I asked you for any favors?"

It's the day before dinner with Faisal. I'm in Vinny's dorm room in Rubin Hall, sitting at his desk while he's hanging off his bed, messing with some of his remixes on his laptop. Vinny's got a basketball net attached to his door and I like tossing the ball when my brain's feeling jumbled.

"At lunch today. An hour ago. You literally asked me for half my chicken tenders. And when I said no, you ate them anyway." *Swish.* The ball flips right through the net. Twenty points for me. Or is it ten points? I don't really watch sports.

Vinny swipes the ball off the floor. "That was a favor to you and you know it. You don't even like chicken tenders."

"Chicken tenders are the best thing at that goddamn excuse for a dining hall and *you know it*."

Vinny throws the ball at me. It bounces off my shoulder.

"Come *on*, D-Money. I like Amy. You've got that magical charm. How many times do I have to ask you to help me win her over?"

"You wanna get laid? Then just be hot and unavailable."

"Don't you mean *available*? Why would I get with Amy if I'm unavailable?"

My God, he's serious. I don't want to correct him. He's too pure. Maybe that's why I like hanging out with him. I met him last year, during freshman orientation. He clung to me on day one and hasn't let go yet. But I don't mind. He talks a lot, and sometimes it's annoying, but sometimes it's . . . kinda nice. He has no secrets. He's like a dog, and I mean that in the best way. What you see is what you get. I went to dinner at his house once and his whole family's like that: open and honest and so, so different from mine. I envy it a little.

"Anyway, it's not about getting, you know, laid," Vinny mumbles. "I like her. I want to *date* her. And I think she feels the same way. Like, while you were getting chewed out by Professor Pryce, Raquel and Amy and I were talking on the couch, and Amy sat next to *me*. Not her friend. *Me*. And then her arm kept brushing against me, even though there was plenty more room on her side. That means something, right? That's, like, a sign, right?"

"Maybe? Maybe not? Look, bud, I am really not the guy to get advice from." Don't get me wrong; I've *been* with women—but lately, the only one I've thought about anything more with is

Kasia. Even if she is, you know, mostly virtual.

"Wow, so helpful."

It's my turn to throw the basketball at him. "I don't freaking know! Just talk to her. Or take Feminist Theory next semester, idiot. Maybe that'll teach you how to read women." Actually, I've been wanting to audit that class myself. Professor Johanssen is *really* hot.

"I'll take your advisement under consideration." Vinny abandons his laptop and hugs the basketball to his chest. "But seriously, what are you so pissy about? You stressed?"

Stressed might be a little bit of an understatement; I'm getting an ulcer just thinking about dinner tomorrow. It's a sick joke that of all the possible people Faisal could have fallen in love with, he chose Kiran's sister.

The thing is, I liked her back then. A lot. Maybe more than that—maybe a lot more than that. But that was also when Faisal started acting different: ignoring my calls and texts, never coming home, snapping at Mom and Dad. Faisal had been bullied at school his whole life, and it wasn't unusual to see him coming off the bus with new cuts and bruises. It wasn't unusual for him to be a little closed off. But this was beyond that. Once he left for college, it was like something in him finally cracked. Like all the cuts and bruises he thought he'd shaken off over the years had given rise to an infection, deep within him. That was when my parents started insisting I attend the local Sunday school, probably as a precautionary measure to ensure I, at the very least, would stay in line. They probably just wanted to feel like they were still in control of something. Of someone.

Kiran was a welcome distraction, a tiny flame that brought me comfort while the cold whipped at my back. Until that day three years ago, when the accident happened and everything went to shit, and we had to pack up and leave. I didn't even get to say goodbye. I couldn't. Because saying goodbye would mean having to give her an explanation, and I sure as hell couldn't tell her the truth and risk putting Faisal in the cross fire. And lying, well—Kiran was always pretty good about seeing through my bullshit.

So yeah, forgive me if I'm a little stressed about seeing her tomorrow.

"Question . . . ," I say carefully. "If you found out someone who potentially holds a grudge against you was standing between you and the happiness of someone you care about, what would you do?"

Vinny's eyebrows float. "Depends on how bad the grudge."

"Er, unclear."

Vinny bites his lip and gets uncharacteristically quiet, like he's deep in thought. I smile, imagining a tiny Vinny-like dog inside his head, running on a hamster wheel.

"My mom always says honey catches more flies than vinegar," he finally answers, shrugging. "All you can do is pick up the pieces and smooth things over as best you can. Dial up that magical charm of yours. Could be they don't even hate you as much as you think."

I wouldn't be surprised if Kiran hated me; any normal person would after being ghosted like that. Then again, I wouldn't be surprised if she'd forgotten all about it, either. She was always tough, definitely tougher than me; I've watched her chase a boy after he threw a monkey ball at her back, tackle him to the ground behind the Sunday school, then act like nothing happened. Me leaving probably didn't even make a dent. For Faisal's sake, I hope that's the case.

"Hey, is this one of those hypotheticals that aren't really hypotheticals—"

"But I don't elaborate because I don't want to talk about it?" I finish. "Yep, one of those."

Vinny grins. "Not like you to stress over someone like that."

"Haven't really been myself lately."

I shake my head violently, clearing away the thoughts. I'm being stupid. How I feel doesn't matter. What Kiran thinks about me now doesn't matter. All I need to worry about is making sure tomorrow's meeting runs smoothly, that my past mistakes don't do anything—literally—to fuck this up for Faisal. If Kiran does hate me, then I'll just have to smooth things over as best I can, like Vinny said. I'm sure Kiran's over it, anyway. After all, it's been three whole years. Everything will be fine.

Vinny's trying to balance the ball on his finger. "Anyway, I was thinking something more direct with Amy. Like catch her at the next party, ask her out to lunch. Or asking straight up how she feels."

I stand and stretch. I should probably go to the gym, run this tension off. Otherwise, I'll risk looking like the shrimpy one in the family next to Faisal. Unacceptable.

"The problem with asking direct questions is it means you'll get a direct answer and be disappointed. Sometimes it's just better to ride the wave, take what you can get." My shoulders let out a satisfying crack. "The last thing you want to do is come off as desperate."

The ball falls off Vinny's finger, and he watches it roll. "I don't know. Sometimes I don't think it's such a bad thing. Being desperate. Just means you want something so bad, you can't even hide it."

"Yeah, but that's not really my style."

"Your loss," he says with an uncharacteristically knowing smile, one that almost tempts me into asking what he means, before he turns his attention back to the remix on his laptop.

LOADING

[CAMBRIA: THE EVOLUTION EXPANSION PACK]
[ROANA GUILD CHAT ROOM]

Kasia Coribund: THERE YOU ARE.

Kasia Coribund: Quick, I need good excuses to not go to a Thing

Devynius Foxx: Sorry, sorry

Devynius Foxx: Some stuff came up

Devynius Foxx: Now, do you need excuses for a Real World thing or a Cambria thing?

Kasia Coribund: A real world thing.

Devynius Foxx: Your dog died.

Kasia Coribund: I don't have a dog, first of all

Kasia Coribund: and second of all, morbid much??

Devynius Foxx: Okay how about

Devynius Foxx: you sprained your ankle

Devynius Foxx: you lost your voice

Devynius Foxx: you caught a highly contagious monkey flu

Kasia Coribund: what's a monkey flu?

Devynius Foxx: no idea

Kasia Coribund: let me rephrase the question

Kasia Coribund: I need a good PLAUSIBLE excuse

Kasia Coribund: preferably one that doesn't involve me being hurt or sick

Devynius Foxx: okay, okay

Devynius Foxx: you went to the wrong location

Devynius Foxx: and have now found yourself stranded in Timbuktu

Kasia Coribund: how do you know I don't actually live in Timbuktu?

Devynius Foxx: Have YOU ever met anyone from Timbuktu?

Kasia Coribund: No, but . . .

Devynius Foxx: Exactly.

Devynius Foxx: how about you had class?

Devynius Foxx: and you got stuck so you tried to sneak out early?

Devynius Foxx: but the professor—ho boy, that eagle-eyed professor

Devynius Foxx: he's a hard man to avoid.

Kasia Coribund: . . . I don't have classes right now

Devynius Foxx: Consider yourself lucky then.

Devynius Foxx: Okay, last option: tell them you needed to talk to your best friend

Devynius Foxx: because he is a clingy bastard who gets lonely when you're not around

Devynius Foxx: and would much appreciate your company.

Kasia Coribund: Heh. I'll try that.

Kasia Coribund: Ugh, gotta go.

Kasia Coribund: Wish me luck.

Devynius Foxx: You and me both.

CHAPTER 5

KIRAN

Saturday, June 12

I'VE NEVER DREADED THE WEEKEND more than I do right now. But I promised Amira I'd meet Faisal, and Saturday comes whether I want it or not. I get ready and ride the Amtrak in a daze—Amira bought my ticket to spare me from the Chinatown Bus—and eventually arrive at some fancy Italian restaurant in Midtown that's all dim lights and violins and it makes me and my wallet sweat.

A lanky maître d' with a well-oiled mustache greets me at the door with a painfully slow up-and-down look of derision. "Can I help you?" he asks like someone who has no interest in helping. To be fair, I do look a little out of place; I had enough sense to wear actual pants instead of sweats, but with my short hair sticking out at odd angles, it probably looks like I crawled out of a sewer and was promptly electrocuted.

I look over his shoulder and find Amira sitting in a round

booth, talking animatedly. Laughing. With a pillar blocking my view, though, I can't see who she's with.

But it's more than one person.

My stomach free-falls, and I almost barf.

Amira spots me, and for a moment I feel like I'm my character on Cambria, when I've accidentally aggro'd way more mobs than I can take on alone, which often results in me full-on sprinting in game while Foxx laughs and the real me screams at my monitor. But before I can decide how to make my strategic retreat, Amira stands so suddenly that she bumps the table. She's not wearing her glasses today, and she's in a flowery skirt that reaches her ankles and a white peasant top that makes her look like she's about to break into song about this provincial life. She waves me over, grinning ear to ear.

I give a little wave back and the maître d' begrudgingly lets me through.

Please don't be here, please don't be here, I beg as I trudge toward Amira's table, my jaw clenched so tightly that my teeth are throbbing. My eyes are fixed on the pillar, waiting for it to reveal *him*. Dreading that it will. What's the point of closure if the universe is determined to open chapters that should *stay* closed?

Closer. *Closer.*

But it's . . . not Deen.

My legs almost collapse beneath me. I'm relieved; there was a chance Deen would show up, I knew, but I don't think I'm ready. I'm not sure I'll ever be ready.

I recognize the man sitting beside Amira immediately, only because he looks so strikingly like Deen. He's Deen, only *not*; even though he's sitting, it's clear he's *massive*—like two hundred pounds of muscle massive—with biceps the size of small honeydews and a light beard peppering his jawline. It's like someone crossed Deen with the Hulk. But the family resemblance is there. He has the same messy pile of dark curls for hair, the same tawny, copper-kissed skin and warm brown eyes.

Faisal Malik.

Across them sits a young, handsome Black guy wearing a suit like he just got out of work; he's loosened his tie and wears an affable smile. I don't recognize him, but he is a vast improvement over Deen—reason number one being that he is not, in fact, Deen.

Amira hugs me and pecks my cheek. "Thanks for coming."

"Yeah, of course." I smile.

Behind her, Faisal doesn't get to his feet to greet me. He eyes me, briefly, and looks away.

Okay, rude.

The Black guy immediately gets to his feet and extends his hand toward me. "Salaam. I'm Haris Ibrahim," he says as I shake his hand.

"Just tagging along for moral support." He glances at Faisal. "I'm Faisal's friend from college. This *dazed and confused zombie* and I go way back."

Faisal blinks a couple of times, as if waking from a nap, and jerks to a stand. "Oh, uh."

He wipes his hand on his pants, then reaches toward me, as if approaching a flame. His hand is trembling. "Assalamu alaikum," he says with a perfect Arabic accent, soft like a breeze through leaves. "It's, uh, good to finally meet you, Kiran."

I take his hand. It's warm and gentle. And, if I'm being honest, a little moist.

"Walaikumu assalam. Likewise," I reply stiffly. The smile on my face feels so painfully artificial that it burns my cheeks trying to sustain it.

He blinks again and retreats to his seat; Amira takes her seat next to him.

There's an open space next to Haris, but I sidle in next to my sister in the round booth, forcing Faisal to scooch closer to Haris and make room for me. A waiter brings in some fresh bread and herbed butter, and Amira and I waste no time snatching a couple of rolls.

"Sorry my brother's not here," Faisal mumbles. "Deen's got summer classes, so . . ."

Hearing his name aloud sends a jolt through me. I break my roll in half.

"I'll catch him eventually. Where does he go again?" Amira asks between mouthfuls of bread.

"NYU." I can't tell if it's a smile or a grimace, but Faisal's mouth turns up slightly at the corners.

"Oooh, smart boy. What's he studying?"

"He's . . . not sure yet," Faisal responds. "Still figuring things out, I think."

I try to imagine an older Deen. Attending classes. Hanging with friends. Living a life I know nothing about. A hard knot coils in my belly.

I chomp into my bread roll.

"He's still got plenty of time," says Amira.

Haris speaks up. "Amira, didn't you decide to be a lawyer when you were, like, twelve? I think I remember Faisal saying that." Amira laughs modestly.

"What about you?" I ask Faisal. "Have you always wanted to do nonprofit . . . stuff?" I don't actually know the details of what Faisal does, other than that he does nonprofit work with my sister with kids in juvenile detention. But I need to find out as much about this weird Hulk-Deen character as I can. I don't care what Asher says; if the man who's upending my entire life has a flaw, I'm going to find it.

"Sort of," he replies. "Yeah, in a way."

I wait for some kind of follow-up. But it never comes. Instead, he grasps a roll from the basket and begins intently buttering every inch with the focus of a painter.

I press on. "So you majored in what, business?"

"No, uh. Poli-sci." He takes a bite of his bread. A period to the conversation.

What is it with this guy? Look, I get that I'm not the most delightful or intriguing person on the planet, but I've never met someone so uninterested in basic politeness. Trying to talk with him feels like watching the slow, sizzling death of a slug sprinkled with salt. As much as I hate to admit it, Deen at least was savvy at keeping a conversation going. He always seemed engaged, kept eye contact. Like he was really hearing you, taking all of you in. At least before he completely ghosted me.

I wonder if Deen told his brother about me. Assuming Deen connected the dots about Amira being my sister. Assuming Deen even *remembers* me.

Whatever. *I'm here for Amira*, I remind myself.

"You know, Kiran's recently figured out what she wants to do," says Amira cheerfully, sweeping away the stilted air. Bless her.

Haris, at least, feigns interest. "Oh? What's that?"

"Medicine," I blurt out.

"Annnnd UPenn's got a couple South Asian dance troupes," Amira presses. "You're going to join one of them?"

"Maybe." I shift uncomfortably in my seat. Amira and Asher both keep saying I should continue dancing through college, but it seems like it would be a waste of time, especially since the only reason we can afford UPenn is because of the premed scholarship I got. I have to keep up my GPA or risk losing it.

"UPenn starts in August, right?" Haris asks, opening a menu. "You excited?"

I shrug. "Hasn't really hit me yet. Plus, I'll still be in Philly, so it won't feel like much of a change." Except now I'll have to live on campus instead of with Amira.

Haris raises a brow. "Not a fan of change?"

My eyes drift to Amira, who's having a moment of lovey-dovey eye contact with Faisal.

"No. Can't say I am."

A voice grabs our attention. "Phew. Made it."

I look up.

And instantly regret it.

Standing at the table is none other than Deen Malik, in the flesh.

No. No, no, *no*.

I swallow painfully, trying to stay calm, trying not to reveal the fact that my body's tugging in every direction. There is a tangible stretch to time and space: the impossible has happened, and I am here, right here, in the center of it. Sitting in this restaurant booth, I am suddenly very aware of the largeness of the universe.

Faisal stands. "You're here!" It's like his entire demeanor changes; Faisal stumbles over Haris's lap and wraps his brother in a bear hug. Deen's legs practically dangle off the ground as he limply pats Faisal's back. "I thought you couldn't come."

"Okay, put me down, big guy," he grunts, until Faisal finally lets him go. "I may have had class, so I may have had to sneak out early." Deen pats his hair down, smooths the olive-green T-shirt he's wearing under his open vest.

Then he smiles the same smile I've seen in my head a hundred thousand times, with the same lopsided dimple, the same tiny mole beneath his left eye, the same long lashes that make me jealous—I used to tell him that all the time. But he's a little taller now, and stronger-looking, too, filled out in all the right places.

He's here. He's actually *here.*

Deen's eyes catch mine. A flicker of recognition. Slowly, the corners of his mouth curl in a smile—like he knows something, like he's in on a secret.

I can't believe this. He must be feeling the discomfort, too. He *must* be. He's just better at hiding it.

"Amira, Kiran," says Faisal, his hand outstretched like he's revealing a priceless new statue at a museum. "Meet my brother, Deen."

"Salaam," he says politely. Oh God, his voice is deeper, too.

Amira beams and gets up to introduce herself, but before she can even open her mouth, Deen's got her in a hug, too. Apparently the Maliks are secretly a huggy people. "I feel like I already know you!" he says, charm dialed up to a full ten as Amira bursts into happy giggles.

I think I'm going to be sick.

Amira sits down next to me, her cheeks a glowy pink. Deen greets Haris with a hard handshake before taking a seat next to him.

Which means I have nowhere to hide.

"I thought Deen wasn't coming," I whisper between gritted teeth.

Amira leans into me. "Is that a problem?" she whispers back.

It's a big fucking problem, I want to scream. God, I knew I'd have to see him eventually, thanks to this cruel and unusual punishment that the world has decided to bestow upon me. But why now? Why now, when I'd finally, finally gotten over him?

"Kiran, right?" Deen says suddenly. He extends a hand toward me. "I don't know if you remember me. It's been a while."

I don't know if you *remember me*? I almost burst out laughing: the evil, bitter kind of laugh where you throw your head back and cackle from the spires of your dark castle just before you destroy your enemy.

One more thing that hasn't changed. He's as infuriating as ever—no, even more than I remember.

I meet his eyes. "Now that you mention it," I say, shoving a bread roll into his open hand, "I think I do."

"You know Deen?" Amira asks. "Since when?"

"Yeah," I say slowly. "From Sunday school." I need damage control, stat.

Maybe it's a little hypocritical to want to keep Deen a secret from Amira. I don't know. At first, I agreed to the pact because I didn't want to burden Amira with another thing on top of her schoolwork and finally learning about Mom's illness. But the longer I kept it from Amira, the more I didn't want her to know. In the end, Deen was a mistake, a mistake *she* shouldn't have to worry about, ever.

I keep my voice level. "It was years ago, three years, maybe? Glad to see you gave up on growing facial hair."

"Glad to see your fashion sense hasn't changed." He's smiling fondly, like he's actually happy about it. I don't like it.

I go for the jugular. "But it's such a shame I never saw Faisal. It was like he never even existed, until now. Why was that?"

Faisal blinks like a dazed owl beside his brother, and Deen's jaw twitches. But before he can respond, Haris interrupts:

"Three years ago? Wait, wasn't that when—"

"When Faisal studied abroad," Deen says quickly. "In Spain. That's why he wasn't around. He's worldly like that. Can't believe you forgot, Haris."

I narrow my eyes at him just as Amira voices the question on my tongue: "What? I didn't know you studied abroad, Faisal!"

Faisal suddenly spills his glass, and ice water glazes the table and dribbles off the sides.

"Oh no!" Amira gets to work and immediately throws her napkin onto the water to soak it up. Deen and I add mine to the pile, while Haris does the noble job of rescuing the bread basket.

"Sorry, sorry, sorry. I c-completely zoned out," Faisal stammers. "I don't know what happened."

"It's okay! A little excitement never hurt anyone," says Amira with a wink. Faisal's ears redden.

"This is what happens when you daydream about your girl all day," Deen adds, grinning.

Faisal clumsily wipes away at his side of the table, but only manages to spread the water around. "Sorry."

Despite the diversion, the awkwardness between me and Deen remains almost unbearable. Amira and Haris, thankfully, act casual. Like they don't notice anything amiss. We all manage to clear away the water, settle back down, get our water refills, and order our food.

But I'm starting to think that I'm not the only one feeling uncomfortable. I sneak a glance at Faisal, whose mouth is pressed in a thin line, like he's lost in thought. He's back to being the Faisal before Deen arrived: quiet and withdrawn, the heaviness on his shoulders so palpable you can almost see it threatening to pull him to the ground.

"You okay?" Amira asks.

"Fine now." Faisal smiles at her, but there's something fake about it.

"Good, because I have a million questions for you, Amira," says Deen. "First of all, I gotta know: *Law & Order* is more or less a perfect representation of the criminal justice system, right?"

Amira grins and cracks her knuckles. And just like that, the awkwardness evaporates. They talk and laugh comfortably. Like friends. Like family.

Deen always was good at doing that.

But I don't laugh with them. I can't shake off the feeling that what Amira said about waiting for my approval was just a farce. That really, in her heart, she's already made her decision. That this stiff, blank-eyed man—who looks like he'd rather be anywhere but here—is the one she's imagining a possible future with. And even though I can feel in my bones that there's something seriously suspicious about this whole situation—Faisal's jumpiness, and the rumors surrounding him, how fast things are moving despite them hardly knowing each other—I'm powerless to do anything about it.

The rest of dinner goes off without a hitch, mostly because Amira and Haris get deep into talking about work while Deen peppers in a question or two. I listen politely. Faisal zones out. Occasionally I catch him staring at me beneath thick, furrowed brows.

I'm at the bottom of a tiramisu that Amira and I are sharing when her phone rings.

"Oh, speaking of work." She stands and gently squeezes Faisal's shoulder. For just a moment, his mask slips and the glassiness of his eyes fades, and he looks warm. Adoring. But then she leaves and it's just the four of us.

Faisal pushes himself up from the table. "Excuse me," he says gruffly, and stands. "Bathroom." And without waiting for a response, he leaves.

Haris chuckles. “Think I might use the bathroom, too. You two good to hold the fort?”

I cringe inwardly so hard I think I almost become a human black hole. But Deen salutes, good-heartedly, and Haris leaves, too.

Silence. I stare intently at the remnants of tiramisu on my plate like they’re the most fascinating things in the world.

I count ten seconds. Fifteen seconds. Twenty seconds. Part of me thinks I should be grateful, in a way, for this chance. For almost a year, my whole world was Deen. I stayed up impossibly late just to talk to him on my phone. Closed my eyes and memorized the cadence, the vibrations of his voice on my ear. He said everything I needed when I needed to hear it most. He was there for me when Mom first got sick, when Amira was cramming for the LSAT and couldn’t be.

And then, without warning, he closed himself off.

I could get the answers I’ve been yearning for, right here and now. I could tell him everything I’ve bottled up inside me for so long. Why did he ghost me? Does he know that I lost all confidence in myself when he left? I was only fifteen, and he made me feel that there was something deeply wrong with me. He made me question myself. I could never forgive him for that.

I look up from my plate and realize Deen’s been staring at me this whole time, his mouth curled at the corner.

“So,” Deen begins, “looks like time’s been pretty kind to you.”

“Are you really flirting with me right now?”

“It’s just a fact. You look good.” He shrugs. “Although you’re still as high-strung as ever.”

“Don’t act like you know me.”

Deen leans forward, cradles his chin in his hands, and smiles. "I did, once."

"So, what, you think that makes us friends?"

"Friends?" Deen snorts. "Men and women can't be friends. The sex part always gets in the way. But that doesn't mean we can't be friend*ly*, right? We don't want Amira and Faisal worrying about nothing."

Nothing? Was that all it was to him?

I want to throw my plate at him. No, my knife. No, my fork.

But the waiter comes back and takes away my dirty utensils and my plate, and it looks like I'm going to have to commit murder with a coffee spoon.

I get up abruptly.

"I am here for Amira," I growl. "And that's it. That's all *this*"—I gesture at the space between me and him—"will *ever* be. Now, if you'll excuse me."

Deen opens his mouth to say something, but I turn on my heel and leave.

I need to put some distance between me and Deen, so I head for the bathrooms because there's no way he can follow me there. I briefly consider drowning myself in the sink.

I hate that he affects me so much, even now. I hate that he knows it.

And I hate that he looks like he's having fun doing it.

The bathrooms are in a quiet, shadowy hallway in the back of the restaurant; as I approach, the faint flush of a urinal from the inside of the men's bathroom clashes with the thin wailing of the violins on the sound system.

Except then I hear voices from the shadows. Familiar ones. I peek over the wall blocking off the hallway.

"What gives?" asks Haris, agitated. "What the hell are you getting worked up at *me* for?"

Faisal takes a step back, looks away. "I'm sorry. You're right. It's not your fault. But I told you not to say *anything* about the past. I *told* you."

"Wait, I thought—you mean she doesn't *know*?" Haris runs his hands down his face. "What the hell, man. Is that why Deen pulled out that bullshit about you traveling abroad? Why the hell didn't you *tell her*?"

"There's nothing to tell."

I panic and press myself against the wall before they see me.

Are they talking about Amira? *Tell her* what? So Deen lied about Faisal being abroad three years ago?

"Come on." Haris's voice lowers. "Does she at least know about Leah?"

Faisal looks at him now, glaring. "No. And right now, it has to stay that way."

Leah? Who is Leah?

"Look, I don't want to tell you how to live your life, but this is idiotic. Is this because of Deen?" Haris asks.

"This is because I love Amira."

Haris paces a few steps. "So, you just gonna hide what happened? Forever?"

"No!" Faisal's voice rises, but he stops, closes his eyes. "No," he says, softer now. "I'll tell her. I want to tell her. About everything.

But with my parents being on my case, the *risk* to them and to Deen—" He sighs. "I'm just waiting for the right moment."

Haris shakes his head, and a disapproving look passes between them.

"I know." Faisal draws in another deep breath. "I know. It's just hard. I tossed my past in the trash, where it belongs. It's been three *years*."

His voice lowers to a sad, desperate whisper. "I don't want to dig it up again."

My knees go weak beneath me and I nearly sink to the floor. My lungs quake. I've seen so many sides to Faisal today, I can't tell which is the real one.

What the hell did I just witness?

And what is Faisal hiding from my sister?

CHAPTER 6

DEEN

Sunday, June 13

I'M TRYING TO IMAGINE KIRAN chasing me from behind the treadmill at the gym, and I'm embarrassed to admit it's making me go full speed.

I can't get the look on her face out of my head. The suspicion in her eyes, the questions beneath them. The fire in them that never left.

So yesterday didn't exactly go the way I planned. For one thing, I think it's safe to say she definitely wasn't thrilled to see me, so I started at a total disadvantage. Fair enough; I'm pretty sure the return of an ex is right up there on people's don't-want lists along with the coming of the Antichrist and literal blights of locusts. She could barely stand being alone with me for two seconds, which . . . stings more than I'd like, even if I expected it.

But if I could just get her one-on-one for a little while, have her hear me out, give Faisal a chance, I'm sure she'd see he's not a bad guy—for one thing, he'd never hurt Amira the way I hurt Kiran.

I'm in way over my head. Smoothing things over with her is going to require more . . . effort.

At least she looked . . . good. Really good. Part of me is happy for her. And part of me . . . well, part of me doesn't know what to feel. Part of me thinks I don't really deserve to feel anything.

I'm halfway into my third mile when my phone starts buzzing.

It's Faisal.

I stop in my tracks as my already high heart rate does its own little sprint. Texts from him are surprising enough, so him just calling out of the blue—that makes me especially nervous.

I swallow and try to even out my breathing before I pick up.

"Hey."

"Sorry to bother you again so soon after yesterday," says Faisal. "And I'll make this quick since Mom's yelling about something and I don't want to take any more of your time. Just wanted to say thanks. For coming."

And true enough, I hear the faint, familiar shouting of a woman's voice in the background. A sound I hate more than anything.

"Oh yeah," I say, wiping sweat from my brow. "Glad I did. Amira's great."

Silence.

"Faisal?"

There's a muffling sound, then a groan. "I blew it."

"What? What do you mean, you blew it?"

"You saw what happened. I freaked out. I don't know why, but it just hit me that all of this is *real* and that it could *happen*—that me and Amira—that we are *happening*. And I freaked out because—because what if I mess this up? What if I do something stupid? I don't know what I'm doing. I'm still figuring things out, I barely know how to take care of myself, and—"

"Whoa, whoa, whoa, Faisal. Hey. Deep breaths." A couple of girls walk by me from the Pilates studio, staring, so I shoot them a forced *Hey, I'm cool, everything's fine!* smile.

"And then you had to lie for me—"

"Hey, I was only using the excuse Mom's been using on relatives who ask about you."

"I wish that made me feel better. Also didn't help that Amira's little sister was looking at me like she thought I was a fraud. And, like, I *know* that. I know I'm not good enough for Amira. I'm trying, I really am, but it feels like I'm starting a hundred feet behind because I fucked up." He takes a long, shaky breath. "Sorry. I'm sorry. I'm just— I'm really bummed."

I sit down on a bench, and I can't tell if summer allergies are fucking with me or if my eyes are prickling from something else. I haven't heard Faisal like this in months. I know better than anyone how hard he tries, so to hear him crack, to hear all the raw stuff pouring out that he keeps locked inside—it hurts.

But what hurts the most is how he's still convinced it's all his fault.

"You . . . you have a lot of experience with women, right?" he asks, a little calmer now. "No judgment or anything—that's between you and God, but . . ."

I chuckle softly. "You calling me a ho?"

"No! God, no." I hear him mutter something like *Astaghfirullah*—

"I seek forgiveness from God." "It's, ugh, how do I explain? Do you think . . . do you think it's fine not to tell your partner everything about yourself? From the get-go? Like what you've done? Or who you were before?"

"What do you mean? Why would you need to?" My voice rises.

"During dinner when Haris almost . . . when he almost mentioned what happened back then and you had to cover for me . . . I lost my cool. Got mad at him for almost blowing it. But what right do I even have to be mad? He called me a coward. And he's right. I *am* a coward. I can't stop wondering . . . would Amira still love me if she knew everything? I haven't told her about the stuff I did; I fell for her so fast and then things just happened and for the first time in my life I felt like I could breathe. But now we're actually here and I don't think I can keep pretending that I'm not terrified of what she'll think when she knows. It's not just about Mom threatening to not pay for me to move to California anymore if people find out, or even losing funding for AFFEY. I'm terrified of what might happen if . . . if I lose her."

Images of him at his lowest rush me so fast I lose my breath: Faisal stumbling home with red-rimmed eyes. Faisal throwing up in the bathroom all night, orange pills strewn across white tiles, begging me not to tell Mom and Dad. Me, fumbling with his phone, trying to call Leah because she was the only one who'd know what to do.

I refuse to see him like that again. Not after everything he's done for me.

"I know it's not fair to put that kind of pressure on anyone," he continues. "But I think that's why I messed up so bad yesterday. I'm scared."

I squeeze the phone so hard it presses against my bones. I swallow. "Jesus. Faisal, I'm so sorry."

"I just don't know what to do."

"You don't have to do anything. Okay?" I say fiercely. "You don't have to do *anything* you don't want to do."

Faisal lets out a soft, wet laugh. "The only thing I want is to marry her."

I close my eyes. I want to remember this moment. Because it's the first time I've ever heard my brother say he wanted anything. And now I think I've found a way to repay my debt to him. A promise I can actually keep. Between carrying all this shame and having to deal with M&D's obsession with appearances, he's had enough to worry about for years. I don't want him thinking about anything else but keeping this person-sized happiness he's found for himself. It's the damned least I could do.

Kiran, with her suspicious, probing gaze, manifests in my head again like a ghost with a vendetta. But I stamp it out.

"If you want to marry her, then you're going to marry her," I declare. "And I'm going to do everything in my power to make sure that happens. Deal?"

"Yeah." Faisal laughs softly again, a real one this time. He takes a breath. "Deal."

THREE YEARS AGO

DEEN: Hey

DEEN: You okay?

KIRAN: ?

DEEN: I dunno, you seemed

DEEN: off somehow?

DEEN: Like something's wrong

KIRAN: Oh

KIRAN: Just tired

DEEN: Not getting enough sleep?

DEEN: Err, is it my fault?

KIRAN: no no

KIRAN: I like talking to you at night actually

KIRAN: it's fun

KIRAN: but

KIRAN: It's my mom

KIRAN: She hasn't been feeling well lately…

KIRAN: Don't tell anyone, okay?

KIRAN: Gossip spreads like wildfire

KIRAN: And I don't want people acting weird around us

DEEN: oh

DEEN: shit

DEEN: I'm sorry

DEEN: is she sick?

DEEN: You don't have to talk about it if you don't want to

KIRAN: I . . .

KIRAN: kind of. Yeah.

KIRAN: It's hard to say for sure

KIRAN: What she has doesn't really have a clear diagnosis

KIRAN: It's one of those weird wait and see kind of things

KIRAN: But

KIRAN: they suspect it might be ALS

KIRAN: since she's having trouble walking and swallowing . . .

KIRAN: I'm terrified.

DEEN: holy shit

KIRAN: we haven't even told my sister about it yet

KIRAN: I think my parents are afraid it's gonna be a distraction from her studies
KIRAN: so . . . I don't even have anyone to talk to about it, you know?

DEEN: wow
DEEN: Kiran
DEEN: I don't even know what to say
DEEN: how are you even going to Sunday school?
DEEN: that's . . . a lot
DEEN: I'm really sorry you're going through this

KIRAN: Me too.

DEEN: Hey, so . . .
DEEN: you know the forest in the back of the masjid?

KIRAN: yeah? Kinda hard to miss it

DEEN: . . . true
DEEN: but I went deep in there the other week
DEEN: I mean deeeep
DEEN: and I found something I think you're gonna like
DEEN: Meet me there next week? During break?
DEEN: I wanna show you.

KIRAN: what is it?
KIRAN: you gonna murder me?

KIRAN: get rid of your Super Smash competition?

DEEN: ha

DEEN: don't need to resort to murder to do that

KIRAN: shut up

KIRAN: . . . but okay

KIRAN: yeah

KIRAN: I'll meet you there.

DEEN: sweet

DEEN: thanks

DEEN: look forward to it

DEEN: and

DEEN: look I know I'm not your sister or anything

DEEN: but

DEEN: if you need anyone to talk to

DEEN: I'm here

KIRAN: yeah

KIRAN: I . . .

KIRAN: thanks, Deen

DEEN: Seriously, anytime.

DEEN: It's a promise.

CHAPTER 7

KIRAN

Sunday, June 13

FOR THE REMAINDER OF THE weekend, I furiously storm my way through the entire internet. At least that's what it feels like: me, stomping around on Facebook like an angry T. rex, upending every rock and roaring into the void as I charge a virtual jungle.

Which I guess sounds a lot better than what I'm actually doing, which is Facebook stalking.

I can't stop thinking about what Faisal said about this Leah, and how desperate he sounded to keep her buried in the past—and hidden from Amira. But I'm going to dig up everything I possibly can. No one gets to lie to my sister. Whoever Leah is, she's the key to unraveling Faisal's Secret™. I can feel it.

At least that's what I'm banking on now. I've already looked up Faisal online, but I can't find anything about him. Not on Facebook, not on Twitter or Instagram or Reddit. I even searched Archive of Our Own, wondering if maybe he was the kind of guy who had secret kinks (no judgment) or fetishes (some judgment, depending). But then I got distracted by some new fan fiction that I should probably delete from my browser history.

So all I've got to go on is the name Leah. I don't have a last name, and unfortunately there are approximately fifty billion Leahs in the tristate area. I'm not even sure how to spell her name exactly (Leah? Lea? Lee-ya?), so I'm running out of steam, fast.

I x out my guild chat window where Nilina and Solen invited me to clear a couple of dungeons with them—sorry, guys!—take a loud chug of coffee, and slam it on my desk. "This is SO annoying! Facebook already knows everything about me. It should know which Leah I'm looking for."

"Man, you type loud. You sound like a hacker but without the actual intelligence of one," says Asher's voice through my computer. We're on Hangouts, talking through our webcams; I can see him at his desk, a tired but amused little smile on his face. The dim light in his surprisingly tidy dorm room casts shadows across the wall behind him. He decided to stay on campus this summer to tutor and take some extra classes, the masochist.

"If you have time to joke, then you have time to help me."

"I did help. I checked Deen's Facebook, and there's nothing. Just a lot of vain selfies," says Asher. "What if Leah *doesn't* have Facebook? What if Leah isn't even a person? What if Leah is actually a pet dog or ferret or something? We can't just search the entire internet on a single name. We need something a little more concrete. If Faisal really does have some secret shady past, do you think it's going to be conveniently posted somewhere for you to find?"

"So what do you propose? I go ask him? *Hey, Faisal, random question, but who is this Leah you're keeping secret and also why are you lying?*"

"I mean . . . yes?"

"Like he's just going to come out and tell me!" I laugh darkly. "He's going to deny it. He got upset with his supposed friend; how do you think he'll react if *I* ask?" My head droops onto my desk and I cradle it with my arms. I'm tired and frustrated. But mostly I'm angry: angry I can't do anything, angry that Faisal has something he's keeping from Amira, all while having the nerve to pretend to love her. As if she hasn't been through enough these past few years. Why did she have to fall for Faisal, of all people?

The prickle of an idea begins to itch in my head. "Wait." I lift my head. "What about Haris?"

Before Asher can reply, I'm already typing his name into the search bar.

Haris Ibrahim.

"Haris? Who's Haris?" I can hear Asher asking in the background.

His name pops up. My heart begins to beat faster, fluttering hopefully.

I click on his profile, and there he is. "He's Faisal's friend from college. He was the guy I overheard talking to Faisal at the restaurant. And I think I've just found him."

Haris J. Ibrahim. Age twenty-six. Associate attorney at Garson, Reese, and Calloway, a criminal defense firm. His profile picture: him grinning ear to ear on a Caribbean beach beneath a setting sun.

Guilt chews on my insides like bad gas, but I shake it off.

"Sorry," I mutter, to him and the universe. I don't enjoy creeping on people through social media, but desperate times, right?

"I'm in," I blurt. "I'm in the Matrix."

"That's not what that means," Asher grumbles.

I find a photo album; Haris takes a ton of photos, all super high quality. For some reason, I can totally imagine him having several DSLR cameras.

Asher's quiet as I click through the first photo album, labeled "Law School Shenanigans." It's really just a bunch of photos of Haris in different suits, standing outside several different courthouses. The guy looks good, not gonna lie. There are a bunch of jealousy-inducing albums labeled "Vacations," "Travels," and "Other Journeys," and I can now safely say I think I know the one human who has visited every single country on the face of the earth.

But then I finally find an album, smaller than the others, simply labeled "College."

My hand is shaking, so I grip the mouse tighter. I click.

Orientation week photos. Selfies from Halloween. Many, many blurred photos from various parties. Villanova University, I quickly learn, knows how to party. But I'm most surprised by how few photos there are of Faisal, especially given that Haris is supposedly his closest friend. Something's not right. Weirder still: Why are there so few photos, period? For someone who clearly loves taking them, Haris totally dropped the ball in college.

"Find anything?" Asher asks softly.

Click. Click. I'm watching a slideshow of four years of a life I know nothing about unfold, and I'm getting dizzy.

"Wait," I say aloud. I click back to a photo I passed.

And then I see it. I see him.

Faisal. It takes me a couple of seconds to recognize him: he's thinner, scrawnier. He doesn't have a beard, and his jawline is sharp. Too sharp, even. Dark, puffy lumps, the familiar result of several nights of sleeplessness, hang just beneath his glassy eyes. He's wearing a dark blue Villanova T-shirt that's at least two sizes too big. He has his arm around a girl: white, with strawberry-blonde hair in a loose bun. Friendly blue eyes. But she also looks tired. Her hand is on his chest, a loving gesture. And he has her pressed up against him, as if he'd stumble without her, as if she's a raft. And he is lost at sea.

Faisal isn't tagged. The girl is tagged as Leah Pearson. But her Facebook page is private. Which means I can't see 99 percent of the stuff on it.

But the worst part is how Faisal's and Leah's faces look *off* somehow—like they're looking at the camera, but they're not really . . . there. I remember a while ago Asher sent me this creepy article about how the Victorians would dress up the newly dead to take photos, as if they were still alive. It gave me nightmares. Their eyes were still open and they'd be dressed in their finest, but you just knew, deep in your bones, there was no life there. The haunting look in Faisal's red-rimmed eyes makes me shudder. I'm fairly certain he wasn't sober when the photo was taken. I've seen people on weed before, and whatever he was on . . . it looks harder.

I'll be the first to admit there are way too many South Asian aunties who love to jump all over stuff like this with their assumptions. I do not condone that. Mom used to get mad whenever gossip would break out at dinner parties—about so-and-so's daughter being caught out with so-and-so's son in some kind of illicit harami-pastrami relationship. "You don't know any of that," she'd snap. "Why would you spread these kinds of rumors?" which of course would start a fight and result in us having to be corralled out of the dinner party by our very apologetic dad.

On the other hand, I can't help but think this photo is pretty damning. Asher was off the mark: Leah Pearson wasn't a pet dog or ferret. She was Faisal's girlfriend.

A girlfriend he maybe did drugs with.

I click the Message button on Leah's Facebook page.

If her page is private, anything I'd send would probably be filtered. I don't even know what to say. Is any of this even my business? Whatever his lifestyle was, who am I to go poking around? And maybe he wasn't on drugs. Maybe he was just really, really tired when they took the photo. And so what if he had a girlfriend before Amira? People are allowed to have pasts.

But then why would he be so determined to hide that fact? And the timing—it sounded like whatever he's hiding, it happened around three years ago. Around the same time those weird rumors about him being cut off from the family started floating around the masjid.

Faisal's voice reverberates in my head. *I told you not to say* anything *about the past. I* told *you.*

I close the Messenger window and show Asher the photo.

Silence. And then: "Well, guess that's all there is to it," Asher says. "Maybe he's ashamed about having dated someone in the past? Maybe their family is conservative about the whole no-dating-before-marriage thing?"

I close out Facebook entirely. The more I look at the picture, the queasier I feel.

"Which would be fair; I mean, a lot of Muslims don't 'date' in the usual sense," I explain. "But it's not exactly uncommon, either, and Amira isn't the type to judge if he'd dated someone in the past, Muslim or non-Muslim. He's got to know that. I keep thinking there's got be more to it than that. That maybe this is just the tip of the iceberg."

Asher sighs. "I still think you should just ask him straight up, especially since things are moving so fast."

"Sure, and then he goes and tells Amira I'm snooping on the love of her life, and then Amira gets mad at *me*. Plus, I did try to ask about it at dinner, and then Faisal overloaded and spilled his water. A coincidence? I think not."

I groan and slump deeper into my chair, until half my body is slouched beneath my desk. "Based on what I overheard Faisal telling Haris, I feel like there's something I'm missing. We've confirmed Faisal's lying to hide . . . something related to Leah, something that happened three years ago, but if I'm going to break this up, I need to know exactly what happened. I need to be sure. I'll be damned before I let Amira be duped and played by another Malik's lying ass."

"Speaking of which, why not confront Deen?" Asher asks. "You've been wanting to for years, anyway."

I sit up suddenly. Asher's got a point.

Faisal won't spill—well, his secret, at least; if the dinner was any indication, he's skittish and paranoid and clearly doesn't want to fuck anything up with Amira. It'd be cute, almost, if it weren't so wrong.

But his brother?

I was hoping to avoid Deen entirely, as unrealistic of a wish as that is, especially after he had the nerve to act so . . . *familiar.* But he's the only lead I've got. He's clearly in on Faisal's lie, too, with that whole *studying abroad in Spain* shtick he whipped out at dinner. If there really is something Faisal is hiding, something that happened right around when Deen left . . . maybe it's all connected.

I swallow.

"I think you're right, Ash," I say slowly. "As much as I hate to admit it, I think it's time I talk to my ex."

CHAPTER 8

DEEN

Sunday, June 20

I DIDN'T PAY MUCH ATTENTION in Theoretical Physics last semester. It's not that I don't find physics interesting—I do, even though I only took it to fulfill lab requirements—but the line between "Hey, that's an interesting way to look at things" and "Okay, this is just absurd" gets crossed a little too often in Professor Calloway's lectures for my liking. Also, class was right before lunch, and it's hard to focus when you're jonesing for some chicken tenders.

I did pay attention when we started to cover Laplace, mostly because his ideas were absolutely batshit even by physicist standards. He's famous for a lot of things, but the one that jumped out at me was the idea that you can unerringly predict everything that's ever going to happen in the universe simply by knowing the state of the universe right now.

"Think of it this way," Professor Calloway explained. "The universe is like a giant supercomputer. To determine the future, all you need to do is enter the input—the state of the universe right now: the position and velocity of *every* particle within it. The computer performs a calculation based on the laws of physics and gives you the output, i.e., the state of the universe a moment later. The universe, in other words, is calculable. Laplace posited that scientists could accurately predict the future of the entire universe, based on observable patterns in the present and past." She paused a moment, for dramatic effect.

"We now know, however, that Laplace may have been a little optimistic. There are cases we've found where it seems you can get a completely unpredictable, random outcome from a perfectly normal series of events. That's chaos theory: the idea that the most infinitesimally small shift in the input of our universal supercomputer can throw everything to hell. So as nice as it would be to predict the future of our lives, Laplace's postulate is currently nothing more than a thought experiment. The reality is, there's just so much we don't know. When you really get down to the base level of the universe, we don't even truly understand things like cause and effect. All we have are vague ideas about patterns. And *that* means we live in a world of infinite possibilities. *Anything* can happen."

I don't know. Our lives are full of infinite possibilities? It sounded like a bunch of new age bullshit to me. At the time, I thought: *If anything can happen, why am I stuck with* this *crappy version of* this *crappy universe?*

But today, as I walk into a tiny Joe Coffee on the Upper West Side, I'm almost starting to believe in the endless possibility of the universe. And, if I'm being honest, fearing it.

I still haven't wrapped my head around Kiran being back in

my life, even though she's sitting right there. I order a latte and watch her fidget in her seat as the sad-looking barista gets to work. Thankfully, her sister isn't here yet. After Faisal's last phone call, I texted Amira, too. Figured I should get to know her better, this woman who has my brother's heart in a headlock.

More important, this gives me the chance I need to talk to Kiran. Alone.

She hasn't noticed me yet. I almost don't recognize her, either, at first; it'll take me time to get used to how her hair is way shorter than before. It actually suits her. She's also gotten a tiny gold nose stud, and I couldn't help but notice how it kept catching the light at the Italian restaurant the other day, like a little sparkle playing across her face.

Her sense of style—or total lack thereof—is definitely still there. Today she's opted for a red sweatpants and gray T-shirt ensemble. This girl does not dress to impress; somehow, that's impressive in itself.

I was surprised when she agreed to come out for coffee. She even said she had something to talk to me about, too, which I'll take as a promising sign.

I could feel Amira's little sister looking at me. Like she thought I was a fraud.

Faisal's dejected voice echoes in my mind. It's not even his fault; if it weren't for me, Kiran could look at him objectively instead of bringing in all this heavy-ass baggage.

If I want to help Faisal, it's imperative to patch things up with Kiran, by any means—without her finding out anything more about Faisal.

I'll be genuine. Up the charm magic. Kiran can be reasonable, right?

I fix my hair using my reflection in the nearby window, grab my latte, and approach her. Here goes.

"Look who it is," I say amicably, pulling the chair in front of her. "Been a while, huh? Just the two of us, out on a coffee date."

Her look of surprise quickly slips into annoyance; her mouth presses into a thin line.

"Do you think you're *funny*?"

My smile falters. Not off to a great start. "I like to think so. But that's the thing about comedy, I guess. It's subjective."

"The situation's already awkward enough without you running your mouth. Oh, and thanks a lot for forgetting about our pact at dinner, by the way. You were supposed to keep us a secret."

"And I *did*," I reply defensively. "All I divulged was that we knew each other."

"How I wish we didn't." Kiran sighs and rubs her forehead.

I swallow, at a total loss. Kiran pulls out her phone and begins scrolling.

Up close, I realize just how little she's actually changed, minus the chilliness. She still holds her phone weird, with both her thumbs hovering just above the screen. She's chewing the inside of her mouth like she always does when she's thinking. There's a gym bag by her feet, which means she probably still dances; she used to be obsessed, back then, and I didn't understand why until I saw her dance at some wedding. I've never seen anything more . . . eyeball-gripping. And the weirdest thing was that I felt proud. Proud of her, but also proud of our culture, our shared heritage,

I guess. Like I was part of something bigger than myself, and she was showing me that without saying a word.

I kind of miss that feeling.

"Well? What is it that you wanted to talk about before Amira gets here?" Kiran asks, not looking up from her screen.

I clear my throat. Right. I'm here for a reason, and that reason does not include ogling, much. Except my head's coming up empty. I've never had to actively get someone to like me before. Not to brag, but I've been told I'm just naturally likable.

But she liked me once before. Surely she can learn to like me again—until the wedding, at least.

I flash my trademark dimpled smile. "I like your nose piercing."

"Okay."

"You start college soon, right?"

"Yep."

"Have a boyfriend?"

"Shut up."

"Thought about your major yet?"

"Yep. Pre-med."

Pre-med? Since when? I always thought she'd focus on dance. She had a gift for it, after all.

My eyes trail to the gym bag by her feet. "But you're still dancing, huh? That's cool. Your mom must be happy."

Her thumbs stop moving. "Maybe. But she died. A year ago."

Oh. My breath leaves my lungs so fast, a punch to the ribs would have been easier. We live in a world of infinite possibilities, and surprise, surprise, I'm an infinite asshole.

I bite my lip, trying to find the words. But I can't.

She goes back to scrolling, casually, like it's nothing. Somehow that makes it worse. I knew, when we first met, that her mom was starting to get sick. They hadn't even told Amira about it yet because her parents thought it would interfere with her studies. I didn't know a thing about ALS at the time, but sometimes I'd research it, and we'd talk about it late at night. It hits me now: the average life span for a person diagnosed is five years, at best. I *knew* that. We *talked* about that.

I try to imagine what it must have been like, watching her mom in the hospital bed. The late nights, the slow and steady march to death. The crying, alone. The crying, with her dad—the weight of keeping it a secret from her sister. I try to relive it all, to imagine it as vividly as I can, and I don't even know why. Maybe because I feel like shit that I didn't realize. Maybe because I feel like shit that I wasn't there. But then again, what could I have said? What could I ever say?

"I'm sorry. I didn't know." I swallow. The words sound stale.

"Yeah, well," says Kiran, putting her phone on the table a little too hard. "It is what it is."

My hand reaches for hers before I realize what's happening. But I quickly yank it back.

Idiot.

"How's Faisal, by the way?" Kiran asks, filling the silence. "He looked a little . . . antsy. At dinner."

"Oh, he's always like that." I chuckle uneasily. "I think he was just nervous. You know. About his potential bride's family."

Kiran's eyes narrow. "Bride, huh?"

"Yeah. Actually, that's what I wanted to talk to you about."

Here goes. I take a deep breath and lean forward, my hands folded on the table, businesslike. "The thing is, my brother's head over heels for your sister, obviously. And—between you and me—he's been wanting to take the next step soon. So I just wanted to make sure, you know—we're okay. You know. You and me."

"Wait, wait. What do you mean, take the next step soon?"

"Propose, obviously. Hopefully in the next week or so. I told him to just go do the whole public proposal thing, get a bunch of flash mob dancers and all that. But I'll be honest, I don't think he has enough friends to pull that off. And he insists we do it right. Islamically. With family." I wanted to ask Amira's schedule once she gets here—keeping the proposal part a secret, of course. "So what I'm thinking is: We do a formal family dinner thing. Get our parents to meet, blah blah blah. And then he can take your sister outside for a quiet, informal proposal thing. I'd need your help, though, just to make sure no one interrupts them. We have this really pretty garden area in our backyard, so I can get some string lights or something set up, make it real, uh, romantic. What do you say? Want to help me make that happen? For them? Might be nice for you to feel more involved in all this, work together, for old times' sake."

"I—" Kiran grips the sides of the table, like she's about to flip it. "I don't understand. I know they're thinking about getting engaged, and I know moving to California is on the table, but—my dad doesn't even know Faisal exists yet."

"Right, and that's why we're going to have a family dinner."

"They've only known each other for three months—are you seriously talking getting engaged in a *week*?"

"What's wrong with that?" My stomach clenches like a fist. I don't know what kind of reaction I expected, but Kiran does not look happy. "They love each other. Why wait? They have the rest of their lives—"

"Stop," Kiran snaps. "This is moving *way* too fast."

"Come on. Isn't that how it usually goes with, you know, love?" Not that I know anything about it.

"This isn't some fairy tale. I can't let my sister get married to some *stranger* and get whisked away to California."

I blink. There's something ugly about the way she says the word *stranger*, and I don't like it. "What the hell is that supposed to mean?"

"It means you and your brother need to slow the hell down. I'm sorry, but this is my only sister. I don't want to see her getting hurt. She's a good person."

"Hurt? What are you saying—that my brother isn't a good person?"

Kiran stares back at me, quiet. But her voice is thick when she finally speaks: "Honestly? I'm not sure he is."

That gets me. "You don't even *know* him."

"That's exactly the problem. I don't."

"Then maybe if you actually took the *time*—" I breathe. The heat's rising from my gut straight to my head and my voice is getting louder. But it's hard to stay calm. Why is she so stubborn?

"Please. Kiran. I don't want to fight you. That's not why I'm here. But you're making it really hard—"

"*I'm* making it hard?"

Shit. This whole thing is spiraling. "That's not what I—" I throw my hands up, frustrated. "This isn't about you. Or me, for that matter! It's about Amira and Faisal. We're here for *them* and that's *it*, that's what *you* said."

Kiran's chin rises. "What about Leah? What do you think *she* would say about this?"

"Wait. *What?*" My heart sprints frantically in my chest. How the *hell* does Kiran know about Leah? Faisal probably hasn't talked to her in *years*. Not since the accident—he told me so himself. Too many bad memories between them.

Just what else does Kiran know?

Or worse, what else does she *think* she knows?

"Leah has nothing to do with anything anymore," I growl. "I don't know why you—" I lock eyes with her, searching for . . . something. "What are you trying to do, blackmail him? Why would you ruin this for him?"

"He ruined it by lying." Her eyes glitter with barely reserved anger. "Makes you wonder what else Faisal's hiding."

The night of the accident comes rushing back to me: flames reaching for the night sky like the hungry grip of hell itself, Faisal's disappointed face, pale and sickly, hollowed out by shadows, the earsplitting cry of police sirens getting closer and closer—

Faisal squeezing my hand. *I'll take the fall for you.*

I swallow hard. "What do you want? What will it take for you to let this go?" My voice sounds more desperate than I'd like.

"I want you to be honest with me. For once. You're going to tell me everything about your brother," she answers, steepling her fingers like a villain with all the cards, "and I'm going to decide whether or not he deserves my sister."

"I . . ."

Oh. I suddenly get it now. Kiran doesn't just hate me. She wants revenge.

Of *course* she does.

But no matter how much she thinks she knows, no matter how much she tries to blackmail Faisal for answers, no matter how much I owe it to her—this is the one thing I can't give her. Faisal was there for me when I needed him most. The least I can do is help him now.

"I'm sorry," I reply, staring her directly in the eyes, "but I don't know what you're talking about."

"I'm here, I'm here!" Amira strides toward us, her long hair bouncing around her. The awkwardness is palpable, but Amira's just waltzed right into the center of a storm, entirely oblivious. "Oh, Kiran! I didn't know you were coming!"

Kiran is dumbfounded; she stares at her sister like she's never seen another human before.

I throw on my most charming smile. "Hey, big sis," I say as I wrap my arms around her in a hug. "How nice to see you again."

"Aw." Amira giggles. "I think I could get used to this."

Situation defused. For now.

Before I let her go, I lock eyes with Kiran. Her mouth remains tight, but her eyes are wild with fury. There's an electric current running between us, sharp and deadly. As much as I can understand her feelings, I refuse to let her do this. I *can't*.

Nothing—no one—is going to ruin my brother's life again.

Not even Kiran.

THREE YEARS AGO

DEEN: Hey

DEEN: :)

KIRAN: Ugh.

DEEN: ???

KIRAN: Sorry

KIRAN: I can't

KIRAN: process

KIRAN: anything right now

DEEN: Wait what??

DEEN: Did I miss something?

DEEN: . . . did I do something wrong?

KIRAN: No

KIRAN: Definitely not

KIRAN: Definitelyyyyyyy not . . .

DEEN: Ohhhhh

DEEN: I get it

DEEN: You keep thinking about . . . you know . . .

KIRAN: Shut up

DEEN: You're feeling all shy now, huh

KIRAN: Shut up!!!!

DEEN: Blushing cuz we kissed, huh

KIRAN: jfsdlkjfksdjfj

KIRAN: STOP

KIRAN: Do you realize how messed up that is???

KIRAN: it's, like, sacrilegious to kiss behind a masjid

DEEN: okay, first of all, we weren't behind a masjid

DEEN: we were behind a tree in a field behind a masjid

KIRAN: omfg

DEEN: SECOND OF ALL, I would argue it's very Sufi

DEEN: I am honoring God by honoring your lips

KIRAN: . . . Allah forgive me

KIRAN: that was my first kiss

KIRAN: and I was fooled by this snake like a chaste and ignorant Eve

DEEN: hey

DEEN: it was mine, too.

KIRAN: Oh.

KIRAN: really . . . ?

DEEN: Yeah. Actually.

DEEN: But I'm sorry

DEEN: the next time you lean in to kiss me

DEEN: I'll be sure to check if it's really what you want

KIRAN: oh my GOD

KIRAN: Weren't you supposed to be helping me feel better??

DEEN: Do you not? :(

KIRAN: . . .

KIRAN: No comment.

LOADING

[CAMBRIA: THE EVOLUTION EXPANSION PACK]

[ROANA GUILD CHAT ROOM]

Kasia Coribund: What would you do

Kasia Coribund: If someone from your past, someone who used to be important to you

Kasia Coribund: Waltzed back into your life

Kasia Coribund: And tried to destroy everything you know?

Devynius Foxx: Wait I've seen this

Devynius Foxx: Is this one of the James Bond movies?

Devynius Foxx: No wait, the plot of Star Wars: Revenge of the Sith?

Kasia Coribund: Yeah. Maybe.

Kasia Coribund: If that makes them Anakin.

Devynius Foxx: Damn, that bad, huh.

Kasia Coribund: Can't say I've ever had an enemy before, exactly

Kasia Coribund: But this is worse

Kasia Coribund: The problem is, they know me.

Kasia Coribund: My secrets, my fears. Etc., etc.

Devynius Foxx: Need me to beat someone up for you?

Devynius Foxx: Cuz I'll do it

Devynius Foxx: I'll do it right now

Kasia Coribund: I wish.

Kasia Coribund: It's just scary, you know?

Kasia Coribund: On one hand, it's kind of lonely, not trusting people

Kasia Coribund: But trusting people is terrifying

Kasia Coribund: Letting yourself be vulnerable and all.

Kasia Coribund: Because what if you showed your heart to someone who might not have deserved it?

Kasia Coribund: Someone who could use that against you?

Kasia Coribund: How do you know when you're actually safe with someone?

Devynius Foxx: Like here?

Devynius Foxx: Like us?

Devynius Foxx: it's a shame there's no suggestive "waggle eyebrows" emoticon

Kasia Coribund: Truly a loss to us all

Kasia Coribund: ugh.

Kasia Coribund: I'm just so, so angry

Kasia Coribund: Angry at them for taking the trust I showed them

Kasia Coribund: And using it against me

Kasia Coribund: But more than that

Kasia Coribund: I'm angry at myself for trusting the wrong person.

Kasia Coribund: And now it's biting me in the ass.

Devynius Foxx: Well . . .

Devynius Foxx: This enemy.

Devynius Foxx: DO they know you?

Devynius Foxx: Do they REALLY know you?

Devynius Foxx: How long has it been since you last spoke to them?

Kasia Coribund: Years now.

Devynius Foxx: So are you still the same person you were then?

Kasia Coribund: I . . .

Kasia Coribund: I guess a lot has changed since then.

Devynius Foxx: Right. Which means they're obviously a very different person, too.

Devynius Foxx: So there's nothing holding you back.

Devynius Foxx: They think they can hold the past over you?

Devynius Foxx: This idiot who has clearly underestimated you?

Devynius Foxx: Hell no.

Devynius Foxx: Show this fool what happens when someone tries to stab you in the back.

Kasia Coribund: And what's that?

Devynius Foxx: You stab the ass in the heart.

CHAPTER 9

KIRAN

Wednesday, June 23

WHEN THERE AREN'T ANY YOGA classes in the group studio at the gym near my house, I use it for personal dance practice.

I used to be shy about it; there's a big open window where people can poke their heads in and watch me, the little brown girl, doing weird twists and turns to loud Bollywood music. But after Mom died, I stopped feeling shy. I was too numb to feel anything.

Now, I'm too *pissed* to feel shy. I turn up the volume on the stereo, feel the vibrations beneath the soles of my feet.

It sounds cheesy, but when I dance, I can let my mind truly wander. Thoughts come and go; I bid them hello, a polite acknowledgment, before sending them off into the void. And slowly but surely there comes a weightlessness to my feet. Every exhale, lighter.

I've thought about going professional. I love dance. Mom loved it, too—she'd been a dancer, a damn good one. But she wanted me to be a doctor, said it would give me more opportunities. Then, when Mom got sick, well. The path became clear.

Left. Right. Spin, step, step. Stomp. The boom of thunder beneath me. The rush of blood and molecules and atoms and life in my veins. One of the dances my mom did for our aunt's wedding was a dance duet: "Dola Re Dola" from the movie *Devdas*, a song about two women celebrating the joy of first love. I was twelve, and watching Mom perform was magic to me, the tiny bells on her ankles like the laughter of birds. I couldn't fully understand the words to the song, but I wanted to be a part of it, too. It's funny, looking back on it now, that a song about first love is the very song that got me into dance.

Seeing Deen the other day was . . . a nightmare.

The plan to glean more info about Faisal was simple, in theory: get Deen alone (ugh), interrogate him à la Detective Phoenix Wright until he either spills or trips up, then comfort Amira after I tell her the truth about her lying, possibly cheating wannabe-fiancé with peanut butter brownies and old Bollywood movies. Of course, considering Deen has made keeping secrets a freaking *art form*, I knew he wouldn't just blurt out the truth easily—which is why I even stayed up late the night before studying investigative journalism tips and tricks with Asher.

But I guess I was doomed from the start, since the first rule of investigative journalism ought to be *Don't go in sweating*. And yesterday? I was drenched. Perspiration-wise. A wet-and-wild bundle of anxiety. Anyway, what the *hell* was Deen thinking, talking about his brother proposing so soon? I've only just met Faisal. Worse, Amira agreed to Deen's family dinner idea, as if it were just an everyday thing instead of a meet-the-parents huge-freaking-deal.

Next week sounds perfect! she said, her face eye-achingly bright and excited and hopeful.

I'm still trying to wrap my head around all of this. I don't understand the rush. And I don't understand why Deen's feigning ignorance about Leah.

More than that, I'm tired of being caught in this antigravity limbo space, watching helplessly as Amira sprints into the dark.

On the dance floor, though, I can move. For now, that helps me think.

I dance harder. Faster. The song finally fades and I'm left standing, a heavily breathing husk. But in the silence, I can still feel the scorch of anger in my chest, the flaring embers that remain.

I've never seen Deen act like that before. I remember three years ago, when he first started to change. It was a warning sign of what was to come, looking back on it: from talking every day and night for hours on end to a slow and steady pull apart. It was pathetic, the more I think about it—*I* was pathetic. I'd text him silly, trivial things like, *Question: Do you think microwaving ice cream is criminal or resourceful?* just to try to get his attention. Eventually, I stopped expecting a response. But hoping. Always hoping. I texted because it hurt not to, because if I didn't, it would mean we were really over.

Then, suddenly, he stopped showing up to Sunday school. The last time I saw him was at the masjid, by sheer coincidence; he and his parents had been talking to the sheikh in hushed tones by the entryway. No one else was there because it was late afternoon on a Monday, and I was only there to drop off some food Dad made for a charity event.

As if he sensed me, Deen turned around. Our eyes met.

It was clear he hadn't slept; his face was ashen, colorless, his eyes dull.

"Are you following me?" he asked in a low voice.

"No. Of course not. But now that you're here, it would be nice if you answered my texts every once in a while."

He stared at me, expressionless. Glanced back at his parents. "I'm sorry. I can't.

"I really, really can't."

And he walked away.

He didn't even give me the chance to ask what the hell was going on.

The other day, when we were arguing at Joe Coffee—I've *never* seen him lose his cool like that, over anything. Or anyone. I've never seen him fight for something like that.

Guess he couldn't be bothered to fight for *me* like that.

I glance into the mirror that covers the entirety of the back wall of the studio. I've recovered my breath now, and there's a tiny rivulet of sweat that runs down my cheek, but I don't have the usual glow of life that suffuses my cheeks when I dance.

I don't look happy at all.

Maybe that's the problem. This is how I hurt myself, every time. I focus so much on fighting, and the longer I fight, the harder it is to learn when to give up. I kept fighting for Deen when it was clear he'd already moved on. I kept refusing to believe what the doctors were saying about Mom, even though it was clear she wasn't going to make it.

Maybe Amira loving Faisal—maybe this is another one of those things.

Maybe this is another battle I'm destined to lose.

I'm home by evening and the house smells like peanut butter brownies because I've gone on a baking spree; these are no longer celebratory Amira-broke-up-with-Faisal brownies but mopey mourning brownies.

The stairs creak. Dad's heavy feet thudding until he reaches the kitchen.

"You're back," he says, adjusting his glasses. The hair on the back of his head is sticking up slightly; he must have just woken up from a nap. He's also got the start of a mustache—it's his "new look." I don't have the heart to tell him it's terrible.

"Yep," I reply, pulling open the oven door. "Want a brownie?"

Dad scowls. He hates peanut butter. He explained peanut butter isn't a thing anywhere outside the US—and since he grew up in Pakistan, he never developed a taste for it. That doesn't stop me from calling him a monster.

He takes a seat at the kitchen table where I left his Philly *Inquirer*. The house feels too quiet, so after I've taken the brownies out to cool, I throw some jazzy lo-fi beats on the TV that Nilina, my guild leader on Cambria, swears helps her relax.

"Have you cleared out the, ah, closet yet?" Dad asks, barely suppressing a yawn. I know he's trying to act casual about it, but I know it must hurt him every time to ask about my mom's closet.

"Not yet."

It's code for *I'm not ready yet,* which is why Dad doesn't push. He nods.

He unfolds the newspaper with a loud crinkle. "I got an interesting phone call today. From Amira." He turns a page. "Did you know anything about this?"

"So you heard." I grab a seat at the table with a fat brownie slice, plus a little extra for love—I need it.

"Have you met him? This . . . Faisal?"

"Yeah. A little over a week ago, over dinner."

Dad's mouth scrunches, like he's thinking. "How is he?"

"Okay, I guess. Not sure I really get it, but . . ." I bite my lip.

"And Amira? How is she?"

"She looked . . . happy. Probably happier than I've ever seen her."

"Good." He exhales. "Then that's all that matters."

I wish I could feel the same way.

That's the only thing that's getting me through this, Kiran—knowing you're all together.

Promise me you'll look after them.

"Don't you think she's moving too fast?" I ask Dad. "Mom just . . . Mom died less than a year ago. We're still picking up the pieces. And she's only been seeing this guy for three months."

Dad goes quiet for a moment, like he's thinking. "Did I ever tell you how your mom and I met?"

"Arranged marriage, right?"

"Yes." He turns another page of his newspaper. "I first met her at a function—an engagement party, I think. Her cousin, Asim

Mamu, was marrying my sister, Reina Phuppo, and there was talk of setting us up next and I was nervous. But then I saw your mom, sitting at a table with one of her younger cousins, making her laugh. I immediately had feelings for her. We talked a little. But I knew something was there. Something special. We got engaged, soon after that."

"So you fell in love right then and there?"

"See, there is no falling in *love*. You can have instant feelings, but love—no. Actually, the first few years of our marriage were rocky. We kept fighting. Once, when Amira was still a baby, I said something stupid to your mother. She took Amira in the middle of the night and snuck out of the house. I couldn't find her for days. Turns out she was hiding out at your nani's."

"*What?*" I try to imagine my mom, younger, out in the cold with baby Amira in her arms. "What did you *say*?"

"We were fighting over the dishes. We were both young and stupid and angry. We had no idea what we were doing." He folds his newspaper back into a perfect rectangle and gently places it on the table. "Years later, when you were born, you had a really bad cold and we had to stay up all night looking after you. It was just a cold, but we were terrified. And one night we were sitting next to each other on the couch: Mom had you in her lap, fussing over you, trying to get you to take your medicine. I was watching over her shoulder, making duas and praying you'd actually take it. It hit us then—how we were both feeling the exact same way. How for once we were on the same wavelength. Because of you."

"I . . . didn't know that." I stare at my lap. My nose suddenly feels stuffy.

"She looked beautiful that night," he adds sadly. "That was the night we decided we were going to do everything we could to make us work. That was the night we decided to love each other."

"What do you mean? You didn't love each other before?"

Seeing my confused expression, he smiles.

"There are millions of shayaris and ghazals and songs that spin beautiful words about what love is: fire, wine, pain," he goes on. "But that is all passion. Feeling. Love, on the other hand, is an act. A practice. A decision."

"Are you saying who you love is a *choice*?"

"No, no. Who you have *feelings* for—that is not a choice. Feelings happen whether you want them to or not. But love isn't a feeling; it's the act of planting a seed and putting in the time and care it needs to grow. It demands hard work and renewal to survive. It demands commitment. By necessity, it cannot be taken lightly.

"That is why in life, the two most important choices you will ever make are your career path, because it's what you will spend every day of your life doing, and your partner, because it's who you will spend every day of your life with. That is the person you have committed to—decided to—love, for the rest of your life. That is *work*."

I snort. "That's definitely not how they show it in movies."

Dad makes a face and waves with his hand, like he's waving off a bad smell. "What do they know? Real love is messy. Messy doesn't sell."

"Someone should warn Amira."

He sighs tiredly. "Perhaps she already knows. Amira is an adult now. She made her first choice very early, to be a lawyer. Now she's old enough to make her second. It is a little fast, maybe, but she is a smart girl. If she chooses this Faisal, there must be a good reason. She has told me a little, and I know this Faisal has been a comfort to her. Who are we to interfere?"

I clench my fists. Deen's words are ringing in my head: *This isn't about you. It's about Amira and Faisal. We're here for* them *and that's* it.

Except what does it really mean to be there for someone? Does it mean supporting them no matter what they do? Or does it mean stopping them before they take a dangerous plunge, even if you risk them hating you forever? Isn't it a sister's job to interfere if you're about to do something stupid?

In the end, it is Amira's choice, and I don't want to take that away from her. But wrong choices do happen, and right now Amira still has the time to look before she leaps. If only she'd slow down.

I might be fighting for a lost cause. But I'll be damned if I don't at least try.

"If you are really worried," says Dad gently, "we'll be seeing him and his family next weekend. People have a habit of letting their guards down when they're in their own homes. If he truly is a bad choice, we'll see it."

My stomach rolls. I don't look forward to seeing Deen again so soon after our fight—especially now that he knows I'm totally against his brother and Amira being together. Especially since he'll be the one orchestrating the proposal.

But a flicker of an idea comes alive in my head. Dad has a point: we'll be in Faisal's house. And even if he proposes, that doesn't make it too late for Amira to pull out. While Deen is busy helping his brother, there'll be no one to stop me from, say, taking a look around, searching for any clue to the truth of what these boys are really hiding.

Who knows what I might *accidentally* stumble into?

"You should get some sleep, beta." Dad smiles. "Think about what I said."

"Oh, I will, Dad," I reply, clearing my plate off the table. "I most certainly will."

CHAPTER 10

DEEN

Sunday, June 27

"HOW DO I LOOK?"

Faisal is wearing a maroon button-down shirt—collar down, because he's not a douche—and some brown khakis. He's thrown in some gel on his hair, too, which does little to tame his curls, but does add a little je ne sais quoi. I haven't seen him this dressed up in years. It feels good to see him so . . . alive.

I grin. "You look like a million bucks. The bee's knees. Dare I say, an absolute unit."

Faisal snorts. "Always gotta be overkill with you."

"Always." I pull a pencil from behind my ear. I even have a clipboard with a list I typed up earlier this morning. I'm not messing around.

"All right, let's go through this again," I say. "Deodorant slathered?"

"Check."

"Teeth brushed?"

"Check."

"Garden swept?"

". . . Is that one of your euphemisms?"

"No, it's about the garden out back. I wanted to double-check in case, like, feral raccoons wandered in and ate the string lights or something. I'll check it one last time." I mark that one with a star.

"What about M&D?" Faisal asks. "Have they been briefed?"

I nod. "Told them about Amira's mom, so they know the situation. No awkward comments. And they're heating up food now like I asked, since Amira's dad likes to eat early. Also, Mom assured me she asked for extra gulab jamun from the caterer, since it's Amira's favorite." Gulab jamun is basically deep-fried doughnut balls soaked in sugar syrup. They're practically *everyone's* favorite.

I cross the section labeled *M&D* off the list. I've been at their place since last night, preparing; it was Vinny's idea to do the checklist. "Makes things *legit*," he'd said.

"Okay. Okay, good." Faisal massages between his brows. "And the brownies for Kiran?"

"Yep," I answer. If I remember correctly, she had a peanut butter brownie obsession, so I tried making some from a box. Don't ask me how they turned out. I'm stressed enough as it is. But I need a peace offering. It's like I told Kas: if Kiran tries to mess with Faisal, then I'll stab her ass in the heart—only, with kindness. Which, honestly, sounds really weird the more that I think about it.

I even asked Vinny for advice yesterday.

"So, I may have confirmed said person from our previous conversation does in fact hold a very bad grudge," I informed him, storming back to his dorm room after my failed coffee "date" with Kiran.

Vinny, sitting at his desk, nodded sagely as he balanced a pen on his upper lip. "Then you gotta do the only thing you can do to make sure they can't ruin everything. Keep your enemy close."

"Okay, but how do you keep an enemy close when they hate you?"

"Make them not hate you," he answered with a grin, which made the pen on his lip fall with a clatter.

It was about as helpful as I should have expected.

Back to the present:

"Lastly"—I take a deep breath—"the ring."

Faisal digs into his back pocket and pulls out a tiny red velvet case. He creaks it open. Inside is a modest gold ring embedded with an emerald. A diamond wasn't an option, with most of the money Faisal's been saving earmarked for the nonprofit. But I have a strong feeling Amira will be perfectly okay with that.

The velvet case trembles in Faisal's palm, and he fumbles to close it.

I pat him on the back. "It's gonna go great. I'll make sure of it. All you gotta remember is she loves you." I loosen his tie a little. "Honestly, anyone would."

Faisal smiles. "Thanks, little bro."

A pinch in my chest. *Don't thank me*, I want to say. But I bite my tongue. He hates it when I say things like that, and I definitely don't want to bum him out, today of all days. The reality is that this, trying to give him this one perfect moment, isn't even a *piece* of what I owe for what he's sacrificed for me. The bare wall of his office should have been covered with his law degrees, with awards, with photos of graduation. Instead, he's had to fight tooth and nail just to recover pieces of what he lost, the future he should have had. He can barely even start a nonprofit to help kids because of his stupid criminal record.

It's funny; so much of Faisal's life has been him trying to hold on, trying to wrangle back his self-control—and yeah, there were many close calls.

But in the end, I'm the one who lost mine. And Faisal had to suffer for it.

The stairs groan; it's Mom who comes down them, her long, curly black hair disheveled. She's wearing a dark blue shalwar kameez and her trademark stone-cold Desi Athena expression.

Her arched eyebrows shoot up when she sees us. "You're both actually ready? This is a first."

"And you're not?"

If she detects any annoyance in my voice, she ignores it. Or maybe I've talked to her that way for so long, she's convinced herself that's just how I sound. "Your dad's still getting ready and I have to go color my grays. Deen, turn on the oven—we need to warm up the naan."

I salute, all fake smiles. "On it."

Mom nods. "And Faisal?"

"Yes?"

She draws out the silence, then: "Does Amira know? About you? About the accident?"

Faisal's face stills, as if while trying to process Mom's words, his brain overloaded. He blinks hard. "N-no," he stammers. "She doesn't."

My hands curl into fists.

"Good. Keep it that way. Weddings invite enough gossip as it is, and people will speculate, but as long as we keep the truth in the family, it'll stay in the family. As far as anyone else knows, you studied abroad."

Faisal swallows and looks away, but Mom keeps her cold eyes on him, nailing him into place.

"You might be tempted to tell her everything, but I need you to understand that if word comes out about what you did, there is no turning back. You think Amira will marry you knowing you have a criminal record, on top of everything else? You think her family will let you anywhere near her? You open that box, you invite our entire family's reputation to destruction. Think about what it would do to Deen."

I flinch.

The line between Mom's eyebrows deepens the way it always does when she's stressed about something. "You open that box, and I can assure you, we won't be paying for your move to California. I need to know that when you leave this house, you'll remain stable. It'll look bad enough if word comes out, but then for you to move, leaving us to clean the mess? What if you relapse? I won't allow it."

Fury sparks a white-hot flame in my belly. As if Faisal hasn't already beaten himself up about his past enough as it is, Mom has to rub it in his face.

"I know," Faisal whispers.

"I need you to tell me you understand," Mom says.

"I understand."

"Good." Mom's dark gaze slides to me, damning me to the same promise. But I already know. I know how people would react, better than anyone.

I'll take the fall for you, Faisal's voice echoes from somewhere in the darkest parts of my brain.

I know to keep our secret. No matter what. After all, we moved just to make sure no one learned the truth.

I think about when I saw Kiran at the masjid that one last time. The broken look on her face. I squeeze my fingernails into my palm.

"Some things are better left unsaid, beta," Mom says before going back upstairs, leaving us both in stunned silence. I know she'll never say it, but she wants this—Amira and him—to happen just as badly as I do. She wants this Faisal thing to be finally laid to rest. And in her eyes, marriage is the most convenient way to do it. Once he gets hitched, people will stop asking about the past. All they'll care about are future babies.

It's about getting past the finish line now.

I force a weak smile. "Welp, I see Mom's just as *wonderful* as ever."

For a moment, Faisal says nothing, but I can see the dark thoughts roiling behind his eyes.

"Mom. Mom never changes," sighs Faisal finally, half exasperated, half making his voice sound like the announcer guy from Fallout 4. He's trying so hard to keep on a brave face, like his own mother didn't just knock him down to the ground. As usual.

Suddenly, the doorbell rings. Confused, I check my phone. It's only 6:00 p.m.

They're early.

"I'll get it," I announce as I'm already running up the stairs.

I throw open the front door, breathless.

But it's not the Nooranis.

It's Mona khala. Mom's younger sister. A menace if there ever was one. And I'm not saying that because she only gives us fifteen dollars at Eid, even though she's a doctor with her own private practice. Faisal once joked that Mona needed to be a cardiac surgeon because of all the heart attacks she gives people. Mom was mad at him for a week.

But he's not wrong. I've found her in my bedroom looking under my mattress for porn (as if anyone keeps porn under their fucking bed anymore). I've seen her yell at her cousin in front of everyone on Thanksgiving for overcooking the turkey by ten minutes.

And when Faisal first started getting bullied in middle school, she was the one who suggested Faisal learn how to better defend himself. As if the bullying was somehow his fault for being too weak.

"What are you doing here?" I ask, trying to keep my voice level. It doesn't work.

"Hi, meri jaan," Mona khala says sweetly, kissing my cheek and pushing past me. Behind her is a parade of her kids: Sara, Salman, and Sohail, all under the age of seven, and therefore the worst kind of human. "Your mom didn't tell you? She invited me. It's a big night! Plus, you know how things like this go. If it's a total disaster, she'll need someone to gossip with."

Bullshit. Mom is many things, but she isn't the type to gossip, especially after what happened with Faisal. She must have let it slip that we were having dinner with a potential match for Faisal, and Mona just invited herself.

I blink away the dizziness. "She did *not* tell me, actually."

Mona's husband, Naveed, stumbles in close behind, carrying some sort of baby basket where, I presume, Sami, my youngest cousin, resides. If kids are the worst kind of human, then babies are subhuman.

"Hey, bud," Naveed says with a wave. *Bud.* People should only call each other bud if they reside in the Deep South and own a pickup truck, or they're itching for a fight, or both. He drops Sami's baby basket by my feet. "Can you put him somewhere quiet? He's going to be napping for the next hour or two. Hopefully. Oh, and could you order a pizza for the kids?"

He doesn't wait for my response; he follows Mona into the kitchen while my little cousins—minus Sami—rush in like a storm and dash straight for the basement, where Faisal keeps the video games.

"Rania!" Mona's screaming for my mom from somewhere in the kitchen. "Are you upstairs?" There's a crinkle of foil. "Oooh, look at all the gulab jamun."

I close my eyes. This is what I get for trying to be prepared, for putting in work. It all went to waste. Maybe it's because I haven't prayed in years. God's definitely punishing me.

This was supposed to be a quiet night. An *easy* night.

"Nothing's ever easy, huh?" I ask the evening air before slamming the door shut.

The Nooranis arrive an hour later—right on time. Amira, wearing a deep red shalwar, comes bearing gifts: flowers, specifically white camellias for Mom (her favorite, which I may have told Amira earlier today), and cookies from Schmackary's for the rest of us. Her dad is a small man wearing a knitted vest and metal-rimmed glasses, and reminds me of a scholarly humanoid mouse. He's a scientist or researcher, I think, so it checks out.

"Young man," he addresses me, shaking my hand.

"Dad. That's *Deen*," Amira whispers with a snort.

"Ah, Deen! Of course. Assalamu alaikum."

I smile. "Walaikumu assalam." The greeting feels strange on my tongue. Unfamiliar. But I'm surprised by how naturally it comes out of me. It's been a while since I've gone to Sunday school, or even hung out with other Muslims; ever since Faisal's incident, my relationship with The Big Guy Upstairs has been strained, at best.

Kiran comes in last. She's wearing a long black shalwar kameez, and I'll admit, she looks . . . good. For someone with no fashion sense, she wears it well. But she definitely chose to wear black on purpose. Like she's protesting. Or in mourning.

"Hello, Deen."

"Kiran." When she practically declared war last time I saw her, I decided to assume she can and will shank me without a moment's notice. Or worse, reveal how much she really knows about me and Faisal, in front of everyone.

"Huh." She stops and stares at my forehead.

My eyes narrow. "What?"

"Oh, nothing. You just don't have that ugly vein sticking out today." She walks down the hall, following her family.

I rub my forehead. It's smooth. "I don't have any ugly veins," I hiss after her. "My veins are *beautiful*."

I know I should be more friendly, but I don't like that she looks confident. On my territory. It's unsettling. Especially because I still don't know what she knows—about Faisal, about Leah. Hell, I don't even know who she *is* anymore; the girl I knew was easy-going, funny. Had a goofy laugh, and laughed at everything.

Now she's an unknown. And I don't like unknowns. But I won't let her get under my skin. Not tonight. Not when I know Kas is also off fighting her own battles, which, weirdly enough, makes me feel less alone.

Everyone greets everyone; Dad offers to take Amira's dad into the living room for some chai before dinner, and they'll get along just fine: Faisal told me Amira's dad has strong opinions about politics—but not too strong. Mona khala makes Amira do a twirl under the guise of inspecting her dress, and even though it comes across as a prospective buyer inspecting a horse, Amira humors her. I triple-check the garden in the backyard; no sign of feral raccoons, and the string lights are still up.

It's gonna go great, I repeat in my head, like a mantra.

Eventually, we all sit at the table in the dining room, where Mom has set up a whole buffet of dishes, still warm thanks to the burners she's placed beneath them—two types of biryani, kabobs, curries, and a big vat of nihari. The house smells like simmered spices and meat. Warm and welcoming, even—it's unrecognizable. The house itself keeps creaking and groaning, as if it doesn't know how to deal with actual movement and life within its walls.

"So I hear Amira is a lawyer." Mom looks at Kiran. "What about you, Kiran?" A softball question. Mom's here to get to know the Nooranis, not scare them away. For once, we're almost on the same page.

Almost.

"I'm . . . nothing right now," Kiran replies. "But I'm starting college in August."

"Soon, then. What do you plan to study?"

"Medicine. Eventually."

I stop chewing. There it is again. I can't help but wonder what made Kiran decide on medicine.

Guess it's not really any of my business, though.

Mona khala makes a face. "Impractical these days. Unless you come from a lot of money. Otherwise, you'll have to spend dozens of years paying off student loans. It's grueling."

Okay, it's definitely not Mona khala's business, either.

"These kabobs, man," I say loudly, in a way I'm begging the universe will change the subject. "I could eat them forever!"

"I see your point, Mona aunty," Kiran answers, as though I don't exist. "But I managed to get a scholarship. And it's what I want to do." She adds softly, a little less sure: "In honor of my mom."

Ah. So that's why.

But is that what she really wants?

"At what cost?" Mona replies sternly. "An undergrad scholarship won't help with med-school tuition. No mother I know would want to see their child drown in debt."

The clatter of silverware ceases. Amira shifts in her seat, and her dad seems intent on scooping as much curry as humanly possible on his naan. As for Faisal, beside me, I can't see his expression, but I can feel it: the tangible awkwardness, the frustration, like a cold shroud. From somewhere in the basement, I can hear the theme of Super Smash Bros. blasting and high-pitched screaming. At least my cousins are having a better time than we are.

"Well," Kiran says slowly, "my mom is dead, so . . ."

My throat squeezes like something's gotten dislodged. Watching Kiran get grilled by Mona khala . . . this doesn't feel good.

"Dead? Uff." Mona khala puts down her fork and looks at Mom. "Cancer? Heart disease?"

Mom gives her sister a meaningful look.

"Anyway—regardless"—Mona begins helping herself to some gulab jamun—"it's terrible, losing your mom when you're young. That must be hard. But God never gives you more than you can handle. We must take comfort in that."

Kiran stares at her plate, as if trying to glare holes through the china with sheer willpower. Beside me, Faisal's holding his head in his hands.

I need to regain control of the situation, fast. We're not exactly the easiest family to deal with (whose is?) but Amira doesn't need to know that—at least not now, not *yet*.

I laugh weakly. "I don't think that's as comforting as you think it is, Mona khala."

"You know, when *our* mom died a few years ago," she continues, also ignoring me, "it was hard on all of us. Knowing we have to live the rest of our lives without her. My kids won't know who their nani is. Absolutely heartbreaking."

"Except Nani lived in Pakistan and we never visited her *anyway*," I say, stabbing a kabob with a fork.

Mona clicks her tongue. "Even so, we could have. And now we *can't*."

I debate throwing something at her.

Mom clears her throat. "So how do you spend your days? Are you working?"

"Um, no." Kiran relaxes, gently puts down a piece of naan she was about to put in her mouth. "I dance a lot. My mom was a dancer, too."

Mona's eyes light up. "Dance! Classical? How cute. Will you be continuing in college, too?"

Stop. Talking, I scream inwardly.

"Unfortunately, I won't have time," Kiran replies. "For now, I do mostly Kathak. Modern, sometimes."

"Well, you know, if these two get married"—Mona gestures between Faisal and Amira—"you'll have to dance at the wedding."

Kiran's eyes go wide. Amira's face ignites in a deep shade of scarlet.

I glare at Mom. *Control your sister.* But she pretends not to see me. Typical.

"If . . . ," comes Faisal's shaking voice, "if that happens, Kiran doesn't have to feel pressured."

Nice one, Faisal.

"Nonsense," Mona khala replies. "If God gives you a gift, you must use it. And what better way to honor her mother than dance? It would be beautiful."

"Don't you think we're getting a little ahead of ourselves?" asks Kiran. "First of all, I haven't danced at any events in years, and—"

"If it's just a matter of nerves—then Deen, what about you? You could do a dance, too."

"*What?*" Kiran and I both say at the same time. Of all the stupid ideas Mona khala has pushed forward, this is by far the worst one.

The situation's already precarious as it is. Forcing her to dance at a wedding she's not exactly excited about—even if it wasn't my suggestion, I just *know* it's going to put me at number one on her to-shank list, if I'm not there already.

Mona dabs her mouth calmly with a napkin. "You *are* the only siblings of the bride and groom. Dancing at weddings has become more commonplace these days. You could do your own dances just before the Nikkah." She looks at Mom, as if she'd know. "What do they call it? Dance-offs?"

"I don't *dance*," I say.

"You're desi. As much as you pretend it's not, it's in your blood."

"That doesn't even make sen—!" I groan. I don't even know how to start arguing with her. I'm starting to remember why I rarely visit M&D's.

Finally, Amira giggles. "I'm sorry, but . . . I do kind of want to see that."

Everyone looks at her like she's sprouted a second head.

"Amira!" Kiran hisses.

"What? I mean . . ." She smiles shyly. "Not to be presumptuous or anything. But I think it'd be cute to see my little sister dance at my wedding. To be honest, I was hoping for it. And I'm sure Faisal would be amused seeing Deen. Right?"

Faisal blinks. "I—I mean, sure . . ."

I glare at him wordlessly.

"Then it's settled." Mona khala plops her napkin onto her empty plate. "Deen and Kiran will dance at the wedding."

THREE YEARS AGO

DEEN: So question

DEEN: when the hell were you going to tell me you can dance?

KIRAN: eh

KIRAN: I dunno, you never asked?

DEEN: I didn't realize I had to!

DEEN: jesus

DEEN: I mean, I can dance a little but that was a whole other level

DEEN: If I could dance like that, EVERYONE would know

DEEN: "hi my name is Deen and I can kick your ass at dancing"

DEEN: "hi my name is Deen and I could try out as one of Beyoncé's backup dancers and not be laughed offstage"

DEEN: "hi my name is Deen, don't talk to me, I'm dancing"

KIRAN: wait, how did you even see me??

KIRAN: Guys were supposed to be in a separate area

DEEN: Separate area . . . how backward

DEEN: there is no separation when it comes to love

KIRAN: unbelievable.

KIRAN: anyway, it's not like I whipped it out of nowhere

KIRAN: I practiced for weeks

KIRAN: Ghazala aunty asked me and a couple girls to prepare something for her daughter's mehndi

KIRAN: my mom can't really dance anymore

KIRAN: so she thought it'd be a good opportunity to try it, see how I like it

DEEN: so what's the verdict?

KIRAN: it's . . . really embarrassing

KIRAN: I think I prefer dancing for myself

DEEN: Noorani, you disappoint me

DEEN: how about you try it again

DEEN: for me

DEEN: . . . . alone

KIRAN: Pretty sure when God says to "lower your gaze" to be modest and not creepy

KIRAN: God was directing it at you

DEEN: damn

DEEN: Do you think that means God actually notices me?

KIRAN: . . .

KIRAN: Tonight was a long night

KIRAN: So I think I'm gonna take off my makeup

DEEN: Go on . . .

KIRAN: change into my pj's

DEEN: yes, I like where this is going . . .

KIRAN: and then pray for your soul.

DEEN: :(

CHAPTER 11

KIRAN

Sunday, June 27

AFTER WE ALL FINISH EATING dinner and another round of chai is brought out, I excuse myself for the bathroom. Just in time, too, because Mona's begun lecturing on the difficulty of raising kids and working full-time, a discussion that she's not so subtly directing at Amira, and I'm five seconds from screaming.

I head for the hall, but I have no idea where Faisal's room could possibly be; the house is insultingly huge: vaulted ceilings, multiple stairways, winding corridors. They even have a separate prep room thing attached to the kitchen, the kind where you'd have servants gossiping à la *Downton Abbey* before bringing you poisoned canapés.

This is a problem, because I have to be quick. I can't afford to leave Amira's side for very long—not only because I want to save her from Mona, but I don't want to give Faisal a chance to be alone with her. It's bad enough seeing them smiling at each other, as if everything is okay, as if Faisal isn't hiding something.

My biggest problem, though, is Deen, who's been watching me like a hawk. And thanks to Mona, I've lost all my earlier confidence; Mona's words about what Mom would want cut deep into my already frayed nerves, exposing them for all to see. In front of the last person I'd want seeing. I'm not a stranger to aunties and uncles giving unsolicited advice—mostly, it's a way to show they love and care about you—but this Mona woman apparently wouldn't know tact if it tactfully strangled her with its bare hands. All the more reason why I can't let Amira be a part of this family.

I figure Faisal's room is either upstairs or downstairs, where I can hear Deen's younger cousins screaming their heads off and blasting some Mario game.

But just as I'm trying to decide where to look first, there's a sudden blast of sound right behind me, and I nearly leap out of my skin. It's the adhan, the Muslim call to prayer, coming from a small gold alarm clock on the wall. My heart slams against my ribs. I can't believe I was nearly murdered by the adhan, of all things. God's sense of irony is astounding.

I try to calm myself before I head deeper into the hallway

and crash

straight

into

Deen.

"Lost?" he asks.

I leap back. My heart's racing all over again.

"Yeah," I reply, as coolly as I can. "Just trying to find the bathroom."

"Down the hall, make a left." He grins. "You should hurry back, though, before all the peanut butter brownies are gone. You like those, right?"

My mouth opens, ready to let out the ugly, excited gasp I make whenever I discover I'm in the vicinity of baked goods, only to catch myself just in time. It'll take way more than brownies to make up for all his thoughtlessness.

I smile politely. "That was a long time ago."

The adhan fades, and there's a beat of silence between us. I wait for Deen to leave, but he doesn't. On the other side of the wall, I can hear our parents talking, Amira laughing—muffled sounds that carry from the dining room into the quiet, dark space where Deen and I stand, alone. It's the first time, I realize, we've stood next to each other in years. He's grown . . . taller. I have to look up to meet his eyes, where I catch a glimpse of something wavering behind them, like a tiny light. Or a flame.

His grin slips away. He's close enough that I can smell his cologne, or his deodorant. It's sharp, like pine or mint.

"I'm . . . sorry, by the way," he says slowly, rubbing his arm. "About Mona. She can get carried away." Deen avoids my gaze, like he's actually ashamed. I did notice him trying to defend me at the table, which caught me off guard; for a moment, I'll admit, I felt a budding gratitude in my chest. But I'm not sure it's a feeling I like right now.

"It's fine," I reply. "It's not like we *have* to dance at the wedding if we don't want to, so there's nothing to worry about." Especially if there is no wedding. But I don't need to tell him that.

"That's not—" Deen makes a sound like a mix between a groan

and a sad, resigned chuckle. "Whatever. I forgot who I'm talking to. The bathroom is over there. Just don't get lost, or I'll have to hold your hand and walk you there myself."

Heat flushes through me in indignation, and a thousand insults come to my lips. But Deen's already gone.

As his footsteps fade, I press myself against the window behind me and take a deep breath. The glass windowpane is cool against my burning skin. I've bought myself a couple of minutes with my bathroom excuse, but that won't be enough to find Faisal's room and dig through it. I need more time.

I turn around. Through the window, a glimmer catches my attention outside: summer night dew on flower petals glittering like jewels, and string lights, hung from the canopies of trees, bathing the backyard garden with a gentle warmth. The lights lead to a wrought-iron gazebo surrounded by white rosebushes and tangled briars, illuminating the structure in buttery-gold glory.

The stinging tug behind my ribs is so sudden, I draw a sharp intake of breath. This must have taken forever. It's elegant. Inhuman, even, in its beauty. Like magic.

The perfect place for a proposal.

I remember now, Deen mentioning something about a garden for Faisal's proposal. Did he set this up? How could someone so obnoxious make something so beautiful? For some reason, it annoys me even more than I already am. I guess Deen must have been serious about wanting it to be perfect.

But this could work in my favor: if this is where he's planning on having Faisal propose, then maybe I can kill two Deen-shaped birds with one stone.

A plan is starting to form in my head, but I'm going to need a little help.

I grab the small gold adhan alarm clock and head downstairs.

Three kids, no older than seven or eight years old, are huddled a foot away from the TV. A Nintendo Switch that they've ripped from the console is splayed haphazardly by their feet, surrounded by wires—I wonder if it's Deen's or Faisal's.

Kids, I've learned, are easy to manipulate once you realize how much less cynical they are than adults. Last summer, I babysat my neighbor's two kids, six-year-old twins Will and Tessa, every day for two weeks, and it would have been hell, except for one thing: they believed almost anything I told them. It became a game for me. How ridiculous of a lie could I make them genuinely believe? By the third day, I had them convinced that the trees outside were actually my long-lost sisters who were cursed by a witch, and that I, too, was an ageless witch. They became very obedient after that. Made almost $750 for doing practically nothing.

I find a window a few feet away from them and hide the alarm clock behind the curtain. Deen's cousins pay me no attention; on the screen, Mario is racing Sonic on a track, while in real life, one of the kids—Sohail, I think I heard Mona call him—is mashing buttons on the controller. They must have just been babies when Deen and I first met.

I clear my throat. "Hey. Do you guys know where Faisal's room is?"

The girl, whose name I think is Sara, gives me a deadpan stare.

"Aren't you the one marrying him?"

"No, the one marrying him is prettier," says one of the boys, squinting up at me.

"I think she's pretty, too."

"No. That's—" *Amira*, I almost say. "My sister might marry him. But it's not official yet."

"Seems pretty official to me."

"Okay." I close my eyes, refocus. "Well, I need to know where his room is."

"Why?" The other brother, Salman, eyes me curiously.

"Because that's where he keeps the holy water," I say. *Got 'em.*

Sara stills. "Why do you need holy water?"

"Because . . ." I bite my lip, look away. "I don't want to say. I already told the adults and they didn't believe me."

"Told them what?" Salman asks impatiently.

"It's just . . ." I take a deep breath. I'm deep in the role now. "There's a jinn, in the garden. He kept staring at me through the window, and I think he wants something, but . . . I'm honestly scared."

Behind Deen's cousins, confetti bursts across the TV screen. Sonic has beaten Mario for first place. Sohail turns around and glares at me, as if it's my fault he, playing an Italian plumber, somehow lost to a supersonic hedgehog.

"Jinn aren't real. You're just trying to mess with us," he says.

Sara shakes her head. "Not true. Mom says they only live in Pakistan."

"That's wrong on so many levels, but I don't have time to argue with you," I retort. "I'm telling you, there's a jinn outside and it's very angry, and I need to know where Faisal's room is or else the jinn will—"

Suddenly—thanks to my turning back the hands by a few minutes—the adhan alarm clock goes off again, full blast. Deen's cousins scream; Sohail grabs his sister's arm and clings tightly.

"It's the jinn. It's trying to scare us," I say calmly, though I bug out my eyes for dramatic effect.

Salman looks at me. "What do we do?"

Sohail lets go of his sister's arm. "Jinns aren't real," he repeats, a little less sure this time. "It's—it's a trick or something."

Sara points down a dark corridor to our left. "Faisal's room is there."

"Perfect." I bend down to their level. "I need you three to go outside and take down"—I gesture at the window—"all of those lights if you can. The louder you are, the more afraid the jinn will be. I'll grab the holy water and join you, okay? But don't be too loud—you don't want to get caught. By anyone."

Sara and Salman nod, while Sohail folds his arms across his chest. But still, he follows them, and I watch as they frantically race up the stairs until they're out of sight. I ignore the pang of guilt in my stomach. I don't feel particularly good about lying just to use them as a distraction, but at least if they're outside and messing with the decorations, Deen will be kept busy.

I flick the light on in Faisal's room, and for a moment, I'm thrown off. It's all beige, with carefully curated splashes of deep blue, too thoughtful and matchy to have been Faisal's choice of decor. There's a sloped ceiling painted black, and a leather reading chair tucked in the corner that looks like it's never been sat on. Matching mahogany furniture: a carved four-poster bed, and a reading desk, surface clear save for a laptop, a couple of leather-bound Merriam-Webster dictionaries, and a tiny terrarium that I'm fairly certain is filled with fake plants. It's all stale, and though the room's furnished, it somehow manages to feel empty—like a staged room in a house for sale. It's almost . . . too neat.

The only sign of normalcy is a laundry basket tucked in the corner that's been left open, revealing a pile of dirty clothes.

Is Faisal a clean freak? I wonder. Or does he just not feel at home here? His mom flashes in my mind: her eagle eyes, her perpetually judging stare. Somehow, I wouldn't be surprised if it were both.

But I don't have time to think. I start looking, heading straight for the desk.

I flip open the laptop, but of course it's password protected, so I yank open the first drawers and shuffle through some folders and papers, though most are empty or blank; apparently he and I use the same fancy tabbed folders, so at least we have one thing in common. Focus, Kiran.

I open a second drawer. The problem is, I don't even know what I'm looking for. More incriminating pictures? Love letters from Leah? Weird porn, maybe? But with as clean as this room is, my chances of finding something on him are dwindling by the dust bunny.

There's not a single thing here. And that's the weirdest thing of all. There's hardly anything. My own drawers are a mess of spare change, of notes and ticket stubs and Polaroids. Old receipts. Either he deeply ascribes to a Marie Kondo lifestyle or he's a serial killer.

Or he's hiding something.

Third drawer. It's just a couple of folders filled with legal stationery for AFFEY, the nonprofit Amira's helping him get up and running. There are some copies of contracts, too, and a couple of bills and statutes. Boring legal stuff. I'm running out of steam by the time I get to the last drawer. I shuffle through some more AFFEY paperwork.

There's a crash and thud from somewhere outside; Deen's cousins are hard at work, from the sound of it, but that means I'm running out of time.

I flip through folder after folder, frantically now, imagining the tips of my fingers leaving sweat marks everywhere.

At the bottom of the drawer I find a bright orange Campus notebook. The cover is water stained, which, given how neat he keeps things, is . . . odd. The pages crackle as I start to flip it open.

There's handwriting. Neat and precise. It's Faisal's notebook, though I'm surprised he has one—not many people write in notebooks these days, unless it's for a school project or they're one of those organizational bullet journal people. But this notebook doesn't appear to be either. I remember Asher telling me something once, back when I used to have a blog that I kept up for all of two weeks. Boys don't do diaries, he'd said. Boys write manifestos.

I suddenly feel nervous. My fingertips burn. Part of me is screaming not to read it, that I have no business reading it. Maybe part of me is afraid of what I'll find.

If he has anything to hide, he has no business marrying Amira, another voice in me presses. A voice that gives me resolve.

I stop flipping; the page I land on is dated November. Three years ago. My throat tightens as I begin to read:

> *Sometimes, it's hard to breathe. I'll wake up in the middle of the night and gasp for air. I can't even scream. M&D tell me they're terrors or nightmares, but I don't think I get enough sleep to dream anymore. You'd think they'd recognize withdrawal symptoms, but I don't think they want to admit it. Like if they pretend it never happened, everything will be fine.*
>
> *Leah stopped replying to my texts. I wonder if she hates me. She has every right to.*
>
> *The fucked-up thing is that if the drug wasn't still in my system that night, I'd have had no hope of getting out of the felony charge. I'm learning a lot about weird legal loopholes these days. Just not the way I wanted.*
>
> *I should be happy. But honestly, all I want is to remember how to breathe again.*

I think of Faisal's face in the picture I saw. I love being right as much as the next person, but this . . .

Just what kind of drugs was he on? And what's this felony charge? The words start to blur on the page. I'm trying to grasp what it all means, but it's too much.

And Leah, again. At the center of it all.

I carefully rip the page out and shove the notebook back in the drawer. I feel sick. Is this really the kind of thing Faisal feels okay hiding from his future life partner? *Why?*

Maybe ignorance really is bliss. The rumors about Faisal hadn't even come close: this is so much worse than I thought.

Faisal is so much worse than I thought.

There's a searing prickle on the back of my neck. And the smell of pine.

I spin around, hiding the page behind my back.

"What do you think you're doing?"

Deen stands beneath the doorway. There's no sign of his usual smile, and his eyes burn. He's furious.

"Nothing," I say quickly. Too quickly.

"Nothing, huh." Deen takes a step toward me. "Want to hear something funny? I thought a bunch of feral raccoons were trying to raze the garden outside, but—surprise—it was just my cousins. Apparently they've gotten the idea that there's a jinn loose outside. Thankfully, I wrangled them off before they could do too much damage."

Another step. "And then I realized you'd been gone an awfully long time, far longer than any normal person should take in the bathroom."

I can feel the rush of blood in my veins, every cell ablaze beneath my skin. I'm wearing a shalwar kameez, which means I have no back pockets and nowhere to hide the paper.

Deen's going to realize I know the truth about his brother. Or at the very least, that I've been digging for it. And I don't want to give him any more reason to keep an eye on me.

The thought hits me, then. Is Deen really in on hiding his brother's secrets from Amira, too? And a sadder thought: Would I be surprised if he was?

A roar of shouts and claps shakes the ceiling above us. The bang of footsteps. Deen stops moving toward me and listens.

"Deen, beta! Kiran! Come upstairs!" comes Mona's voice from the top of the nearby stairs.

Deen and I share a look, then walk up without a word. I crumple the page in my fist, letting Deen walk ahead of me, and tuck it into my sleeve.

"Faisal proposed!" Mona shouts when we reach the kitchen, clapping her hands together. Behind her, Faisal is talking to Dad, face flushed, while Deen's parents flank him with wide smiles.

"What?" Beside me, Deen has an expression that I can't read.

Amira suddenly rushes me and envelops me in a hug.

"I said yes," she says into my hair, laughing.

My head spins, and her voice echoes in the empty space of my mind. I hold her to me, an anchor to something real. Like it's the last time I'll ever hold her.

LOADING

[CAMBRIA: THE EVOLUTION EXPANSION PACK]
[ROANA GUILD CHAT ROOM]

Kasia Coribund: So marriage is a thing that people do, right?
Devynius Foxx: Oooh, Kas . . .
Devynius Foxx: This is awkward, but
Devynius Foxx: I'm just not ready for commitment right now
Kasia Coribund: Ha ha.
Devynius Foxx: Everything all right?
Devynius Foxx: Sounds like things have been hectic on your end.
Kasia Coribund: To say the least.
Kasia Coribund: I've just been thinking about marriage a lot recently
Kasia Coribund: Not for myself, but for someone important to me
Kasia Coribund: You know how I asked you how you know when you can trust someone?
Kasia Coribund: But then I remembered the best way to find out if you can trust somebody is to trust them.
Kasia Coribund: Except then I remembered it was Ernest Hemingway who said that, and the guy isn't exactly number one on

my list of inspirational people

Devynius Foxx: pretty sure he shot 400 rabbits in a single day

Devynius Foxx: just to prove he really could

Kasia Coribund: . . . . . . there you have it

Kasia Coribund: the thing is, people actually live like that

Kasia Coribund: baselessly trusting people and hoping for the best.

Kasia Coribund: And I almost envy them.

Kasia Coribund: I wish I knew how it felt.

Devynius Foxx: If we met in real life

Devynius Foxx: Would you trust me?

Kasia Coribund: . . . What?

Devynius Foxx: Maybe trust is something you have to practice.

Devynius Foxx: Maybe you could practice on me.

Kasia Coribund: what are you saying Foxx, lol

Devynius Foxx: Sorry, sorry

Devynius Foxx: Lack of sleep is hitting me HARD

Devynius Foxx: But for what it's worth

Devynius Foxx: I trust you, Kas

Devynius Foxx: Right here, right now

Devynius Foxx: I gotta go

Devynius Foxx: Talk later?

[**Devynius Foxx** has logged off]

CHAPTER 12

DEEN

Friday, July 2

VINNY SLAPS MY BACK, HARD. I stumble forward. "Where you at, Malik?"

I can barely hear him over the spine-throbbing rumble of music blasting from the speakers. It's 1:00 a.m. and we're at a party at some warehouse in Brooklyn. I recognize clusters of people from my classes, with a couple of international students thrown in—but since it's the summer, it's mostly faceless, nameless bodies moving to the bass-heavy beat, aggressively grinding their loins together like they're trying to start a fire. On a giant sofa shaped like a pair of lips, and sitting far too close to me for my liking, at least four, maybe five people fumbling through a sloppy make-out session that's one pair of limbs away from becoming a human centipede. In the middle of it all, someone's set up a beer pong table; every time someone takes a shot, regardless of whether they score or miss, the horde bursts into screams that rattle my skull.

I'm no prude, thank you very much. Tonight, though, it's . . . a lot. I've found a slightly quieter, less-crowded spot by an empty coatrack near the bathrooms to take a breather.

I wonder if Kas would ever come to a place like this. Probably not.

"Seriously, who invited this zombie?" Vinny laughs, all good cheer.

"You did, Vinny."

Tonight, Vinny's wearing jeans and a sleeveless white T-shirt, which normally is straying into jackass territory. But Vinny just looks like a happy dude; even though he's got booze on his breath, his cheeks are flushed, and drops of sweat glitter across his hairline. We've been here for almost an hour, and though I'm wilting, Vinny's thriving like a weed. My theory's that he's just used to crowds, coming from that big-ass family of his single-handedly taking over Long Island.

"You should be celebrating your brother's engagement. Or are you still stressing over that enemy of yours?" he asks.

"Who knows." And by that I mean, he's hit the nail right on the head. The guy's weirdly perceptive about the strangest things.

"Did you up the magic charm? I *told* you to dial up the charm." Vinny, buzzing with energy, is drumming his fingers at the bar to the beat of the music. "Wait, does this person have anything to do with your brother's engagement?"

I stiffen. Yep. Weirdly perceptive. "Uh, maybe?"

"Yikes. Grudges and weddings don't mix. Trust me, I know; my aunt Jules *hated* the girl her best friend Mike was marrying. Needless to say, the wedding was a hot mess. I told Ma it was because she was in love with the guy, but—"

"Anyway, you sure you don't want to call it a night?" I say, changing the subject. "We could still celebrate. Like, at a bodega. With egg and cheese bagels." Seriously. I'm hungry, tired, and would much rather be on Cambria, playing a couple of rounds with Kas. Something to distract myself.

But Vinny ignores me. "The *point*, D-Money, is that you gotta find the source of the grudge and face it head-on. The longer you ignore it, the more likely someone's face will get bashed into a wedding cake."

He's probably right. But my head's a load of static and nothing, not even good advice, can penetrate it. I don't even feel like drinking tonight, and it's not because I hear the angels on my shoulders tutting and shaking their heads in divine judgment. Right now, lack of sleep is making me picture them as angelic Professor Pryces, their round-framed glasses glinting as they jot down my sins in their little leather notebooks. Deen Malik, a shit Muslim *and* a shit student.

I just can't stop thinking about Kiran.

Seeing her last week has thrown me off my axis. Something about her just riles me up with the enthusiasm of a drunk with an egg beater. And look, I know it's my fault for leaving things the way they were. Of course she'd be mad at me. Bitter, even.

But trying to dig more dirt on Faisal? That's going too far. It's bad enough she knows about Leah. Faisal's entitled to his privacy, to live without being bogged down by his past. I wish Kiran'd leave well enough alone.

"No, you need a night out. You, my good man, have been tense as *hell* lately. And I'm not quite ready to call it quits just yet." Vinny looks over my shoulder, into the crowd. Searching.

Oh. "Is Amy here?"

"I'm glad you asked. But first, here." He shoves a glass into my hand. "I got you a drink."

I shake the glass, eyeing it suspiciously. Particles swirl before floating to the bottom. "What's in it?"

"Something to get you drunk."

I take a tentative sip and splutter it back out. It tastes like sugar and gasoline. "What the hell is this shit?"

"I dunno, man, I panicked and I know you don't like your vodka straight up, so I might have added some stevia packets I found." He wraps his arm around my shoulders. "Look, Amy's over by the back. You warmed up now? I need you to play wing-man tonight. Turn up the eau de Deen-ette, the social potpourri, if you catch my drift."

I sigh, rub my eyebrows. "Fine. Yeah. I got you." I'm actually *far* from warmed up, but Vinny's nervousness is vibrating off him in waves, and I don't need to give the lovesick bastard a reason to be even more high-strung than he already is. I consider setting the drink down on a nearby table, full of empty and crushed red Solo cups and glass bottles, but decide against it. I'm going to need it. I follow Vinny to the back of the warehouse, shaking thoughts of Kiran out of my head.

Amy's on a sofa in a relatively quiet corner, drink in hand. She's with Raquel, who's wearing some tiny glittery gold dress ensemble;

her back's half turned to us, covered by little more than some strips of fabric and strings.

Right. *Raquel.* With everything that's been happening, I'd almost forgotten about her. But I suddenly remember the part where Vinny said she was into me. Only it doesn't ignite the same kind of, we'll call it excitement, in me as it normally would. Maybe the stress is getting to me. Or maybe it's Kasia.

"Look who it is!" Amy smiles wide, her curls bouncing when she sees us. "Our favorite pool team."

I shove Vinny ahead into the open seat on the sofa, next to Amy, and grab a stool to sit by Raquel. Even with the smell of sweat and booze permeating the air, I catch a whiff of her vanilla-scented shampoo.

"Hey." Raquel raises an eyebrow. "Why do you two look like you're up to no good?"

Vinny laughs nervously and takes a swig from his beer.

"Us? No good?" I put my hand on my chest in mock indignation. "Perish the thought. We were just casually discussing how we're gonna kick your ass in pool again."

Raquel laughs. "I'll believe it when I see it."

"Sounds like a date." *Right. Live in the here and now, Deen.* I take a long sip of my drink, trying to blur my thoughts.

"Speaking of which," says Vinny, "*this* guy's older brother just got engaged."

"Oh yeah? Is that why he looks like someone died?" asks Raquel.

My fist tightens around my drink. I'm relieved that Faisal and Amira are officially engaged now, but I can't get rid of this nagging nervousness itching in the back of my head. I still don't know what Kiran might have found in Faisal's room. After Mona khala called us upstairs, she never left Amira's side, so I didn't have a chance to grill her. Even amid all the celebration, she was quiet. Too quiet.

How much does she know? I have to find out. Knowing about Leah is one thing, but if she finds out about the fire—God, the stress of it all, of waiting for a potential shoe drop, is *killer.*

Vinny reaches over to whack my shoulder. "Seriously, why are you so bummed? Your brother's getting hitched! It's going to be the wedding of the century! Seriously, his parents are loaded." He said the last part at Amy and Raquel. "You're going to be the Prince Harry to Faisal's—whatever the hell the older prince of England's name is. Which means *you*, Mr. Grade A, USDA-certified Hot Shit, are the one everyone's going to be throwing their hot single daughters at."

I waggle my eyebrows. "Hardly necessary."

"Yeah, but it also means your brother can be someone else's problem."

I bristle. "What's that supposed to mean?"

"Hide it all you want," Vinny starts, "but I know when you're staring at your phone, it's because of him. When you get a phone call and you gotta leave the room? That ain't a booty call—no one would look that upset." Vinny looks at Amy. "This guy worries about his brother like you would not even believe. Probably the only person he cares about."

"Yeah, well." I'm annoyed Vinny's running his mouth so much, but he's not exactly wrong. I throw back the rest of the drink Vinny handed me, even though it burns. "The thing about the wedding? They want me to do some kind of dance-off. Against my future sister-in-law."

"Is that a common thing at Pakistani weddings?" Amy asks.

"Dance-offs? Some do it, yeah, depending on community beliefs and whatnot. Usually in groups." Though Kiran would outshine everyone in a group without even trying. I run my hand through my hair, and I have one of those moments where I realize how hot and sticky and dark it is in here. I sigh. I guess it's time to come clean to Vinny. "I think the more uncommon thing is my future sister-in-law also being my ex."

Vinny sits up. "Whoa. Whoa, whoa, whoa, hold up. Your *ex*? As in, a person *you* formerly used to *date*? You never told me this." His eyes bulge. "WAIT, is this ex the enemy in question? The one you've been trying to smooth things over with?"

"Maybe. Yes." I run my hands through my hair again. "In any case, I didn't think it was pertinent to bring up because it was a long time ago. I was, like, fifteen."

"Long time ago my ass. I still haven't gotten over my first girlfriend from day care." Vinny looks ahead, wide-eyed, like the processor of his mind can't keep up. "No shit, was she your first?"

"Yeah, and it ended badly and now she hates me."

"What did you do to her?"

I look away. "Uh, I might have . . . ghosted her?" God, why is it that some things sound ten times worse when said out loud?

Raquel's and Amy's eyes widen in horror while Vinny's face becomes a perfect impression of the cringe emoji.

"I know." I rub the back of my sticky neck. "I'm a tool."

"I, for one, don't believe that for a second," Amy offers as comfort. "You must have ghosted her for a reason, right?"

Faisal's gaunt face flickers in my mind. "Something like that."

Vinny shakes his head. "Damn. No wonder she hates you. That's *cold*, D-Money. No offense, but I don't know if this is the kind of problem you can smooth over."

"Thank you for the vote of confidence, buddy ol' pal." I clench my jaw. The thing is, he's right. But I still have to try, for Faisal's sake.

"Oh my God, so what," says Raquel, "you're going to have to dance-off at the wedding with your ex? We're talking, like, a Bollywood-type dance thing, right?"

Amy grins. "That could actually be kinda cute."

I laugh bitterly. "I don't know about cute. Kiran's a dance pro, which means I'll be made to look like a dying fish on the floor in front of five hundred people. Plus, Kiran doesn't want her sister to marry my brother. She's practically declared war."

"You could always dance with her instead of against her," says Raquel. "Choreograph something together. Then she can't make you look bad."

I snort. "A single guy and girl dancing together would be too scandalous, unfortunately. Plus, she'd probably *want* me to look bad. To get revenge."

And if dinner last Sunday was any indication, by any and all means necessary.

I know I shouldn't panic yet; just because Kiran knows about Leah's existence doesn't necessarily mean she knows about everything else. But Mom meant it when she said she wouldn't fund

Faisal's move to California if things got out. If Kiran keeps digging, losing Amira wouldn't just be the end of a relationship. It could be the end of everything Faisal's worked for, everything Faisal's dreamed of. It could be the end of Faisal, and all the sacrifices he's made to get here. How could Kiran not give him a chance, not see how important Amira is to him?

Or maybe she does. Maybe she doesn't care.

I grip my glass tighter. Right now, it doesn't matter if I'm the reason why she's doing this. Rage overtakes me like a fever. Maybe it's the booze, but I'm suddenly pissed about everything: our parents not being there for Faisal when he needed their support most, and then threatening to take away everything if his secret gets loose, all because of their stupid obsession with appearances. And Kiran—she pisses me off, too. So freaking judgmental. Unlike me, Faisal's been doing his best; he doesn't deserve to be haunted by his past mistakes. He deserves to talk about it on his *own* terms.

The nerve of her, looking at me the way she did when I caught her looking through Faisal's stuff. Confused. Ashamed. And *vulnerable.*

Vinny grabs us another round of drinks and things start to get hazy. Numb. I know I should eat something, but right now I don't care. Words spill more easily. I don't tell them anything about Faisal, of course. But Kiran? Nothing's off-limits: I tell them about our past, our fight at the coffee shop, finding her in Faisal's room. The warehouse spins and blurs at its edges, and I feel myself rocking back and forth on some invisible wave. The anger is still there, though, like dull glowing embers.

I say something; Amy's laughing hard, the kind that quakes her body. It reminds me of Kiran, the old Kiran. Raquel's got her arm draped around her. Vinny watches, his mouth stretched wide, showing teeth.

Amy's eyes drift to mine. "She could just be doing this to get your attention, you know."

"Attention? No way." I take a long pull of vodka. "There isn't a drop of love in her. Only pride."

"Then what about you?" Amy's hand is on my knee. "She's clearly getting under your skin. You sure you don't still have feelings for her?"

I laugh. I don't know why it's so funny; of all the wild thoughts I could have about this whole situation, that is one that hasn't crossed my mind. Maybe it's because there's no way I could ever remotely care for someone who refuses to give Faisal a chance. Maybe it's because Amy snorts when she laughs, like Kiran used to. Maybe it's because I've known for years I don't have a right to feel anything.

Kas pops into my head. The funniest thing about not knowing anything about her is that it means she could be anyone. She could be Amy, for all I know.

"For Kiran? Nah, m'afraid I feel next to nothing. And maybe a teensy bit of guilt; I'm not *that* bad." I put my hand on Amy's. "Teach me how to love again?"

Amy and Raquel holler, dissolving into a fit of giggles, and for a moment, I feel a little lighter. White blurs my vision. Softens it. I reach for my glass, which I've set on the floor somewhere, but to my disappointment, it's empty.

"We should do group therapy more often," Raquel chokes out through her laughter.

"You know, we're having a dholki in a couple weeks. It's technically like a bridal party, but they're opening it to everyone." I lean forward, like I'm telling them a secret. "You all should come." In my woozy state, I decide having them there would be nice. Friends on the inside and all. More distance away from Kiran. "Vinny, you in?" I flash him a lopsided grin.

But Vinny's jaw tenses.

"Maybe," he replies weakly.

I blink, confused. The annoying itch in the back of my brain is back, only it feels worse this time. But the cogs of my brain are slogging through my thoughts too slowly to understand why.

Vinny stands. "I'm going to go find some water," he announces. His eyes shift to me, unreadable. They linger for a moment, as if waiting for something.

Then I watch him stumble and disappear into the crowd.

CHAPTER 13

KIRAN

Friday, July 2

I'M SITTING BENEATH A SACRED camphor tree that sits at the heart of a forest just outside Coralei, the capital of Cambria. Birds trill and chirp; leaves rustle softly overhead. My Mecha leopard lets out a low, fluttery purr beside me, as she always does when we're idle in game. My computer speakers aren't top quality, but the sound is soothing, mind-numbing. I watch two level-fifteen Warriors and their Mechas—a dog and a monkey—swing their swords at some low-level monsters.

Footsteps come from behind me in the game and my heart quickens despite itself. Of course it's not Foxx. Foxx hasn't logged on in two days now, and his name is still listed as offline in the guild. A third player, a Healer with a peacock Mecha, runs to join the Warriors. They defeat the monsters easily. One of the Warriors breaks into a victory dab.

I shuffle through my inventory, sorting and resorting. I keep glancing at my message window. I've already cleared a couple of group dungeons with some strangers, but I'm tired of that. I hate that I'm waiting for him. I hate that I can't enjoy the game without him. But my chest aches. There are a thousand knots suspended behind my ribs, and these days, talking to Foxx is the only thing that undoes them.

I slide the ripped page from Faisal's notebook into my drawer for safekeeping. Deen kept watching me that night, after our encounter in Faisal's room. Like he knew I knew something, and it was driving him mad trying to figure it out. Hopefully he hasn't discovered I stole a page from his brother's diary. The reality is, I don't know what to do with it. I don't even know how I'm supposed to look Faisal in the eye after this. I'd figured Leah was something more along the lines of a dirty romantic secret, or worse, that Leah was still in his life—that maybe Faisal was cheating on Amira somehow. I didn't think I'd have to tell her the love of her life had a far darker past than any of us could have imagined. What kind of crime—no, *felony*—did Faisal commit, anyway? Even if a judge dropped his felony charge, my imagination runs wild with possibilities, and it's all *bad*.

Scratch that: I know exactly what I have to do. I need a new plan, a new approach to break Amira and Faisal up. Something more drastic. Faisal's criminal background wouldn't throw her if she knew—she's a criminal justice lawyer, after all. But that's not the real issue anyway, is it? A little beep catches my attention, the sound of someone in the guild logging in to the game. My breath catches in my chest. Foxx?

[Nilina Torby signs on.]

My chest falls. Where are you when I need you, Foxx?

On screen, the Warriors and their Healer have disappeared, probably off to some mission together, and I can't help but feel a little envious.

Another beep. Someone's sent me a DM, so I pop open my message box.

Nilina Torby: Ayy
Nilina Torby: Sol and I are gonna try some high-level dungeons
Nilina Torby: Wanna come?

I sigh and begin typing.

Kasia Coribund: Nah
Kasia Coribund: Probably gonna call it a night, actually
Nilina Torby: ohhh, I see
Nilina Torby: you were waiting for Foxx
Kasia Coribund: . . . .
Kasia Coribund: Maybe?
Nilina Torby: Hoho
Nilina Torby: Sorry, luv
Nilina Torby: He hasn't been on in a bit
Nilina Torby: But I'm sure he'll be back soon
Kasia Coribund: Yeah . . .

I bite my lip and type out my question a few different times before closing my eyes and pressing Enter.

Kasia Coribund: Hey, can I ask you a weird question?

Nil replies right away:

Nilina Torby: those are my favorite kind
Kasia Coribund: You've actually talked to Foxx, right?
Kasia Coribund: Back when the guild did voice chat?
Nilina Torby: oh yeah
Nilina Torby: that was a while ago, before you joined
Nilina Torby: but we stopped to make Foxx more comfortable
Nilina Torby: he's a shy one, that boy
Nilina Torby: why do you ask?
Kasia Coribund: he didn't sound like an old pervert or something, did he?
Kasia Coribund: like, he didn't want to stop voice chat to hide the fact that he's a 90-year-old dude with a foot fetish, right?
Nilina Torby: lollllllllll
Nilina Torby: Granted, it's hard to tell on voice chat but
Nilina Torby: I can promise you he sounded very normal
Nilina Torby: and very nice
Nilina Torby: definitely not an old fart
Nilina Torby: why
Nilina: Torby you startin to get curious about the real him?
Kasia Coribund: not . . . exactly . . .

I sit back in my chair. Even though Foxx and I both agreed not to share anything specific about our real lives, right now I'm regretting it. It was almost charming, at first, not having to get bogged down in the unnecessary details of who we are, getting straight to the meaty stuff. He knows the important things, intimate thoughts I haven't shared with anyone else. So I guess I shouldn't be surprised the urge to tell him my name is getting . . . unbearable. Like a final wall between us that I'm itching to demolish. Out of curiosity, maybe. Or something else.

I don't know when I started thinking about him as something beyond just pixels on a screen, or as a stranger in some video game. But over the past few months, I've found myself waking up and wondering what he's up to for the day, what his life is like—I keep looking at people I pass on the street and wondering if they're him. Stupid forbidden thoughts.

Worse, I keep hoping he's wondering the same things about me.

I can't tell him about Amira's engagement, exactly, but it'd be nice to talk to him. To know that he's still there, the warm, sympathetic voice on the other side of the screen.

The opposite of Deen in every way.

The garage door rumbles downstairs. There's a creak of wood from the side door, and the security alarm lets out a little chime. Dad must be home.

Kasia Coribund: anyway, I gotta run
Kasia Coribund: talk to you later?
Nilina Torby: ;D
Nilina Torby: See you soon, luv

In game, my character gets to her feet, and my Mecha leopard stretches out on her pads, eager to get moving. Maybe she misses Foxx, too.

No, she doesn't feel *anything*, I correct myself. *It's all just pixels.*

I take one long final look at Foxx's name on my screen before logging off.

I head downstairs. But it's not Dad, to my relief, because he asked me to clear Mom's closet before he got home.

It's Amira.

I'm suddenly out of sorts. I think of Faisal's notebook page hidden in my room upstairs, separated from us by some wood and carpet.

Her face splits into a smile when she sees me. "Hi." She's carrying several grocery bags; she hoists them one by one onto the kitchen counter.

"You're . . . here."

She didn't even tell me she was coming tonight. Not that I'm upset about it—I've wanted to have her here, living a normal life with me and Dad, for so long. It just feels weird now, seeing her home, standing in our kitchen like nothing's changed. I can't even remember the last time she visited.

"Thought I'd spend the Fourth of July weekend here for a change." Amira answers my question before I can even ask, and stretches out her fingers for me to see: they're red from the weight of the grocery bags. "Did you just come back from dance? You look like . . . what's the word . . ."

"Crap?" I haven't gotten to brushing my hair yet, and I'm

once again wearing my favorite oversized hoodie and sweatpants. Hadn't even realized it was Fourth of July weekend. "Was just playing games." I lift my arms and stretch, and my back lets out a satisfying crack. "And sleep's been avoiding me lately."

"Hmmm," she says thoughtfully. "Where's Dad?"

"At work. Should be here soon."

"Perfect. Help me make dinner?"

I shuffle in closer, peering into her bags. Amira is a wonderful cook, as you might expect. "Wow. Homemade dinner? You should come home more often."

"I know. It was hard to make time during school, you know, but now"—Amira pulls out a couple of tomatoes, onions, tiny boxes of masala—"I have no excuse. I want to make the absolute best of my time before—"

She pauses. A tiny breath slips from between her teeth. It hits me then, too: she's home because she wants to spend time here before she moves to California. With Faisal. The beginning of the end.

"Well, I'm glad you could make it," I say, and she smiles weakly.

Amira tosses me a tomato; I know the drill. I've never been much of a cook, but Amira has always loved cooking, and I'm more than happy to play sous-chef if it means I get to eat something other than mac and cheese from a box. I start dicing the tomatoes as she rolls up her sleeves and starts peeling the onions.

It's quiet, save for the tap and scrape of knives hitting chopping boards. But despite everything, a warm glow blooms in my chest. The silence isn't oppressive; it's easy and natural. It's . . . nice. It's how things should have been.

Except now there's a new ring on her finger, gleaming under the kitchen light. Teasing me. Goading me.

"Mona khala's hosting a dholki for us in two weeks." She scrapes the diced onions to one corner of her chopping board. "I can't believe this is really happening."

"Me neither." I'm struggling to find words, any words. I don't want to think about wedding stuff. I just want to enjoy this moment, with her.

"I've always loved going to dholkis, you know? The singing, the dhol drums—and the smell of henna. Heaven."

"And the sweets."

"And the sweets," she repeats in agreement. "And now I'm having my own." She stops chopping for a moment and reaches for a paper towel; tears are streaming down her face.

"I wish Mom were here. You know she'd have a killer dance for us," Amira says softly, sniffling.

It's probably just the onions; Amira doesn't cry, not even in front of me.

I wish Mom were here, too. She'd know exactly what to say about Faisal and the notebook. Maybe Amira wouldn't be with Faisal in the first place. Things would be normal. Us, living together. Like a family.

Amira finishes wiping her face and goes back to chopping onions. I glance at her; she looks like she's going to say something, but changes her mind.

"What?"

A small smile plays across her face. "Deen seems nice," she says slowly, testing the water.

My face warps in horror. "*Please* don't finish that train of thought."

"I'm just saying," she says, shrugging. I don't know how she does it, but even her shrugs look innocent.

"He's a menace."

"A good-looking menace. Plus, I don't know about that. He can't be all that . . . menacing."

"Trust me, I—" I stare at my hand, white-knuckled on the hilt of my knife. "I know people like him."

"Well, I, for one, am excited to see you dazzle everyone on the dance floor."

"You cannot be serious. I thought you were just saying that to make nice with Mona."

"It's my wedding, so you have to do what I say. Let me be Bridezilla on this one thing." She giggles, as if pleased with herself. "Plus, let's be real: I was never going to have a wedding without you dancing in it, anyway. And if you, say, decided to give Deen secret dance lessons, I wouldn't tell anyone. You may be having an innocent little dance-off at the wedding, but behind closed doors, he could be the Baby to your Patrick Swayze."

"Astaghfirullah. Sorry, but he's on his own." I go back to chopping tomatoes, more violently this time. My hair falls, covering the angry flush on my cheeks. In *Dirty Dancing*, Patrick Swayze lifts Baby for their final dance routine. If I *could* lift Deen, I'd immediately yeet him into outer space. "You don't expect me to do a dance at the dholki, too, do you? One dance is enough torture as it is."

"No . . ." She throws the chopped onions into a pot on the stove. "But I do expect you to go to the masjid with me next Friday."

I blink, confused. "For . . . jum'ah prayer?" Jum'ah is a special Muslim prayer that happens on Friday afternoons. I try to catch most of my prayers, especially since Mom died, but I usually avoid the masjid. As much as I love the feeling of being inside a masjid—the melodic call to prayer that fills the walls like a sea of voices, the feeling of community—I have too many distracting memories there. Just one more thing Deen Malik has ruined forever.

"Faisal suggested we meet the imam for premarital counseling, so we're going to our old masjid here—you know, the one you went to for Sunday school?"

My throat tightens. The masjid where Deen and I first met. Great.

"But the imam said we should try to bring family, get everyone's perspective."

"Really?" I'm surprised Faisal would suggest that, considering those counseling sessions are supposed to be for putting everything on the table: your thoughts on morals, religion, careers. Then again, if he's prepared to keep lying, this could all be part of his plan to keep up the charade of honesty.

I roughly chew the inside of my mouth as I chop another tomato. Just thinking about it is infuriating. Faisal really thinks he can get away with lying. I've heard horror stories of men marrying "good Muslim girls" just to get their hands on green cards, or marrying to keep their parents off their back. Maybe that's why Faisal's marrying Amira: so his parents will think he's all settled down, that they won't have to keep an eye on him anymore because he'll be Amira's problem now.

What if he runs away with Leah? What if they run away together and go on a crime spree? Like Thelma and Louise?

I close my eyes and try not to revel in the image of Faisal and a faceless Leah flying off a cliff in a car, with Deen in the back seat.

"So, you're really set on him, huh," I say suddenly, the words spilling from my mouth despite my better judgment. "This really is happening. Even though you barely know the guy."

Amira tilts her head in question. "Maybe not as much as I'd *like*, but that's what premarital counseling is for."

"I guess I just don't understand the rush. You just graduated law school. You still have so much ahead of you."

Amira lowers the heat on the stove and turns to me. Her eyes are soft, like warm brown pools.

I want to show her the journal page. I really want to. But I'm worried about what she'll think of me. Snooping in Faisal's room, reading Faisal's private journal? Just to prove that she's made a poor life choice? I don't want her to feel like I'm attacking her or controlling her. I have to tread carefully; even with Faisal's journal page proving he's got a shady past, there are still too many uncertainties. I need to be undeniably clear with the facts if I'm going to bring this up and crush her heart.

So no, I won't show her yet.

But I will test the waters.

"You've known him for three months," I continue. "I get wanting to keep things kosher and wanting to make sure you're married before you move to California together and live together or whatever, but—you don't know him." *Felony felony felony*, says my brain.

"I guess . . ." She trails off and looks up at the ceiling, like she's looking for the right words. The kitchen smells like roasting onions and cumin. Smells that should be comforting. "I guess I think about it this way. How could you not want to rush in when you've found the one?" she says finally.

"But *three months*? You can't decide the rest of your life in three months. There were rumors about him, you know. *Bad* ones. How can you feel good about any of this?"

But Amira looks calm. Almost like she expected this. She wraps her arms around herself, as if she's cold.

"You know that day you found me in the closet?" she starts. Her voice is low, soft. Like a mother speaking to a child. "That day, that moment—it was the worst day of my life. I was so scared. Terrified. Everything came crashing down on me at once. I wasn't able to be there at the hospital like you were, Kiran. I didn't see Mom dying a little more every day. Because of school, because I was in New York, I had distance. God, honestly, I *wanted* distance. But then one day she was gone, just gone, and then everything I wanted to say, everything I needed to hear—that was gone, too. Before I knew what was happening. So that day when I went into her closet, I just . . ." She looks past me, like she's seeing something I can't.

"We were just kids." Amira breathes shakily. "We're *still* just kids. How the hell are we supposed to live without our mom? We're too young. There's so much left she needed to teach us. And I know we still have Dad, and I love him and he's great, but—"

"It's not the same." My eyes burn. I had no idea she had these thoughts, ones that so closely mirror mine.

"Right. Exactly." She smiles sadly. "And then I met Faisal. That's when it hit me. You know that passage in the Quran that goes, '*And of everything, we created you in pairs, so that perhaps you may remember*'? I met Faisal, and suddenly, that passage made sense. Faisal helps me *remember.* Who I was, who I wanted to be. And what I love. I decided that the bar exam, my career—all of that could wait a couple more months. I can always start my law career in California. I have connections. But people won't always stick around, and I don't want to risk losing someone again."

My chest tightens. But I have to say it. "What if he's not as perfect as you think he is? What if he has a past, and if you just took the time to—"

"We *all* have pasts."

"Yeah, but what if his was *really* bad?" I stare straight at her. I'm trying to hint as clearly as possible without saying things outright, but she's not taking it.

Amira looks back at me, her eyes a mix of a hundred emotions I can't read. Affection, maybe. Pity.

"You worry too much. I promise you, Faisal has everything that's important. And honestly, Kiran, I—I don't know how I would have gotten through losing Mom without him." She squeezes her eyes tight for a beat. "Whatever he might have done, it's in the past now, and that's between him and God. I know he's not a bad guy. That's enough for me."

Is it, though? I want to ask, but the words won't come.

I suddenly feel very tired. There's just a dull throb in my forehead, a mind-numbing emptiness that pulls me in. It sinks in: her saying these things about Mom—saying she couldn't have done it without Faisal—it hurts. Because what about *me*? *I* needed her. I needed her to share that pain with me before, not now. Why was Faisal the one she turned to? And is that really the reason she's marrying Faisal now? Faisal hasn't made her remember anything. Only forget that she has a choice. That she has a real family, despite everything.

She puts a hand on my shoulder, gives it a gentle squeeze.

"I know you're not a hundred percent on board with Faisal yet. But you don't have to protect me. Whatever you're worried about, whatever your notions about him are—I want you to let it go. For me."

I look away.

"Oh!" Amira jumps, suddenly remembering the pot on the stove. "Damn. Burned the onions a little too much. Let's try a second take."

She smiles and reaches her hand toward me. "Start over?"

THREE YEARS AGO

KIRAN: If you could have any superpower

KIRAN: what would it be and why?

DEEN: O_O

DEEN: Huh.

DEEN: Why, are you handing them out now?

KIRAN: Ha ha.

KIRAN: Tell me!!!!!

DEEN: I'M THINKING

DEEN: I don't do well under pressure!!!!!!!

DEEN: . . . Well, I do SOME things well under pressure, but

DEEN: okay okay

DEEN: Maybe flying

DEEN: I'd wanna fly

DEEN: Or teleport

DEEN: Something to do with transportation

DEEN: So I could get the hell out of my house without my parents ever knowing

DEEN: . . . or maybe invisibility

DEEN: What about you?

KIRAN: Hmm . . . seeing the future!

KIRAN: I want to be able to see the future.

DEEN: Feeling anxious about the future?

KIRAN: Yeah. Always.

KIRAN: Especially lately.

DEEN: How's your mom, btw?

KIRAN: To be determined.

KIRAN: It's just a waiting game now.

DEEN: OKAY I know my real answer now!!!

DEEN: Healing powers.

DEEN: Definitely healing powers.

KIRAN: Heh

KIRAN: You're a good guy, Deen.

DEEN: Only for you.

CHAPTER 14

DEEN

Friday, July 9

I HAVEN'T BEEN TO A masjid in years; two, at least. Maybe three. Who's keeping count? Ever since we moved from the Philly area to north Jersey, my parents and I stopped going to any masjid for anything. Even for Eid, we'd opt instead to visit Mona khala's house in south Jersey—which is saying something.

Mom and Dad never said it outright, but after everything that happened with Faisal, I think they wanted to avoid the masjid community just as much as I did. People took notice of Faisal never being there, of the inconsistencies in Mom's excuses. Rumors spread like cockroaches on fire, and they were just as hard to kill. Running away from it all was the better option; it's probably the only thing me and my parents have ever agreed on.

That's the one problem I have with masjids. You can never just walk in to pray. No, you cleanse yourself of God's judgment only to receive the judgment of hundreds of rando aunties and uncles. I still remember the day I caught Aunty Noreen trying to pry information out of Kiran: *You're friends with Deen, right? His brother, Faisal—is it true he's a sickly boy?* I can still see Kiran shrinking beneath her stare, confused, uncomfortable: *I'm sorry, I really don't know anything.*

That was the last straw for me.

So for Faisal and me to come back to the one masjid where it all began, after all this time, when all the compound stress is one pascal away from ripping my skull in half? Put me out of my misery.

"You coming?" Faisal calls out to me, holding open the door. He looks nervous, like he doesn't want me out of his sight.

"Oh. Yeah." I throw off my shoes, gripping the wall to help me stay balanced. Could God smite me for entering His holy domain considering how shitty of a Muslim I've been these past few years? Probably. And I wouldn't blame Him. But I *have* to be here; I'm Faisal's emotional support sibling. "Just pray I don't royally screw up," he said on the phone after he asked me to come.

I toss my shoes in a cubby in the masjid's mudroom, hold my breath, and follow Faisal into the main prayer area. I wish I had the heart to tell Faisal I stopped praying a long time ago.

But as soon as I enter, my breath's knocked out of me. The masjid hasn't changed at all. It feels a little smaller than it used to, but everything's the same: the smell of mothballs and perfume, the plush red carpet designed to look like a hundred prayer rugs stitched together, the white domed ceiling that carries voices. Whispers.

I get why people say nostalgia is seductive. There's something about the air here that settles on me like a warm blanket. So many memories in this masjid. Good memories. But I was a better person back then, too.

Now? I just feel out of place.

Across the hall, I spot a sight for sore eyes: Amira, wearing a sunny yellow scarf over her hair, already sitting down at the front of the prayer room. There's a bearded guy in a white kurta next to her, who looks somewhere in his late thirties—the imam, probably, the one who leads prayers in the masjid. I don't recognize him, though; they must have brought in a new guy since I was last here. He smiles and waves us over to take our seats.

Faisal's shoulders unclench a little as he sits next to Amira, a few respectful centimeters away from her. Still, their knees are close enough to touch. Amira glows at him. I've never seen anyone look at my brother that way.

"Brothers! Assalamu alaikum. It's good to finally meet you, Faisal," says the imam, shaking Faisal's hand heartily. "My name is Imam Obaid Rehman. Sister Amira was just telling me about you."

Faisal smiles shyly, scratches his nose. "Good things, I hope."

The imam's eyes land on me. "And Deen; it's nice to see you again. I remember you."

I freeze. Good things rarely follow when someone says *I remember you.*

"You were just a boy. You were only here at the Sunday school for a year, were you not? Then you moved?" The imam chuckles. "You were always running around after prayer time, God knows where."

To flirt with Kiran. How times have changed.

"Yeah," I say, relaxing, though not much. "Sounds about right."

"But it's a shame we never met sooner, Brother Faisal."

Faisal's face goes pale. "When my family moved here for that year, I, uh, was in college, so . . ."

My fists clench. It's hard to drag yourself to a masjid when you're going through shit like an addiction, with no help from your parents. But people never know how to respond to that.

"Oh, me too," Amira pipes in. "I rarely even had time to come home, so I only came to the masjid a couple times. But this was where Kiran went to Sunday school."

"Yeah, and it feels like *centuries* ago," a familiar grating voice says from behind me.

Kiran is wearing a loose white scarf over her hair and a rumpled, long-sleeved T-shirt. Her dark crystal-orb eyes are decked with puffy bags beneath them. Apparently I'm not the only one having trouble sleeping lately.

She's *here*. It's a good thing I came, then. I still don't know everything she's got on Faisal, or what she's planning on doing with that info. What I *do* know is that with the four of us here, now would be the perfect time to show all her cards. The thought makes me want to throw up in my mouth, which I'm pretty sure I'm not supposed to do in the house of God.

But at least I'm here, too.

"Salaam, Kiran." I pat the space beside me. "Fancy seeing you here. Come, *sit*."

A muscle in her jaw twitches. "Walaikumu assalam, Deen." She doesn't look at me as she sits down on the other side of her sister.

I wonder if she feels just as awkward about being here, if the memories of *us* feel as foreign for her as they do for me.

"Now that we're all here," says Imam Obaid, "let's just get a few things settled. I know it's a bit unconventional to have siblings involved, but I think it's important to start establishing yourselves as family from the beginning. Get used to the idea that this is a joining. With that in mind, right now, I want you all to think of me as your coach. Love is a team sport, you see. It requires skill and endurance and partnership. I'm here to make scrimmage easier."

Silence.

Imam Obaid laughs. "Man, that sounded so much more profound in my head."

I snort. Okay, I officially kind of like him.

"Let me start over. You see, there's this myth I hear often from couples that premarriage counseling means airing your dirty laundry in front of me and your potential spouse. You might have this image of me lecturing you on this and that, telling you about your shortcomings, your wrongful actions. But I'm not here to lecture you. If you wanted to hear lectures, you'd come to the Friday khutbah more often. I'm only here to help facilitate the beginning of what we pray will be a long and trusting future together."

Kiran's staring daggers into the carpet.

She's clearly getting under your skin. Amy's comment from last week intones in the back of my mind. I hate that she's right, about that at least. It's gotten so bad, I've been wanting to talk to *Vinny* about Kiran. But lately, he's been weirdly . . . clammish compared to his usual self. Even this morning, when I told him I was going out. Normally he'd be all: *Pray take me with you, good sir, so I can live among the bourgeoisie for but a day.* But not today.

"It sounds like you two have already settled on the wedding

date?" asks the imam, pulling out a small notebook from a bag beside him.

"Yes," Amira replies. "August twenty-second. My best friend, Rizwana, managed to get us in at the Ballroom at the Ben on a last-minute cancellation."

Kiran blanches, bites her bottom lip. Guess it's the first time she's heard of it, too.

It's official now, I think with some relief. *Almost.*

"About six weeks, hm." Imam Obaid jots it down, slams the notebook shut. "Not much time, then. You'll have homework. I want you both to keep journals. I have found that writing one's thoughts and feelings is therapeutic in itself."

Amira nods enthusiastically. I get the impression she's always been a good student. Faisal, on the other hand, gives a weak, stiff smile. He's never been good with keeping track of journals.

"Now let's begin," Obaid says.

I glance at Kiran from the corner of my eye and hide my nervousness by trying to slip her my most charming, familial smile (Vinny's tip number four for wooing: smile often), but she doesn't notice. Instead, her head is turned, gaze trained to the window—to the cluster of trees behind the nearby Sunday school building.

I hate to admit it, but for brief a moment, I want to know what she's thinking. A need so bad, I'm almost tempted to pray.

Premarriage counseling, apparently, is just an extended Q&A session, a giant game of Would You Rather? that lasts over an hour. Imam Obaid goes easy on them, though, tossing mostly harmless questions like, "What does a day off look like to you?" and "What's an accomplishment that you're proud of?" or "Babies: yes, no, maybe so?

"I think this is a good place to start wrapping up," the imam concludes. "I'd like to open it up to the floor now, to Brother Deen and Sister Kiran. Do you have any questions you'd like to add into the mix?"

"I'm good, actually," I reply quickly, and scramble to my feet. "And I'm sure Kiran has nothing to add, either. I'm sure everyone's eager to stretch their legs. But this was a great sesh. Very enlightening."

My legs are cramped and I'm ready to head back to campus. I've been itching to play Cambria; it's been days since I've last logged on. Plus, the sooner we finish, the less chance there is of Kiran—

"I have a few questions," says the demon in question.

Fuck.

"Oh? Great! Sister Kiran, let's hear it. Deen, sit down, please."

My eyes dart over to Faisal. I see panic, clear as day, all over his face.

Slowly, I sit.

"Kiran? Your question?" Amira probes.

The corner of Kiran's mouth tilts up. "Do you think married couples should keep secrets?"

Amira blinks. No one says anything for a beat.

"We usually keep those harder questions for future sessions," Imam Obaid says calmly. "Without other family present. But if you feel comfortable answering now . . . ?"

"It depends on the secrets," Amira answers slowly.

"Oh?" Kiran presses.

"Actually," I chime in, "can we go back to talking about practicing patience, because I think that's a really important top—"

"Deen, please," interrupts Imam Obaid. "Let Sister Amira speak."

I suck in my mouth, frustrated.

Amira continues: "I think it's okay to have a little mystery, especially in the beginning. I also think I shouldn't have to disclose things like everyday purchases to my husband. I also think everyone has a right to privacy." Amira laughs, but it sounds a little strained.

Kiran's lips thin, like she's dissatisfied with her sister's answer. "Hmm, okay. Your turn, *Brother Faisal*."

Kiran coats that last bit with subtext so palpable it could drip all over the carpet. "Same question. Secrets between loved ones. How do we feel about those?"

"I—I don't really . . . ," Faisal stammers.

"And how do we feel about—oh, I don't know—not disclosing former exes and lovers to your future wife? For example?"

Amira looks at her in confusion. "Kiran, what—?"

"On a scale of one to ten," Kiran continues, "how appropriate do you think it is to marry someone just to use them to hide *who you really are*?"

That's it.

I grab Kiran by the elbow and pull her to her feet. "Excuse us for a second."

Kiran tries to wrench herself from me. "Hey, what the *hell*?"

"Come, my dear future sister-in-law," I say, tightening my grip before dragging her out of the prayer room.

I take her outside behind the masjid (not the first time). Thankfully, on a Friday afternoon, not many people are here.

Kiran whips her arm out of my grasp and spins to face me.

"You can't just—"

I take a step toward her, backing her against the wall of the masjid. "What are you doing?" I hiss.

Kiran holds my gaze with equal hatred in her eyes. "Asking questions."

"Asking questions. Right, right." I run my hand down my face. "I think what the imam meant by letting us ask questions is that we ask important questions pertinent to their future marriage. Not leading questions like we're in some kind of interrogation room. What is your freaking problem?"

"You know damn well what my problem is," says Kiran. "It really doesn't bother you? That your brother is lying—that he's been lying?"

I choose my words carefully. "I regret to inform you," I say, "there seems to be a misunderstanding. Maybe you think you know something about his past. But he's not a liar." *Don't let her get under your skin.* "Has it ever occurred to you that, I don't know, maybe you're wrong about him?"

"Don't try to paint me as overdramatic," she snaps.

"I don't have to. If you don't have any proof, then don't you think you're being just as ridiculous as the stupid aunties and uncles who go around spreading rumors because they're bored with their own lives? Isn't gossip supposed to be, I dunno, *un-Islamic*?"

"It's not just gossip. I *have* proof."

A knot swells in my throat. My thoughts whirl in a panic. "What are you talking about?" I struggle to keep my voice steady.

"I don't have to tell you anything. You'll just deny it, anyway."

If she's trying to rile me up on purpose, it's working. "I don't know what you think you know," I say slowly, "but if it's about Leah, it's nothing. You want the truth? She's just someone in Faisal's past. That's it. The rest is between Faisal and Amira." I place my palm against the wall, next to her head. "But I swear to God, if you keep trying to dig shit up for the sole purpose of ruining my brother's life, I'll . . ."

No. What am I doing?

I take a deep breath and pull away.

But the damage is already done. Kiran's face falls, and her fists, clenched at her sides, unfurl. She hesitates before speaking, her voice like a strangled sob. She takes a shaky breath. "What the hell happened to you? You were never this—this *mean*."

Her words knock me back. I was supposed to be giving her a reason *not* to hate me, but then I go and lose my temper? Vinny was right about one thing. This isn't the kind of problem I can smooth over. Because the problem, as usual, is me.

"Maybe you never really knew me." I let out a hard, bitter laugh. "And you certainly don't know *him*. You hate me? Fine. I get it. But I am begging you to stop bringing Faisal's past into this when you're clearly still hung up on ours. Those two"—I point toward the masjid—"actually have a good thing going. They deserve to be happy together."

"Oh my God. I'm not digging into his past because I'm pissed about you ghosting me three years ago. I'm not some bitter ex-girlfriend. I just don't want you to ruin my sister's life!"

"Then allow me to give you some friendly advice: you really might want to rethink your strategy here."

Kiran lets out a barely stifled, frustrated scream. "Jesus, you're *insufferable*, you know that?"

"Who says the word *insufferable* these days? What are you, the protagonist of a Jane Austen novel?"

Kiran laughs bitterly. She doesn't look angry anymore, exactly; she's just blank. Just an expressionless, thick layer of ice covering a terrifying, nameless undercurrent.

"If this were a Jane Austen novel, Deen," she says frigidly, "you'd have a shred of decency in you somewhere. But you're just a selfish, shallow shell of a person who lashes out at others because it's easier than looking inside and accepting that there is *nothing in there*."

For once, I'm speechless, and as I scrabble for the right words, she spins on her heel and leaves.

LOADING

[CAMBRIA: THE EVOLUTION EXPANSION PACK]
[ROANA GUILD CHAT ROOM]

Devynius Foxx: Do you ever get the sense that you don't know yourself at all?
Devynius Foxx: Yesterday, I was talking to one of my friends about something that happened
Devynius Foxx: I got into an argument with someone and it became really, really heated
Devynius Foxx: And instead of taking my side and getting angry on my behalf
Devynius Foxx: My friend tells me I might have gone overboard.
Kasia Coribund: Yikes.
Devynius Foxx: Which, of course, made ME angry . . . at first
Devynius Foxx: But the more I thought about it, the more I realized
Devynius Foxx: That maybe I've BEEN angry
Devynius Foxx: about a lot of things
Devynius Foxx: and the person I fought with got caught in the cross fire

Devynius Foxx: which is why, even as we were fighting, I could feel my conscience knocking on the door to my brain

Devynius Foxx: "Hi, remember me? Your neighbor? Could you stop being an asshole for two seconds and keep it down?"

Devynius Foxx: But I ignored it, because I could barely comprehend what was happening.

Devynius Foxx: My friend called me stubborn

Devynius Foxx: I never thought of myself that way, but he's probably right.

Devynius Foxx: And that terrifies me because if I don't even know myself

Devynius Foxx: I feel like all of this *stuff* is bubbling in me, set to go off at any moment

Devynius Foxx: I wish there was an easier way to know yourself

Devynius Foxx: So at least if I'm aware of my flaws

Devynius Foxx: Maybe I could be, I dunno, more mature

Devynius Foxx: Keep myself in check.

Devynius Foxx: Jesus, I'm rambling–sorry.

Kasia Coribund: I wish I could say I had no idea what you were talking about

Kasia Coribund: But I do.

Kasia Coribund: I think that's why I like taking those "What animal are you?" or "What color is your soul?" quizzes on BuzzFeed

Kasia Coribund: They probably don't mean shit, but I take them because I'm desperate: maybe this will be the thing that tells me exactly who I am!

Kasia Coribund: It's also probably all egocentric and I'm just looking for confirmation that I'm a cool or interesting person

Kasia Coribund: Maybe the fact that I'm taking those quizzes for confirmation means I'm actually a terrible person

Devynius Foxx: Or that you're just bored?

Devynius Foxx: Because you're definitely not terrible

Devynius Foxx: Not when you're sitting here, listening to me.

Kasia Coribund: Maybe I'm just doing it for selfish reasons because I want you to like me.

Kasia Coribund: But maybe what we're doing right now is the key

Kasia Coribund: I'm analyzing myself now because we're talking about it

Kasia Coribund: I think there's a reason why they say "Your friends are a reflection of who you are"

Kasia Coribund: The more you talk to them, the more you open up to them

Kasia Coribund: The more they can tell you who you are.

Kasia Coribund: Maybe that's how we get better.

Kasia Coribund: We keep talking.

Devynius Foxx: That, I can do. Gladly.

Kasia Coribund: Or you could drop acid

Kasia Coribund: That might be easier

Devynius Foxx: Ha

Devynius Foxx: I think I'll take my chances with you.

CHAPTER 15

KIRAN

Tuesday, July 13
40 Days Until the Wedding

A FEW DAYS AFTER AMIRA and Faisal's premarriage counseling session at the masjid, I'm standing outside an intimate little izakaya on the Upper West Side, playing lookout and trying very hard to look casual even though I'm sweating profusely and wearing sunglasses that are way too big for my face.

Asher is late, and every second he's not here is another noticeable rip at my facade of calm—I know because two different people have asked if I'm lost.

I'm full-on pacing now, and then I hear heavy footsteps behind me—it's Asher, to my relief, jogging up, breathing hard. His mane of hair is slick with sweat, his sideburns two chestnut-brown tributaries on either side of his head. But at least he's dressed the way I told him: a button-down collared shirt, a tie, dark slacks that somehow make his long birch-tree legs even longer. I'd never tell him to his face—probably because he'd never let me live it down—but Asher is good-looking, and worse, he's the casual, effortless kind; he's almost a foot taller than me, for starters, and his honey-beige skin has always been smoother, more pristine. To add insult to injury, the summer sun has graced his face with a dusting of tiny chocolate freckles that play across his knife-sharp cheeks like gold powder on a croissant. It's no wonder he's been popular ever since we were kids.

"I'm seriously regretting"—Asher heaves—"ever agreeing to this. Why'd you have to pick a restaurant all the way on the Upper West Side?"

"I didn't. Faisal did. Apparently it's one of his favorites. And it makes it more believable when he chooses the place."

Asher groans. "On a Tuesday, no less. I should be working. Or preferably, sleeping."

"It's almost five, first of all. And second, you *did* agree, so you can't back out. You're the one who said you'd do anything to help me." I slip my phone into my pocket. "Amira should be here any minute now. Hurry up and get in there," I say, already shoving him toward the door.

"Wait, wait." He stops and spins around to face me. "Walk me through this again because I need to see if it sounds just as stupid as when I first heard it the other night, or if I just completely misheard, which I'm really, really hoping I did."

"This is step one of three of the new Save Amira plan. We're going to make Faisal so jealous he shows his true colors."

After my talk with Amira the other day, I realized if she doesn't care about Faisal's past, I can't exactly *make* her. I needed a *new* plan of action.

Then it hit me: she doesn't care about his criminal past because she doesn't believe it affects them now. But that's just the thing: if Faisal is insecure enough about his past to hide it, then he's probably insecure about a lot more. His past is only a symptom of a much bigger problem. I don't have to uncover the details of the felony, or the drugs, or Leah. I just have to show that once a liar, always a liar.

"Why are plans always either three or five steps?" says Asher. "Why not four, or six? Or, for the sake of convenience, one?"

"Focus, Ash. We've got less than six weeks until the wedding, and Amira's friends from college are coming tomorrow to hit the ground running with wedding prep. This plan needs to be underway, like, yesterday."

"Don't you have wedding prep to do, too? Like for your cute little dance routine with Deen?"

"If all goes according to plan," I mumble, "I won't have to." To be honest, after our tiff behind the masjid, the only thing I want to do with Deen is fist fight. I'm sure he feels the same way.

Asher sighs. "Okay. Let's hear the rundown again."

"People lie about their pasts because they're ashamed, right?" I begin. "This plan just happens to be a very effective way to bring all of Faisal's insecurities out. Make him show his true colors so I don't have to. The best part? You don't have to do anything. Just have a nice dinner. Be yourself. Make her laugh. I'll take care of the rest."

"So you had Faisal pick the place so that when you and him walk in and see us, it'll feel more like a horrible coincidence," says Asher in slow realization.

"Exactly. If I picked, he'd be more likely to figure that I planned everything out."

Asher lets out a huge breath. "I can't say I feel great about you using me to make Faisal jealous. This whole situation is messed up and I want to see her break this thing off just as much as you do. But I don't know, doing *this* feels . . . in poor taste. To both of them."

"What's *in poor taste* is Faisal's lack of honesty," I say with a huff. "Faisal's done bad things. Amira's safety is at stake! I mean, the guy committed a crime, a *felony*—who knows what he's capable of? You think he'd go to such lengths to hide it if he'd just stolen an apple? All we're doing—all *you're* doing—is taking one of your childhood friends out for a nice meal. If Faisal freaks out, then it's his own damn fault."

"I know." He sighs. "I'm doing this because I agree with you, to an extent. Hell, you two are like sisters to me, and I don't like the idea of anyone lying to you. But don't ask me to get involved again, okay? If this doesn't work the way you seem to think it will, you're done. After today, you're going to be a good little sister and help Amira prep for her wedding. That's it."

I nod, barely listening.

"And since you're basically whoring me out, I want something in return."

"What do you want . . . ?" I ask hesitantly.

"Buy me Cambria," he says, smiling. "So we can play together. And it better be the Collector's Edition."

I laugh softly at the unexpected gesture. "Deal."

"Okay." Asher rolls out his shoulders, his neck. Then he throws open the door to the izakaya.

"Here we go."

Asher texts me once he's settled inside; he got a booth in the back corner, where he and Amira will have some privacy, but still be easy for me to spot.

Outside the restaurant, my heart rustles nervously against my chest, and the constant pacing I'm doing is only making it worse. Thankfully, I discover a bench at the corner of the street, so I take a seat and just breathe raggedly for a while. From the nearby park I can hear a dog barking, the squeals and giggles from a bunch of kids running through a water fountain. Sounds of summer.

Six weeks. I still can't believe Amira already picked an official date—without even telling me. Maybe I shouldn't be surprised anymore. But every day that passes, every day we get closer to August 22, will make it that much harder to put the brakes on. The sooner I put a stop to this—the sooner I can get Amira to see what a mistake marrying Faisal is—the cleaner it will be. I really don't want to make this any harder than it needs to be. Amira's been through enough. *We've* been through enough.

You don't have to protect me, Amira's voice echoes in the back of my mind.

But she hasn't given me much of a choice. She's the one determined to bring a total stranger into our family. Mom *told* us to stick together.

I rub my fingers against the edge of the bench beneath me. Damn it, Amira. If we'd handled this right, if we'd looked out for each other like we were supposed to, maybe she wouldn't be barreling into a wedding like this to cope with her grief.

My phone pings with an incoming text message:

Should be there in a couple minutes

I haven't put his name in my contacts list yet, but I recognize the number: Faisal, whose contact info I got from Amira. I shot him a message that night about wanting to get to know him more, saying how the two of us hadn't had a chance to really talk, one-on-one. Pretty convincing stuff, if I say so myself. If medicine doesn't work out, maybe I should be an actor.

Faisal bought it without question. Seemed excited about it, even, in his Faisal way. I get the impression he doesn't emote much, like a big gargoyle who's only recently been magicked into being human.

I see Faisal's form emerge across the street and wave him over. His face breaks into a shy smile and he jogs over, waving back. I get why he named his nonprofit AFFEY—the guy is certainly affable. It'd almost be cute, if he wasn't trying to destroy my family.

"Assalamu alaikum," he says in his deep, rumbling voice, and after some awkward fumbling with arm placement, he gives me a limp hug.

"It's good to see you," he says. "Thanks for waiting. And for coming all this way to have dinner with me. I, uh, was surprised when you texted out of the blue like that, but I'm really glad to get a chance to hang out, just the two of us."

I force a smile back. "My pleasure. Seriously. I thought about inviting Amira, too, but it sounded like she had plans. It works out, though. I figure it's better this way."

"I agree. And I'm happy. About this. It's a good chance for me to get to know you. For you to get to know me."

My smile falters a little. For someone who doesn't really emote, he sure knows how to sound genuine. Like he means every word, from the pit of his stomach. It catches me off guard. I don't know what to say, so I reach for the doorknob to the restaurant.

"Hey, I just want to say," Faisal starts, his voice shaking. "I really appreciate this. I know things haven't been easy. On you in particular."

My skin prickles and I pause, pull my hand back from the door. I turn to face him. "What? No, no. Not at all. I mean, I'm perfectly fine," I say nervously. "Where's that coming from?"

"I dunno, I just—" He exhales. "It's nothing. Never mind. Forget I said anything." He smiles to reassure me and opens the door. "Shall we?"

"Lead the way," I say, and muster my strength back into my feet, trailing Faisal into the restaurant.

Inside, the smoky air is thick with the fragrant, tongue-tingling smell of soy sauce and fresh rice. Even though Faisal picked a weird time, almost all the tables are full—even the bar, which is illuminated with dim gold light from paper lanterns. The walls are painted in rusty reds, with stark black wooden beams propped across the ceiling. It's a small restaurant, and the laughter and talk mix in with the hiss and slap of metal spatulas on griddles. It's cozy. The kind of place Amira and I would both love.

I'm surprised. I have to hand it to Faisal. Did he know it'd be the type of place I'd like? Or do we have the same taste? I don't know which thought is more unsettling.

"Excited?" asks Faisal. In the dim light, his features look softer, for some reason. "I'm pretty hungry myself."

"Oh. Yeah," I reply, trying hard to keep my face neutral. But I can tell that my voice sounds strained.

Faisal grabs the attention of a waiter to let them know about our reservation, and my throbbing heart crescendos as we near the back of the restaurant.

This is it. This could be the moment that fixes everything, the moment of truth. I just wish it didn't have to feel so painful, so *wrong*.

Familiar voices grow louder ahead of us, and I stop in my tracks, abruptly, as though my own body were resisting. Faisal bumps into me from behind, making me stumble forward.

In the booth in front of us sits Amira in a cute yellow dress, her arm reaching across Asher's chest to scoop at the mochi ice cream they're sharing. He slides the plate closer to her and she grins with childlike satisfaction.

"Dumbass," says Asher, laughing softly. "You have something on your mouth."

Amira's face falls. "Where?"

"Here," he says, and dabs at the corner of her mouth, gently, with a napkin.

My cheeks burn. They look like an actual couple, a beautiful one at that. When I was younger I used to imagine them getting married—one of my best friends getting married to my big sister, the fantasy!—but right now it looks so convincing I'm *ashamed*, like I walked in on something I shouldn't have.

I'm not the only one; next to me, Faisal's shoulders stiffen, his face freezes. The human has turned back into a gargoyle.

Amira is the first to notice us.

Her head tilts, like a bird, and she frowns. "Faisal? Kiran? What are you doing here?"

Beside her, Asher's face is locked in a grimace.

"Oh. I—I thought—" The ball in Faisal's throat bobs up and down. "I'm sorry. I didn't know you were here." He takes a step back. "I should—I should get out of your hair." He looks at me, his dark eyes nebulous. "Rain check, Kiran?"

I say nothing because every muscle in my body has turned to lead.

Amira gets to her feet. "Wait, Faisal—"

But Faisal's already gone.

The three of us say nothing for what feels like minutes.

"That was . . . weird," Amira finally says, blinking hard.

"Yeah," I reply. My mouth is dry. "Very weird."

I should feel a lot of things. Satisfaction. Gratification. My plan worked, after all. Faisal's obviously shaken up.

But I didn't expect to feel something that feels an awful lot like guilt.

Asher looks at me, his lips still pressed in a thin line.

He doesn't have to say a word.

I already know.

LOADING

[CAMBRIA: THE EVOLUTION EXPANSION PACK]

[ROANA GUILD CHAT ROOM]

Devynius Foxx: Random question

Devynius Foxx: Do you ever think about how weird dancing is?

Devynius Foxx: Like as a concept?

Devynius Foxx: The idea that people just get up onstage

Devynius Foxx: and move their bodies around

Devynius Foxx: and the audience claps

Devynius Foxx: "Thank you!! Thank you for moving your body in such a compelling, delicately patterned way!"

Devynius Foxx: "And thank you for watching! I have trained years to move my body in this way!"

Kasia Coribund: Are you okay Foxx

Devynius Foxx: LISTEN

Devynius Foxx: Isn't it WEIRD?

Devynius Foxx: And yet

Devynius Foxx: I find dancing to be, like, one of the coolest forms of expression

Devynius Foxx: It's mesmerizing

Devynius Foxx: Why is it so mesmerizing?

Devynius Foxx: What even IS IT?

Devynius Foxx: What makes something a gesture versus a dance?

Devynius Foxx: These are the things I think about before bed

Kasia Coribund: Wow, I . . .

Kasia Coribund: I've never really thought about it that way

Kasia Coribund: I mean, I love dancing, personally

Kasia Coribund: But, hm

Kasia Coribund: I guess I'd like to think

Kasia Coribund: Dance is a person's soul reaching out to talk through the body

Kasia Coribund: That's the difference between just, a physical gesture and dance

Kasia Coribund: You're *talking* in dance.

Kasia Coribund: You're baring your soul,

Kasia Coribund: conveying meaning in a way we just can't with words.

Devynius Foxx: Just another way to throw open our trench coats and reveal the bare-naked truth of ourselves, huh

Kasia Coribund: I hate you

CHAPTER 16

DEEN

Tuesday, July 13

40 Days Until the Wedding

"YOU LOOK LIKE YOU'RE SEIZING."

It's a few days before the dholki, and I'm in Vinny's summer dorm room, in front of the full-length mirror hanging on his door. My room doesn't have a mirror like this, for whatever reason, making Vinny's room the perfect place to practice dancing.

Or at least, what's *supposed* to be dancing. Apparently the line between aimlessly flailing your arms and actual choreography is thin.

"Then tell me what I'm doing wrong," I say, gritting my teeth. "Because I'm following the exact moves the guy's doing in this stupid movie." On a chair I've strategically placed next to the mirror, I've propped my laptop up with some Bollywood movie called *Bajirao Mastani*. Mona khala was the one who recommended it, since I know approximately jack shit about Bollywood. I look over my shoulder, but Vinny's tapping away at his laptop. "What are you doing?"

"Looking up the symptoms of a stroke."

I stop moving and wipe the sweat from my brow. "You think you could do better?"

He pulls down his headphones from his ears. "Bollywood dancing? Nah, man, there are *many* things I can outperform you in, but that's, like, in your blood."

I roll my eyes. "So people keep saying." I wipe my forehead with the bottom of my shirt and try to catch my breath.

The truth is, I don't dance much these days. I mean, I'll dance at clubs. But I used to dance a lot more as a kid, at weddings and stuff. Almost everyone dances at weddings. I'm not talking "Cha Cha Slide" bullshit. At desi weddings, people pull out the bhangra drums, the ones that beat in syncopation to your goddamn heart and set the floor, your body, hell, your very *being* on fire. You can't *not* dance. Your body just reacts to the beat, like it's been waiting for it all this time.

If there is some magical thing about my blood that can make me dance, though, it's not working right now. Maybe it's performance anxiety or something.

"You just need a better coach. Why don't you shove your pride in that special sock drawer of yours and text Kiran?"

"No way. It's a dance-off, a competition. I'd rather make a fool out of myself than ask her for help." I sigh. "Plus, the last time I saw her we had a huge fight."

I still can't believe half the things I said to her at the masjid. I of all people should understand why she's snooping around Faisal, to some degree. She's like a freaking hound catching a whiff of *something*, hoping to catch a big one at the end of the trail. Determined on a whole other level. She doesn't like me, same. She's hurt about what I did to her, fair.

I know Kiran said she was only doing this to protect Amira, but I don't believe it. There's too much fury wafting off her for it not to be personal. But hurting Amira and Faisal to get back at me, sabotaging their relationship—it's way too much. Can she not just take it back a notch or two or ideally ten?

If Faisal detects even a *hint* of Kiran hating him, it'd probably crush him.

At the very least, it seems like things are going along smoothly with the wedding preparations, including the dreaded task of digging up Faisal's baby pictures for some slideshow Amira's friends want to make, and sorting invitations to our side of the family (which according to Faisal, resulted in heated arguments between M&D). And with the way Kiran conveniently sidestepped giving any specifics, she was probably just bluffing when she said she knew more beyond just Leah.

I hope.

Except there was something about her face that doesn't give me much hope to go on.

"Your pride's showing, D-Money." Vinny, presumably done looking at WebMD, goes back to clicking at his laptop, where he'd been making another one of his remixes. "Well, I'm sure you'll eventually win Kiran over. Just like you do with everyone else."

I pause. There's something about his tone that feels . . . off. "Hey, are we cool?" I ask. "You've been acting kinda off ever since that party in Brooklyn."

"Yeah. 'Course. Of course we're cool."

I sigh and ignore the nagging feeling that for once, Vinny has learned how to lie.

"Well, this is going nowhere, so I'm heading back to my dorm." In any case, I'm taking the train back to Jersey in the morning, which leaves me tonight to catch up on some much-needed Cambria time. It feels like it's been forever since I've had time for a proper hangout with Kasia, and it's making me feel . . . itchy. Pretty sure I have dozens of notifications even from Nilina and Solẹn on the guild, asking if I'm okay.

It's times like these I wished telepathy were a thing so I could shoot Kas a message. Tell her that even though I'm busy, I'm still here. That I still care.

Vinny puts on his headphones again and turns back to his laptop, so I open the door and collide right into none other than Amy.

I stumble forward. "Ow."

"Oh, hey. Glad I caught you," she says after she straightens up.

"Hey yourself. You looking for Vinny?"

"No, actually . . ." She bites her lip. "I was looking for you. You weren't in your dorm."

I blink. "Oh." I think back to the last time I saw her, at that party with Vinny and Raquel. I can't remember what happened. That whole night was kind of a blur.

I quickly close Vinny's door behind me before he notices

anything and lead Amy away from his room.

"Here's a totally random question," I say in a slightly-less-than-panicked whisper. "I didn't say something stupid the other night, did I?"

"No! No. It was really fun, actually." She laughs softly. "Even if you spent most of the night raving about a girl."

"Feels like I've been doing that a lot lately."

We reach the common area on Vinny's floor, and Amy takes a seat on the couch. I remain standing. I'm too antsy to sit. The common area is empty, thankfully, and quiet. Too quiet. I still haven't gotten used to the emptiness of campus during the summer.

"Any updates on that front?" Amy asks, twirling one of her curly locks of hair. She looks cute, like a doll, and I get why Vinny's into her.

"Huh? With Kiran?"

"Yeah. I mean, it sounded like you were really stressed out about that dance you have to do together. You kept going on about how your brother's wedding *has* to be perfect or you'd never forgive yourself. Pretty dramatic language coming from a guy like you."

"Ah. That. Well. That was a bit of an exaggeration. I do that."

"I think it's sweet, though. Admirable."

"That why you wanted to see me? To compliment me?" I ask. "Not that I'm complaining."

"In a way." She smiles. "I want to get to know you better."

Ohhh boy.

I feel my mouth go slack, and it all comes together. Vinny. No wonder he's been pissy. How could I not have seen?

I clear my throat. "I, uh. I'm actually pretty busy—"

"Right, that thing you mentioned before—that's Saturday? The dole-key?" She butchers the word so hard it makes me wince.

"The dholki."

"Yeah, that. We're still invited, right?"

Oh, hell. And my drunk ass thought it would be a good idea to invite her and Raquel. As if things aren't already balancing on the edge of a precipice. What the hell was I thinking?

You don't think. That's the problem, says a voice in my head that sounds far too much like my own.

I run my hand through my hair. "So the thing is—"

My phone vibrates in my pocket. I pull it out and my eyes go wide at the name flashing on my screen.

Faisal. Calling me.

I hold up a finger at Amy. "Actually, put a bookmark in that. We'll, uh, chin-wag later?" I tell her, already heading out of the common room.

I throw open the doors of Brittany Hall and plunge outside. New York is humid and dusty and dense with sound: the occasional bellow from an angry pedestrian, the symphony of honking cars, the rattle of a jackhammer cutting concrete from a nearby construction site. The sun's already drooping below the cityscape, illuminating the backdrop of skyscrapers in tangerine hues and liquid shadows. I narrowly miss stepping into a puddle—of rainwater or piss, I can't tell.

"Hey, what's up?" I say into the phone, plugging my other ear with my finger.

"Hey." There's silence on the other line. "Are you coming tonight?"

Faisal's voice sounds shaky. Wrong. I tense. "My train's for tomorrow morning. Why?"

"I just saw Amira. With another guy."

"What?" My insides turn to ice. "No. Are you sure you're not misunderstanding something? Are you sure it was her?"

"I'm a hundred percent sure. She said my name—she saw me. We go into a restaurant, and as we're walking to our table, there's Amira. With a guy. Having dessert, laughing, just the two of them. She looked just as surprised to see me as I was to see her." Faisal exhales. "God, I don't know what to do."

I close my eyes. I can practically see him right now: in his office, slumped in his chair, head in his hands. Defeated.

"Wait, what do you mean, *we*?" I ask.

"Kiran—" He groans. "Oh God, *Kiran*. I ditched her, too. And after she invited me out for dinner. Said she wanted to get to know me."

"*Kiran* invited you?"

"Yeah. I was really excited, too—I mean, I don't know, I thought she didn't like me, and I haven't exactly made an effort to talk to her, either, so I guess I can't blame her—but I guess I've ruined it."

I dart into a Starbucks, where it's quieter, and grab a seat at a small table by the window. A flock of thoughts whirl in my head, but words don't come.

"I was an idiot." Faisal lets out a wet laugh. "I panicked and ran away, like a coward. We're supposed to be getting married and I can't even talk to her like a normal person. No wonder she's seeing someone else."

"Don't pull that bullshit on me. It was obviously a misunderstanding. She loves you, you love her. You just need to talk to her and clear things up like adults. That's all."

Easier said than done, though. I would know.

"I feel like I can't really do this anymore," he whispers.

"Do what?"

"This. All of it. I don't know, I keep thinking—I keep thinking it's karma or something. What if I don't deserve her? I haven't exactly been completely honest with her, you know. It's like Kiran said at the masjid. Secrets. But I keep running. Pretending to be something I'm not."

My pulse quickens. I've seen Faisal give up. I was there the last time he gave up on something important.

I'm not letting him destroy everything he's worked so hard to build.

"The dholki's soon; this is just nerves or something," I assure him. "Plus, you're the last person karma's gonna chase down. You're a good dude, Faisal. I know it, Amira knows it. And that's all that matters."

"Am I? Sometimes I'm not so sure."

"Faisal, you're not hearing yourself. Amira's the best thing that ever happened to you. And you're the best thing that happened to her. Don't give up everything for a little bit of nerves. Don't slide, man."

"Don't worry. I wouldn't talk about what happened with you. Your secret will be safe."

"It's not about that *at all.*" My voice rises, and I catch a couple of irritated glances from other customers trying to enjoy their burnt coffee.

"I can't believe I'm saying this," I hiss. "Even if it's true, even if she was out with some other guy today, you *have* to fight for this. She's worth it, right? You being happy, for once—that's worth it, right?"

Silence on the other line. I exhale.

"In any case, the dholki is in a few days. Go hang out with Haris. Get your mind off things. Then call Amira."

I need time to think. The fact that he was with Kiran—invited by her, no less—feels like too much of a coincidence. Did Kiran set the whole thing up? It seems weird, like something out of a bad Bollywood movie maybe. Would Kiran do something like that?

I should tell Faisal. But he's barely keeping it together as it is. Staged or not, seeing the love of your life with another guy is a punch to the dick. Not to mention learning that said love of your life's sister wants you to perish.

No. I got this.

"I'll see you tomorrow when you've cleared your head, okay?" I tell him. "Talk to Amira and stop being so hard on yourself. You're the firstborn son, the pride and joy of the Maliks. Act like it."

"I think we both know that title has always belonged to you," he says softly.

There's a familiar, painful throbbing in my chest.

"Yeah," I say, chuckling, "but you always deserved it."

LOADING

[CAMBRIA: THE EVOLUTION EXPANSION PACK]

[ROANA GUILD CHAT ROOM]

Devynius Foxx: SUPERPOWERS

Kasia Coribund: SUPERPOWERS!!!!!

Kasia Coribund: What about them?

Devynius Foxx: If you could have any superpower

Devynius Foxx: what would it be and why?

Kasia Coribund: oh damn

Kasia Coribund: That's a good one.

Kasia Coribund: Hmmmm . . .

Kasia Coribund: To see the future.

Devynius Foxx: Oh.

Devynius Foxx: Yeah.

Devynius Foxx: Guess that's a pretty popular one, huh

Kasia Coribund: Makes sense

Devynius Foxx: So why?

Devynius Foxx: Why that power?

Kasia Coribund: I want to be able to see the future

Kasia Coribund: because . . . I want to make sure it's safe

Kasia Coribund: that everything I'm doing right now is right

Kasia Coribund: that everything I'm working for means something.

Kasia Coribund: I want to know what to expect

Kasia Coribund: so I can do what I can to protect what I have now.

Devynius Foxx: Heh, it's funny

Devynius Foxx: When someone asked me this question before, I never knew the answer

Devynius Foxx: But I think I know now.

Kasia Coribund: Yeah?

Devynius Foxx: I want to be able to change the past.

Devynius Foxx: It's not unlike your power, in a way

Devynius Foxx: But I want to be able to go back in time, slap my old self for the mistakes he's made

Devynius Foxx: and live differently.

Devynius Foxx: I want things to be different.

Kasia Coribund: Sounds like someone has a couple regrets

Devynius Foxx: Yeah.

Devynius Foxx: Yeah, I do.

Devynius Foxx: You don't?

Kasia Coribund: Maybe.

Kasia Coribund: I don't know.

Kasia Coribund: I'd like to think

Kasia Coribund: The mistakes I've made only become regrets if I don't use them as fuel to make me stronger.

Kasia Coribund: Or at least strong enough to never repeat them. To do better.

Devynius Foxx: Damn

Devynius Foxx: Put that on a mug

Devynius Foxx: Put that on a wooden sign for the kitchens of white women everywhere

Kasia Coribund: Idiot

Devynius Foxx: But yeah, it's funny

Devynius Foxx: Whenever I feel . . . powerless

Devynius Foxx: I always find myself wondering about superpowers.

Devynius Foxx: Would I feel so powerless all the time if I lived in a world where I had some badass superpower like x-ray vision or flying or superspeed?

Devynius Foxx: Or would I just feel as pathetic as I ever did

Devynius Foxx: because either way, I'm still human?

Devynius Foxx: Sorry

Devynius Foxx: I'm just tired of feeling powerless all the time, you know?

Kasia Coribund: If it makes you feel any better

Kasia Coribund: I'm pretty sure even superheroes have regrets

Devynius Foxx: TRUE

Devynius Foxx: I mean just look at the Batman comics from the 70s

Devynius Foxx: a jockstrap over tights????

Devynius Foxx: Who hurt you, Batman?????

CHAPTER 17

KIRAN

Saturday, July 17
36 Days Until the Wedding

THE MASTER BATHROOM IN THE Maliks' house is, in a word, obscene.

It's colossal enough to double as a Turkish bathhouse, complete with white marble floor, pillar-flanked bathtub fitted with jets (spacious enough to fit four people, if you were into that sort of thing), and a shower with not one but two showerheads. There's even three floor-to-ceiling dressing mirrors so you can see yourself at every conceivable angle. I'm starting to understand why desis push for their kids to be doctors; the Maliks probably have enough cash to fill an actual, literal money bath.

But at least they're generous enough to lend us the space for Amira to get ready before the dholki, so we can pretend that we, too, are rich and fabulous socialites getting ready for a night out. I'd be lapping it up if not for the fact that this was all in service to my sister's accursed bridal shower. And that we're in Deen's house.

I dig for my phone at the bottom of my embroidered cloth purse, an old finicky thing Mom got me a few years ago with a latch that doesn't quite close right. No new texts. Hopefully Asher is already here. I know he's been reluctant to help, so I even brought the copy of Cambria he asked for—well, a sixty-day time card, since I couldn't afford the full game.

"Can you stop your phone addiction for two secs and help me hold Amira's dupatta?" Rizwana's voice snaps me to attention, even though she's got a safety pin between her lips.

Rizwana is Amira's best friend. They met in middle school, and according to Amira, bonded over being two brown girls in a world that liked to imagine them as poor, unfortunate souls oppressed by their terrorist fathers. What most people don't know is that you'd have a better chance having a face-off with a wild tiger than telling Riz what to do; it's why she went to school all the way in Chicago despite her parents' protests. She's also the eldest of three sisters, and has the uncanny ability to take charge no matter where she is and who she's with. Which is probably why Amira asked her to take charge of the wedding planning. Riz flew in the next day.

I don't argue with her. "Yes, ma'am," I say, flouncing over to her and Amira, who's sitting in a chair. I hold Amira's dupatta in place over her shoulder as Rizwana carefully pins it down.

Amira is decked in a rose-pink lehenga adorned with delicate, flowery gold-and-bronze embroidery, as was Riz's suggestion. Riz also did Amira's makeup, emphasizing Amira's full lips and tracing her cheekbones with a dusting of gold glitter, letting her dark, curly hair flow untamed over her shoulders. A gold tikka—a forehead ornament—shimmers beneath the bathroom light. Amira looks like a Mughal princess.

We finish with her dupatta, and I catch her gaze in the mirror. Her face breaks into a faint, tired smile. My breath catches in my throat. How many times have we stood in front of a bathroom mirror together, getting ready for school or dinner parties or family trips, sharing combs and lip glosses, venting about Mom and Dad or simply chatting about the first things that popped into our heads?

This, though—this is different. We're both quiet, like we know in our guts something between us is about to change forever. Something I can't see. Something I can't quite grasp. The logic in me says we'll still always be sisters, sure, but part of me can't help but feel she's about to go on to some plane of existence where I'll never be able to reach her, at least not in the same way.

Amira once asked me if I'd ever want to get married. I shrugged, threw her some noncommittal answer: *Maybe when I'm, like, twenty-five or something.* I imagined I'd feel like an adult then. I'd *be* an adult. But Amira is twenty-six now, and the idea of her getting married . . . it suddenly feels too early. Like she couldn't possibly be ready yet.

Riz puts her hands on Amira's shoulders. "How do you feel? Ready?"

Amira lowers her face. "Just tired. Faisal and I were on the phone till late last night."

Riz raises a brow, concerned, but doesn't press it. Guilt prickles in the pit of my stomach.

I wonder if Amira and Faisal were able to resolve things. Then again, is seeing Amira with another guy, especially a very cute, very single one you grew up with, the kind of thing you can resolve overnight?

I guess step one of my plan was a success. But that's a good thing, right? At least, good enough for now; finding out the details of Faisal's felony has proved impossible, so I'm at a dead end. I'm starting to suspect that the Maliks did something to keep it all buried.

I just wish Amira had listened to me in the first place. Maybe then I wouldn't feel like such garbage right now seeing her face like this.

There's another knock at the door; Riz glares at it. "If it's that Mona woman checking in again, I swear—"

"Knock, knock," says a soft, deep voice.

The three of us relax. It's Dad.

He pokes his head in; through the open door, I can hear the steady rhythm of a dhol drum like a heartbeat.

"Are you—?"

"Come in, come in," say Riz and Amira at the same time.

Dad hesitates, then enters. He's in a dark blue sherwani, his gray-flecked hair carefully combed to the side. The smell of his cologne tickles my nose from across the other side of the bathroom, but it's not bad. It's a familiar, gentle smell, like jasmine and musk. He's holding a single red rose in his hand.

He pushes his glasses up the bridge of nose and smiles at Amira. "You look beautiful," he says softly.

The gloom on Amira's face dissipates like sun-chased clouds.

Riz moves to step outside. "I'll meet you guys downstairs," she says, winking at me, before leaving the three of us alone.

Dad coughs. "I just wanted to see you before you went down. God knows I'll have trouble getting any alone time with you both. It's a madhouse down there."

"Are there a lot of people?" I ask.

"It seems the Maliks decided to invite a lot more guests than we thought."

I scowl. "Can't say I'm surprised." Apparently, not giving a shit about what other people want is a side effect of being filthy rich. Which, come to think of it, explains a lot about Deen.

"Well, that's fine," says Amira, shrugging. The glass bangles on her wrists clink softly. "It's a dholki, after all. The more people, the more fun it'll be."

Except it'll be all friends and family of the Maliks, I argue in my head.

Dad steps toward Amira and hands her the rose.

"I also wanted to tell you how proud I am of you. Both of you. You know I'm not good with words—your mom was the one . . ." He drifts off, looking past us. "I wish she could be here to see what I see."

Amira gets to her feet and throws her arms around him. "Me too, Dad."

My eyes burn. How long has it been since the three of us have been in a room together, talking? No, wait. I remember now: we haven't held each other like this since the funeral.

I'm brought back to the hospital one year ago, at Mom's bedside: *That's the only thing that's getting me through this, Kiran—knowing you're all together.*

Yes. Mom wanted *this*. This, right here, this life we share, the seeming impossibility of it, despite everything. This is why I have to keep us together. At the end of the day—at the end of your *life*—can you say you're a family if you weren't together? Even in this strange bathroom, even if Mom is gone, as long as we stay together, we'll always have a home.

Amira looks over her shoulder at me and waves me over.

I don't waste a second; I jump in and squeeze the two of them, tight.

And I close my eyes, breathing in the familiar smell that makes me remember everything.

According to Amira, the plan for the dholki was to invite around forty or fifty people—a small event, by desi standards.

But apparently Amira's future mother-in-law didn't agree with her, and there are at least a hundred people in the Maliks' house.

The crowd fills the entire living room, with surplus pooling in the kitchen. Upstairs, the rumble of little kids—a lot of kids, judging by the sound—shakes the ceiling, and throngs of men form their own congregation in the parlor room on the other side of the house, where Dad will no doubt be occupied for the rest of the evening. There's even a catering staff diffused through the masses, offering trays of various sweets and pani puri, tiny fried bread cups filled with a spicy potato filling. My stomach roars, awakened by the promise of something that isn't instant mac and cheese.

But the main festivities are being held in the living room, where dim string lights, hung across the vast ceiling and dangling down the walls, cast a warm, gold glow. Every inch of the floor is taken by people, mostly women, swaying and clapping to the beat of the dhol drum that sits in the very center of the room. My Urdu is atrocious, but I recognize the tune to a popular folk song; the singers' voices are slightly-less-than-harmonious, but they're loud enough to rattle my ribs and wake every cell in my body, like the heavy bass on a stereo. I'm itching to dance, even though I shouldn't. But I guess that's the magic of dholkis. Originally, they were for the bride's and groom's families to banter at each other through song, to extol the happy couple's virtuous qualities. A way to show off that ends in song and dance-offs. They're fun.

But I can't allow myself to get caught up in it. I have more important things to do.

Rizwana leads Amira into the fray of the dholki, with me and Dad bringing up the rear, and the energy of the room, as palpable as heat on my skin, rises in full force. Riz sets Amira onto a red velvet love seat on a makeshift platform that sits beneath a tent of colorful, twinkling scarves threaded with gold, and strings of fresh marigolds.

The women in the room change the song: *Rasool-e-paak ka saaya, Mubarak ho Mubarak ho*, something that roughly means, *With the blessings of the Prophet, congratulations, congratulations . . .*

I find Asher in a gray suit and thin black necktie, eyeing the buffet table. His plate is already towering with samosas. I grab a flute of thick mango juice off the table.

"Not wearing the kurta I bought you?"

"You got me that when I was sixteen," he says, dabbing yogurt onto the side of his plate with a spoon. "I grew out of that thing a long time ago, thank you very much. Kind of a shame, though. Kurtas are mad comfortable. Like the barong I wore at my tita's wedding."

"Aren't those see-through?"

"Whatever you're imagining, I want you to stop right now."

I laugh, but the sound quickly withers in my throat when I catch Deen skulking on the other side of the room. For some reason, he's decided to don a dark blue blazer and matching pants instead of traditional clothes, like a kurta or sherwani. A shame. Strictly biologically speaking, I've always considered him . . . acceptable. Handsome, even. But he always looked better in traditional clothes. Just another sign he's changed.

Next to him is Haris, killing it in a in a deep purple velvet blazer, and Faisal, who, unlike his brother, at least had enough sense to opt for the traditional route and deck himself in a cream-colored sherwani, even though it's barely containing his beefy arms. He's staring at Amira like a lost fawn—if a fawn was built like a tank. A baby rhino?

"So? What are you scheming for tonight?" comes Asher's voice at my ear.

"Me? Scheme?" I slap my hand on my chest. "Heaven forbid. I'm just a good little sister who's helping Amira prep for her wedding. Like you said."

"Uh-huh. See, I have trouble buying that when you very adamantly demanded this morning I 'look nice' and 'jealousy-inducing' for the dholki."

I mouth a polite *salaam* at a white-haired aunty who's smiling at us, though I have no idea who she is. "Sir! Whatever could you be implying?"

"That you're terrible." He takes an angry bite of a samosa.

"Whatever you're planning, can you at least keep me in the loop?"

"Well, since you're asking . . ." I fish out my phone from my purse and open my Notes app:

PLAN TO SAVE AMIRA:

STEP ONE: Sow the seeds of jealousy & insecurity

~~—Dinner with Asher~~

STEP TWO: Build distrust between Amira and Faisal

—Catch Faisal in a lie! Something that makes Amira question his integrity!

STEP THREE: Bring out the Dark Horse

—Find Leah's phone number/contact info!!!!

Asher runs his hand down his face. "Is this your grand plan? Catch Faisal in a *lie*? How the hell are you going to do that?"

"I'm still working on that." I have an idea, but Asher's definitely not going to like it. I'll have to brief him later.

"Can we not just, I dunno, have fun? I had to drive all the way to New Jersey for this. Jersey!"

"I'll have fun once I save my family."

Suddenly, Deen catches my gaze, and his eyes narrow. He says something to Haris and Faisal, and saunters over to us.

My heart bangs nervously. Step two, go.

I down my mango juice, grit my teeth, shove my phone back in my purse. "Look sharp," I tell Asher, and wipe my mouth with the back of my hand.

"What—?" he starts.

But Deen's already here.

"You seem very focused on your phone instead of your sister's dholki," he says, his dark eyes sharp on mine. "Checking your Minder account?"

I fold my arms across my chest. "Why, are you hoping we'll match?"

Asher frowns. "What's Minder?"

"Muslim Tinder, though I heard they changed their name recently. Shame." Deen's gaze slides to Asher. "I don't think we've met." But the look in his eyes says he knows exactly who Asher is. At least, he should; I'm pretty sure I mentioned him, back when we dated.

"Deen, this is Asher," I say. "Asher, Deen."

"Ah yes, your, uh, *friend*, right?" Deen barely restrains his sarcasm.

Asher wipes his hand on his pants and shakes Deen's hand with a smile. "Nice finally meeting you. I've heard a lot about you from this one," he says, tipping his head at me.

Maybe I'm imagining it, but it almost seems Deen's grip is a little too tight.

"Oh?" Deen replies coolly. He's smiling back, but his eyes are glinting with something unfriendly. "Well, we can't believe *everything* we hear, can we?"

Asher rips his hand away with a nervous laugh.

Before I'm ethered by whatever the hell tension this is, Faisal sidles his way from behind Deen, Haris following close behind. "Sorry, sorry—oh, Kiran! Assalamu alaikum." Faisal's forehead is damp with sweat, and the dark circles beneath his eyes match Amira's.

"Salaam, Kiran," Haris greets me. He notices Asher. "Oh! And you're . . . ?"

"The guy who caused a big misunderstanding the other night, apparently," Asher replies.

"Oh. That guy. Gotta say, it's, uh, nicer meeting you this way," says Haris.

"Yeah, about that." Faisal's ears redden. "I'm sorry, Kiran, for leaving you high and dry the other night. I kind of . . . misunderstood the situation a little and panicked. But Amira explained you're childhood friends." He looks away, genuinely remorseful.

"Well, I'm glad that's been cleared up," Asher pipes in, all friendly smiles. "And I'm glad to be here. I'm a big fan of the Noorani sisters."

"Uh, yeah. Same," agrees Faisal, blinking hard.

Seeing Asher and Faisal standing together, the difference between them is . . . apparent. Asher plays the part better than I thought.

I clear my throat. "It's funny," I say, even though it's not really funny. "We grew up with Asher. Me and Amira. It was cute because Asher's four years older than me, and Amira is four years older than him. 'Course, Asher and Amira were always closer. So it's no wonder you misunderstood the situation. Most people do."

Faisal nods weakly. "The two of them did look picture perfect."

"Everyone says that. Actually, my mom was sure the two of them would end up together. Lawyer, future doctor."

Faisal's eyes widen. "Oh. You don't say." Even over the din of the music, I can tell his voice is thin.

"Oh yeah, Asher's going to med school next year," I throw in casually. "And get this: when they were younger, they'd finish each other's sentences. They liked all the same things. They were really cute together."

The ball in Faisal's throat bobs up and down. "I'm jealous. I'm always saying I wish I'd met Amira sooner."

"Crazy, though, that you all chose the same exact restaurant out of the hundreds of thousands of restaurants in Manhattan, at the same exact time," Deen cuts in, his voice like red-hot iron.

The back of my neck prickles.

"Crazier things have happened," I say, smiling, keeping my voice level.

"Have they, though?"

"Maybe it's a sign from heaven," I reply, doubling down. This is my chance. Time for step two of my plan. "Actually, you know what would be good? If you guys get to know each other a little better. You guys could do your own little bachelor party thing. Right, Asher?"

"Oh, I don't know . . ." I feel Asher's eyes on me, ignore the angry bite of them.

"I like that," Faisal says. "If you're—if you're special, to Amira, then I want to get to know you, too. What if we did something next Friday? On Saturday we're all supposed to be going to Edison to get wedding clothes, but Friday could work. Haris, you're in, yeah? What do you think, Asher? Wholesome little night out?"

"What a great idea," says Asher weakly.

I clap my hands together. "So it's settled." Faisal almost makes it too easy.

Haris pats Faisal's shoulder. "I should get this guy to his bride-to-be. We'll finalize things later?"

Asher nods, still chewing his samosa. He looks pale.

But I catch Deen staring at me as if he's trying to burn holes through my skin.

Before I can process, Deen spins on his heel and disappears into the throng of people, leaving me standing there. Dumbfounded.

The music suddenly picks up behind me; the crowd has edged to the already-packed corners of the giant living room, leaving space around the dhol drum and the older woman playing it. Leaving a lot of space.

Enough space for a dancer.

Oh no. I have a bad feeling about this.

I hear someone call my name; it's Mona, elbowing her way through the crowd. She grabs my arm, breathless. "Come, Kiran. You have to dance."

"What?" I stare at her in disbelief. "I only agreed to dance for the wedding."

She tuts in annoyance. "It's your sister's dholki. Think of it as a practice round for the actual wedding."

I look back at Asher.

"Please. *Asher,*" I plead.

But he shrugs. *Have fun,* he mouths.

Okay, so maybe I deserve that for pushing him into the bachelor party thing, but that's *cold.* I try to worm my way out of Mona's grip, but the woman is strong. I realize there's no winning this.

I toss Asher my purse for safekeeping before I'm dragged away by Mona.

She shoves me into the center of the living room and I'm dizzied by the sheer number of people around me, the loudness of the music.

And then I see Deen, leaning against a back wall behind the crowd, a knowing sneer plastered on his face.

THREE YEARS AGO

KIRAN: lolllll

KIRAN: I can't believe you fell out of the tree

KIRAN: like a goddamn coconut

DEEN: Ok first of all

DEEN: I thought it would be romantic

DEEN: We'd get some PRIVACY

DEEN: And then you go and laugh at me!!!!

KIRAN: Because you FELL

KIRAN: And then Zahira ran over because she thought you were DEAD

KIRAN: omg I have never laughed harder in my life

DEEN: Couldn't you have at least PRETENDED to be worried???

DEEN: I could have died!!!

DEEN: I could have broken my neck!!!

DEEN: I could be HAUNTING you right now

KIRAN: lolololol

KIRAN: I made sure you were okay first!!!

DEEN: Ugh

DEEN: Serves me right for trying to be romantic I guess

DEEN: I used to be amazing at climbing trees, I'll have you know

KIRAN: Oh yeah?

DEEN: Yeah

DEEN: We used to have a bunch of A+ climbing trees in our backyard

DEEN: But then my parents went and chopped half of them down

KIRAN: Oh no, I hate that :(

DEEN: Honestly? I'm still in mourning

DEEN: Parents, man.

KIRAN: Parents, man.

KIRAN: Guess you don't really have a good relationship with yours, huh?

DEEN: lol

DEEN: Never.

DEEN: My parents only had kids to uphold their legacy

DEEN: Like they're 15th century monarchs

DEEN: They only care about their image

DEEN: And that I meet their expectations.

KIRAN: :(

KIRAN: My parents don't really have expectations for me

KIRAN: My big sister's always been the perfect one

KIRAN: At first, I was fine with it because they never give a crap what I did but

KIRAN: Lately, I kind of feel . . . I don't know.

DEEN: Forgotten?

KIRAN: Exactly.

KIRAN: Part of me has always wanted to be a dancer

KIRAN: But I want to do something better

KIRAN: Something that would make them proud, just to show them I can.

KIRAN: Maybe then they'll care.

DEEN: Well, whatever you decide to be

DEEN: I hope it's because it's what you want

DEEN: And not because of your parents.

KIRAN: And whatever you decide to be

KIRAN: I hope it's not a professional climber.

DEEN: You monster.

CHAPTER 18
DEEN

Saturday, July 17
36 Days Until the Wedding

SO MAYBE IT'S MY FAULT that Kiran got roped into dancing.

But I need her distracted. Plus, Mona khala had already been lamenting the lack of dancers—"These youth are killing our culture; no one even remembers the old folk songs anymore!"—so really, what choice did I have?

I cup my hands around my mouth. "Break a leg, Noorani."

She rewards me with a glare.

Someone turns on the surround-sound stereo and the entire living room vibrates to the bass line; Anum phuppo, my dad's younger sister, bangs away at the dhol, adding another layer to the beat that makes the song richer, more vibrant.

Mom and Mona khala stand on the sidelines, close enough for Kiran to see them, their eagle eyes trained on her. And behind Kiran sit Faisal and Amira, perched together on a red velvet love seat on a platform I helped put together out of some old planks of wood and bricks I found in the garage that were probably originally meant for the tree house Faisal and I wanted to build when we were kids. But Amira and Faisal look . . . awkward together, the inches between them like miles. I told Faisal to talk to Amira about what he saw at the restaurant; I wonder how it went. It looks like they'll need more time, though. Guess it's only natural; they haven't been together long, so unfortunately, it wouldn't take much to shake them.

Do I have Kiran to blame for that?

I glance over at Asher, who's watching Kiran intently from the other side of the room. Asher sets his plate and Kiran's purse down on the kitchen counter and squeezes closer for a better look.

Perfect.

I haven't been able to shake off what she said to me at the masjid about having undeniable proof about Faisal. And then with what happened at the restaurant with Faisal seeing Amira and Asher together like that—it's too much of a coincidence. Whatever she knows or doesn't, the girl isn't backing down anytime soon.

It's up to me to slow her down. Plus, I'm allowed to mess with her a *little*, right?

Kiran closes her eyes and goes very still, almost meditative, like a runner just before the bang of a popgun. I don't recognize the song, but it's clear she does; I can see it on her face. The focus. The zoning out into another world.

The room goes quiet.

Vinny would have eaten this all up—especially the food. If there's one thing my parents can do right, it's a buffet. But Vinny never showed, which might explain why, thankfully, Amy and Raquel aren't here, either. I'm wondering if I should have told him about Amy. He texted me this morning with some lame excuse about not feeling well and needing to take it easy, except I've never even seen the guy develop so much as a sniffle: not when the flu took out most of campus last semester, not a cold, not even a hangover. I don't think the guy *can* get sick. A fool and his cold are soon parted, I guess. Come to think of it, when was the last time I got sick?

Anyway, not having him around makes me feel uneasy. It's been years since I've gone to an event like this, and I feel out of place. I don't even know half these people; some are family, I think, but others are just friends of M&D's. Some maybe from our old masjid in Philadelphia. But these people keep wishing me *mubarak*, congratulating me and hugging me and telling me how great it is that Faisal found someone like Amira. They pretend like they know us. Like they care about us.

But these are also the same people who, if they really knew about Faisal—if they knew the truth about our pasts—would be the first to toss us in the sin bin and write us off as hopeless cases.

It's all bullshit. And Mom and Dad are eating it all up. They've finally found the distraction they've been looking for, the perfect opportunity to show everyone that they have nothing to hide.

This is exactly why I didn't tell Kiran three years ago. I didn't want to get her involved in this bullshit.

Kiran begins to dance.

Arms flowing in graceful, fluid arcs around her, her hips swaying to the rhythm like the vibrato of strings. With every twirl, her flowing lehenga spins around her legs, teasing the shape of them. Right now, she *is* the music—as it increases in cadence, so does she. Even from across the room, I can feel her like a live wire, the unspent energy ready to spring from her body.

I've seen her dance before, once. Three years ago, to a song from some ancient Bollywood movie—*Devdas*, I think. But her moves are sharper now, more confident. Like a person who knows exactly what they want, has found exactly what they love doing. I find myself a little jealous. I don't think I've ever felt that way about anything.

I catch her smiling, and our eyes meet.

Dance is a person's soul reaching out to talk through the body. Kas's words echo through my mind.

Only I don't understand what Kiran could be saying. What either of us have to say to each other anymore. Or what I'm feeling.

This is my chance to get what I need, while everyone's distracted. But my eyes won't look away. My feet won't move. She feels so far away, and yet I—

"Yeh larki kaun hai?" says a voice next to me. "Wo kiski beti hai?"

I turn my head; it's an older woman with stark black hair and lined, warm brown skin, wearing a bright purple sari. I don't know her, but I think she was the one leading the songs earlier.

"Kiran Noorani. Bride's sister."

"Oh ho." She smiles knowingly. "Friend hai? Dost hai?"

I'm even more irked, and not just because she's wasting what precious time I have. "No. Not a friend. Or anything." I know I said I'd play nice, especially in front of people. But right now I don't care. Rumors about me and Kiran being friends, more than friends, are worse than the alternative. I don't want any hint of that going around the rumor mills.

With Asher still distracted, I excuse myself from the old woman, yank myself from the dance floor, and make my way to the kitchen.

I wasn't expecting Asher here; honestly, I'm surprised he'd show after what happened. He irks me, too. I didn't expect Kiran to have a partner in crime.

And if what happened at the restaurant was Kiran's fault, as I suspect it was, then she's definitely not finished. I know her well enough to know that, at least.

I find Kiran's purse shoved in a corner on the kitchen counter. It's a big, strangely heavy bag of round cloth, with flowery embroidery and tiny beads embedded in the fabric, although some are missing.

The metal clasp doesn't seem to be working, either, because the purse just falls open in my hand.

I slip into the butler pantry and peek inside. There's her phone (bingo), some lip gloss. A Nintendo Switch. I snort. Of course she still plays games. Some things never change.

But her phone—that's the gold mine. She's been glued to her phone all night, and I saw her showing something on the screen to Asher.

Except there's something stuck on the back of her phone. She's installed a small pocket in the back, the kind that holds credit cards and her driver's license. My fingers find something thin, a white, glossy piece of cardboard. A business card?

Carefully, I dig into the pocket and manage to yank out the card. I flip it over.

It's a sixty-day time card for Cambria.

What the hell is she doing with this? Does she play Cambria?

The thought stings a little; something that I thought was my private getaway, my secret oasis, suddenly feels a little less sacred. It's just weird, coming across it in Kiran's purse.

Well, whatever. I don't think she used to play MMOs, but even if she does, hundreds of thousands of people play Cambria, all over the world. There's nothing special about that.

I turn my attention to her phone, in my palm.

Okay. She never used to keep a lock code on her phone, so it's time to do what I came for. My thumb grazes the power button, hesitating.

Suddenly, the entire house bursts with applause that makes the walls shake. The song is over.

My heart leaps back into my throat. Shit, shit, shit. I sneak out of the pantry, purse tucked under my armpit, and carefully shove the purse and phone back where I found them.

Kiran is standing in the center of the room, breathing hard, her chest rising and falling. Her cheeks are pink and she looks like she feels truly alive.

At least that makes one of us.

LOADING

[CAMBRIA: THE EVOLUTION EXPANSION PACK]
[ROANA GUILD CHAT ROOM]

Nilina Torby: You two are so weird

Devynius Foxx: Ma'am, I resent that

Devynius Foxx: I am perfectly normal.

Kasia Coribund: HEY.

Nilina Torby: Seriously, every time I come in here

Nilina Torby: You're asking each other icebreaker questions like a coupl'a middle schoolers out on a date

Kasia Coribund: They're fun, though!!!

Kasia Coribund: Oooh, actually that reminds me

Kasia Coribund: I thought of a really good one today

Kasia Coribund: Foxx! And Nil, feel free to answer too

Kasia Coribund: If you could summarize your entire existence with a single song, what would it be?

Devynius Foxx: Oh man

Devynius Foxx: This question

Devynius Foxx: Can't go wrong with the classics

Devynius Foxx: Right now . . . hmm . . .

Devynius Foxx: I'm feeling "Bitter Sweet Symphony" by The Verve

Kasia Coribund: Yessss, I can definitely see that

Nilina Torby: NICE, that's a good one

Nilina Torby: I'd have to think about it a little longer

Devynius Foxx: What about you, Kas?

Kasia Coribund: This is kind of breaking the sacred no-real-life rule, but you need to understand the context before I answer

Kasia Coribund: But basically, when my parents met one on one for the first time at some diner, my song of choice was playing in the background

Kasia Coribund: And, as you said, Foxx, you can't go wrong with the classics

Nilina Torby: Well, don't leave us in suspense!

Kasia Coribund: "I Wanna Dance with Somebody" by Whitney Houston, baby

Nilina Torby: LOL really???

Devynius Foxx: Huh.

Devynius Foxx: a popular favorite tbh

Nilina Torby: IS IT THO??

Kasia Coribund: Excuse me, I will NOT stand for this slander!!!

Kasia Coribund: It's my parents' SONG without which I would not EXIST

Nilina Torby: shit, now it's stuck in my head

Devynius Foxx: OHHH I WANNA DANCE WITH SOMEBODY

Kasia Coribund: I WANNA FEEL THE HEAT WITH SOMEBODY

Devynius Foxx: YEAHHH I WANNA DANCE WITH SOMEBODY

[**Nilina Torby** has logged off]

Kasia Coribund: . . .

Devynius Foxx: Guess she doesn't love us :(

CHAPTER 19

KIRAN

Saturday, July 24

29 Days Until the Wedding

EDISON, NEW JERSEY, IS A desi immigrant's dream.

What you need to know about Edison is that it's home to the bustling Oak Tree Road, aka Little India, an entire two-mile district crowded with desi shops, banquet halls, restaurants, and wholesalers, with names like Raj of Sweets, Green Chutney, Dosa House, and my absolute and popular favorite, Desi Fashion Bazaar. The true mark of an Asian immigrant community is its sheer disregard for creativity, opting instead for stark, utilitarian conventionality. It's part of its charm.

Amira takes a hard inhale after we crawl out of Riz's car, like bugs through molasses, into the humid afternoon air. "Oh man, do you smell that?"

"What?" I ask.

"Home."

"Home," Riz repeats, deadpan. "We drove an hour from home, to . . . home?"

Amira pouts. "Home in like, a spiritual sense! The home of our ancestors! The home of our blood."

Riz snorts. "Calm down. It's just Edison."

We follow Riz down the main road, passing storefront after storefront. The architecture in Edison is plain—mostly crammed row-home-type buildings from the sixties and seventies, flat storefront paneling made of a hundred shades of white and beige. But what the architecture lacks in color, the signs and awnings more than make up for. Bright oranges and greens and reds, bold lettering, made only more striking against an overcast, somber gray sky. To Amira's point, there is that familiar smell wafting through the air, an intoxicating combination of spices and overripe fruit and charred meat that seeps through the store windows.

When I woke up this morning, Amira and Riz suggested coming with them to go dress shopping. Dad said he'd be busy with work anyway, so I jumped at the chance. It feels like it's been ages since the three of us have just hung out, even if it is to get Amira's wedding dress. Still. Days like these are starting to come less and less. And if Amira actually gets married to Faisal, they might end altogether.

With the gentle chime of a bell to welcome us, we enter Bebak Boutique. It's a clothing store but probably one of the coolest clothing stores I've ever been in. The lights are dim, first of all, with tiny spotlights on the ceiling that shine directly on giant wall-to-wall poles, from which hundreds of glittering lehengas hang, layered from floor to ceiling. The gold-painted walls are carved with Mughal-style flowers, and the entire expanse of the floor is carpeted with an ornate, plush Persian design. Unlike most desi clothing stores, which smell like mothballs, this one smells faintly of jasmine, and I see why: there are huge, jungle-green pots in every corner of the store, brimming with fresh jasmine flowers. Mom would have loved it.

"Are you sure you don't want to just order a dress from Pakistan?" Riz asks. "I have the names—Kiran, stop trying to steal the flowers!—of a few designers who would be perfect for you."

Amira walks down the line of lehengas, occasionally running her fingers down the embroidery. "Except they cost a fortune. It'd be cheaper buying a ticket to Pakistan, getting one made at some tailor, and buying a ticket back."

"Tell your rich in-laws to pay for it, since they keep insisting on controlling everything else."

Huh? Are Deen's parents giving Amira a hard time?

"I can't do that! I can pay for it myself, but it's just—money like that is better spent elsewhere." Amira pauses at a traditional red lehenga. Her voice lowers. "Speaking of which, I was kind of thinking, if Kiran's okay with it—"

I pull my face away from the bouquet of jasmine flowers.

"I was thinking of wearing Mom's wedding dress." She stares at the floor, her eyes downcast. Like she's afraid of my reaction.

I smile. "Of course you should wear it. Mom would love that. Just promise me you're not going to, like, chop off the sleeves to make it more modern or something."

Amira laughs and I feel warm. I think she'd look beautiful in Mom's dress, to be honest.

Just not getting married to this guy.

The bell on the door chimes again and I turn around.

My heart sinks. It's Faisal. And then my heart dive-bombs right into the floor.

Because behind Faisal is Deen.

"You made it!" Amira bounces into Faisal for a hug.

Faisal looks surprised for a moment, then hugs her back, hesitating. I feel my jaw twitch in annoyance. I don't detect an ounce of awkwardness between them. Did they patch things up, or is Amira pretending everything's fine?

"It was only a thirty-minute drive from M&D's," Faisal replies.

Amira's eyebrows furrow. "M&D's?"

"Mom and Dad's," Deen interjects. Then he grins at Faisal, like it's their own private joke. I guess despite their differences, they really *are* siblings. It's weird, thinking about it; Deen had been so secretive about his family; I still haven't quite wrapped my mind around the fact that he has a brother—that he, too, has inside jokes with him, memories with him, like Amira and I do. And secrets. Definitely secrets.

"Didn't know the guys were coming," I say. "I thought it was just gonna be us."

"Sorry," Deen says. "Not sure about our taste with this kind of stuff, but we wanted to help pick things out. Hope that's okay?"

I don't answer him; only stare at him with unbridled annoyance.

He's wearing a white T-shirt and some jeans, and his hair, which normally looks painstakingly combed and product'd and lovingly spoken to, is a wild, untamed mess of black strands. Today he's even sporting a little stubble around his chin, and I can't tell if it's because he didn't get to shaving, or he missed a couple spots.

He seems . . . genuine, though. Or maybe he just wants to play nice in front of Amira and Faisal.

"All right, people," says Rizwana, clapping her hands together, "we need to get proper outfits for the mehndi. But we also need to find a sweets vendor because I am not allowing stale laddoo to be shoved in Amira's face on my watch. So, divide and conquer: Amira, Faisal, you stay here since, you know, I need you to try on outfits. But Kiran, I need you to be my taste tester."

"Sure."

"I'll go with her," Deen says suddenly. "I'd be no use here."

Something in my chest does a horrible panic dance, like my heart's walking on coals.

"All right, all right, but"—Riz wags her finger at Deen—"don't even think you can get out of trying on shalwars. Just head to Raj of Sweets on the other side of the road. Check it out, make sure it's still good; my cousin catered from them last year and it was pretty decent, but you never know. Then come straight back."

"Fine," I say with a resigned sigh. "Let's get this over with."

Amira throws me a friendly wave, and I march out of the clothing store, not bothering to check whether Deen's following me.

"Say you're there for the Noorani-Malik mehndi!" Riz calls out. "They know you're coming."

I scowl. Noorani-Malik. I hate the sound of it.

Outside the store, Deen trots up behind me.

"Do you know where you're going?" he asks once he's matched my pace.

"Do you?" I snap, which shuts him up.

Except I can feel his eyes on me, a smile tugging at his mouth while they dig into me.

"So, if you're helping your sister," he finally asks slowly, "does that mean you finally approve of the wedding?"

"I bet you wish," I say. "Just wanted to get out of the house."

"Our little bachelor party thing is happening on Friday," he says. "I'm super excited to talk to *Asher*."

The way he says Asher's name makes me tense.

"For someone you've claimed to be your best friend," he continues casually, "it sure is a shame I never met him earlier. You know. When we dated."

I abruptly stop and stare at him. "Why? Are you jealous?"

He stops a few steps ahead. Then he looks over his shoulder, smirking. "Oh, so we're both sharing our wishes now?" He looked tired earlier, but now there's this living glint behind his gaze, a tiny flame, that brightens his whole face. It's annoying not being able to read him. And to think I was once so sure I knew everything about him. What a joke.

I keep walking, narrowly missing him with an elbow.

We find Raj of Sweets about a half mile away from the boutique, on the other side of Oak Tree Road. It's not exactly as grand as the name implies; it's a small hole-in-the-wall, with cracked linoleum flooring and bizarrely textured walls that might have been white at one time, but are now the color of expired milk. Over the whirring fan and hum of the row of coolers, old Bollywood tunes play on the dusty stereo, and the owner, an older, wispy-haired man in a stained cotton-white shalwar kameez, has to keep slapping the top of the stereo with a rolled-up newspaper when it skips.

But the place smells like rose water and sugar, so thick I can practically feel it coating my skin.

I approach the counter, channel my inner Rizwana. Take charge, Kiran. Don't let Deen see you sweat.

"We're here for"—I swallow—"the Noorani-Malik order?"

The wispy-haired store owner doesn't get up from his stool. "Atcha. Kya aap dulha aur dulhan hai?"

My Urdu is garbage, but I recognize the words *dulha* and *dulhan*. Groom and bridegroom.

I feel my face burn. "O-oh no, no, we're not—"

"Nahain, janab," Deen steps in, "wo humare bhai aur behen hai."

"Ahh, theek hai, theek hai," the man replies with a little head bob. He finally gets up from his stool and rummages through one of the coolers.

I raise an eyebrow. "You still know Urdu?" Deen doesn't strike me as the kind of guy who's in touch with his culture. He's more the kind of person who's ashamed of it, even, which pisses me off. And yet, his Urdu is still better than mine. Which pisses me off even more.

Deen shrugs. "Yeah, well. It's not something you forget."

The wispy-haired store owner pulls out a white cardboard box and opens it on the counter, revealing an assortment of different desi sweets: marigold-colored laddoo, glittering topaz jalebi, pink and white chum chum. I can already taste the sweetness on my tongue, and my mouth starts salivating with barely controlled greed. Let the record show that I would not be against having a permanent rose-flavored sugar syrup IV drip. I freaking *love* this stuff.

"Try it," the store owner says, and I decide I love him, too.

"Want me to feed it to you?" offers Deen, breaking me from my reverie with a fake sweetness that almost puts me off my appetite.

I snort. "Sorry, the only person who gets to feed me mithai is my future spouse. On our wedding day."

"And waste all that time waiting for Mr. Right when I'm Mr. Right Here?" He tuts. "*Shame.*"

I roll my eyes and reach for a pink chum chum, a small, coconut-flake-covered, oval-shaped dessert made of curdled milk soaked in sugar syrup. I take a bite down the middle and get a burst of syrupy rosewater-flavored goodness.

Ohh, sweet Lord!

Beside me, I hear Deen snort.

"What?"

"Nothing. You're certainly enjoying yourself."

I swallow. "What? People can't enjoy things?" I snap.

"No. I'm just . . . never mind."

His mouth quirks up in a smile that ignites the glow in his eyes, familiar and heart-aching all at once. A real smile. An echo from the past. It catches me off guard.

Panicking, I quickly open my purse and rifle through it to find my wallet. "I'm gonna buy some for my dad," I say.

What is wrong with me?

Deen translates the order for me before peeking into my purse. "What games do you play?" he asks, eyeing my Switch.

He suddenly feels way too close. "A little bit of everything." I wonder if he remembers that time I brought my Nintendo 3DS to the masjid. It feels like centuries ago.

"Hm." He stares at the floor, deep in thought. "You play any MMOs?"

I feel my back straighten defensively. I hand the store owner some cash. "Sometimes," I reply hesitantly.

The store owner slides the bags of samples and my order for Dad toward us.

"Come on," Deen says briskly, swiping the bags off the counter. He props open the door for me. "We should head back before Amira's friend kills us."

I glance at the counter, expecting another bag.

But he's carrying them all.

LOADING

[CAMBRIA: THE EVOLUTION EXPANSION PACK]
[ROANA GUILD CHAT ROOM]

Devynius Foxx: soooo

Devynius Foxx: any updates on that enemy of yours?

Devynius Foxx: you fight em yet

Devynius Foxx: challenge em to a duel

Devynius Foxx: better yet, challenge one of those ol western showdowns

Devynius Foxx: you know, with the pistols and the tumbleweeds and the long jackets

Kasia Coribund: Those showdowns require fast reflexes

Kasia Coribund: If my enemy challenged me to a western showdown, I would fumble, drop my gun, and promptly burst into tears

Devynius Foxx: ooo yes, MIND GAMES, good strategy

Devynius Foxx: make them feel like a total dick!!!!

Kasia Coribund: I don't think that would work tbh

Kasia Coribund: my enemy's Mind Game game is too powerful

Kasia Coribund: like the other day . . .

Devynius Foxx: uh-huh . . .

Kasia Coribund: they were being . . .

Devynius Foxx: yes . . . ????

Kasia Coribund: . . . nice?

Devynius Foxx: NO!!!!!!

Devynius Foxx: the WORST

Devynius Foxx: NOT . . . NICE!!!!!!!!!!!

Devynius Foxx: ANYTHING BUT THAT!!!!!!

Kasia Coribund: . . .

Devynius Foxx: That sick bastard . . .

Devynius Foxx: What are they planning?!?!?!?!

Devynius Foxx: Is it all part of their sick mind game?!?!!?!

Kasia Coribund: . . . I . . .

Devynius Foxx: you gotta fight the motherfucker

Devynius Foxx: end their reign of tyranny!!!!!

Devynius Foxx: let them know their kindness will not stand!!!!!!

Kasia Coribund: OKAY BUT SERIOUSLY, IT'S VERY CONFUSING

Devynius Foxx: OMG WHAT IF

Devynius Foxx: you really fucked with their head

Devynius Foxx: and you . . .

Kasia Coribund: I . . . ???

Devynius Foxx: hear me out . . .

Kasia Coribund: I'm listening . . .

Devynius Foxx: you . . .

Devynius Foxx: were nice to them BACK

Devynius Foxx: REALLY throw them off!!!!!!!

Devynius Foxx: THAT'LL SHOW EM

[**Kasia Coribund** has logged off]

Devynius Foxx: I WAS KIDDING, COME BACK!!!! T____T

NOW

⸭ Sunday, July 25 ⸭
11:53 P.M.

KIRAN: So, I have one more part for you to play for my Save Amira plan

ASHER: oh no
ASHER: I thought you said I was done
ASHER: What do you need now?

KIRAN: Uhhh
KIRAN: Please don't mad
KIRAN: But I need you to take a picture for me

ASHER: . . .
ASHER: A picture of what exactly?

CHAPTER 20

DEEN

Friday, July 30
23 Days Until the Wedding

"DO YOU THINK THEY HAVE mozzarella sticks?" asks Vinny, opening a leather-bound menu.

Across the table, Asher stares at him, dumbfounded. "I don't think it's that kind of restaurant," he says slowly.

The Laughing Bard is more than a restaurant; it's an experience. The ambience is staid and classy: Victorian architecture, dim lighting, extravagant paintings in gilded frames, red leather seats that pop against black walls. The second floor is home to a massive, hand-carved oak bar—something the Laughing Bard is apparently famous for—that sits in front of a wall of glittering bottles of vintage scotches and whiskeys. We're in a private room on the first floor, themed to look like some rich nobleman's library. It smells vaguely of cigars and hypermasculinity.

The restaurant was Asher's choice. I'll admit, it's not a bad one for a pseudo bachelor party.

Vinny pouts. "Aw, man. You might be right. They didn't even laminate their menu, which means they probably update it, like, weekly. That's some bourgeoisie shit." He sets the menu down and longingly eyes Faisal's mojito. "Bet the drinks are killer."

Faisal laughs. "You won't want this one. This is nonalcoholic." He gives his drink a swirl. "I think they call it a Gentleman's Tonic? Weird aftertaste, but they're good; this is my second one already."

Vinny gives him a puzzled look. "What makes it a Gentleman's?"

"No idea, but one of the waiters recommended it when I asked for nonalcoholic drinks."

"They serve it to you with a '*here you are, old chap*,'" I reply.

Vinny grins. "You mad lad, how absolutely cheeky of you."

There he is. My own grin widens. "I admit to enjoying a good bit of drollery hither and thither."

Vinny and I share a loud, mirthful guffaw, and for a moment, things don't feel so . . . off between us. He's always wanted to meet my brother, but with the way things have been, I wasn't even sure he would show up. I still haven't talked to Vinny about Amy yet, and I don't know if he's heard anything from her. It's not exactly a conversation I'm looking forward to. I mean, how do I even start? *Hey, old boy, you know that girl you've been fancying? Well, it appears she fancies me instead! Blimey!*

So yes, I'm putting it off. I have too much on my proverbial plate, anyway. The only thing I want to see on my plate tonight is fish and chips.

Haris clears his throat. "Shall we toast?" he asks, sitting to Faisal's left at the head of the table. "To the man of the night?"

Everyone stands awkwardly and raises their drinks. Pretty sure none of us have ever been to a bachelor party, most of us being Muslim and all, and I think it shows.

"To Faisal!" I say. "Congratulations to you and Amira, and khuda hafiz to his virginity."

Faisal's eyes widen in horror, while Haris and Vinny burst into laughter.

I smile. It feels good, being this much closer to his dream. Like it might actually happen. Just a few more weeks, and he'll be in California. Free of M&D, free of his past. Just, free.

"So what's the plan?" asks Haris after we all settle down. "After dinner, should we catch a movie or, I don't know . . . go bowling?" He looks at Faisal. "I genuinely don't know what's fun anymore."

"Question: Is this a bachelor party or a ten-year-old's birthday party?" asks Vinny.

"How about we just see where the night takes us?" Asher offers quietly, taking a sip of water. He seems like a pretty chill guy, but he's been kind of reserved since we got here. Maybe he feels out of place; he's been distracted by his phone a lot.

I watch Faisal from the corner of my eye, who's been pretty quiet, too.

Hopefully Faisal's silence is the result of wedding planning nerves, and not something else.

A waiter comes in with plates of deviled eggs, a cheese platter, marinated olives, and Welsh rarebit, and our table becomes a mess of passing plates and bumping hands. The waiter takes Faisal's empty glass of Gentleman's Tonic and swaps it with another full-to-the-brim drink.

Haris looks at me and smirks. "So, Deen, I hear you have to do a wedding dance. How's practice going?"

Ugh. I sink in my chair. "Practically nonexistent."

"It's true," says Vinny, mouth full of egg. "I saw him practice once and it was Sad, capital *S*."

"Uh, not to be the bearer of bad news," says Haris, "but . . . the wedding's in three weeks. Is that enough time to get it down?"

My forehead throbs. "Don't remind me." I wonder if I should just accept the inevitable: that Kiran is going to do some spectacular dance and I'll be following up with a "Hey, look what I can do!" and make fart noises with my armpit or something.

Across from me, Asher puts his phone down, eyes glazed over, like he's lost in thought.

"That sucks." Haris reaches for a slice of bread. "Everyone's going to be expecting it, right? I mean, you can't have a South Asian wedding without dancing. And with you and Kiran being the only siblings of the bride and groom, the pressure is all on you."

Faisal sits up in his chair suddenly, spilling some of his tonic. "But not *too* much pressure. Amira's friend Rizwana said she and her sisters might do a dance, too, so if you don't want to do one, that's totally okay."

"No! No. It's fine. I want to," I say. Faisal gives me a lopsided smile that forces a smile to my own face.

And it's true. I do want to do this. It's rare that I get the chance to do anything for him, and this is certainly nothing compared to half the sacrifices he's made for me. He's always been looking out for me, taking the brunt of Mom and Dad's harshness. The only reason why they're not on my case for school these days is because he's there at home, fending them off. Even if he did slip for a couple of years in college, can I really blame him? With everything he's been enduring, he deserved a little slip. He's more than made up for it since. So if he tells me to jump, fuck yeah, I'll ask how high. If he asks me to dance for his wedding, well . . .

I'll figure it out.

Haris is asking Faisal about Rizwana when I feel Asher staring at me.

"Can't keep your eyes off me?" I ask.

"What? No. I was just thinking."

"About me?"

"Ha. Kiran did mention you were like this."

I don't ask what he means by that, and honestly, part of me doesn't want to know.

Asher's gaze flicks to Vinny, Faisal, and Haris, who are busy chatting away.

"I was thinking," he says softly, careful not to be overheard, "you and Kiran, you're both overcomplicating things. And not just with the dance. Kiran told me you two used to be a thing."

My muscles tense. I guess she went back on our pact to keep things secret. Then again, I guess I can't completely fault her—it has been three years. I'm just annoyed she had to go and tell this guy.

Asher continues: "There's all this anger, and a lot that's been left unsaid. But why don't you just . . . tell her you're sorry? I get that there's a whole other side to the story that I don't know. But I don't think you're a bad person. It's just, Kiran's hurt. You can get where she's coming from, right? It might be good to acknowledge the elephant in the room, before someone gets hurt even more. Maybe I'm wrong, but . . . I think she'd forgive you. Hell, I think you could be friends."

"I think you're giving me too much credit."

"What do you mean?"

"I mean, if she has friends like you, then why the hell would she need me?"

Asher's thick eyebrows crinkle, like he's about to say something else, but Haris's voice snaps me to attention: "Whoa, you okay, big guy?"

At the head of the table, Faisal's head droops.

"Huh?" Faisal blinks. "Yeah, I just got really sleepy all of a sudden."

"Does someone need a nippynap?" Vinny asks.

Faisal laughs. But it's not his normal laugh. It's more like a loud, hysterical giggle, uncontrolled and sloppy, as if he were—

Oh no.

I stand up. "Hey, can someone call the waiter in?"

Something like understanding flashes in Haris's eyes; he throws open the velvet curtains that hide the door to the rest of the restaurant and leaves the room. A few minutes later, he returns with the waiter.

"These are nonalcoholic, right?" he asks, pointing to Faisal's empty Gentleman's Tonic glass.

The waiter's eyebrows furrow. "No. Why? He's over twenty-one, right? Did Mark not check his ID?"

"He's over twenty-one, but he—" Haris pinches the bridge of his nose. "Shit. How many of these has he had?"

The waiter thinks. "Uh, not sure. Four? I think? Sorry, I'm not the one who took the order, so . . ."

Vinny snorts. "Yooo, someone's gonna have fun *tonight.*"

My jaw tightens. "Faisal doesn't drink." Faisal's gone respectably sober for the past few years, and for good reason. He's been really proud of it, too. How did he not taste something off? Have all those protein shakes destroyed his sense of taste? Shit. What if Kiran finds out and tells Amira?

I glance at Asher, suddenly suspicious, but he doesn't notice. "Get some water," Asher orders the waiter. "He barely ate anything, so could you also bring a soup or something?"

The waiter leaves without another word.

Faisal bangs the table with a loud, crack-of-thunder slap that makes us all jump. "No, guys, guys. I've never felt better. Everything's great!" he says, his words slurring. He can barely keep his eyes open. "You know, I haven't felt like this in ages. It's been so long since I've just had fun with my boys, you feel?"

On some level, this is the funniest thing in the world. I've never actually seen Faisal *drunk* before, and I gotta say, this happy drunkenness is an adorable look for him, even if it is completely wrong. But I'm worried. Amira *can't* find out about this. It's not exactly a good look for Faisal to get wasted out of the blue when he's supposedly straight edge.

"I've just been feeling so stressed with the wedding—not the planning, 'cause I'm useless at that, but—I just wanna make Amira happy, you know? She's great. So great, you know? So fuckin' great."

Haris rubs his back. "All right, big guy, just hang tight." He looks at me and shrugs.

I shrug back.

Good thing I don't have class tomorrow.

There's a knock at the door. The waiter?

"Come in," says Asher tiredly, and the door opens.

Someone pushes apart the curtains and struts into the room. Panic hits me like a hot iron, flattening me to the ground.

It's a police officer.

She's wearing dark aviator sunglasses. Blonde curls pop against the trench coat layered over her gray-and-black uniform. She looks around the room, taking us in without a word.

Haris is already backing away. "Did someone freaking call the cops on us?" he mutters.

"It's either that or the haram police," I mutter back. "Wait, aren't you a *lawyer*?"

"You think that matters?" he snaps.

After a painfully long stretch of time, Asher finally speaks. "Can we help you?"

The police officer rips off her sunglasses, revealing big eyes framed by even bigger fake lashes. Dim light reflects off shimmery pink lips.

Then it hits me.

Vinny's eyes go wide. "By Jove, old boy," he says, his jaw slack. "She's a *stripper*."

"Oh *hell* no," I hear Asher mumble behind me.

"Fay-zal Malik?" she asks, in a booming, authoritative voice.

Faisal blinks blearily, and raises a hand. "I'm Faisal."

"You're under arrest." The woman smiles and strides up to him, the heels of her boots clicking. "For getting married." She whips out a pair of fuzzy red handcuffs.

Haris is stunned, as if a stripper mere inches away from grating her ass on his very Muslim friend's abs right in front of him isn't much better than the sudden appearance of a cop. Vinny whoops. "Yeah, read him his Miranda rights!"

But Asher gets to his feet, a vein in his forehead twitching. He looks . . . strangely pissed.

"Ma'am, pardon me," he says, moving between the woman and Faisal. "What's your name?"

"Trudy."

"Hi, Trudy." Asher gently pulls her trench coat back over her bare shoulders. "Look, I'm very sorry to have wasted your time, but I don't think we'll be needing your, uh, services tonight."

"But I was hired for the hour."

Asher licks his lips. "Well, I'm afraid there's been a mistake. Let me walk you to your car and I'll write you a check."

I round on him. "Did *you* hire her?"

"No! No. Not—it's complicated. But for what it's worth, I'm sorry." Asher grits his teeth. "This *shouldn't* have happened."

Vinny laughs. "Dude, you're amazing."

"That's one word for it." My voice lowers. "I guess you didn't get the memo, *Asher*, but my brother's as straight edge as they come. We don't even usually *have* bachelor parties. Especially not like *this*."

Vinny stops laughing. "Yo, don't shit on sex workers. My cousin paid her way through college as a call girl. Now she's an econ professor."

"You know what I mean."

"Am I getting paid or what?" Trudy asks.

But Asher's barely listening; instead, he's looking at his phone. He's taller than me, the asshole, so I can't get a good look at his screen, but he looks like he's texting someone. He wipes at his brow.

"What are you doing?" I ask, irritated. My suspicion's growing.

"Nothing, just—getting a Lyft." He puts down his phone. "Something tells me bowling isn't going to be happening tonight." He smiles weakly.

"Yeah, no shit."

"I'm going to escort Ms. Trudy out of here and pay her. Just make sure your brother gets some water in him, okay?"

"Fine. Just, don't tell anyone about what happened tonight, okay?" I look at him in a way I hope is intimidating to show that I mean business . . . even though he's a little taller than me.

Asher raises an eyebrow. "Obviously. I'm not an asshole. Is he always so distrustful of people?" he asks, addressing Vinny.

Vinny nods solemnly. "Yes."

"Sounds like someone I know." Asher grabs his wallet off the table, pats down his pockets, and prepares to follow Trudy through the curtains to the main restaurant area.

Before he leaves, though, he pulls me aside. "Hey, Deen?" he says in a low whisper.

"Yeah?"

"Just . . . reach out to her, okay?"

His eyes catch mine and hold them. Like he's serious. Like he's pleading.

I stare back, confused, before exhaling.

"Sure," I reply. "I will."

LOADING

[CAMBRIA: THE EVOLUTION EXPANSION PACK]
[ROANA GUILD CHAT ROOM]

Kasia Coribund: Was there something absolutely bonkers you wanted to be when you were a kid?

Kasia Coribund: Like a total pipe-dream job?

Kasia Coribund: Like you know how most kids want to be an astronaut or president when they're young

Kasia Coribund: before reality slaps them in the face?

Devynius Foxx: Ha

Devynius Foxx: I think I wanted to be a judge

Devynius Foxx: I like the idea of getting paid to judge people

Devynius Foxx: Still do, tbh

Devynius Foxx: What about you?

Kasia Coribund: I wanted to be a ballerina

Kasia Coribund: That was before I saw how mangled their legs and feet get after years of intense practice

Kasia Coribund: But yeah, definitely a dancer of some kind.

Kasia Coribund: A ridiculous pipe dream.

Devynius Foxx: Dancer, huh

Devynius Foxx: Is that really such a pipe dream?

Kasia Coribund: Doesn't exactly pays the bills, unfortunately

Devynius Foxx: What about teaching dance?

Devynius Foxx: Wouldn't that be more stable?

Kasia Coribund: Those kinds of jobs are rare . . .

Kasia Coribund: In any case, that was a childhood dream

Kasia Coribund: I've got something else I need to do now.

Devynius Foxx: Well, if you ever change your mind, Teach, let me know.

Devynius Foxx: Would love to be your first student ;D

Kasia Coribund: Unfortunately that would be . . . a little difficult, given the circumstances

Kasia Coribund: But I'll teach you the first rule of dance

Devynius Foxx: Which is?

Kasia Coribund: There are no rules.

Devynius Foxx: . . .

Devynius Foxx: I want my money back.

CHAPTER 21

KIRAN

Saturday, July 31

22 Days Until the Wedding

I'M IN THE KITCHEN, WRANGLING some leftover rice and dal into an old Donald Duck cereal bowl when my phone buzzes.

Thinking it's Foxx, I snatch the phone. But it's Asher. And I'm in trouble.

What the HELL were you thinking???

I cringe at my screen. To be fair, I *knew* he wouldn't like my stripper idea. Which is why I didn't tell him *all* the details.

Any chance you took a picture of the lucky lady? I type.

OF COURSE NOT, he replies, and I can practically feel the flames coming off him.

Jesus, woman

I don't like what this is doing to you

Hiring a stripper? Really? Isn't Faisal religious? Not cool, Kiran.

Hey, you said you would help, I text back. Step two, remember? Build distrust between Amira and Faisal. It's a worthy cause.

Not if it means springing a sex worker on an unwilling participant. You should know better, Asher says. I swallow down what feels a lot like shame. Then I remember the crucial question:

Did anyone figure out who hired the stripper?

Don't worry, I'm not going to rat you out. As much as you deserve it, Asher adds.

Good ol' Asher. Even though he's mad, he still exudes big brother energy.

There's a pause before Asher's next response:

I appreciate and respect your loyalty to Amira, but I feel like you're going overboard. Are you sure this isn't personal?

I feel a sourness in my belly worse than cramps. I don't like the insinuation. But Asher's mad at me. No, scratch that. He's not mad at me. He's disappointed. And everyone knows that's worse.

I start typing *I'm sorry*, but delete it, replace it with a diplomatic Thanks for your help, Ash, and put my phone back on the kitchen counter.

A part is me *is* sorry—for disappointing Asher, for making him question my reasons for doing this. But Asher doesn't have any siblings of his own. He could never really understand the lengths I'm willing to go to protect mine. Even if it means asking him to take pictures of Faisal with a stripper.

No matter, though; I don't need the pictures, anyway.

Amira bounds down the stairs and lands in the kitchen with a graceful hop. Her long hair is tied in a high ponytail, and she's wearing a cream-colored pullover, sleeves folded, over dark red leggings. Casual, but somehow still high fashion.

"Hey. Dad said we should clear out some stuff in our rooms," she says. "He'd like us to get started on Mom's closet, too."

"Yeah, okay," I say, not really paying attention. I flatten my rice with a spoon until it becomes almost paste-like.

"He's called in some junk collectors to come in next week, so we have to be quick."

"Junk collectors?" That's random. "Why? Late spring cleaning?"

She shrugs. "No idea. He mentioned it on the way out to work, so I didn't ask. You know, I feel like Dad's working way too hard these days." I feel her eyes graze over my face. Her forehead creases. "What's up? You're making a face."

I let out a long exhale. The thing about lying is it never gets easier. I think in order to lie well, you need to be okay with ripping your soul into tiny pieces—especially when you lie to people you care about. I imagine that every time you do, one of those pieces of soul—one more little reason to like yourself—dies. It's the price you pay. And the more you do it, the less there is left.

Although, ever since Mom died, I haven't been good about keeping track of those pieces anyway.

"Just got a text from Asher. Apparently the bachelor party was last night."

Amira's eyes gleam. "Oh God. A Muslim bachelor party. It sounds like an oxymoron. So? What'd Asher say? Was it any fun?"

"Something like that." I look away. "It sounds like someone invited a stripper."

"A stripper?" Amira blinks. "Who would invite a stripper?"

"No idea," I lie, even though every time I lie to my sister it tastes like chalk on my tongue. I don't know how Faisal does it. Speaking of which: "Have you heard from Faisal?" I ask in a low voice.

She shakes her head. "No, I . . . haven't. He hasn't texted me since last night."

I glance at the clock on the oven. It's already almost 5:00 p.m. Faisal is playing right into my plans, digging himself into a hole. I chew the inside of my mouth.

"At least the boys enjoyed themselves?" says Amira with a soft, sad laugh.

"I'm sorry," I say this time. This time, I really, really mean it.

Amira turns and leans on the counter and stares up at the ceiling.

"Yeah. Wow. It's . . . weird." She laughs again, but it sounds tight. "I'm genuinely surprised. Faisal's a pretty straitlaced guy, you know? Never misses a prayer, does everything by the book—that kind of guy. At least I thought he was. So him being with a stripper, and then not texting me is, um"—she swallows—"it's really out of character."

"Yeah."

"I mean, I wasn't there so I don't know the whole situation, but I'm kind of bothered by this. Actually. Yeah. I'm pretty bothered. A whole day's gone by, too, and he hasn't said a word about it." She goes over to a chair and just sort of falls into it. "I kind of wish he just gave me a heads-up, just so I wasn't blindsided days before the mehndi."

Her head falls backward, her long hair plunging behind her, revealing the length of her neck.

"Want me to drop you off at a strip club so you can get revenge?"

She lets out a wet snort. "Sure." Her voice sounds a little raw and hopeless. A sound that makes me wonder, for just a moment, if Asher is right.

It's quiet. I can hear the bustle of moving cars outside, the creaking of our old walls, the gentle hum of the fridge behind us. Comforting sounds. Usually.

"You don't think he—" Amira's rubbing her right wrist, running her thumb down her veins.

"What?" I press.

She looks up at me. "You don't think he did it because of what happened with Asher, do you?"

"I don't know. You'd have to ask him," I answer diplomatically. "But something does feel a little . . . weird."

"Yeah, and the timing. It's very . . . weird."

Seeing her sitting there, forcing a casual conversation with me, cracks my chest open. I rub my arms. I'm suddenly cold.

Amira sighs. "Thanks for telling me, though. Sounds like he and I need to have a chat soon."

"Yeah."

Amira pushes herself away from the counter. "I'm going to go upstairs and start on my room. Lots of junk . . . to clear out."

"Right. I'll meet you up there in a sec," I say as she disappears back upstairs.

I open the phone to look at the Save Amira plan on my Notes app, and cross out step two.

Amira's right about one thing.

Lots of junk to clear out.

⌘

The throbbing pulse of the tabla and sitar reverberate through the empty yoga studio, and I stretch out my bare feet on the cool wood floor beneath me, taking in the vibrations. It's a song from *Bajirao Mastani*. The kind of dance that'd be perfect for Amira's wedding, if I were actually planning to let it happen.

My limbs become fluid around me. My breath inflates my veins, filling me with life. It's just what I need right now to shake the image of Amira's face out of my head, the hard pit in my gut that feels too much like guilt for my liking. I know I shouldn't feel guilty. Exposing Faisal—I have to do it, for Amira's sake.

But just because I have to do it doesn't make it easy.

Behind me, I hear the click of the studio door opening. Someone's coming in. That's weird—yoga isn't supposed to start for at least another hour.

I glance over my shoulder. "Sorry, I'll be done in a few—"

But then I recognize the person standing in the doorway.

Deen.

I freeze and slowly turn to face him. I'm suddenly hyperaware of how I look right now: staticky hair splayed outward across every conceivable plane; the pool of sweat in the small of my back; the lovely sweat mustache I'm sporting; the old black sweatpants from ninth grade I'm wearing, the ones with the hole on the left knee.

He's wearing a tight-fitting black T-shirt and light blue jeans, and the hint of an infuriating smirk plays on his lips.

"Please. Don't stop on my account," he says, folding his arms across his chest.

My voice flies up five octaves. "What are you doing here?" I know Asher said no one's connected the stripper to me, but seeing Deen so soon after feels . . . *ominous*. Wait, did Asher tell him I'd be here? Or was it Amira? Ugh, it must have been her. Deen probably texted her and buttered her up for the intel, the sneak.

"Is this the song you're dancing to for the wedding?" asks Deen, ignoring my question. "Needs a little pizzazz, honestly. I got a friend who's good with remixes—want me to ask him to remix it?" But before I can answer, he's already texting.

"*What are you doing here?*" I demand again.

"Dance practice, obviously." He puts his phone away, closes the door behind him, and approaches me. "I've been thinking—oh, come on, don't look at me like that—I've been thinking, What if we did the dance together?"

"*What?*"

"Look, I know we've . . . gotten off on the wrong foot, and you have reason to dislike me, but—we could use this opportunity to, you know, get reacquainted."

I ignore him and lower the volume to the *Bajirao Mastani* soundtrack. I'm scrolling through my playlist for something to replace it with, but I don't feel like dancing anymore. I want to listen to something raw, something angry. Like death metal.

"Admit it, Noorani," he continues, "it'd look cooler if it was the both of us dancing. You can't tell me Amira wouldn't love it. And isn't that what this whole wedding is about? Making her happy?"

"I want her to be happy more than anyone," I mutter between

gritted teeth. "*Unfortunately*, us dancing together is going to make aunties freak out over the impropriety of it all and put a gossip target on my back, which would *not* make Amira happy."

He blinks. Realization settles on his face. "Ah. I . . . didn't think about that. But, okay, what if I said I wouldn't let that happen? What if I told people it was my idea, that I *forced* you to do it because I was nervous about dancing alone?"

I snort. "Yeah, because that would help."

"Please?" He takes another step forward. His eyes catch mine, and he almost looks . . . genuine. I look away.

What is Deen doing? I don't buy for a second that he wants to do a dance with me. It's not like him. It's not like him to make the first move, to extend the olive branch.

I want to hit him with it.

"What do you want from me?" I snap.

"Nothing. That's all there is." He looks around the room, taking in the space. "And in any case, why can't I just enjoy your company? I thought we really bonded in the sweets shop the other day."

"No."

"Fine, fine." The old floorboards of the yoga studio creak with Deen's every step. He looks at himself in the mirror and smooths down his hair. "The truth is, I just don't want to look like a complete dingus in front of five hundred people at the wedding. People are going to be evaluating prospective mates for their daughters. You know how many times my mom's told me that in the past week?"

That, I can believe. For as long as I've known them, Deen's parents have seemed overbearing and image obsessed. It explains why he's always been so vain.

I put my hand on my hip. "How do you know there even will be a wedding?"

He stops smoothing his hair and turns around to face me. "Why wouldn't there be?"

I swallow. "I don't know. Things happen."

"You sound like a mafioso."

"Not like that," I say quickly. "I'm just saying, you don't know what's meant to be," I say, hoping that I sound like I'm speaking in the vague, cosmic sense.

"I do know what's meant to be," he says, with more power than I expected. "Ever since my brother and Amira met, they've been drawn together with the force of a freight train. You don't even know. Those two are meant to be together. I believe that with all my soul. He's my family. Blood of my blood."

The sitar in the song croons softly in the background. My jaw clenches.

"Now who sounds like a mafioso?" I'm acting on pure emotion now, but I can't help it. Rage bubbles up in me, scathing and uncontrollable. Deen has the nerve to walk into *my* space, messing up *my* flow—

"The way I see it, things wouldn't be moving so fast if Amira knew the whole truth."

Deen flinches as if he's been slapped, but he quickly regains himself.

"You don't understand the situation."

"Then help me understand. Because Amira's about to give everything up because of him, and she deserves—*I* deserve—to know why he's pretending this *Leah* person doesn't exist, or the *felony* he committed—"

I stop. The song's ended, and the studio is completely silent.

"How did—?" Deen bites his lip. But it's too late. Whether it's shock or adrenaline, his mask has slipped.

So it's true, then. It's really, really, true. I *knew* that, but . . .

Deen starts again. "Look, Kiran. I wish I could explain all this, but I can't. I just can't. I swear."

My insides curl. It's the same goddamn line from three years ago.

"I'm tired of you saying that to me," I say.

We stare at each other for a long time, at an impasse.

"Okay. Fine," he says, cutting me off. "Fine. Then what about this?" He takes a few more steps to meet me in the center of the yoga studio. I hate that I have to lift my head to meet his gaze. "All I'm asking for is a chance to get to know me. Which means no more questions about Faisal, no more digging, no more sneaking around. We do the wedding. We do the dance thing." He breathes in, then out. "And I give you an explanation. The truth of what happened three years ago." He reaches out his hand. "Deal?"

I stare at it. Excuses crawl up my throat, but none of them stick. I want to say yes—I've wanted to know the truth for so long—but I can't let this wedding happen, no matter what. I can't let my sister be torn from me again. This is a promise I can't keep.

But I've come this far; might as well lie once more. Especially if it means I finally get the truth.

Cautiously, I extend my own hand. "Fine," I say, ignoring the sound of shredding paper in my mind. Just another piece of soul, gone.

But his skin is warm against my cold, clammy hand. He gently squeezes it, then lets me go. My fingers flex at my side.

"Great." Deen grins and slaps his hands together, a crack that echoes through the empty yoga studio. "All right, Teach. Shall we get started? Show me the ropes, the rules?

"Then again, the first rule of dance is that there are no rules, right?" he adds with a wink at my reflection in the mirror.

My heart does a strange, frantic dance behind my ribs. I blink, confused by the familiarity of the words.

But I shake off the sense of déjà vu.

I've got enough to worry about right now.

THREE YEARS AGO

KIRAN: So we just got back from the hospital

KIRAN: the neurologist is pretty sure Mom has ALS

KIRAN: I haven't slept

KIRAN: I keep researching, trying to find the tiniest bit of hope

KIRAN: but the more I learn about it

KIRAN: the more terrified I am

KIRAN: Five years.

KIRAN: Mom has five more years

KIRAN: at best.

KIRAN: what the hell am I supposed to do?

KIRAN: In a few years I'll be a freshman in college

KIRAN: just starting my life

KIRAN: and she'll be done.

KIRAN: how are we supposed to live without her?

KIRAN: I keep thinking about all the things she'll miss

KIRAN: how empty it'll feel without her

KIRAN: you know, I haven't called her mommy since I was, like, four

KIRAN: but right now, that's all I can think about

KIRAN: I'm back to being four and I just want my mommy

KIRAN: I'm so scared

KIRAN: I'm so fucking scared

KIRAN: We haven't even told Amira yet because we want her to focus on school but

KIRAN: what am I supposed to do?

DEEN: hey, sorry for the late reply

DEEN: and I'm sorry you're going through this

DEEN: I can't really talk right now

KIRAN: I really need you right now, Deen

KIRAN: I know you've been swamped lately

KIRAN: but can you just hop on the phone for, like, a minute?

DEEN: I'm sorry

DEEN: I can't

DEEN: Things at home are mad busy

DEEN: Talk later, okay?

KIRAN: . . . okay

KIRAN: Fine

KIRAN: You know how to find me.

CHAPTER 22

KIRAN

Saturday, July 31

22 Days Until the Wedding

"I'M HOME," I YELL, PEELING off my shoes. I'm greeted only with silence.

I hate always coming home to a dead house.

At least the lights are on. Most nights I come home to total darkness, with Dad at work, or locked inside his bedroom watching TV or reading the newspaper—once he's in there, the rest of the world is shut out.

Half-packed boxes labeled AMIRA'S ROOM form mini skyscrapers in the mudroom. This must be the spring cleaning Amira mentioned.

"Anyone home?" I yell again. Amira must have gone back to New York already. I check my phone and sure enough, there's a text from her: Had to run home for some errands! See you next week for the mehndi? Xx. Maybe I'm looking into it too much, but something about her texts feels not as . . . chipper as her usual self. I wonder how she's doing since she found out about the stripper.

I get my answer when I slip into the kitchen. Amira's left the kitchen spotless: a newly vacuumed floor; the counters cleared of Dad's biscuit crumbs and globs of peanut butter from this morning's breakfast; the puddles by the sink wiped down. The lingering lemony scent of disinfectant tickles my nose. It's what the house used to feel like, when she was part of it. Whenever she got stressed, she'd go on a mad cleaning frenzy. I'll have to tell Asher the plan is working.

I drop my duffel bag on the landing by the stairs and flip on the teakettle. The oven light blinks: 9:07 p.m. Deen and I were choreographing the wedding dance for a full hour. I expected another fight within the first five minutes, but the time actually flew: mostly me demonstrating and him making stupid, snarky remarks about what I look like. I'm a little surprised how attentive he was—unnecessary comments aside—and how much he seems to care about getting the moves down. Either he really does want to make sure his brother's wedding is perfect, or . . . or he's really decided to be pleasant for once.

I drop a bag of cardamom tea and pour boiling water into a mug.

The boy I saw today—he didn't feel like the same person I fought with behind the masjid. He felt more like an old, familiar friend. Or worse, like the old Deen. I don't get how a person could turn charm on and off so easily, like a light switch. Maybe Deen really does have a superpower.

My fingers start to burn.

"Shitshitshitshit." Lost in thought, I've managed to overfill the mug and make a mess all over the clean counter.

I run over to the other side of the kitchen and shove my hand under some cold water from the sink. For the first time in a while, the roll of paper towels has been refilled—thanks, Amira!—so I gently dry my burned hand and start wiping the mess down.

That's when I notice a small flash of red on the counter. A card? No, a business card.

THE FORREST GROUP, PHILADELPHIA
REAL ESTATE AGENTS

My face crumples in confusion. Realtors? Why does Dad have a business card for Realtors?

No.

It hits me over the head, a series of seemingly disconnected events rapidly materializing into a single conclusion: the push to empty out Mom's closet. The junk collectors. And Amira coming over, despite being busy with work and wedding planning. Did she already know?

The sudden pinch in my gut forces a fistful of breath out of me. I don't even feel the pain from my burned fingers.

I swipe the card off the counter and storm upstairs.

Dad, predictably, is in his bedroom. He's sitting up in bed with his phone in his lap and his glasses precariously hanging on to the tip of his nose. It bothers me a little that he still only uses his side of the bed. He won't go anywhere near Mom's. As if he's waiting for her to come back.

Right now, he's listening to some old recording of some qawwali—basically desi slam poetry, times ten—done by Nusrat Fateh Ali Khan. I only know because I recognize the voice. He's been obsessed with Nusrat Fateh Ali Khan since Mom died.

He lifts his head and pushes his glasses back in place when he sees me.

"Oh. I didn't know you were back," he says.

The Dad from a few years ago would have known exactly where I'd gone, and furthermore, demanded an exact time for me to report back. He'd be waiting by the door until I slinked back home, with Mom laughing and calling him overprotective. I almost prefer that to this apathetic shell of a man.

"What is this?" My voice comes out all barbed and pitchy. "Are you selling the house?"

Dad pauses the qawwali and puts down his phone.

"Yes," he replies, perfectly calm, as though he expected this. "The house isn't on the market just yet, but soon. With Amira moving to California and you going to college, it makes no sense holding on to all this empty space. I've always wanted to live in the countryside, too. We have family in Texas. My brother's there. After the wedding, I'll move."

"Texas? You're moving to Texas?" My head spins. "What about me?"

"You'll be living in the dorm. It'll be good for you to live on your own, especially your first year. Stand on your own two feet."

Except I don't *want* to live on my own. I don't *want* to stand on my own two feet. What's the point of family if it's so easy to dissolve one?

"Dad," I plead in a panicked whisper. "This is moving way too fast. If you leave, where will home be? Where am I supposed to go for the holidays? What if I get sick? What if—"

He coughs into his hand. His skin looks pallid.

The ball of anger in me unfurls a little. "Are *you* sick?"

"No, no," he replies, waving his hand. "Just fighting off a small cold."

My shoulders slump. "Okay, if—if you're sure." The house creaks and groans, the usual sounds of the old wood and foundation settling for the night. Downstairs, the washing machine churns water, adding to the soft hum of white noise.

"I don't want to give up the house," I continue. "This is our house. We can't just leave now. We grew up here. I don't want other people to live here." The idea of strangers running through these halls—our halls—feels like a violation.

"I understand how you feel. And I'm sorry for not telling you earlier—I've been thinking things over for a long while now. But I think it'll be good for us. This house—it stopped being a real home when your mom died. You know that. It's time to move on."

Dad taps the space beside him, beckoning me, so I walk toward him and lean against the mattress. He takes my hand in his.

"Where you live, where you love, where you breathe—that is where your home will be."

My ribs draw tight, as if someone's pulled on their shoestrings. I don't think Dad understands at all. Yes, we lost Mom, but isn't that all the more reason to hold on to the house?

Have we not lost enough?

"This isn't what Mom wanted," I say, gritting my teeth.

"Life changes, Kiran." He closes his eyes and lets out a tired sigh. "That's the one thing you can count on. We'll talk about this in the morning, okay, beta? Between work and trying to coordinate with the Maliks for the wedding—I'm too tired."

He doesn't open his eyes. I watch the steady rise and fall of his chest, the subtle flare of his nostrils.

I pull his phone away from him, set it gently on the bedside table.

"Okay, Dad," I say. "Get some rest."

I turn off the lights and leave him alone, closing the door behind me.

Later that night, I sit at my desk and crack open my laptop. The screen casts an eye-aching blue glow over my bedroom.

A cheerful ding, louder than I expect, makes me nearly jump in my seat. It's a message notification in the guild channel.

A message from Foxx:

Devynius Foxx: Hey. You're up late.

Normally when I get a message from Foxx, my heart flickers with life and my veins tingle like they're filled with molten gold.

I remember the relief on Deen's face when I shook his hand, promising to stop digging into Faisal's past. I don't even feel guilty about lying anymore. Tonight, I'm just numb.

I minimize the chat box, and instead open up Facebook to Leah's page one more time.

Step three: Bring out the Dark Horse.

It's the final step in my plan to save Amira, the one I've been dreading the most. I've thought about messaging Leah a hundred times. But each time I sit down to write it, the words won't come out. I don't even know where to start. Would she even reply? Would I reply if I were in her shoes?

I guess part of me was hoping it would never come to this.

But right now, with the house and everything, I don't care anymore. Despite the empty pit in my belly, the words spill out from me like water.

> Hi Leah,
>
> You don't know me and I don't know you, but we both know Faisal.
>
> This probably sounds ludicrous, but . . .
>
> My sister is getting married to Faisal in August and I have a couple questions. About him. Frankly, there's some things I'm worried about and I don't know who else to turn to.
>
> I was hoping we could talk.

I press send.

Then I throw myself into my bed, sinking deep into my plush comforter, and I pretend that the maw of the world is eating me whole.

CHAPTER 23

DEEN

Monday, August 2
20 Days Until the Wedding

AM I BEING PARANOID IF I suspect that Kiran was behind the whole stripper incident? I text Vinny.

He texts back immediately; he must be out of Statistics already. Unlike me, Vinny is a good boy who does not text in class.

If Kiran was behind it, why would Asher stop it?
Also let's be real, you said Kiran hates you
So why would she hire a stripper to get back at you??
Isn't that more like a GIFT???

I chuckle. He has a point. But I can't shake off this bad feeling.

Faisal said Amira called him to ask how the bachelor party went. He said he panicked and told her he didn't remember much, then backtracked and said he'd eaten too much and passed out.

Or something like that; he was talking too fast on the phone when he told me. The way she questioned him, though—it was like she knew about the stripper and was waiting for him to mention something. But if word got out that a stripper was there, on top of the fact that he accidentally got wasted, M&D would *kill* Faisal. Frankly, it's a miracle they haven't found out already.

I don't think the Kiran I know would ever have pulled a trick like that, but she has always been headstrong, and absolutely fearless. The kind of person who sways as hard as they can on a swing set just to see if they can go over the top bar—and hopes that they do. So if she really, really wanted to destroy Faisal and Amira's relationship . . . No. I don't want to pursue that line of thinking anymore. It only rubs my face into what I already know: that I'm at the center of it all. The jerk who ghosted her three years ago. The cause of this whole mess.

But I got her to promise no more schemes. At least, I *think* she did. She had that look in her eye when we shook, one that said this wasn't the end of the story.

Btw, that remix you asked for is almost done

Glad to hear you've dropped your pride to get jiggy with your ex in front of 500 people ;D I for one look forward to it

I grin. Vinny, you scoundrel, I text back. Kiran doesn't know this yet, but the song we've practiced to isn't *exactly* the one that's going to be playing that day.

I let Vinny know I'll be heading out of the library soon, and get to my sore feet. I'm at a table in the Bobst Library where I'm supposed to be studying for my upcoming finals. August is already here. Which means just a few more weeks until I'm done with summer school. And a few more weeks until the wedding. But I can't focus on finals right now. Hell, I can barely focus on anything. Dancing with Kiran the other night proved to be a success. I took Asher's advice; I reached out, made the first move. Now I just have to keep upping the charm factor and smoothing things over. It's working so far. Regardless of whether she keeps her promise, at least with us spending so much time together, there'll be less time for . . . mishaps.

But goddamn, my legs are tired.

I slip my phone into my pocket and start heading out to the humid death trap that is Rubin Hall.

My phone dings again, but this time, it's a message from Kasia in the guild chat:

Kasia Coribund: If you could live anywhere in the world right now, where would you go?

I've thought about this question for years, but I'm disappointed to announce that my answer has always been, and will always remain:

Devynius Foxx: In my bed. In my room. In my house.

I smile. I love that about her, about us. She's always interrupting my day-to-day with some seemingly innocent question that secretly has a thousand layers to it. I find myself excited to learn more about her, in ways I've never gotten to know anyone else before. Somehow, it teaches me more about myself, too.

I guess . . . I guess Kiran also had that effect on me. Except the

Kiran of today teaches me about myself by testing my limits. And what I learn about myself is rarely good.

Let's talk more about your bed, I start typing, when I nearly crash into someone around the corner of the hallway.

There's a flurry of folders and notebooks and textbooks that fall to the ground with a spine-jolting clatter.

It's Amy.

"Hi!" she says, brushing her curls out of her freckled pink face.

"Hey." I look at the mess of paper around her. "Woof. Sorry about that."

I bend down to help her collect it all, my legs throbbing in protest. Of all the people to bump into right now.

"It's okay! I'm a little scatterbrained, too, lately, with finals and all."

"Yep, those finals." I look away.

"You haven't really studied, have you?" she asks, laughing.

I hand her back her folders. "How'd you guess?"

She laughs again, like I've said the funniest thing in the world. "Raquel and I were thinking of doing a group study thing since exams are coming up. You free on Sunday?"

"Nah," I reply, rubbing the back of my neck. "That's when the mehndi's happening." I see her confused face and explain: "Er, it's the ceremony thing that happens before a wedding. It's like a bridal thing, but also not? It's hard to really paint a clear picture. It's like you have to experience it to understand what it is."

"Lots of wedding stuff, huh? A shame we never ended up going to that other thing you invited us to; Vinny was supposed to give us the deets but then he got sick." Her smile wavers a little. "Well, what about Saturday?"

"I'll have to be heading home to help set up, make sure my brother's not stress-eating in his bedroom—that sort of thing."

"How about lunch on Monday?" she asks again, undeterred.

"Ah." My stomach churns uncomfortably. "See, the thing about mehndis is that they usually go pretty late, so I might not even be back on campus then. The last mehndi I went to when I was a kid, back in Pakistan, lasted until three a.m."

"Oh." Amy hugs her notebooks and textbooks closer to her chest. "Okay."

"Yeah, sorry. You know how it is," I say automatically, even though she obviously would have no idea how it is. "But I bet Vinny'll be free. He's been looking for excuses to hang out with you and Raquel more"—nice, smooth—"so I'm sure he'd appreciate the invite."

Amy's mouth folds, making her lower lip disappear. "Sure. Yeah. Maybe I'll do that."

Has she gotten the hint? I have no way of knowing. Maybe I should just come out and tell her: *Hey, so I'm not really into you that way, but do I have just the boy for you!* Or is that one of those things that's going to sound a lot worse out loud?

Movement from the other side of the hallway snags at my line of sight, and my soul leaves my body so fast, rigor mortis would leave me standing.

It's Professor Pryce.

Shit.

Okay, so what you need to know: ever since he gave his little pep talk, I *have* been better about showing up to Professor Pryce's class on time. Sort of. But between everything that's been happening with Kiran and the hours I've spent talking to Faisal, making sure he's okay, I've kind of fallen off the ol' homework train. And it's not even that I forget to *do* it, I just keep forgetting to bring it . . . finished.

"I don't understand how you can write the most brilliant essays I've ever seen for my class one day, and then turn in *this* the next," said Professor Pryce last week, thrusting back a piece of paper with a poorly drawn cat on it and the caption, *Oops, I forgot! :3*

I do realize I'm on thin ice. Trust me, I do. I just don't need to hear about it for the hundredth time. I don't want to hear about how disappointed he is. Even worse, I'm scared of the alternative—that I'll see it in his eyes and his voice, that he's given up on me.

"What's wrong?" asks Amy. But I'm already running.

I dart into a darkened hallway, into a quiet row of bookshelves labeled MAPS/ATLASES that smells like the mustiness of ten centuries. Pretty sure no one's opened any of these atlases in years, so it's empty. The lights here are dull, practically running on a single watt. I lean against one of the bookshelves, my chest rising and falling at a frenetic pace.

Footsteps. Getting closer.

Closer.

"What are you doing?" Amy's head suddenly pokes out from behind one of the shelves.

"Gah!" I throw my hand to my chest. "Why'd you follow me?"

"I don't know! I figured if you're going to react that way, you must have seen something horrible. Like a ghost."

My breathing starts to slow. "No, just Professor Pryce."

Her face crumples with confusion. "But Professor Pryce is really nice."

"I'm sure he would be if I actually went to more of his classes." I wave her closer. "Get in, get in. If he sees you, he'll find me."

Amy sidles next to me into the maps section, our shoulders touching. We crouch, and she cradles her books to her chest tighter. For a moment, I think she leans into me a little more. Or maybe she's having trouble balancing.

"Shouldn't you just talk to him?" Amy whispers. "Might be easier if you get it over with."

I swallow and train my eyes to the doorway, saying nothing. It reminds me of something Vinny said. About me and Kiran. But *just talking* always sounds so much easier than it actually is.

I hear the echo of more footsteps, harder this time, the click of new, fancy, Professor Pryce–style shoes.

I hold my breath.

Professor Pryce walks past the doorway.

He's gone.

"Holy fucking shit," I say, letting out a sigh of relief. I lean against the book stack and close my eyes. I think I just lost ten years of my life. More, if I'm lucky.

Amy giggles softly. "You all right?"

"I swear, the universe is testing me," I mutter.

Amy goes quiet. That's when I feel something warm against my mouth.

My eyes open.

Amy's kissing me.

I freeze, my mind on overload. What is happening? What is happening? I'm willing my hands to move, to stop her, but they're lifeless. I don't want this. Not like this, not with her, not while—

Kasia. The name appears in my head like a jolt of reality.

"Whoa." I finally break away. "What—?"

"Wow, I—sorry. I didn't mean to interrupt," says a voice behind me.

I turn around, only to be greeted by Vinny, wearing a broken expression I've never seen on him before. His blue eyes have glazed over, cold and unfeeling. As if something behind them has shattered.

"I was trying to come find you to warn you about Professor Pryce, but. Clearly you didn't need help."

"Vinny."

Vinny turns to leave.

I jump to my feet.

"Vinny, *wait.*"

Except Vinny is fast; he's actually *running*—is he crying?—sprinting out of the library. I follow close behind, watching him zip straight into the road, narrowly missing a taxi, before running into Washington Square Park.

I will my already sore legs to move faster. But Vinny's actually in much better shape than me, and he's pulling away.

I hate sports, I scream in my head. *I hate sports I hate sports I hate sports I hate sports.* It's a chant that gets me through the pain of my muscles burning, and slowly, surely, I catch up to him.

Finally, I grab him by the shoulder. "Stop," I wheeze. "Jesus, just stop."

To my relief, Vinny actually does.

He looks at me, breathing hard, with a tightness in his eyes that feels like a slap. I curl forward, hands on my thighs, desperately gasping to catch my breath.

"How could you, man?" Vinny's voice is low. "You know I like her."

"I know. I know." I wipe the sweat off my forehead with the back of my hand and stand a little straighter. "But it's not what you think. It's just, she's kind of been coming on to me, and we keep bumping into each other, and—I don't know, maybe she got the wrong idea."

"How did she get the wrong idea? She knows I like her, right?"

"I—" My shoulders slump. "I've hinted—"

"It's a simple yes or no answer."

I sigh. "No." I shove my hands in my pockets; my fingers are shaking, even though I can barely feel them. "I don't think she does. But that—what you just saw—that didn't mean anything."

"I don't know if that's better or worse." He rubs at his eyes and lets out an exasperated breath. "You were supposed to help me. How was that helping? In no way, shape, or form was that helping."

"I meant to help! But I've been swamped with Faisal's wedding and stuff with Kiran—I'm trying to make sure she doesn't ruin everything, I can't focus on everything on once! I've been trying. Doesn't that count for something?"

Vinny laughs. "Man, I really hate this about you, D-Money. Was *this* really why you wanted wooing advice? I don't get it. You're the kind of guy who could have anything he wanted, but you don't take any of it seriously. You could have any girl you want, but you just had to go after the one I liked. I'd say it's because you only care about yourself, but I think even that's a lie. The only thing you ever give a shit about is your brother. That's a recipe for a lonely-ass life, right there."

"You don't understand the situation." Ugh, God I feel sick. "You don't understand what we've been through. I *swear* I didn't mean to hurt you."

"Wooow." Vinny folds his arms across his chest. "You know, all this time you've been talking and giving me excuses, but not once have you even said you're sorry."

I flinch because he's right. Saying sorry now would just sound fake.

But if Vinny doesn't believe me, who the hell could?

"You know the sad thing?" asks Vinny. "A few weeks ago, when we were hanging with Amy and Raquel, and you called yourself a tool—I thought it was just some bullshit you were telling yourself. Being hard on yourself because of what you did to Kiran. Which you should. I mean, who the hell just ghosts the person they're dating on a whim like that? But now, I think you're actually right." He walks past me, his shoulder banging mine. "You're actually a freaking tool."

My shoulder throbs.

This time, I don't chase after him.

LOADING

[CAMBRIA: THE EVOLUTION EXPANSION PACK]
[ROANA GUILD CHAT ROOM]

Devynius Foxx: Remember how we were talking about getting to know yourself

Devynius Foxx: I've been thinking about it more lately

Devynius Foxx: And I'm starting to realize something.

Devynius Foxx: What happens when you wake up one day

Devynius Foxx: And you've finally figured out who you are

Devynius Foxx: But you look at yourself in the mirror and think

Devynius Foxx: Damn

Devynius Foxx: I really don't like this guy?

Devynius Foxx: How do you even begin to track where it all went wrong?

Kasia Coribund: Oh, Foxx.

Kasia Coribund: That's awful.

Devynius Foxx: I'm tired of so many things

Devynius Foxx: My parents, my average day to day, moving toward an amorphous future that I don't know if I really care about

Devynius Foxx: More than all that, though

Devynius Foxx: I think I'm tired of the voice in my head

Devynius Foxx: Of me.

Devynius Foxx: Does that mean I'm actually the problem?

Devynius Foxx: Is it actually all my fault?

Kasia Coribund: That reminds me of when people say things like

Kasia Coribund: The only thing you can control is your reaction.

Kasia Coribund: Which like, yes, okay

Kasia Coribund: No one should sit there and feel sorry for themselves when they can do something about it

Kasia Coribund: But at the same time, having to get up again and again and again, despite the crappy circumstances around you . . .

Kasia Coribund: It's a lot.

Devynius Foxx: Honestly, I don't know if I have an excuse.

Devynius Foxx: I'm lucky. Most of what I want in life, I get.

Devynius Foxx: Even if I don't deserve it.

Devynius Foxx: So how do you be better?

Devynius Foxx: How do you make sure you're moving in the right direction?

Devynius Foxx: If you don't like who you are

Devynius Foxx: How do you get a refund?

Kasia Coribund: Be the person your dog thinks you are

Devynius Foxx: . . . um.

Devynius Foxx: Unfortunately, like you, I too lack a dog in my life.

Kasia Coribund: Then pick one!

Kasia Coribund: Pick the dog in your life

Kasia Coribund: The person who is your proverbial Good Boy

Kasia Coribund: And be the person THAT pup thinks you are.

Kasia Coribund: Keep doing the things that they'd hope you would do

Kasia Coribund: And keep doing it until it becomes second nature

Kasia Coribund: That's my advice

Kasia Coribund: Though tbh, I'm in no position to act like I know any better =_=;

Devynius Foxx: Heh

Devynius Foxx: The dog in my life, huh

Devynius Foxx: What happens if *they* don't even like you anymore?

Kasia Coribund: They always will.

Kasia Coribund: As long as you're always trying, at least.

Kasia Coribund: And if you do happen to lose that person for good

Kasia Coribund: I'm still here.

CHAPTER 24

DEEN

Saturday, August 7
15 Days Until the Wedding

"YOU SEEM DISTRACTED."

Kiran's voice shakes me out of my head.

"What?" My voice comes out like a wheeze.

It's the day before the mehndi, and Kiran and I are in the yoga studio near her house. I wasn't sure I was feeling up to it—after the fight with Vinny, all I've wanted to do is call him up and beg him not to be mad at me anymore. I miss playing pool together after class, goofing off in his room. Him filling the silence with music and weird stories about his family. Thinking about how his face looked that day is literally giving me a stomachache. Aah, what's wrong with me? Even in my own brain, I'm thinking about it in a selfish way. Vinny's mad, and he's got a good reason. He's asked me so many times to help him with Amy. Every single time

I promised I would, and like the good, perfectly naive friend he is, he believed me.

I get where he's coming from, I really do. I just wish he'd understand where *I'm* coming from. I've been so busy trying to put out fires around Faisal that I haven't had time to notice the situation with Amy. I've texted Vinny a hundred times since she kissed me, but no response.

So more out of frustration than anything, I texted Kiran. Dance practice?

Kiran laughs quietly, a barely perceptible huff of air. "Welcome back, space cadet. What are you thinking about?"

"Hey, you've been on your phone, too." And it's true. We've been dancing for nearly an hour now, and she's taken a phone break at least five times.

"That's because I have a life."

"If you're checking your Minder account again, a tip for you: no one likes a desperate girl, Noorani."

She punches my shoulder. "If you have time to be rude, you have time to practice. You're still fumbling all over the place."

"Ow."

"And whatever bullshit *you're* mulling over in *your* head," she continues, looking pointedly at me, "you need to clear it out. We don't have room for it on the dance floor. Mental distractions will mess with your focus, and God knows you need to focus if you want to get it right." She groans. "I could be doing summer homework right now."

"You got summer homework?"

She nods. "It's premed stuff. A bunch of reading, mostly. Apparently they're going to be giving us tests as soon as we step on campus."

"That sounds like abuse." I rub my shoulder. "You're really set on going to med school, huh." I don't know why, but the thought annoys me. She has this thing that she's really good at, and she's just going to toss it away to do something typical. As if we don't already have a billion desi doctors. It makes no sense.

"I'm not here for your opinions," she answers, peeling off her hoodie and tossing it by her bag. "Now remember. Move your hips more. Exaggerate. It's okay if you feel ridiculous. Dance is about letting yourself be—I don't know—*vulnerable*."

"At what *cost*?" I reply, exasperated.

"It's the only way you'll get any better." Kiran blasts on the music. "You're not as cool as you think you are, anyway," she shouts over it.

"Lies and slander."

She ignores me and gets in position.

It's that song from that Bollywood movie *Bajirao Mastani* again—I watched the clip from the movie, and Deepika Padukone can *get* it—but it's slow and not right for a duet. It's missing something.

I sigh. I wonder if Vinny ever finished that remix.

Kiran is standing in front of me, facing the mirrors. My hands slide down her arms, hovering just above them.

I swallow hard. *Focus, Deen. You're here for Faisal. Nothing else matters.*

The singing begins in earnest, and Kiran's head falls suddenly, my own arms rising in opposition. She crouches, extending a leg and twisting in an impossible pattern I can't quite follow. Behind her, I lunge and turn right—

"*Left*," Kiran barks—

I correct myself and turn left, until eventually we reach a flow, finding a rhythm in our steps. Kiran shoots up and dips her hands down, and I cross the room to reach her, our fingertips just grazing. I narrowly avoid stepping on her bare toes. Her back curls while mine straightens, and we spin away from each other—mine a messy, dizzy twirl of limbs, while hers is a graceful, intentioned movement. A breath, a pause, a suspension—before I reel her back in, my right hand on hers.

This time, I pull her closer, catching sight of her mouth. She's breathing hard and her lips are parted, pink with exertion. Familiar lips.

"Hey, are you wearing makeup?" I find myself asking before my thoughts have time to catch up with my tongue.

She stumbles and glares at me. "No. You think I'd waste makeup for you?"

I chuckle softly.

The truth is, I find Kiran really easy to talk to. With her, I don't feel the need to fill the silence. Maybe it's because she doesn't expect anything from me, or even want anything from me, but now that I think about it, that year we dated, she never asked anything of me, either. Never once complained that we had to hide what we were doing. All she ever wanted was for me to be there.

And I couldn't even give her that.

What would she be like, I wonder, if she did expect something? What would she look like if she wanted something from me? Wanted me?

She looks at me, and a crash of cold water and memories come flooding: us climbing trees, laughing over video games, stealing quick kisses in the parking lot.

Deep down, you actually feel guilty about what you did to Kiran. I imagine Vinny's voice echoing in my head, because I guess he's the voice of my conscience now.

I lose my balance, trip over my feet, and fall backward.

Kiran bursts into laughter.

"Don't laugh at me, you monster!" I groan and flop over. My butt hurts. "Damn, Noorani, and you had the nerve to call *me* mean . . ."

Her laugh falters a little. We're both remembering our fight behind the masjid, I think, and the warm buzz between us fades away like it was never there.

She wipes the sweat off her brow, and that's when I notice her fingers, pink and raw, like they've been burned.

"Looks like I'm not the only clumsy one," I say, reaching for them.

But she tears her hand away.

We stare at each other, wordlessly. Like we're both baffled by something, but we don't even know what, or why.

She stands and slams the off button to the stereo. "I'm going to go pee," she announces.

"Oh. Uh, sure," I reply eloquently.

She nods, slips on her shoes, and shuffles away, her back stiff, like she's a puppet on strings.

The door slams behind her.

Silence.

I look at myself in the mirror. I hadn't even noticed it until now, but I'm breathing hard, too.

What is wrong with me? The stuff with Vinny and the lack of sleep must be messing with me. I'm here to keep Kiran under control. That's why I'm playing nice. Right now, the line between playing and reality is getting a little too blurry for my liking.

I pick up my phone off a table in the corner of the yoga studio, trying to calm myself. There's a message from Kasia in the guild chat. I slide my phone open and read.

Kasia Coribund: Hope you're having a good day today, friend :)

I take a deep breath. Right now, her voice is a steady anchor.

I type out a response: Well, could be better.

The seconds crawl by as I stretch my legs. But out of the corner of my eye, I notice a glow from Kiran's hoodie on the floor.

The glow quickly fades, and I walk over to get a closer look.

Kiran left her phone.

My heart does its own little dance in my chest. This is it. The chance I've been looking for. I could look through her phone, read through her texts. Maybe see if she hired the stripper, or sent something to Asher about the restaurant, something that implicates her in it all. Maybe I could see the proof she's said she has against Faisal. See her plans—I bet she has them stored in her Notes app, like always. I could see it all.

Except it's a huge invasion of privacy!! the voice in my head screams.

But Kiran could be doing things that are much, much worse. She could be trying to ruin Faisal's life. The worst thing that could happen is that I find nothing and learn that she's actually innocent. And if that's true, well—I'll never bother her again.

Plus, what's a little invasion of privacy between family, right?

Just one peek.

Hands shaking, I slide my hand into her hoodie, gingerly, as if it might bite me, and yank her phone from the front pocket.

The sixty-day time card for Cambria is gone, for one thing. But her phone screen lights up, and for a moment, I'm confused.

Because on her screen is the same gray bar that was on my screen.

A notification. From a guild chat.

My mouth goes dry as I click the bar. It leads me to a chat room. Our guild chat room.

The last message I sent to Kasia Coribund sits in Kiran's mailbox:

Devynius Foxx: Well, could be better.

I'd laugh if I remembered how. Instead, my knees go weak and my head goes white.

Kiran. Kiran *is* Kasia.

I drop her phone; it lands with a thud on Kiran's hoodie and I stumble backward. No way. No fucking way.

There's a click by the doorway and my head swivels. The door's thrown open.

"Okay, sorry, I'm back." Kiran walks in, wiping her hands down her pants.

I clear my throat, shoving everything down, all the emotion and shock, in one swift gulp. "Hey. Great. Yeah. Good. Cool."

Her shoes tap against the wood floor as she approaches me. She gives me a weak smile.

"You ready to go again?" she asks.

I don't return the smile.

"Yeah," I croak. "I'm ready."

CHAPTER 25

DEEN

Saturday, August 7

15 Days Until the Wedding

AAAAAAAHHHHHHHHHHHHHHHHHHHHHH HHHHHHHHHHHHHHHHHHHHHHHHHHH HHHHHHHHHHHHHHHHHHHHHHHHHHH HHHHHHHHHHHHHHHHHHHHHHHHHHH HHHHHHHHHHHHHHHHHHHHHHHHHHH HHHHHHHHHHHHHHHHHHHHHHHHHHH HHHHHHHHHHHHHHHHHHHHHHHHHHH HHHHHHHHHHHHHHHHHHHHHHHHHHH HHHHHHHHHHHHHHHHHHHHHHHHHHH HHHHHHHHHHHHHHHHHHHHHHHHHHH HHHHHHHHHHHHHHHHHHHHHHHHHHH HHHHHHHHHHHHHHHHHHHHHHHHHHH HHHHHHHHHHHHHHHHHHHHHHHHHHH HHHHHHHHHHHHHHHHHHHHHHHHHHH

HHHHHHHHHHHHHHHHHHHHHHHHHHHHHHHHH
HHHHHHHHHHHHHHHHHHHHHHHHHHHHHHHHH
HHHHHHHHHHHHHHHHHHHHHHHHHHHHHHHHH
HHHHHHHHHHHHHHHHHHHHHHHHHHHHHHHHH
HHHHHHHHHHHHHHHHHHHHHHHHHHHHHHHHH
HHHHHHHHHHHHHHHHHHHHHHHHHHHHHHHHH
HHHHHHHHHHHHHHHHHHHHHHHHHHHHHHHHH
HHHHHHHHHHHHHHHHHHHHHHHHHHHHHHHHH
HHHHHHHHHHHHHHHHHHHHHHHHHHHHHHHHH
HHHHHHHHHHHHHHHHHHHHHHHHHHHHHHHHH
HHHHHHHHHHHHHHHHHHHHHHHHHHHHHHHHH
HHHHHHHHHHHHHHHHHHHHHHHHHHHHHHHHH
HHHHHHHHHHHHHHHHHHHHHHHHHHHHHHHHH
HHHHHHHHHHHHHHHHHHHHHHHHHHHHHHHHH
HHHHHHHHHHHHHHHHHHHHHHHHHHHHHHHHH
HHHHHHHHHHHHHHHHHHHHHHHHHHHHHHHHH
HHHHHHHHHHHHHHHHHHHHHHHHHHHHHHHHH
HHHHHHHHHHHHHHHHHHHHHHHHHHHHHHHHH
HHHHHHHHHHHHHHHHHHHHHHHHHHHHHHHHH
HHHHHHHHHHHHHHHHHHHHHHHHHHHHHHHHH
HHHHHHHHHHHHHHHHHHHHHHHHHHHHHHHHH
HHHHHHHHHHHHHHHHHHHHHHHHHHHHHHHHH
HHHHHHHHHHHHHHHHHHHHHHHHHHHHHHHHH
HHHHHHHHHHHHHHHHHHHHHHHHHHHHHHHHH
HHHHHHHHHHHHHHHHHHHHHHHHHHHHHHHHH
HHHHHHHHHHHHHHHHHHHHHHHHHHHHHHHHH
HHHHHHHHHHHHHHHHHHHHHHHHHHHHHHHHH
!!!

THREE YEARS AGO

DEEN: If you could summarize your entire life using one song, which song would it be?

KIRAN: No
KIRAN: NO
KIRAN: I hate this question
KIRAN: There are too many options
KIRAN: It DEPENDS on too many things!
KIRAN: The person I am in the morning and the person I am at night are two completely different people
KIRAN: It changes by the day, by the hour!!!
KIRAN: In the morning, I'm something chill, like lo-fi jazz. But at night??

KIRAN: I'm wired like, I don't know, Dua Lipa or something with a heavy bass.

KIRAN: Ugh

KIRAN: What about you?

DEEN: "All Star" by Smash Mouth.

KIRAN: omfg

KIRAN: first of all, you answered that WAY too quickly

KIRAN: Second of all, REALLY???

DEEN: HOLD ON, HOLD ON

DEEN: READ THE LYRICS, BRO.

DEEN: It is a work of ART

DEEN: grow up!!!!

KIRAN: I—

KIRAN: I really can't tell if you're kidding or not.

DEEN: lol j/k it's actually "Starboy" by The Weeknd

DEEN: Btw, it's cheating to use more than one song

DEEN: It's an easy enough question:

DEEN: What is the ONE song of your SOUL?

KIRAN: Fine FINE

KIRAN: Okay . . .

KIRAN: Hmmm . . .

KIRAN: "I Wanna Dance with Somebody"

KIRAN: by Whitney Houston

KIRAN: I dunno, you can't go wrong with the classics.

DEEN: Heh.

DEEN: Yeah.

DEEN: Now that is a proper answer.

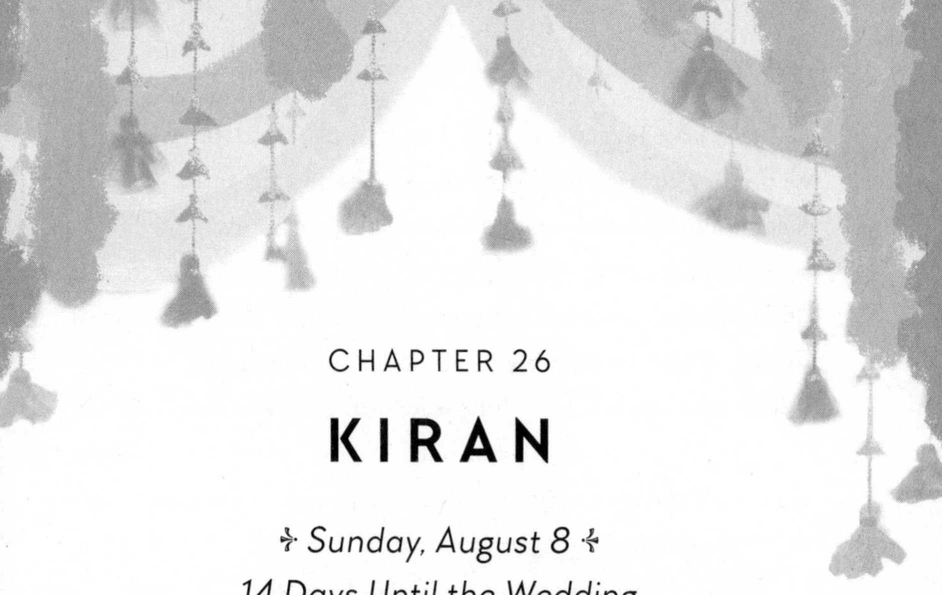

CHAPTER 26

KIRAN

Sunday, August 8

14 Days Until the Wedding

I'VE LEARNED MORE ABOUT MEHNDIS today than I have ever cared to know.

Rizwana explained that the big difference between a dholki and a mehndi is that the latter has more of an important ceremonial feel. The word *mehndi* literally refers to the henna paste put on the bride-to-be's hands and feet, and besides the designs being absolutely gorgeous and ornate, there's a symbolic significance, too: the deeper the henna color, supposedly, the deeper the love the bride feels for her groom. If only.

Technically, mehndis are done closer to the wedding, too, but due to the rush and the fact that this was the only date that worked for everyone, here we are. According to Riz, Deen's mom was not happy about it and kept going off about how they'll have to redo the henna before the wedding.

But I have bigger concerns. I try not to think about how I'll be needing to pack my bedroom soon—and find a safe place for Faisal's journal entry—and instead help Riz clear away the family room to make more space for tonight. Still, it'll be a tight fit. Riz promised to keep it a small affair this time, with only thirty or so close friends and family (again, much to the dismay of Deen's mom), but even that is pushing it for our humble little row house.

After Riz drops off a giant bowl of water filled with floating rose petals and tea candles, and I thread a couple more string lights across the ceiling, we get to the pièce de résistance: the sofa.

"Put down your phone for one sec and help me," Riz says.

I nod and drop my phone on the table. I've been obsessively refreshing my Facebook in-box since I sent a message to Leah a week ago, hoping for a response.

Still nothing.

The floor groans beneath us as Riz and I uproot our cream-colored sofa—also the least-stained sofa in our house—and slide it against the wall, now a colorful backdrop of curtains and floating, glowing mason jars, and trellises of real jasmine flowers, at the front of the room. The sofa is now a makeshift throne for Amira. It must be weird, watching your friends and family celebrating your own wedding festivities while you just sit there, like some kind of puppet king. I remember Nani saying she wasn't even allowed to smile during her wedding, because that would be seen as disrespectful to her own family. Knowing Amira, though, she'd last one minute playing the meek bride-to-be, and ruin her own freshly hennaed hands to join in on the singing, even though her Urdu's as bad as mine.

We're debating whether it would be creepy to hang a photo of my mom on the wall—"Does not that feel, I don't know, vaguely pagan or something to you?" Riz asks—when I hear Amira's voice.

"Oh my God."

Her hands are over her mouth as she descends the stairs. She's wearing glasses and loungewear, and her bramble forest hair is barely tamed in a fat bun on her head. Not even close to being ready for tonight.

"You're not supposed to be here!" Riz barks.

"Don't look! We're not even done yet!" I whine.

"I'm sorry, I'm sorry—I just needed to come down for some water." Amira beelines for the kitchen, throwing not-so-subtle glimpses over her shoulder at the string lights overhead.

She pauses at a stack of printed Quranic prayers and wedding schedules that I've shaped into a star and gently traces a finger across them. I look at her curiously.

"God, it's starting to feel real now," she says softly. But her voice is laced with something else, something . . . sad.

Riz grins. "Good. Because it is real."

"Where's Dad?" I ask.

Amira blinks hard, as if just waking up. "Oh, I had to force him to rest up in his room. I think he might be coming down with something." She rubs her tired eyes. "I'm a little worried about him. He's been working himself too hard." The way she looks, though, I wonder if she's worried about a lot of things.

"What? But the wedding's in, like, two weeks." Dad's clinical research job is rough, but he's rarely had trouble taking time off when he needs to.

"I know." Amira pours herself a glass of water. "But Hamza chacha's flying in from Houston this evening. Nani, too. Actually, Kiran, you'll have to pick Nani up from the airport soon, so maybe she can stay on Dad's case. Hamza chacha will stay out of the way and make sure Dad doesn't push himself."

Our uncle Hamza is Dad's younger brother. He never got married, claiming he was too handsome for anyone, but I think it's because he's actually married to his work as a genetic counselor. And Nani, our mom's mom, is the closest grandparent we've got; Dad's parents still live in Pakistan. But I haven't seen her in months.

I'm excited to see them, but I'm also dreading it. On one hand, I know they're here for the wedding—they wouldn't miss it for the world. But on the other hand, I know they're also here to help Dad move to Houston. To take him away.

"Any word from the hubby-to-be?" asks Riz, lighting some tea candles. "I'm sure he's counting down the hours now."

Amira shakes her head. "He's been busy trying to wrap up some AFFEY stuff before the move to California. There's still a lot to sort out, so we haven't really . . . been talking lately."

"That's understandable," says Riz comfortingly. "You two will have the rest of your lives to spend chatting each other to death, anyway."

"True." Amira's eyes are cloudy. Distant.

I wonder if Amira's told Riz about the stripper. Hell, I'm still not sure if Amira's talked to *Faisal* about the stripper. I haven't really had a chance to talk to Amira about the aftermath; for the past few days, she's been busy with Riz and a bunch of her old college friends, doing last minute wedding prep, and I haven't even had the chance to ask her about Dad's big move.

And as usual, I can't get a read on what Amira's really thinking.

"It's normal to feel . . . nervous right before a wedding, right?" Amira murmurs suddenly. For a moment, Riz and I stop moving, stunned.

Riz is the first to regain her composure. "Of course it's normal. Everyone gets cold feet. It's a huge commitment!"

"I guess. Yeah. Between the radio silence and things feeling a little . . . out of sync between us, I'm feeling antsy. And then with Dad moving, and me moving . . ." She swallows. "It's a lot at once."

My head's a whirlpool of emotions. I can't believe it. The Plan to Save Amira is working. It's just like I thought: all it took was a few pokes and prods at their relationship and already things are starting to fall apart. And with the wedding fourteen days away, it's not a moment too soon. But if she's doubting whether she can make it work with Faisal, then all they need is just one more push. One final blow.

I glance at my phone.

The Dark Horse.

Except I've never seen Amira doubt herself, ever, about anything. And even though I'm happy my plan is working, seeing her like this is a little . . . painful.

But it's for the best.

"These are the kinds of things you should talk to your imam

counselor guy for," says Riz before waving Amira away. "But one step at a time. For now, go finish getting ready. We still need to wrap up here."

Amira bites her lip.

"Right. Okay," she says finally.

Amira starts for the stairs, then turns around. She opens her mouth, as if to say something else, but decides against it.

I watch her finally retreat upstairs and bite down the guilt sprouting in me like a sharp weed.

The house is so stuffed with people, I can feel the walls straining, and the music is so loud, I can feel the floor trembling beneath me.

Amira is on the sofa, surrounded by giant plush pillows. She's wearing a pastel, sunshine-yellow lehenga, and a translucent, silver-threaded dupatta that covers her long hair. Her neck is weighed down by multiple flower garlands. Mona khala is sitting next to her, and I try not to let the annoyance show on my face because she really should be sitting on the floor, where all the other guests are sitting. That's why there are pillows there, damn it.

Nani's holding a tray of laddoo when she finds me leaning against the kitchen counter, on the far edge of the crowded family room. "Kiran, my jaani, you keep looking at your phone." She points a finger at the henna artist Riz hired from Edison, already hard at work on Mona's feet. "Go, sit down with your sister. Get your hands done."

I smile in a way I hope she can't see right through. When I picked Nani up from the airport earlier, she was quiet the whole ride. Of course she was; the last time she'd come to Philadelphia was for Mom's funeral. When she walked into the house, I could see the way her eyes lingered on all the spots Mom used to frequent. As if waiting for her to reappear. Just seeing her like that was enough to tear at barely healing wounds.

"Maybe later, Nani," I tell her. Plus, if I get henna on my hands, it'll be hard for me to check my phone, and I need my phone to keep distracted.

The music shifts to "Ghungroo," a song that was popular, like, a couple years ago. People have already started dancing. It's hot in here and I need some air; the back of my shalwar kameez is damp with sweat and my makeup already feels like it's melting—the Maliks hired a professional photographer, surprise, surprise—though it's barely been an hour since the mehndi started.

I know it's my sister's mehndi and everyone's expecting me to be happy and involved, but right now, I can't bring myself to do it.

Honestly, I just want to talk to Foxx. I want to play Cambria and pretend Amira is okay and that things are normal and that the wedding isn't happening, that what remains of my family suddenly moving for no good reason isn't happening.

I sneak to the back of the house, to another, less conspicuous staircase.

That's where I find Deen, sitting on the middle landing, staring at his phone. He looks up, startled, and puts his phone away when he sees me.

Panic flares in me—did he sneak into my room? What if he finds Faisal's journal page? Do I need to start carrying it on my person at all times now? But then again, there's something off about him. Like if I look close enough, I'll see a storm cloud floating above his head.

I raise a brow. "Hiding from the party, Deen? How unusual."

"Mehndis are mostly for women, anyway. I'm only here for Faisal," he says. "Plus, I can't be the life of the party all the time." He laughs almost . . . self-deprecatingly.

"I didn't even know you were here. Where is Faisal, anyway?"

"Apparently your uncle Hamza convinced him to have a cigar with him out back because your uncle carries cigars around with him like a mobster, I guess?" says Deen, shrugging. "But for a relative of yours, he seems pretty chill."

I roll my eyes. "Somehow, I'm not surprised you'd think that."

Deen smiles weakly. He's got a bad case of sunken, purple bruising beneath his eyes from lack of sleep, and a smattering of facial hair on his cheeks and chin where he missed a couple spots. For a guy as obsessed with his own looks as Deen, it's a bit of a shock.

"You all right?" I ask, approaching him.

Deen recoils, surprised by my question. But after a beat, he relaxes.

"I appreciate you pretending to care, but I'll be fine, Noorani."

"All right. It's just, you look like death."

Deen looks away, a pained expression on his face, like I've pointed something out that he'd rather be ignored.

He grips the railing.

"Actually, do you have a second?" he asks, so softly I can barely hear him over the music.

Then he looks at me so earnestly, in a way so unlike him, that I find it hard to breathe. For so long, it's felt like the two of us have been locked in some weird game of chess that I'd forgotten what it was like to be seen by him with something other than hate in his eyes.

But suddenly, I feel my phone vibrate in my pocket. I fumble for it and yank it out, nearly dropping it from my trembling fingers.

A Facebook message notification. From Leah.

My stomach's churning so hard I can feel my bones rattle, like a wash cycle on an old washing machine.

She replied. She actually *replied.*

"Sorry," I say loudly. "I need to take care of something."

Before Deen can say another word, I move past him and practically throw myself into my room, locking the door behind me.

I lean against the door for balance and open the message, holding my breath:

Hi Kiran,

I appreciate you reaching out, despite the stranger-than-fiction circumstances. Unfortunately, I haven't been fully in touch with Faisal in some time now, but. Yes.

Let's talk.

CHAPTER 27

DEEN

Thursday, August 12
10 Days Until the Wedding

THE PROBLEM WITH MISSING SOMEONE is that you start seeing them everywhere.

Not just in person—I've caught eyes with Vinny a couple of times now, between the library and the dining hall, and each time he's literally run in the opposite direction—but in everything I see or do. Right now, I'm on the bus I grabbed after class to meet Kiran in Philly for our last dance practice. But I can't stop glancing at my phone, wondering if he's finally going to reply to my texts. Earlier, I thought I heard his voice on the street, but it was just another guy with an equally strong Long Island accent. Before that, I got melancholy seeing chicken tenders in the cafeteria. Because of him.

I even can't log into the guild chat room without thinking of Vinny, either. Hell, the name Devynius—it was *Vinny's* idea.

Set the stage: My dorm room, first semester, freshman year. I'm sitting at my desk, waiting for Cambria to finish downloading, while Vinny is perusing my closet and my extensive collection of sneakers. Insert transcript:

ME: Hey, if you had to make up a badass fantasy name, what would it be?

VINNY: Fantasy name? What, you playing D&D? You holding out on me?

ME: No, no—nothing like that.

VINNY: Yo, are you downloading Cambria?!

ME: No! I mean, yes, but just to try it. Maybe. Anyway, answer the question. Fantasy name ideas. Go.

VINNY: How about . . . Vinné.

ME: Absolutely not. Actually, never mind. Clearly, I've asked the wrong person. I'm going with Deenius.

VINNY: DEENIUS? ARE YOU SERIOUS, DEENIUS?

ME: What's wrong with Deenius? It rhymes with genius.

VINNY: Veto. Let's spice it up. How about this: Devinnyus.

ME: That's literally just Deenius with your name stuffed in it.

VINNY: Like the delicious pimento to your olive. The jelly to your doughnut. The cream to your—

ME: You know what? Fine. FINE. I give up. We'll go with Devinnyus. But I'm spelling it differently, damn it.

And thus, Devynius was born.

I want to talk to him, especially after everything's that happened with Kiran. I can't talk to Faisal about Kiran, but Vinny—Vinny would get it, react exactly the way a best friend should upon hearing the maddening news that Kiran is actually Kasia: throw open the window and scream.

"God, I suck," I say out loud, groaning, which makes the middle-aged woman sitting next to me on the bus stare at me with undisguised revulsion.

I even tried to talk to Kiran about it last night, but then she retreated to her room for the rest of the mehndi. I had half a mind to knock on her bedroom door. I even rehearsed what I'd say: *Hey, you know that guy you talk to every day on Cambria, the guy who's totally crushing on you even though he's never met you in real life? Surprise! It's me, the guy you hate [finger guns].*

Except I don't have a death wish.

Thinking about it now, though, maybe it's a good thing I haven't told her yet. I don't know how she'll react. She promised not to poke around Faisal anymore, but who knows how this news would change things. Maybe I'll wait until after the wedding, when I know for sure things are safe and settled.

It's in ten days. I won't have to wait long.

My phone vibrates in my pocket.

Vinny: Sent you the song. It's finished.

I look at the screen, staring intently at the three little dots that follow, a sign that he's typing something else. After a beat, though, they disappear. He's gone.

But he actually came through.

I let out a sad huff of a laugh.

I dig through my bag for my earbuds, shove them in place, and turn up the volume.

Then I click play.

The familiar song that Kiran and I have been practicing to runs through the background, but with a heavier weight to it, an intensity that wasn't there before. And now there's the beat of a second song deftly, seamlessly layered into the first. It's modern and classic, East meets West, to create something entirely new. Before I know it, my foot's already tapping to the rhythm.

I can't help it; I grin, which I'm pretty sure makes the woman next to me inch further away.

The song is *perfect*.

I can't even imagine what Kiran's face will look like when she hears it, in front of all those people.

I let out a long exhale through my nose.

The wedding is so close. So close.

And if it all goes right, soon, everything will finally go back to normal. To what it should be. For me *and* Faisal.

I just hope this time, I don't trip over the finish line.

"I have never been more insulted in my life."

Kiran is scowling at me as I enter the yoga studio. She's standing by the sound control table in the corner of the room, her arms sitting across her chest. Today she's opted for black sweats and a boxy camo T-shirt under an open black hoodie. Like she's ready for battle.

"What's wrong?" I ask, keeping my voice level. Did I do something wrong again? I wouldn't be surprised, at the rate I'm going.

"This!" She seizes a Starbucks coffee cup off the table and shoves it in my direction.

In a messy scrawl, someone has written her name for the order on the side of her cup.

I squint, and then I see it:

Karen.

I look at her exasperated expression, then back at the cup. I burst out laughing.

"I hate it! My name isn't that difficult!" Kiran slams the cup back on the table. "You're lucky. You probably never have to deal with people getting your name wrong."

"At worst, I get people adding an *a* instead of the double *e*. But poor Faisal—he keeps getting called Fieval." I wipe at my eye.

"Oh, man. Never a dull moment with you, Noorani."

"Yeah, well. At least *someone* finds it funny." She stomps to the center of the yoga studio. "You ready? I've got a bunch of angry energy I need to burn off."

Kiran begins to stretch her arms behind her. Already, her eyes are focused in the mirror. Even if she did promise to stop meddling in Faisal and Amira's relationship—*assuming* she'll keep it—she still doesn't approve of their marriage. I wonder if she's also using dance practice as a distraction.

I set my bag down in the corner and watch her. Just like that, she's in work mode now, any trace of annoyance already gone. She ties her short hair back in a tiny ponytail and takes a deep breath, muscles tightening, back straightening. Her stance screams *confident*. The body of a dancer.

Kasia. I remember: Kasia wanted to be a dancer, too. What'd she call it again? Right. A ridiculous pipe dream.

I stand at Kiran's side and stretch out my legs, clumsily balancing on one leg. "You know, you look different. When you dance," I say.

Kiran pauses and looks over at me suspiciously. "What do you mean?"

I avoid looking back. "Just, you look happy. You look like someone who's found their thing." I swallow hard. "I'm envious, I guess."

"Thanks, I think." She shrugs. "It's just a hobby, though. Anyone would look happy."

"Does it have to be? I mean, I know it's hard to find a job as a dancer, but you've got the talent for it. And let's be real, you mostly choreographed the dance yourself, too. That's amazing."

"Have you been talking to your Mona khala?"

The last time I tried to talk about this with her, she totally shut me down. But this time, I can't help myself. "I'm serious. Being a doctor—that's going to take, what, at least seven, eight years? Is that really something you want to do? Because if you don't, if you have any doubts, it's not going to be easy."

"You think I don't know that?" she lashes out.

"I think it's a waste. That's all."

"Except it's what I want to do."

I rack my brain, trying to remember my conversation with Kas—well, with Kiran. At that first dinner with our families, she'd said becoming a doctor was something she *needed* to do. An obligation, in honor of her mom.

"Is that really true?" My heart thrums nervously. "Is it something you really want to do? Or is it because you feel guilty or something?"

I remember vaguely, years ago, talking to her about this, back when we were together. I have no right to say anything now. But I know a thing or two about doing things out of guilt. The crushing pressure of it. And how it often leads to mistakes.

Kiran tosses off her black hoodie and takes a swig from her water bottle. Her eyes are unreadable.

"You don't have to answer that," I say softly. "It's just that I don't want you to have to make hard choices when you could have it all. Dancing doesn't have to be a pipe dream."

I don't dare look at her, but from the corner of my eye, I think I see her stiffen.

Geez. What am I doing? I'm not even sure who's talking anymore: me, or Foxx.

Kiran clears her throat.

"Hate to cut this short, but we're running low on time. Should we try one last run-through?" She presses play without waiting for my answer, and the music starts.

"Fine," I mutter, and stand straight.

We've gone through the song dozens and dozens of times—I've lost count—but it doesn't slow my heart rate or my nervousness.

I stand behind her and close my eyes for a moment, focusing.

We start to dance.

Already, I notice something . . . strange. Usually, I have to force myself to stay completely alert, taking in every movement, every change in music, every step and variation. It gets me tired halfway through the dance. But this time, it feels different. My body's responding on its own, falling into step, feeding off a rush of adrenaline.

I graze my fingers on the small of her back. I know she's tough, but I still touch her like she's made of paper. I haven't gotten used to the idea of touching her yet. My arms leave her body as the music grows louder. At least, I think it's getting louder. But I feel it swelling, growing, surrounding us. Like the cadence is coursing through our veins.

I twist my torso, and beside me, Kiran's elbows glide through the air, in perfect rhyme with her feet. She reaches her arms toward me, and for a moment, her warm breath tickles my cheek. We catch each other's gaze.

A spin here. A turn there. It's all perfectly in sync now.

I grin. Shit, this is *fun*. And Kiran? She grins back. The world spins around us and I'm dizzy and my muscles buzz, but it feels good.

The music finally begins to slow, and I reach for Kiran one last time, breaking our choreography. I dip her, hugging her hips in close. The music stops and it's just us, breathing hard. Against my chest, I feel the steady tick of her heartbeat.

Her lips are parted in shock, but her cheeks are flushed, with the hint of a blush creeping down her neck.

I want to kiss her. The thought sparks a flame in me that surges like a roar, overpowering and unstoppable.

Oh.

No. No! I can't kiss her! I shouldn't. Wait. But—why does she look like she might want me to? At least, I think. I can't tell. Maybe? But that expression, that drunk-on-fire look in her eyes—a look that dares me to let it all come tumbling down.

Except I'm not sure what she wants. Right now, I'm not sure of anything.

Reluctantly, slowly, I pull myself away.

Kiran straightens herself and blinks, dazed.

I turn my back to her, but I think I hear her mutter something like *Astaghfirullah* under her breath.

Seconds seemingly turn to minutes. Sound itself has stilled. I'm too afraid to make a sound.

I can't believe I almost lost myself for a second there. I know I'm supposed to keep my enemies close, but this . . .

Nostalgia is seductive. *Too* seductive.

"Well, that's a wrap." Kiran's voice is tiny. She takes a breath and shakes off the strangeness between us. "Next is the wedding. And for you to hold up your end of the deal."

I turn to face her. The hazy warmth, the afterglow between us, begins to fade.

"I guess you're right," I say. I'm not as quick to shake it off as she is.

Ever since I found out she was Kas, I've been wondering what would happen if I just told her . . . everything. Wondering if maybe she'd understand. But no, I can't take that kind of risk. Even after the wedding, I can't give her the full reason why I ghosted her without revealing Faisal's secrets or risking my parents' wrath. Luckily, I don't have to spill everything; I just need to give her a plausible enough answer to hopefully satisfy her curiosity.

But will it be enough to stop her from trying to ruin Faisal's dream once and for all, from holding his past over his head like an ax?

I hold my breath as her round dark eyes study me closely, like she knows something's wrong.

I can see it now, the wall that's been built between us. The one I built all those years ago. Looking at her now, though, so close—my fingers itch to tear it all down.

"If I *had* said something"—I lick my lips—"if I never ghosted you . . . do you think we'd still be together?"

Kiran's breath hitches.

I backtrack. "Sorry." I laugh, a forced, choking sound. "I'm not making any sense." *What are you doing? What are you* doing, *D-Money?*

"I . . ." Kiran draws back toward the door. "Gotta go."

There it is. The wall.

I smile sadly. "Pee break?"

Kiran nods. "Pee break."

She marches stiffly to the bathroom and leaves me alone, the door slam an echo in her wake.

My eyes glide to the hoodie she'd been wearing earlier, now left crumpled by the mirror. A familiar lump catches my attention. She's left her phone again.

Right. I need to focus. The only reason I'm here is to protect Faisal.

I shift uncomfortably. But I don't want to look through her phone. It's not just Kiran's phone anymore—it's Kas's phone, the one she uses to talk to me, or at least, to Foxx. To breach that feels like a breach of trust that I actually really, really care about.

But I've been breaching a lot of trust these days.

I have to.

This time, when I open her phone, I go straight for her Notes app. My first thought is this girl needs a separate server for all her notes: there's grocery lists, song lists, even lists for favorite inspirational quotes, but also notes on movies she's watched, games she's played—Cambria being her number one—and charts on plants good for different light conditions.

Finally, I find one labeled simply, PLAN. A recent note.

I swallow, my throat tight. I click and begin to read:

PLAN TO SAVE AMIRA:

STEP ONE: Sow the seeds of jealousy & insecurity

~~—Dinner with Asher~~

STEP TWO: Build distrust between Amira and Faisal
—Catch Faisal in a lie! Something that makes Amira question his integrity!
~~Hire stripper~~
STEP THREE: Bring out the Dark Horse
—Find Leah's phone number/contact info!!!!

No way. It's like the world's snapped off its orbit, not unlike the way it did when Kiran and I were dancing. But this time it's too fast, too violent, draining blood from my brain so fast that I feel sick.

Step one. Dinner with Asher. When Faisal saw Amira and Asher together—so she *had* set it up. And catching Faisal in a lie, making Amira question his integrity—so Kiran really was behind the stripper? Which means Amira probably knew about the stripper this whole time.

But step three is the one that scares me the most. Did Kiran ever find Leah's contact info? Leah is the only one who knows the truth, the only one who was there when everything happened. It's why Faisal stopped talking to her.

Is Kiran going to invite her to the wedding?

I clutch my chest; inside, I'm searing hot with anger, splintering to pieces. I *should* feel victorious; I found exactly what I came for: proof that Kiran was behind everything. But part of me feels disappointed. Sad, even. Maybe part of me hoped I wouldn't find anything.

I knew she was likely behind it all, but the reality of it is too much. All of this just to expose Faisal? Why would anyone go to such lengths? Why would she—?

Does she hate me that much?

My fingers graze something on the back of the phone; there's something new in the pocket where the Cambria time card had once been. Except this time, it's a folded piece of composition paper. I carefully unfold it and recognize Faisal's handwriting. It's an entry from his journal, the one he used when he had to go to therapy after the accident.

It's not just gossip. I have *proof.* Kiran's voice echoes in my head.

I exhale through my nose. At least now I know how she found out about Faisal's felony.

I pocket the journal entry and set down her phone. I can't look at the list anymore. I hold my head in my hands, trying to regain some semblance of calm.

It's just, Kiran's hurt. You can get where she's coming from, right? I remember Asher saying.

I can be mad at myself later. Right now, my only priority should be stopping her, any way I can.

The door opens, and in walks Kiran. *Kasia.*

She smiles lightly; her lips shimmer like she's put on a new coat of ChapStick. I want to scream. Everything feels so maddeningly false, so mind-numbingly fake.

But that's what this was supposed to be, right? Playing nice for the sake of the wedding?

"Did you want to do another practice round?" she asks.

Except I don't think I can play anymore.

I shake my head. "I'm supposed to go see Faisal after this. I'm thinking I'll just head over early. The big day's coming up soon, ya know?"

Something in her face goes rigid. "Oh, okay. Yeah. That makes sense." She rubs her arm, looking strangely . . . lost. "See you later, then?"

"Yeah," I say, my jaw tight. "Later."

DEEN: Hey. Thanks for the remix, V-man

DEEN: Question: if it's not too much trouble, could I ask you to remix it a little differently?

VINNY: . . . Seriously?

DEEN: I know. I'm sorry

DEEN: I won't bug you again after this, I promise

VINNY: [. . .]

DEEN: Please

DEEN: It's for Kiran.

VINNY: [. . .]

VINNY: What do you need?

CHAPTER 28

KIRAN

⸭ Friday, August 13 ⸭
9 Days Until the Wedding

I'VE MADE A MESS ON the kitchen counter.

I've been sitting here for at least a couple of hours, staring at my computer, with a giant soup bowl I've filled with Honey Nut Cheerios. I'm surrounded by towers of notebooks and folders, printouts of core competencies for entering med students, lists of possible clinical volunteer opportunities. On the chair beside me sits a summer reading list of fiction and nonfiction books they've recommended for us as a way to get a "head start," except it's four pages long and single spaced and with enough content to cover several college courses.

But I'm grateful for the distraction. There's nine days until Amira's wedding, and even though it feels the rest of the world is in a flurry to prepare, Riz let me stay in after I dropped a vase of flowers delivered to the house from some cousins in Michigan who can't make it for the wedding, shattering glass everywhere.

"Are you always this clumsy?" Riz asked. I blamed it on the book I'd been reading earlier that was on the summer reading list, a depressing story about a neurosurgeon who'd been diagnosed with stage IV lung cancer. And although it did make me cry, the truth is, I can't focus. On anything.

Deen's been plastered all over the walls of my brain like cheap wallpaper, and I hate it.

Something changed about him yesterday. First he had to go and say all that stuff about me being a doctor, about how he doesn't think it's what I really want to do. It pissed me off at first. But he sounded so heartfelt. Like he was genuinely worried. Like he genuinely cared.

And most important, like he could see something I couldn't.

Then there was that dance, a new, painful awareness between us: of the hair in my eyes, the air in my lungs, fading, the outline of his mouth. Memories of kissing him three years ago bubbling in the back of my mind, soft and warm lips, so vivid I can practically taste it. But mostly, it was the smell that got to me, the familiar scent of pine, of mint—and something else, something sweet I could never put my finger on. Pheromones, maybe?

Ah, fuck. My pulse spikes just thinking about it. I have to ignore it. He's just trying to incite a reaction from me, trolling me. But, as much as I hate to admit it, dance practice with him has been . . . really fun. Maybe it's the way he watches me—not in a creepy way, but like he's genuinely impressed, like he sees and appreciates the hard work that goes into it. It's *confusing.*

The garage door rumbles and the mudroom door opens. It's Amira.

She trudges into the kitchen and plops her purse on the counter. She looks exhausted. Her skin is tired and dull, like I'm viewing her through a hazy filter, coloring her in muted grays and taupes. Her messy, tangled hair, normally tamed in a neat ponytail, falls loosely over her shoulders like she's just woken up.

"Whoa. Everything okay?"

"Yeah. I'm good," Amira answers, her voice a few octaves higher than usual.

"Then why do you look like you're getting ready for your own funeral? Should I be singing a dirge?"

"Don't be silly. Really, I'm fine."

"Amira."

"Really." She moves some of my books out of the chair beside me and takes a seat. Deep, dark lines of mehndi stain nearly every square inch of the skin of her hands with intricate swirls and geometric designs of flowers and vines. "I just got back from talking to the imam, so I'm good." She rubs her bleary eyes fiercely. "Did Riz leave already?"

I know she's just changing the subject, but I don't press it. "Mhm," I say through a mouthful of cereal. "She's checking out the venue one last time." I swallow. "I keep saying we should be paying her for everything she's been doing, but she told me to mind my own business. I remember her saying something about having an easy rotation schedule this month. Pretty sure she's lying, though. Isn't the point of residency to like, suffer?"

"I guess you'll be finding out soon enough, huh?" Amira gestures to my books.

"I guess so," I say, ignoring the knot in my chest.

"You know Mom wanted to be a doctor?" Amira says suddenly.

"What?"

"Yeah. She was already on track to go, back in Pakistan. But she met Dad and they got married soon after that. A few weeks later, Dad got a job here, so they moved here together." Amira tugs her long hair over her shoulder. "And then I came along."

My throat tightens. I didn't know any of this. But now it makes more sense why she wanted me to become one.

Amira continues. "Thinking about it now, I feel pretty guilty. Like I ruined her plans."

"I sincerely doubt she ever felt that way."

"Maybe." She sighs. "She was actually telling me she was thinking about going to PA school."

"PA school? To be a physician's assistant?" My eyes widen. "When?"

"Like, a year before her symptoms started. It's not exactly the same as being a doctor, but the program is only two years, and it's a lot cheaper—still makes good money, too. For all intents and purposes, she'd still be able to practice medicine and do pretty much all the same stuff as any other doctor, albeit supervised by one."

"Huh." I put down my spoon, watch it sink into my cereal bowl. "She never told me."

Amira puts up her hands. "It was just a thought she'd had—I don't know if she was actually serious! She probably didn't say anything because she wasn't sure, and I happened to be there."

I'm only half listening; the gears in my head start to whirl with life. Becoming a physician's assistant—I had no idea Mom had ever even considered it. But it's not a bad idea.

I don't want you to have to make hard choices when you could have it all.

I bite my lip. It's not a bad idea at all.

We fall into a long stretch of silence.

Amira is the first to break it.

"Things are changing, but"—she lets out a shaky breath—"women are still always the first to upheave their lives for others, huh? Certainly doesn't help when your in-laws seem to expect it."

She looks stressed. Deen and Faisal's mom must be giving her a harder time than I realized. I'm not sure what to say, so I look at her and let her go on.

"Do you remember the other day when we were in the kitchen, right here, and you told me you didn't understand the rush to marry Faisal?" Amira asks.

I swallow nervously. "Yeah. I think I said something about three months not being a lot of time to really know someone."

Amira nods. "But Mom and Dad barely knew each other when they got married, and it worked out for them. At least, that was the logic.

"But just because it worked out for them doesn't mean it'll work out for us, does it? I keep wondering if—if three months really isn't a lot of time. I know I'm probably saying all this because I'm nervous and it's all starting to feel so real, and Faisal's been too busy getting ready to move to California and there have been more and more . . . questions cropping up in my head. About him. About us."

Her eyes are a vast emptiness that clenches at my heart.

"You mean the stuff with Asher? And the bachelor party?"

"Right. I'm not saying it's enough to call off the wedding or anything. But I'm wondering if those . . . incidents are simply little bumps in the road, or are indicators of a much bigger iceberg of problems hiding under the surface. Red flags that I've been trying to ignore." Amira stares at her lap.

"We work so well together. That's why I fell for him, I think. His nonprofit idea—AFFEY? It's exactly the kind of work that I want to do. Trying to help kids get back on their feet after serving time, giving them a second chance? What's more noble than that? And his passion for it, it's infectious. I mean, he's poured so much of his savings into building the center in California that his parents have to cover the cost of the move. That, plus the timing of it all, too—it felt so right. But is that really enough?"

Amira's fingers clutch the fabric of her pants. "It's a little over a week before our wedding. I thought I'd feel more ready than this."

Guilt tears into me, cutting away at all the pent-up determination. I'm left drained. And cold.

I've never seen Amira like this, so torn and confused and unsure of herself. She's always known exactly what she's wanted. It's what I've always admired her for, what I've always been jealous of.

But because of *me* . . .

Faisal didn't do this to her. *I* did.

"I wish Mom were here," Amira says softly, wilting like a flower.

I close my eyes tightly. "Me too."

I find myself wanting to tell her everything: about Deen and me dating, about my stupid plan, and all the thoughts and fears I've been keeping locked inside. I want to tell her that everything she feels right now is my fault.

But I can't be selfish. I won't dump all my mistakes on her

so soon before her wedding.

For now, I need to clean up my mess. I'll send a message to Leah and tell her not to come. I shouldn't have invited her, anyway. Making her come to Amira's wedding . . . God, what was I thinking? I was so caught up trying to expose Faisal that I didn't think about how it would affect Amira.

I underestimated how much she really cares about him.

Maybe he did commit a felony. Maybe he does have a shady past. But for all I know, he really could be a changed man. If Amira, a freaking social-justice lawyer, thinks so, shouldn't that be enough?

I can't trust Faisal. But I can trust her.

I'll message Leah. I'll erase the three-step plan. I'll shred the journal entry, as soon as I find it—I think I dropped it somewhere, but I'll try not to worry about that right now.

I'm done worrying.

"Boys are the worst," I say.

Amira laughs wetly. "The absolute worst."

"Whatever. Tonight is your night. And tomorrow is your day. Cishet dudes can go suck it. They're all officially grounded."

"Except Dad."

"Except Dad," I say, nodding. "Speaking of which, I should probably go check up on him." Plus, I have some messages to write.

I slide off the chair and make my way to the staircase.

"Hey, Kiran?" Amira's voice stops me.

I look over my shoulder to see her, a small smile on her face.

"I love you," she says.

My eyes burn.

"I love you, too."

CHAPTER 29

DEEN

Saturday, August 21
One Day Until the Wedding

I FIND FAISAL IN HIS room in the basement. He's on the ground in a plank doing dumbbell rows, and besides his cheeks being a little darker than usual, he's hardly working up a sweat. Normally, I'd be rolling up my sleeves to show that I, too, am an unstoppable beast. But if I tried to lift a thirty-pounder in my current state, I'm pretty sure I'd drop through the floor like a freaking Looney Tunes character. Plus, there's only one reason why Faisal would be working out this hard, right before his own wedding.

"I was going to come in and check on you, but I think I know the answer," I say, leaning against the doorjamb.

Faisal lets out a sad huff. "You know me too well." He drops his weights and gets to his feet. He takes a swig from a gallon of water before eyeing me over.

"I thought *I* was tired, but you—you look exhausted. Everything okay?"

I almost laugh. *Not at all*, I want to say. *Not even a little bit.*

Vinny's still not talking to me, and despite the mad whirlwind these past few weeks, I really miss the guy. And the girl I've been crushing on in Cambria is in fact the same girl who hates me more than anyone—enough to write up an entire plan to ruin my brother's happiness.

All the while, every time I blink, I see Kiran, a tiny dancer spinning around in my head, single-handedly churning all my thoughts into an anxiety-laden smoothie.

But I can't let him worry. "Yeah, of course. Have you even met me?"

The stairs above us thump, announcing that we'll be shortly joined by someone else.

It's Mom. She must have just come back from work; typical she would still work even up till the eleventh hour.

"You left your phone upstairs," she says. Her face hardly shows any emotion, other than that her mouth is in a thinner line than usual.

"Oh. Thanks." I reach for it, take it, and immediately sense something very wrong.

Mom looks me in the eyes and I feel myself shrink. Because behind her eyes, I feel the familiar fury.

"Why is your professor emailing you?" she demands, her voice like a bitch slap of freezing wind. "What is this about you not turning in your essays?"

Fuck.

"You went through my email."

It's my fault for leaving my phone around, I guess. Knowing how M&D are. But I wanted to put some distance between me and my messages. For whatever stupid reason, I keep waiting for a message from Vinny. And Kiran.

She smooths at the knot forming between her perfectly manicured eyebrows. "He's going to dock your grades if you keep doing this. You're supposed to be better than this, Deen. Why aren't you taking school seriously? Do you want to end up like Faisal, han?"

I swallow hard. She's telling me things I already know. But I don't like that she has to tack on a jab to Faisal at the end. When he's standing right here.

"You're not even a sophomore yet. You can't afford to slack off. We're paying for your tuition, and we expect—"

"Ami, you can't put that kind of pressure on him all the time," comes Faisal's voice. He stands beside me. "It's not healthy."

"You are the *last* person I want to hear that from," Mom snaps.

Faisal's head lowers. "I know. But Deen's had a lot on his mind lately. Cut him some slack. I'm sure he already knows."

Mom practically puffs up with hot air. "We've seen firsthand what happens when I give any of you boys some slack."

"I know, but—"

"You have *no* right—"

"Ami, please—"

"Faisal, what has gotten into y—"

The thoughts in my head spin faster and faster. Churning and bubbling and spilling . . .

I'll take the fall for you.

"Stop it!" I shout. I'm breathing like I've just run a hundred miles and my exoskeleton is too damn tired to hold in the anger anymore. I round up on Mom, squeezing my phone with all my strength. "Stop it. Holy *shit*. You always do this! You're never home and when you are, you jump down our throats. Why even *have* kids, then? Seriously? Faisal has gone through actual hell to get himself back on his feet with literally no support from his own parents and here you are, treating your own flesh and blood like *shit*."

Mom looks like she's ready to slap me, and frankly, I almost want her to.

"We supported him all throughout college," she says, dangerously low, "before he threw it all away. And even then, we've put a roof over his head, let him stay with us without expecting anything in return—"

"So you could control him! The only reason why you keep him close is to keep an eye on him. You made us move because of the rumors about Faisal at the masjid and you didn't want your precious reputation being tarnished."

"Don't you *dare* speak that way to me," Mom hisses. But I ignore her because I'm on a roll and I can't stop.

"And you—" I start, looking at Faisal, "I didn't ask you to defend me. You're too quick to throw yourself in the fire for others, but how is that actually helpful? Think about *yourself* for once."

Faisal stares back at me like a puppy I've just hit.

"Deen . . . ?"

His voice breaks something inside me. The expression he's making—it reminds me of the night of the accident. The last time I completely lost it.

"Look," I continue, shaking, "I *get* that you take crap from our parents because you think you owe them, or out of some filial piety bullshit, and I get that we're taught that 'heaven lies under our mother's feet.' But can you really say that applies if she's going to trample all over you, if she's going to keep kicking you when you're down? You don't think that's going to affect Amira eventually? The people who love you?"

"Deen!" Mom finally yells and it's like a jolt to my brain. "Tumhe kya hua? What has gotten into you?"

"Nothing." I run my hand through my hair, and I realize my forehead's damp. "Nothing. Forget it. I'm just . . . tired." My throat feels impossibly tight. What the hell am I doing? I must be losing my goddamn mind.

"I can't believe you—we don't have *time* for whatever the hell this is. We will talk about this *later*," Mom promises through gritted teeth. It feels more like a threat. Like everything that comes out of her mouth.

I look her in the eyes. It feels like the first time in forever. "There's nothing more to talk about," I respond. "Either you change the way you act, or I'm done being your son. Trust me. It'd be better for all of us that way."

Mom huffs, her glare digging into me. She's so furious, she's actually at a loss for words. But to my surprise—and relief—she simply storms out of the room, leaving me and Faisal alone.

Neither of us speaks for what feels like minutes.

"You're one to talk, you know," Faisal says finally.

"What do you mean?"

"I'm not the only one with a habit of throwing myself to the wayside."

I blink. "Me? Please. I love myself too much for that."

"Heh. Maybe," says Faisal, smiling weakly. "Go get some rest, Deen. We're going to be busy tomorrow."

"You too." I pat him on the shoulder. "You don't want to show up at your wedding with dark circles and give Amira reason to call the whole thing off."

"At least, not any more than I already have."

Before I can respond, he escapes into the bathroom next door.

And I take a deep breath.

CHAPTER 30

KIRAN

⸎ Sunday, August 22 ⸎

Amira and Faisal's Wedding Day

THE SWELL OF VIOLINS SIGNALS that it's time, punctuated with the beat of a dhol that reverberates through the ballroom. My heart responds in kind, thrumming in an uncomfortable syncopation to the bass.

Riz grins at me. "Shall we?"

Behind us, Amira sucks in a breath. She's wearing a cream-colored lehenga that trails behind her, its shimmering fabric embroidered with delicate gold and pink flowers. On Mona and Mrs. Malik's insistence, she's swathed in heavy jewelry: a gold-plated tikka adorns her forehead; emerald droplets dangle from the wide choker on her neck. A hoop hangs from her nose, with a delicate chain connecting it to her long pink-sapphire-and-pearl earrings. Thick gold bangles chime on wrists with her every movement. It's not unusual to wear so much jewelry at a Pakistani wedding, and Amira looks undeniably beautiful in it all. But still. I can't help but feel she looks weighed down, like a bird chained to a gilded cage.

The only comfort is her lehenga. Mom's lehenga. It fits her perfectly. When Dad saw her for the first time in the dressing room, he cried. Which, of course, made us cry. God bless waterproof mascara.

"I'm ready," says Amira, her voice soft as silk, but strong.

I nod and muster a grin back at Riz. "Let's do it."

A small group of us form the wedding procession, and together, we're holding a blush-pink dupatta over Amira like a tent: Nani bringing up the rear, with Amira's college friends, Cara and Rebecca, sharing the right side. Asher is the only guy, standing just behind me on the left, while Rizwana and I flank the front corners of the dupatta.

We walk forward. Ahead, Faisal's younger cousins, led by Sara, Mona's daughter, toss white flower petals along the path. I hardly notice; I move mechanically, one foot in front of the other, trying not to trip on the length of my own coral-red lehenga.

The doors to the ballroom open, and for a moment, I'm momentarily stunned by an assault of light. *Cameras.* I blink, hard.

And then my eyes adjust.

The ballroom is vast, with gilded walls and a scallop-patterned ceiling where spotlights dance around crystal chandeliers suspended like colossal jellyfish overhead. Roman pillars border the room, their alpine forms blanketing by living vines, and between them, latticed archways reveal a second floor with more seating. White-clothed round tables—filled with people—punctuate the main floor, their surfaces adorned with massive glass vases featuring bouquets of moss and white chrysanthemums and lilac wisteria. But the center of the room is bare: the dance floor. Though the rest of the ballroom is aglow in plumes of shuddering gold candlelight, the dance floor alone is swathed in gentle, ethereal purple.

And at the front of the ballroom is a stage, domed with dangling strings of pearls and more wisteria, filling the hall with the smell of flowers. Two gilded thrones made of black velvet and gold trim sit under a dome, separated only by a thin, opal-studded table and two white feather quill pens. To sign the marriage contract.

My ribs clamp inside my chest. Traditionally for Muslims, the bride's family pays for weddings, but Faisal's mom and dad insisted they cover it. I knew the Maliks were rich, but this is ridiculous.

The violins reach a swell as we approach the dome, where a solitary figure stands beneath: Faisal, in a matching cream-colored shalwar and a pink-and-blue stitched scarf draped over his shoulder. The gold-embroidered turban sits a little lopsided on his head.

Amira takes a seat beside Faisal on an enormous tufted Chesterfield sofa, so gaudy that I'm half convinced the Maliks must have pilfered it from a Mughal palace.

Dad puts a garland of pink roses and white carnations over Faisal's bowed head, while Mrs. Malik places a matching garland over Amira's. To their left, Imam Obaid takes a separate chair, a Quran in his hands. There's a small table beside him, and I spot the official nikah papers: the marriage contract.

Faisal squeezes Amira's hand; she smiles back nervously.

I hesitate.

"Come." Dad puts his hand on my back, gently nudging me.

I linger a little longer before squaring my shoulders and finally plodding offstage.

Dad's led away by Mr. Malik, and Asher and I head for the table closest to the stage, labeled *#1*, the table reserved for family of the bride.

"So, here we are at last," Asher says.

"Yeah." I plop myself into a gilded chair while Asher takes the seat beside me. I know I told myself to let go, but still. It's hard to be happy.

"So is it true that at Pakistani weddings, it's tradition to steal the groom's shoes for ransom? Would that make you feel better?"

I let out a puff of air, blowing my bangs off my forehead. "Pretty sure Faisal barely has money to spare. A lot of it's going toward the nonprofit." And now with Amira involved, I'm sure she'll be dragged along with it. It'll probably take her twice as long to pay back her student loan debt. Just another reason why they shouldn't be together. On top of everything else.

But I promised I'd stop interfering. I even deleted the plan off my phone, wrote a message to Leah telling her the plan was off. I meant to shred Faisal's journal page, too, and I looked everywhere for it. Except I was never able to find it. It must have fallen out the back pocket on my phone.

It makes me feel uneasy. I don't like loose ends.

My eyes trail behind us, to the dozens of tables filled with guests, most of whom I don't recognize—friends and family of the Maliks, I guess—though I do spot Cara and Rebecca and Rizwana, chatting with Haris under one of the archways, and Hamza chacha hanging with Nani by the buffet. And my cousin Adeem, who's face-first in a bowl of biryani.

But my eyes eventually land on a familiar face, one that stands out among the others: Deen. Guess he opted against wearing a shalwar; instead, he's wearing a dark blue suit that brings out the warmth in his skin, adorned with a black-and-gold tie. His sharp jaw is set tight. Purposeful.

"You okay?" Asher asks softly.

I shrug. "Does it really matter now?"

Asher's forehead creases. He opens his mouth to say something, but a loud tapping sound swallows his words.

Onstage, Imam Obaid has a microphone to his lips. He smiles, and the ballroom falls to a hush. My heart skitters nervously.

"Bismillah al Rahman al Rahim," Imam Obaid begins. His warm voice resonates through the expanse.

"On behalf of these two beautiful souls, I thank you all for coming and bearing witness to their marriage, God willing. I have had the privilege of working closely with Sister Amira and Brother Faisal for the past six weeks, and although it has only been a short while, I feel confident that these two have exactly what they need to move ahead on this journey they have committed to undertake, together.

"So what are the tools one needs on this journey? you may wonder. In a world of instant gratification, the very concept of marriage and the level of commitment required to maintain one feels . . . tricky. Like too big of an investment. After all, marriage is so much more than a partnership. So much more than sunnah. So much more than the thing we do to get the items we can't afford on our registries. There is a magic to it, a metaphysical weight to it. We know this to be true, in the movies we watch, the books we read.

"But though the key to a successful marriage has a hidden depth to it, it is also very simple:

"To marry—to love—is to be vulnerable. To have a mutual willingness to put it all out there in every moment without hesitation. To promise to knock down the walls you keep up for other people. To vow to no longer allow the past to remain as a shackle of shame and regret, but the place from which your shared future springs."

I glance over at Deen. We catch each other's eyes, let them linger, until I feel a bloom of heat on my cheeks and turn away.

"To be vulnerable together is the only way we see the best of humanity: patience and understanding, communication and trust. Whether it be a fight over who forgot to do the dishes, or learning to comfort one another after the loss of someone dear.

"*That* is love. That is marriage. And tonight, these two beautiful souls have decided to be vulnerable in front of everyone they know: their family, their friends, their peers. Which, in times such as these, is truly a miracle."

Onstage, Amira and Faisal stare at the floor, as if afraid to look up. I wish I could tell what Amira was thinking.

Imam Obaid puts his hands together in prayer. "Baarakallaahu laka, wa baaraka 'alayka, wa jama'a baynakumaa fee khayrin. May God bless you, and shower His blessings upon you, and join you together in goodness," he says.

The entire ballroom murmurs in assent.

Imam Obaid grabs the nikah papers off the table, hands Amira and Faisal their own pens to sign. Dad and Faisal's dad watch over, acting as witnesses, per tradition. The Imam whispers something, gaining a hesitant smile from the bride and groom. I want to look away, but my eyes are glued to Amira as I watch her pen move across the paper.

And then, at least in the eyes of Islamic law, it is done.

Haris hops onstage, all smiles as he takes the mic from Imam Obaid. "Now, if you'll all join me in a round of applause for the happy couple!" The roar that follows puts me in a daze. "Next, we'll have a few words from the esteemed Dr. Margaret Kline, Amira's professor and mentor. But first."

He searches through the audience. Spotlights graze the center of the room. And that's when it dawns on me.

It's time.

I look down at the table, where a small printed program—the ones I printed for the wedding—laid out on my plate spells it out clearly:

7:30. *Dance.*

Across the room, Deen gets to his feet and begins walking toward the dance floor.

"I'm going to throw up," I mutter, dread settling in my stomach.

"I almost threw up the other day," replies Asher, side-eyeing me. "You know, when someone decided to hire a stripper without telling me."

"I need you to make me feel better, not worse," I whine.

He smirks. "My advice? The sooner you get it over with, the better."

And with that, Asher yanks the chair out from under me and I stumble off it.

I barely manage to catch myself in time. Ignoring the curious stares around me, I throw Asher a dirty look, smooth down my lehenga. He gives me a thumbs-up.

I march toward the dance floor with all the enthusiasm of a person walking to a guillotine. It's not like I haven't danced in public before, obviously—I danced at the dholki, and before that, I've danced at a couple of smaller events. Except, that's just the thing: they were smaller, like thirty or forty people, tops. And I'd usually be dancing alongside Mom. Here, though, there are easily over five hundred. And I'm not dancing with Mom.

The spotlight fades as I step onto the edge of the dance floor; Deen approaches from the opposite side.

My heart begins to pound.

I can't read his expression, which only makes me more uneasy. But Deen reaches his hand out toward me. I stiffen.

"Nervous?" he asks, amused. "After all the practice we've done?"

"How are you *not* nervous?"

"Other things on my mind, I guess. Come on." He pulls me onto the center of dance floor.

"We just have to get through tonight and then . . ." A sad smile flits across Deen's face. "You might not have to see me again for a while."

My eyebrows furrow. "What's that supposed to mean?"

He stands next to me. There's nothing but silence, save for the rapid pounding in my chest. I try to ignore all the confused looks in the crowd or, worse, the judgmental glares. This was supposed to be a dance-off; I was supposed to be alone. But I'll deal with it if it means I finally get the truth.

The music bursts into life.

Except something's off. The beat is still the same, but—

"Wait, this song . . ." I spin to face him, panicking. "This isn't the right song!"

"Isn't it more exciting this way?" he asks, a laugh teasing his mouth.

My eyes widen. Of *course* he's behind it, the troll. "Why the *hell* would you change it at the last—" I stop and listen. "Wait. This song."

It *is* the right song, sort of. The familiar thrum of the tabla intertwining with electronic strings and synth, a splice of East and West. A remix?

Another familiar melody begins, and I recognize it now. It's not a remix. It's a mashup. He's mashed up a song from *Devdas* with "I Wanna Dance with Somebody."

What the hell? Is he trying to mess with me?

I stare at Deen, confused. He grins, his eyes taunting, daring me.

The vocals kick in. I don't have time to ask questions and I certainly won't let Deen get away with trying to throw me off, not in front of all these people, several of whom stare at us disapprovingly. Deen's mom—I shudder—is one of them.

My body responds to the music.

We fall in step, spinning away from each other. As we begin to move, my nervousness and tension fall away like flecks of old paint. My limbs feel light. His feet fall back, mine give chase; when I retreat, he hunts in kind. Our arms sweep in opposition, mirroring each other, two halves to a whole. His arm encircles my waist, hovering just without touching—I arch my back before he whirls me away again, my hair whipping around me; as the song quickens, with every movement, my lehenga floats in a fan shape around my legs. My body is a conduit for the waves of music flowing through me; I take it in and send it back out. If I don't, I'm sure I'll explode. And there's Deen, propelling me through it all.

Our dance feels different this time, and it's not just the song. The audience, the stage, everyone and everything—it's like they don't even exist. It's just me and Deen, goofing off side by side in our own little world. I can't put a name to the warm tension between us, and honestly, I'm afraid to, but it crackles, a living, uncontrollable thing. Playful. People will talk. I don't even care.

Deen shimmies over to me with an exaggerated hip sway and grabs my dupatta, yanking me back, and I laugh because it's ridiculous. We're hardly keeping up with the original choreography. I don't care. I've never felt so loose, so open, so free.

The music begins to slow, and even though my muscles burn, I never want it to end.

Finally, it stops. I fall back limply, sinking into Deen's hand supporting my back. He holds me up and his dark eyes glitter with that unnamed something. I'm hyperaware of the closeness of his lips on my cheek, especially as the people around us come back into focus. Oh God. Embarassment and maybe a little shame rise up in me like a bad burp. This was a *mistake*, what are people going to *say*, why did I—

"Kas," he whispers.

My eyes snap to his. He pushes me back up.

I blink hard. My head's gone numb. "What did you just say?" I ask shakily, rounding on him.

Suddenly, the whole room explodes in applause. Someone at a table near us lets out an ear-piercing whistle; I look over, and it's Asher. Deen's parents can't seem to manage hiding their scowls, but they do manage half-hearted claps to keep up appearances. Onstage, Amira and Faisal are standing, Amira cupping her face in shock, revealing only her crinkled eyes, and Faisal is smiling wider than I've ever seen him. He hops offstage and runs toward his brother before enveloping him in a bear hug.

But Deen—did I hear him right . . . ? No. I couldn't have. He must have said something else. Like . . . gas. Or mass—because I'm heavy? Or badass?

"Deen—" I start, but the crowd storms him, most of it made of unfamiliar aunties—perhaps wondering if he's taken, fishing for his biodata. I can't see him over the throngs of people. I'm completely shut out. Talk about a double standard.

Haris takes to the mic again. "Well, that was a heck of a surprise performance from none other than the bride's and groom's younger siblings, Kiran and Deen! And hopefully that excitement's riled up your appetite because we'll be serving dinner before letting our next speaker, Dr. Margaret Kline, say a few words for the couple," he says, mostly ignored.

I stand alone, dumbfounded. I want to ask Deen. Something about the way he's acting tonight feels off. And then to hear him say Kas . . .

I'm being ridiculous.

It's like Deen said. After tonight, after he finally tells me the truth about what happened three years ago, we won't really have a reason to see each other. Other than the occasional Thanksgiving. After tonight, we'll go back to being strangers. Whatever spell we were under during the dance, it's broken. Or maybe I imagined it.

I leave Deen to be swallowed by the crowd.

CHAPTER 31

KIRAN

⸙ Sunday, August 22 ⸙
Amira and Faisal's Wedding Day

I MAKE A STRATEGIC RETREAT to the bathroom. I need to wash my face, and it's the only place I can get a moment of privacy. A place where I can cool my head.

One of the waitstaff, who is busy serving dinner now, gives me directions, so I leave the ballroom and find the hallway that leads to a separate restroom area. But when I turn the corner, I hear an angry, familiar voice and am hit with a sense of déjà vu.

"Why are you here?" Faisal growls. "How did you even find out?"

A woman's voice. Timid and soft. "I'm sorry. I've been trying to reach you, but you never call me back or respond to any of my messages."

It's quiet. Like Faisal's thinking. "No, I—I'm sorry. But you can't be here," he pleads. "Please. You could ruin *everything*."

I can't see the woman's face; Faisal's shoulder is blocking it. But I can hear her redoubling her efforts. "If you'd just listen to me—"

"*No.* This isn't the time or place. Look, I still care about you, but it's my *wedding*, for God's sake. If my parents find out you're here . . ."

"I'll leave. I promise. I just wanted to talk."

"I can't," says Faisal. "Not anymore." He backs away from her. "Please leave."

He moves toward me, so I press myself against the wall, blending in with the shadows. He passes me, so close I can smell the roses wafting from the garland around his neck.

I peek over the edge of the wall.

My heart shoots up to my throat. I recognize the woman's face immediately.

It's Leah.

She looks better than she did in that photo I saw of her: her eyes are clearer, and her cheeks have filled out a little more, with a tinge of color, of life in them that wasn't there before. She's wearing a simple mauve wrap dress, and her strawberry-blonde hair is tied in a neat ponytail.

But why is she here?

I fish for my phone in my purse and open my Facebook messages. There it is, the message I'd been avoiding sending until last night: *I'm so sorry to cancel on you last minute, but circumstances have changed. Again, I'm really sorry.*

And beneath that, a new message, from her: *I'm here.*

I inhale, steeling myself. Then I step out of my hiding spot.

"Hi, Leah," I say.

Her eyes narrow. ". . . Kiran?"

I nod. "I wasn't expecting you to come. Did you not get my last message?"

"I, uh—" She rubs her arm sheepishly. "I didn't see it until late. Not that that would have changed anything." She sighs before looking at me, her blue eyes glimmering. "I needed to talk to Faisal. You just happened to come along with exactly where I could reach him. I just . . . didn't realize I'd be crashing his wedding. All you gave me was a time and location. It wasn't until I came in and saw the sign that I realized what this really was."

"I'm sorry you wasted your time," I say, because I don't know what else to say.

"Me too." Her shoulders dip. "Though I can't say I'm surprised. He hasn't replied to a single message from me in years now."

I bite my lip. I know I should probably talk to Deen first, but Leah is *here* and Deen's probably busy meeting aunties' daughters and curiosity's getting the better of me.

"Why won't he talk to you anymore?" I ask.

Leah smiles weakly. "It's a long story."

"No one will notice I'm gone," I reply, shrugging. I hate to admit it, but Deen has a certain charisma about him that draws people in and keeps them there. For now, people will be focused on him and dinner and the other speeches. The bride's plain little sister stuck in limbo? Entirely forgettable.

Leah hesitates. She closes her eyes, like she's digging deep in her head for memories.

She starts to speak:

"I met Faisal in high school. Back then, he was a completely different person. A human beanpole. Super quiet, awkward. I don't think a single day passed when he wasn't bullied.

"There were two boys at school in particular who used to bully the crap out of him. It started with the typical stuff: stupid, hateful comments in the hallway, tripping him in the hall, destroying his textbooks, that sort of thing. But over time, it got worse. They'd beat him up, threaten him if he even thought to tell anyone about it. One night, they went to his house and graffitied the front door with something . . . something disgusting. Something Islamophobic."

My fists clench.

"The worst part is," she continues, "one of those boys? That hateful, evil monster? He's my older brother."

My eyes widen in horror. "Seriously?"

"I wish I was kidding," Leah murmurs. "That's how Faisal and I met, actually. I felt bad for him. My brother was always a bully, but he went extra hard on Faisal. I couldn't stop him. So instead, I'd leave bandages or an ice pack in Faisal's locker, or give him my spare change so he could buy lunch. Pathetic." She chuckles self-deprecatingly.

"I thought eventually, my brother would stop, get bored of bullying Faisal. Move on to someone else. But it kept escalating. At the same time, I think Faisal was also getting a lot of pressure from his parents. I haven't met them, but they sound super . . . obsessed with their image. More than they care about Faisal, maybe. That's when Faisal and I started to get closer." Leah sees my reaction and waves her hands. "Not what you're thinking, though! We were just . . . friends. Or maybe the more accurate term is accomplices."

"Accomplices?"

Leah's eyes grow dark. "I started taking Adderall. My own family situation, as you can probably imagine, was pretty fucked up. My parents were assholes to everyone but my older brother and treated me like I was nothing. I couldn't focus on school. But the meds helped.

"So I started giving Faisal Adderall, too. At least, enough so he could keep his grades up, please his parents. It also helped him . . . forget."

The drugs. Of course. I can feel the pieces aligning in my brain. What Faisal said in his journal entry, something about the drugs in his system—he'd been referring to Adderall?

I feel . . . sorry for him. I'd been imagining shady back-alley deals, tiny bags of white powder, Faisal driving away in a convertible with trunks of cash. Not a kid just trying to survive under pressure.

Not *this*.

"It became an escape for the both of us," Leah continues. "We were in a dark place and it was the only thing that kept us numb. So we continued, even until college. Nearly four years of this hell. Then one day, Faisal went back home to visit his family for the weekend, and my brother cornered him in a parking lot. He beat him up so badly, he broke Faisal's jaw. And Faisal had to be put on OxyContin for the pain."

Deen—did Deen know all this was happening? Was he watching all of this, helplessly seeing his brother fall apart? The thought seizes me like a vise.

"That's when Faisal reached his limit. The addiction was getting worse and I think he realized he couldn't continue like this much longer. Of course it was my brother's fault; he'd done nothing but torment Faisal in the most horrible of ways for so long, but . . ." Leah swallows hard. "In the middle of the night, Faisal went over to my parents' house. My brother still lived with them; he worked at my dad's auto shop."

Leah leans against the wall, like she doesn't have the strength to keep standing. "I don't know the details. All I do know is, Faisal said in the deposition that he'd only meant to set his car on fire. But he lost control of the flames. Luckily, we weren't home that night. My brother had an away game and my parents decided we'd all go to support him. But I don't know if Faisal knew that."

She folds her arms across her chest. "That's why I had to come. After the fire three years ago, I stopped talking to Faisal. On one hand, I understand where he's coming from, more than most people would. But I didn't know what to believe. I get all the anger, all the years of pent-up rage toward my brother. Still. What if . . . what if my family *was* home that night?"

My pulse quickens. So it was arson, the felony in his journal entry. My pity for Faisal evaporates. Quiet, awkward Faisal, finally snapping and setting someone's house on fire.

The pain he was going through is no excuse. He could have *killed* people. Maybe he was pushed to the brink. But when push comes to shove—knowing he's capable of turning around and doling out revenge, with no warning, and tenfold—it's unstable.

It's dangerous.

"I think I hurt Faisal pretty badly. It's been three years. I've lost my chance to get answers," Leah says softly, as if only now realizing. "But I'm sure none of this would come as a surprise to your sister—Amira, right? I mean, the nonprofit they're working on together is kind of a big tip-off. I'm sure they've worked it out already."

The realization strikes me like a slap.

No. Amira *doesn't* know. Hell, even with Faisal's journal, even I couldn't have known it was this bad.

No wonder Faisal's been trying so hard to keep it all under wraps.

If Amira really knew . . .

Promise me you'll look after them.

The sound of clapping from inside the ballroom breaks me from my thoughts. The next speaker must have finished.

I force myself to breathe.

"I should go," says Leah.

I nod slowly. "Yeah. Thank you, though. For telling me the truth."

Leah's eyes go downcast. "If you ever need anything . . ." She walks past me and pauses. "Well. You know."

I say nothing as her footsteps retreat and fade away.

I can't let Faisal get away with this. Amira has to know. But how? I let out an angry, frustrated curse and dig through my purse.

If only I still had Faisal's journal page. Except it's gone.

My head's a whirlpool, but my feet begin to move on their own, even before a plan coalesces. Maybe I'll tell Asher. He'll know what to do. And then I'll tell Amira—

"Don't."

A tangled whisper of a voice stops me in my tracks. I raise my gaze, and my eyes meet the one person I don't want to see right now, his usual cocky smirk replaced by something that looks a lot like anguish:

Deen.

CHAPTER 32

DEEN

✢ Sunday, August 22 ✢

Amira and Faisal's Wedding Day

"PLEASE."

I take a step toward her. Kiran retreats, taking a couple of steps back from me. She's eyeing me warily.

The Kiran I danced with is gone.

"I don't know what you're talking about," she says.

I lean in closer and lower my voice. "I saw you talking to Leah."

Kiran stops breathing and looks away.

I'm so glad I looked through her purse that second time; if I hadn't found the plan on her phone, if I hadn't found that page from Faisal's journal, I would've been holding on to hope that the worst was behind me, instead of watching Kiran like a hawk. But as usual, she's a slippery one. I panicked when I lost sight of her, when dozens of extended family—most of whom I've never seen in my life—decided to form their own mosh pit around me and bombard me with increasingly irritating questions: *You go to NYU, right? Your parents still own their own private practice, right? You're going to take over, right?*

I joked with Vinny about how aunties would be throwing their hot single daughters my way all throughout the wedding, but the reality is less sexy than I'd hoped. All those people—they'd be backing away like Kiran if they knew the truth about me.

"I know what you heard from Leah doesn't . . ." I exhale. "It doesn't sound good. But believe me when I say there's more to the story that she isn't telling you."

"Are you saying she's *lying*?" Kiran snaps.

"No. Just that she doesn't know the *full* truth." How could she? Leah wasn't there. Not like *I* was.

"I'll take my chances. She's the only one willing to tell me anything, so why shouldn't I believe her?" Kiran's eyes widen suddenly. "Oh my God. The other day . . . all that stuff you said about Faisal not lying to my sister—you were fucking gaslighting me!"

Damn. No wonder she hates you.

She's right. I was. And yet, the truth is so much more complicated. I had to stick to the story. Faisal made me promise. My parents made me promise.

Keep the secret. No matter what.

I clench my fists.

Earlier, when I was dancing with Kiran, my head felt like a never-ending round of neurotic Ping-Pong with my thoughts.

Because I was also dancing with *Kas*. My Kas, the one who knows me better than anyone, who's been there when I needed someone.

On the other hand, it's still Kiran, determined as ever to bring Faisal down.

On the other hand, it's my fault.

On the other hand, isn't she going totally overboard?

On the other hand, she's fucking *beautiful* in that lehenga and it's a lot to take in. On the other hand, she betrayed our pact. On the other hand, this feeling between us—am I imagining it?

I need a drink. No I don't!

Until finally, the song stopped and I looked her in the eyes, breathless and glowing and for that moment, *mine*.

Kas. The name fell from my lips before I could swallow it. For that moment, I didn't have to care about what people thought. For that moment, we were just Kas and Foxx, and nothing else mattered. Maybe that's the real reason why I wanted to dance with her. It was an excuse to be with her. To forget.

"God, the timing—" Kiran's eyes look raw. "The fire was three years ago. Is that—is that why you ghosted me? Because of what happened with your brother?"

"Please. I know. You're not wrong." My voice cracks. "But please, I'm begging you. If you break up the wedding, Faisal won't be able to move to California. The nonprofit, this chance to start over—this is his dream."

"I'm sorry. But that's not my problem."

Kiran elbows me out of the way and charges ahead.

No.

I grab her wrist.

"Don't touch me!" she shrieks.

Kiran rips her arm out of my grip and shoves me out of her way. I stumble backward like she's a human tempest and getting in her way again would mean sudden death. I let go and watch her disappear into the ballroom, the doors swinging behind her.

My legs can barely hold me up. A bead of sweat rolls down my cheek.

I can't help but wonder: if circumstances were slightly different—if the fire never happened, and I didn't have these secrets I needed to keep—then would seeing her again after all these years have felt like a sign, one even my heathen ass would have believed in? Would all the faith I've lost over the years come rushing back when I found out that of all the people in the world it could have been, Kasia was Kiran?

It all makes me want to scream.

Just like that night.

No. No. No, no, no, no.

I can't let it end like this.

It's my fault.

I can't let it end like this.

You're a tool.

I can't let it end like this.

Some things are better left unsaid, beta.

No.

I burst into the ballroom, scanning the crowd.

Amira's best friend, Rizwana, has finished her speech, so chai and dessert's in full swing; most people are sitting at their tables now, plates piled high with ras malai and gulab jamun and laddoo. Ahead, I see M&D, talking animatedly with some uncles and aunties I don't recognize. They're practically glowing, taking in the attention, until Mom spots me and immediately her expression grows cold. The band she hired is hard at work, filling the ballroom with the steady pulse of the dhols, the rush of violins, the sound so alive I can practically feel it in my chest like a warm vibration. In any other circumstances, it might have been fun to listen to. But Kiran's already onstage, deep in conversation with Amira and Faisal. I can't see her face, but her arms wave animatedly. Purposefully.

I run toward them. I don't need to hear what she's saying. Faisal's expression says it all: mouth squeezed in a tight line, and his eyes—like he's watching his entire life shatter before him. It's an expression I've seen once before, a few years ago. Gaunt cheeks shadowed by flickering flames.

"Stop!" I blurt, winded. Kiran throws me a dagger-eyed glare.

But she doesn't stop.

"He's been lying to you this whole time, Amira," she says, her back turned to Faisal like he doesn't exist. "I heard it all from one of his close friends. You can't do this. Being with him would be the worst mistake of your life. Please. You have to believe me."

"You don't even know the full story!" I argue.

Amira frowns. "These allegations—well, they're a lot to take in, Kiran. Faisal—what she's saying about . . . about your addiction—about this Leah, and the arson. Is it true?"

"I . . ." Faisal's cheeks drain of color and his knuckles tighten on the arm of his chair.

Seconds come in a slow trickle.

"Deen?" Amira asks.

"Kiran is going off secondhand information."

"It's a simple yes or no answer, Deen."

"It's . . . it's not untrue." My jaw clenches. "But there's more to the story. Important details. Most of which I can't tell you. We can talk more about it after the wedding."

"Or we can talk about it right now," Kiran growls. "You heard it from him; Faisal's been hiding all of it from you. If he's been lying about that, who knows what else he'll lie about?"

Frustration bubbles in my veins. "Faisal isn't a *liar*."

"Hiding a past, especially one as colorful as his, is the same damn thing."

"His past is *his* past," I retort, my voice raised. "If he wasn't ready to talk about it, no one should force him." Maybe Kiran has every right to be mad, but the way she's talking about Faisal is *really* getting under my skin.

"If you even took just a minute to get to know him, you'd see what I see. But you don't care because you've been too busy trying to prove he's some bad guy since the beginning. Like when you looked through Faisal's room at the family dinner. When you went through his private journal, ripped a page out of it. How is that fair?"

I can feel Kiran's body tense beside me.

"Kiran," says Amira, the worry lines deep on her face. "Did you really?"

"Okay, *yes*, but—" She turns on me, hackles practically raised. He committed a huge crime, and Amira deserves to know. He could have seriously hurt people!"

"You don't think he *knows* that? You don't think he has to live with that for the rest of his life?"

"Deen, stop," Faisal pleads weakly.

"But he hid it from my sister, the person he's supposed to be marrying!" Kiran retorts. "If he can't be honest with her, then who the hell else is he supposed to be honest with?" Her eyes shimmer with barely checked tears of frustration. "The only logical explanation for why he'd lie is because he's ashamed."

"You have no idea what you're talking about," I say.

"Or *maybe* he's using my sister as a tool to please his parents, to act the part of a 'good son.'"

I laugh darkly. "My parents weren't there for him when he needed them. All that time, he had no resources, no help. God, it was *one* mistake. He was just a kid."

"Or he's a pyromaniac too unsafe and unstable to ever marry Amira."

That does it. Kas or no Kas, this girl is going way too far. "Or *maybe* your judgment's clouded because you're still pissy I ghosted you," I spit back.

Amira blinks. "Wait, ghosted . . . ?"

"We used to date," I explain. "Three years ago."

Amira looks at Kiran. "Is this true? Why didn't you tell me?"

"Because it doesn't matter. It *shouldn't* matter," Kiran says through gritted teeth.

"Deen, enough," says Faisal.

"No! I'm tired of sitting back while other people try to ruin your life. And that's all Kiran's been trying to do these past few months." The words come pouring out now, and for once, I let them. "She even had a whole three-step plan to sabotage your relationship with Amira. Everything that's gone wrong, all the doubts you've had—it's because of her."

"How did you—?" Kiran's shoulders quake. "Did you look through my phone?"

"Only because you looked through Faisal's private journal first!

Do you see what I'm talking about?" I point at Kiran. "As if *she's* in any position to tell other people how to live their lives!"

"*Deen!*" Faisal shouts.

It slaps me like a bucket of ice water. This is nothing like our little argument yesterday. I jerk my head up at him in shock. I've never heard Faisal raise his voice over anything, or at anyone.

He's gotten to his feet, his shoulders trembling with fury. I draw back.

"You have done enough," Faisal says in a low voice.

For a tense moment, Kiran and I regard each other in stunned silence. That's when I notice: the music has stopped.

Slowly, I turn around.

My breath is knocked out of my chest.

Because we have an audience of over five hundred pairs of eyes.

All of them staring at me.

Kiran's dad, ashen faced at a nearby table, sitting beside Mom and Dad, fury and shame contorting their features. Haris, his mouth gaping. Even Asher, his usually calm veneer shattered, head in his hands.

I close my eyes tight before finally sliding my gaze back to my brother.

His shoulders slump. "Acting this way . . . it's beneath you," he says softly. "I don't need you to protect me if you're just going to hurt people in the process. Apologize. Apologize to Amira and Kiran right now."

"It doesn't matter."

Amira stands, her face eerily calm and stony.

"It's over.

"We're done."

LOADING

[CAMBRIA: THE EVOLUTION EXPANSION PACK]
[ROANA GUILD CHAT ROOM]

Devynius Foxx: Question
Devynius Foxx: How do you make someone forgive you when you've royally fucked up?
Nilina Torby: You're asking me?!
Nilina Torby: Isn't that a Kasia question?
Nilina Torby: You two and your cute little Q&As
Devynius Foxx: Unfortunately, this is the one question I can't ask her right now.
Nilina Torby: . . . Oh, honey :(
Nilina Torby: Well, let's see
Nilina Torby: You want to make someone forgive you?
Nilina Torby: That's the problem.
Nilina Torby: You can't.
Nilina Torby: The only thing you can do is give them space.
Nilina Torby: Do everything you can to make it up to them
Nilina Torby: And hope one day they forgive you.
Devynius Foxx: I see

Devynius Foxx: All right

Devynius Foxx: Thanks, Nil

Nilina Torby: Of course, luv

Nilina Torby: I don't know what's happened but

Nilina Torby: I know you two will work things out.

Devynius Foxx: <3

[**Devynius Foxx** has logged off]

CHAPTER 33

KIRAN

Tuesday, August 24

I'M SO GODDAMN TIRED.

Seriously. I feel like someone played Operation with my insides, stitched me back together, and then forced me to run a marathon. Asher says it's stress-related, that after a summer of being on edge and with the smackdown with Deen two days ago, I probably shortened my life span.

Right now, I'm not sure it's the worst thing.

First of all, even after the marriage was annulled, Dad announced he was still moving to Houston. "The house has already been sold, so I can't back out now. And even if I could, I wouldn't. We know better than most that we can't stop bad things from happening, but we can stop them from getting worse. If I changed my plans now, if we put our lives on hold, Amira would only blame herself." The next day, he went to work like nothing happened, and when he's been home, he's been up in his room, packing in silence.

I almost admire the man's tenacity, even though it'd be better for him to take some time off and rest, like a normal human.

If there's *one* good thing that's come of Dad's upcoming move, it's that it gives me something to do other than buying stuff I don't need for my college dorm room, listening to melancholy lo-fi hip-hop beats playlists while stuffing my face with leftover wedding cake, or crying over videos of lost baby animals that would surely perish if not for their timely rescue and friendship with a significantly larger, motherly dog. Thanks to my efforts, the entire basement is now a mini-city of boxes I've stacked to look like skyscrapers. Call me Sadzilla.

But the other strong contender for worst thing that's happened since the wedding is that Amira hasn't spoken to me once since she called it off. After her pronouncement, we drove her back home—our home—in total silence. Riz spent the night with her, the two of them locked in Amira's old bedroom. At least she had someone to talk to, I guess.

Someone who wasn't me.

"You all just need a few days to cool your heads," Asher assured me over FaceTime on that first night. "Would it help if I GrubHub'd you some ice cream?"

Last but not least, I can't focus on any of my summer reading and I move to campus in less than a *week*.

It all comes back to Deen.

At this point, Deen could assert squatter's rights and gain full ownership over my brain space, if he wanted. To be honest, I'm still in a daze over what happened, over how angry he was at me.

As if she's *in any position to tell other people how to live their lives!*

It was a low blow. But I can't help feel like he's right. It didn't exactly come from nowhere, either; Deen even tried to talk me out of my decision to go to med school, as if I was making some terrible decision that was obvious to everyone but me. Foxx had said something similar, too, when I told him I wasn't going to pursue dance. *Is that really such a pipe dream?*

It was as if at the wedding, all of the hidden feelings Deen locked inside came bursting out from him in a way I'd never seen before. There was something about him that was strange from the get-go. Like before the dance, when he'd said that I wouldn't have to see him again. At first, I thought he was being sarcastic, or facetious, like he always is. I mean, regardless of the wedding's outcome, we wouldn't have much of a reason to see each other, anyway. Not that I minded.

But thinking about it now, there was something much more final in his tone that night. As if he knew the fight would happen, or maybe was afraid it would. If he saw the plan on my phone, he must have known that I'd try to stop the wedding. That he would have to try and stop me. Is that why he looked so unbearably sad? Because the dance was actually a goodbye?

But then, why would he look so miserable?

And speaking of Foxx—he hasn't logged on to the guild chat for the past few days, either. It worries me. For Foxx not to log on, right after the fight with Deen, and right after Deen said Kas's name . . .

It feels like too much of a coincidence. But if he is Foxx, then why didn't he say anything sooner? Then again, if he did, would it have changed anything?

The dance, too—I can't stop replaying the dance in my head, only the image is tattered and blurry, like film that's been exposed to too much light. Like there's something I'm missing.

What am I missing?

It's the question I've been wrestling with since the wedding.

Kas.

I dunk a cinnamon graham cracker into a glass bowl of half-melted cookies and cream like the gremlin I am, before scooping a glob of ice cream into my mouth.

But does it even matter anymore?

The stairs creak and I snap my head toward the sound, graham cracker still jammed in my mouth.

It's Amira. With her hair down, she's ghostlike in an old blue bathrobe she's had since she was in high school.

"Hey," she says in a voice that doesn't quite sound like hers.

I suddenly choke on my graham cracker and bang at my chest with my fist. After what feels like the longest minute of my life, I manage to dislodge the cracker and swallow it back down. I take a loud gasp of air.

"H-hey," I manage finally.

Amira floats over to the fridge. She lugs out a jug of mango juice like it's too heavy and pours herself a glass. Her big brown eyes are half-lidded, like she's in a daze.

"Is Riz still with you?" I ask carefully.

Amira takes a long, slow sip. "She flew back home to Chicago late last night. But she says bye."

"Oh." My chest rattles with a shaky breath.

"Have you . . ." My throat is tight. I clear it, though it doesn't really help. "Have you been sleeping well?"

She laughs dryly. "I've slept better."

"I'm sorry."

"Mm."

Amira takes another sip as guilt bites at the pit of my belly.

There's a thick, hanging pause, and it's quiet. The house has never been so lifeless with Amira in it. Even the sound of my own breathing feels too loud.

"What are you going to do now?"

Amira's gaze glides to the ceiling. She lets her head dip for a while before answering.

"That's a good question. I'm honestly not really sure yet," she says. "But I'll take my time. Postpone the bar exam. Maybe head back to New York for now. Try to pick up the pieces."

She leans against the counter and swirls the mango juice in her glass, seemingly deep in thought.

"It was supposed to be one of the happiest days of my life," she whispers.

I wish I had the words to say to make her feel better. I wish I could let my guilt melt into white-hot righteous fury: toward Deen for interfering, toward Faisal for not being forthright in the first place. It'd be so much easier to say it was all their fault. But the reality is, I'm the one who stormed that stage. I'm the one who egged Deen on.

Amira looks at me, letting her long hair trail on the countertop. "When I heard everything Faisal did, you know what I felt, more than anything else? I was . . . disappointed."

I stare at my bowl, at the creamy dregs of melted ice cream. "He lied. Of course you'd be disappointed. He wasn't the guy he pretended to be."

"The funny thing is, it's not the content of the lie that upsets me, but the fact that he lied at all."

I look up at her, confused.

"I'm upset because he felt like he couldn't tell me. I thought by now, he'd feel comfortable enough to talk to me. About everything. Did I make him feel like he couldn't be honest with me? Did he think I couldn't handle it? That my love is that shallow?

"I guess it's like you said all along. He and I had only known each other three months before we decided to marry. Maybe I rushed it a little without even realizing because I was still coping with losing Mom. And maybe that wasn't enough time to build that trust."

But then Amira's eyes flicker with light. "See, but the thing that *really* gets me is, Faisal might have an excuse. So my question is, what is yours?"

I go still.

"You're my *sister*," she continues. "You of all people should know me. So why didn't you say anything sooner? Why didn't you talk to me?"

"I—" My head goes blank and I scramble for words. "I tried. I tried, but . . . every time I did, I felt like you were so happy. For the first time since Mom died. I didn't want to ruin that."

"And how's that working for you?" Amira shoots back.

My eyes begin to flood. I blink the wetness away. But she's right. She's so right.

Amira's face softens. "I'm sorry."

"No," I whimper, shaking my head. Fat tears leak down my cheeks. "*Please* do not say sorry to me right now. Please. I will *cry.*"

"You're already crying."

"I *know.*"

A teardrop plops into my melted ice cream and I wipe away at my face with the hems of my sleeves. I shouldn't be crying. I have no right to cry—Amira's the one with the Free Tears for Life card, and I really don't want to be one of those assholes who make things all about them. But it's like this dam has been broken inside me and I can't hold it all back in.

"I'm sorry," I manage. "I'm sorry I ruined your wedding and I'm sorry I didn't tell you from the start and I'm sorry I didn't tell you about Deen. I'm *sorry.*"

Amira sets her glass down—at least, I think she does, because it's hard to see right now—and walks over to me. She tugs on my arm and pulls me into a hug.

She's warm. "Don't hug me, I'll cry harder."

"I know." She rests her cheek on my quaking shoulders. "But if you're really sorry, then promise me that from now on, you'll talk to me. That's all I ask."

I nod, and more fat droplets escape from my eyes.

"No matter what. No matter any reservations or worries you might have. Even when we get older and it gets harder and harder to stay in contact. With Mom gone, who else are we going to talk to anyway?"

I make an ugly sound, something between a wet laugh and a sob. A slob, maybe. It'd be fitting.

"Promise me?"

"I promise."

"Good." She holds me a little tighter.

I squeeze my eyes shut and just let her hold me. And for the first time in forever, I feel like Amira's baby sister, and I'm okay with it because right now, in her arms, in this kitchen, it's like I remember how to breathe again.

I'm upstairs in Dad's room.

After our talk, Amira went back to New York, and Dad isn't home yet, so I take the opportunity to do something I've been putting off for over a year now.

I take a deep breath, steeling myself, and open Mom's closet door, which swings open with a groan.

I step inside and I'm immediately swept by the familiar smell of antibacterial Softsoap and jasmine oil.

But the smell feels weaker today, for some reason. Time is fading it away.

The thought makes my chest ache.

But.

I drop a big, empty cardboard box in the center of the closet, and let the other flattened boxes I've tucked beneath my armpit fall to the ground.

"The sooner you get it over with, the better, right?" I tell the closet.

The closet doesn't answer back, and for that, I am grateful.

I click play on a jazz-hop playlist on my phone, roll up my sleeves—still damp from my earlier sob fest—and begin folding up Mom's clothes. Each piece has a memory attached to it: the white T-shirt with the Cal State logo that Mom wore to my school picnic in fifth grade. The black dress Mom wore to that anniversary dinner Amira and I planned for her and Dad. The baggy jeans with the green paint stain on the left leg was from when Mom had to help me with my third-grade class project, when I had to build a leprechaun trap. I find a fake pearl necklace in one of her sweaters, one she'd let me borrow for my high school performance of *Beauty and the Beast* (I played one of three feather dusters). All pieces of our life, stitched in fabric and leather and beads. An entire existence, reduced to a single closet.

Slowly but surely, though, the closet begins to empty. It's when I reach the back corner of her closet that I hesitate—not because I'm tired, but because this was where we put the clothes that were easier for her to put on as her disease progressed.

All bad memories.

I check the pockets of her cardigans and find tissues and wet wipes, vitamins and pills. An old prescription card. A number for another ENT specialist. Seeing these again—the memories are too painful, too raw. Grief starts to claw its way up my throat. But I can't let Dad and Amira do this.

So it's up to me.

My hands graze a soft black cardigan, one Mom asked me to cut holes in the sleeves of so she could stick her thumbs through. She wore this one the most. Except, instead of her, it smells stale, like disinfectant. Like a hospital.

My fingers reach into the pocket and find a crumpled, roughly folded piece of paper.

I pull it out, expecting another doctor's note. Slowly, I unfold the paper. It's a page from the legal pad I gave her so she could communicate.

My ribs knit tightly together as I recognize the shaky handwriting. I begin to read:

My little Kiran, my sweetest heart,

I'm sorry to leave you so soon. I've tried so hard to steer you, and there's so much more I want to tell you. This letter will have to suffice for now.

I know I told you to look after Amira and your dad. But that doesn't mean you take on the world by yourself. You've always been so strong. But being strong means trusting them to take on their own battles once in a while. Do that for me and I promise everything will be fine. That's what it means to be family.

I'm so proud of you. Even though I'll be gone, take a deep breath and don't be afraid. No matter how you might feel, you are ready to go off on your own, to follow your heart. I hope that you will. But most important, don't let anyone make you feel like you can't do what you want to do. Not even me. Not even you.

It must have taken her forever to write this. My hands tremble. It's like the rest of the world has fallen away. Like nothing and everything suddenly makes sense. Like Mom was giving me the permission I didn't even know I needed.

The permission to just *be*.

And yet, it was so like her to say exactly what I needed to hear, exactly what I needed it most.

It was so like her.

Alone, in the safety and quiet of my mom's closet, I hug my mom's letter to my chest, and I cry again.

Only this time, I'm smiling, too.

CHAPTER 34

DEEN

Thursday, August 26

"BROTHER DEEN!"

Imam Obaid's voice catches my attention, and I find him standing at the main entrance to the masjid. He waves me over, his toothy grin a crescent moon against his black beard.

I can't believe I'm back where it all started: the masjid.

I shove my hands into my pockets and lumber over to him.

"Come, come, don't be shy!" calls the imam cheerfully. "Although after the wedding, I guess you can't really help it, huh?" He laughs loudly, slapping my back so hard I stumble into the masjid.

It's been four days now, but it feels like a year since Amira called off the wedding. Yesterday, I had to take Professor Pryce's Intro to Poli-Sci exam at eight in the morning, which I'm pretty sure has to constitute some kind of labor law or human rights violation. When I expressed this to Professor Pryce, he rubbed at his temples and informed me that if I'd bothered to be better about my attendance, I would have learned that no such laws exist. We agreed to disagree.

But when I wasn't studying at the last minute, I was in New Jersey, hovering by Faisal's door.

"*You've humiliated us all,*" Mom had said the night of the wedding as we drove back to the house; Mom driving with her high heels in her lap and the hair she'd gotten done at the salon completely frazzled, Dad staring ahead, his glasses reflecting the reds and greens of traffic lights. And Faisal, in a dazed silence, sitting in the back. Alone.

I cradle my head in my hands as my temples throb. Mom didn't care that Faisal had just lost the love of his life. All she cared about was that I'd embarrassed her, that I'd ruined her perfectly laid out plans to regain her status as community linchpin, plans that hinged on Faisal's big redemptive wedding.

The last time Faisal locked himself in his room like this, I was afraid he'd never come out again. The only hope I had was that this time, the protein drinks in the kitchen fridge were disappearing at the usual steady rate. Still, though. I got so worried, I almost responded to one of Kas's dozens of messages on the guild chat asking if I was okay. Except I don't even know how to talk to her anymore. As much as I might want to.

Even Haris tried to coax Faisal out. To no avail.

But on the third day, Faisal finally stepped outside, went into my room, and charged at me with a pointed finger.

"Masjid."

I fumbled for my phone, which I'd nearly dropped when he threw open the door. "W-what?"

"Go to the masjid. Imam Obaid is waiting for you."

And with that, he left, retreating to his bedroom again.

Which is why I'm here at the masjid now. Even with all those muscles, I've never seen Faisal hurt a fly. But lately I've been feeling like less than a fly—a runty maggot, maybe—and I really don't want to test him.

I slip off my sneakers and shove them in a cubbyhole before following the imam deeper into the masjid, into the prayer area. It's a Thursday afternoon, so it's pretty quiet, and the air is stagnant, smelling faintly of sweaty socks and spicy pakora. Weirdly comforting smells. Now that Kiran's not here and I can actually look around, I start remembering things I'd tucked in the back of my head, seemingly insignificant, at the time. Like how after Sunday school classes ended for the day and I'd finished the afternoon prayer, Dad would pick me up and we'd stop by this local Mexican joint for fish tacos. Maybe it was his way of trying to bond, even though we'd usually just eat in silence. Or when prayer would begin, there'd always be some guy correcting everyone's positions, telling us all to stand shoulder to shoulder. At the time, it was annoying being shifted around on the floor, being sternly told that to leave space between a brother in prayer was to leave space for the devil.

But in its predictability, in the unwavering routine of it, it became comforting, too. Like the chirrups of morning birds. Or the evening call to dinner at the table.

It'd been a while since I'd heard any of it.

I take a seat in front of the imam at the front of the prayer room. I half expected Faisal to be here, too. But it's just the two of us.

"Do you know why your brother wanted you to come see me?" the imam asks, hands on his knees.

I jut out my bottom lip and shake my head. "N-nope."

"I thought as much." He watches my wandering eyes and smiles softly.

"You don't come to the masjid, do you?"

"Well, I'm in college in New York, so . . ." I shift uncomfortably.

"Do you go to the masjid there?"

"I, uh . . ." I stopped going to the masjid after the fire. At first, it wasn't an intentional thing. There'd been so much happening all at once that I didn't have time to think about anything else that wasn't right in front of me that wasn't Faisal. And when I tried to pray again, months later, my body felt stiff. Like it'd forgotten how to pray, or worse, like my body was resisting. I didn't want to pray anymore. I didn't want to talk to God anymore. As far as I was concerned, God didn't want to talk to me.

And then I went to college, and Friday prayer became Friday night happy hour in my dorm.

"Hmm." Imam Obaid runs his fingers through his beard. "You know, I find that there is something about returning to the masjid after so long that feels like coming back home. Maybe it's because, in a way, it is a home. A place for us. And there will always be a space for you here. You need only ask. God's words, not mine."

I'm not sure how to respond, so I don't. I'm still not even sure why I'm here.

The imam seems to sense this. "I know about Faisal," he says. "In our marriage counseling sessions, we talked about his past, one-on-one. He told me everything."

My eyes widen. I get that Faisal would have to talk about at least some heavy stuff for marriage counseling, but I'm shocked he'd risk telling anyone, even an imam, the full truth.

. . . Which means the imam knows my secret, too.

I suddenly feel naked. In a masjid, of all places.

"Don't look at me like that," says Imam Obaid. "I'm not going to cast you out or stone you to death."

"Sorry. Reflex."

The imam sighs. "Based on what has happened to you and Faisal, I also understand your outburst at the wedding. And Faisal does, too. *That* is why he wanted you to come here today. So we could talk about it."

"Oh." I don't know if that's comforting or not.

"Deen. What happened at the wedding—it's a symptom of what you've been going through for the past three years. The pressure you've been putting on yourself. And when you let that kind of pressure build, we get outbursts with a very, very wide impact zone." His voice is calming. "If you spend your life hung up on the guilt you feel for your brother, you're going to forget the people around you. The people who actually need you."

"Who said anything about guilt? I have a clean conscience, thank you."

"Deen."

I exhale. "Okay, sure. Fine. Maybe I do feel a little guilty." A lot guilty. "But it's easier said than done. I can't just not feel anything anymore. Trust me, I've tried."

"Your guilt is a bad habit you need to break."

"But why? What's wrong with it? It just means that I'm genuinely bummed out for him. And for good reason. Even when we were kids, our parents constantly compared the two of us, and let's be real, I was the favorite. He'd get bullied at home by our parents, and if he wasn't at home, he was at school, getting bullied by other kids.

"And yet, despite it all, despite how much my brother should theoretically hate my guts, he's still the most selfless person I know. So yeah, of course I'm gonna feel guilty—how can I not, when life's only served him a never-ending buffet of Bad Times?"

And there's nothing I've been able to do to help.

"It's not up to you to ease Faisal's pain," the imam says.

"Sure. *Sure.* Is this the part where you tell me all the bullying Faisal's endured was some kind of test? That God only tests the righteous and all that?" My voice betrays how frustrated I still feel. "The thing is, after God tests you, you're supposed to get rewarded, right? Like when God commands Abraham to kill his kid, and just before Abraham actually agrees and goes to kill his own son, God replaces his kid with a goat and says that he and his son will now become prophets as a reward for their faith. This wedding, being with Amira—that was supposed to be the *goat.*"

And I ruined it.

"The reason why I feel like shit all the time is because I've watched my brother be the nicest person in the world, but the world keeps doling him punishment after punishment. It makes no sense. If bad things keep happening to good people, then either there's no God or there's no justice in the world, so what the hell is the point? How is that *fair*?"

My fingers grow numb in my lap. Talking about it now sets off a spiral of feelings in motion: Guilt. Anger. Frustration. Helplessness. Sadness. It all whirls in my belly in a mocking dance with no sign of easing up, and I feel like I might just vomit it all on the rug. More reason for God to forsake my heathen ass.

"Do you think that means he should *stop* being good?" the imam asks.

"No. I don't know. Maybe?"

"Hmm." The imam looks thoughtful. "Regardless of your feelings on Allah subhanahu wa ta'ala—whether or not you believe it makes sense to do 'good' because it's your ticket to heaven—society would fall apart if people stopped trying to be decent human beings. It's the Hobbesian idea of a social contract: if we all didn't agree on a set of basic morals, we'd all descend into a war of all against all.

"Plus, in a world like ours," he adds softly, "trying to do good is all we *can* do, and keep doing. And I believe it's how Faisal feels, too."

I meet the imam's steady gaze.

"You know your name, Deen? What it means?" Imam Obaid asks finally.

I sigh and nod tiredly. "Faith."

Imam Obaid clicks his tongue. "A common misconception. But I don't think it quite captures the nuance. The word *deen* comes from the Arabic root *dayana*. One meaning is to discipline, like to discipline one's soul. More simply, though, it means debt. The debt we owe to God. Like in the Day of Judgment, Yawm al-Din. The day we must pay our debts.

"Your problem, I think, is that you live up to your name far more than any person should have to. Tell me honestly, Deen. Do you think your brother knows you're sorry? In your heart of hearts, do you think your brother has forgiven you?"

The question makes my breath hitch. I close my eyes briefly, and something in me softens.

Faisal's hopeful eyes.

The way he still asks me to pray with him.

The way he thinks I'm a better person than I am.

This is beneath you.

"Yes," I answer. And I think I believe it.

"Then the issue here is that you need to forgive yourself so you can move forward." He smiles. "I would say, first start with the people you've hurt, other than your brother. Gain their forgiveness and work your way up."

He gets to his feet, his knees cracking.

"What you feel right now—it seems to me that it means the test isn't over yet."

I blink, confused. It's something so profoundly simple, so painfully obvious, that I'm at a loss for words.

Professor Pryce. Vinny. Kiran.

Even Kas, if she's finally realized who I am.

I've been shitty to them all, letting it all pile up. I was so busy trying to make sure the wedding was perfect that I didn't care who

I stepped on to do it. *No matter what.* A total M&D move. And I nearly lost everyone because of it.

But I want to be better.

Imam Obaid glances at the clock on the back wall.

"Ah, zuhr time. Shall we?"

He reaches a hand toward me.

I look at it warily. But there's no fighting it.

And maybe part of me doesn't really want to anymore.

"Sure," I reply.

I grab his hand, and Imam Obaid pulls me up.

Later, when I get home, I open my laptop and log on to Cambria.

And I type out a final message to Kas.

LOADING

[CAMBRIA: THE EVOLUTION EXPANSION PACK]

[ROANA GUILD CHAT ROOM]

[Private Message:]

Kas,

Thank you for being my best friend these past few years.

But now I have to go. This place has been a dumping ground and a safe space to process a lot. And I've had a lot to process.

It's time for me to stop running and face things head-on. I'm ready to.

And I have you to thank for that. Whether you meant to or not, you've been a great teacher, for many things. I'm glad I took a chance on you.

I hope someday, I'll be able to throw open my proverbial trench coat and reveal all the bare-naked truth of myself to you.

Until then, I mean it when I say
I'll miss you.

See you on the other side.

Foxx

CHAPTER 35
KIRAN

Thursday, August 26

THE DOORBELL RINGS, MAKING ME jump in my chair.

I'd been reading a message from Foxx for the hundredth time, trying to make sense of it. *What do you mean, you have to go?* I type back. But Cambria pings back with an alert:

[The Player Account you are trying to Private Message has been deactivated.]

I don't know what to make of it. Why would he delete his account? Unless it really is . . .

And what does he mean, he'll see me on the other side?

The doorbell rings again.

"I'll get it!" I shout, hopping onto the landing of the stairs and leaping every other step.

I'm hoping it's the GrubHub delivery person with Asher's promise of prepaid ice cream, which, right now, I could really use.

Except when I throw open the door, it is *not* the GrubHub delivery person.

"Assalamu alaikum," says Faisal. He puts a hand up, and I can't tell whether he means it as a greeting or if he's trying to reassure me that he comes in peace.

I implode on the spot.

I'm in my pj's: black-and-pink flannel bottoms and an old gray jersey cotton tee with an obvious peanut butter stain over my left boob. I'm wearing my glasses, too—the ones with the chipped lens that I'm too lazy to get fixed. Pretty sure I haven't brushed my hair all day, either, so. Keeping it classy, Kiran.

"What are you doing here?" I ask, my voice shooting up five octaves. Oh God. Is he here to kill me for ruining the wedding? Strangle me with his big beefy arms so my dad can find my body, like a warning?

"Um . . ." Faisal blinks hard and looks away.

I grip the door tighter. "Are—are you here for Amira? Because she's not here!"

"No," Faisal answers. He bows his head. "Actually, I was hoping I could get a chance to talk to your dad. I owe him an apology."

Huh. That's . . . unexpected. And brave. If *I* ever saw my in-laws again—or, almost in-laws—I'd turn tail and sprint in the opposite direction.

Still, I'm wary. But I open the door wider and let him in.

Faisal takes off his shoes and I wait for him. I forgot just how tall he really is. Most of the times I've seen him, he's been sitting down, or slumped over with that crappy posture of his. But although his features are less sharp than usual, and his eyelids are swollen and red-rimmed, his back is straight. Alert. Determined, even.

He smells a little like Deen, I realize.

He sets his shoes neatly by the door. "Is your dad—?"

"Oh! Sorry. Yeah. He's upstairs."

Faisal follows me toward the stairs, and I try not to think about how hyperaware I am that he's behind me and could easily ninja-chop my neck if he wanted. I guess I couldn't blame him if he wanted to. At first, I thought Deen was exaggerating when he said ruining the wedding would mean ruining Faisal's life, but after seeing Faisal's face that night—how broken he looked—I can't help but feel like there might have been some truth to it.

I wonder how he's holding up. Not that it matters now.

What's done is done.

We reach Dad's bedroom door. I knock. "Dad? Faisal's here to see you."

Silence.

I knock again. "Dad?"

When I still get no response, I crack open the door and peek inside.

"Hey, Dad—?"

And then I see him.

A crumpled body, lying on the floor at the front of his bed.

My heart leaps to my throat.

"Dad!"

I throw the door open and run to him. He doesn't stir.

Carefully, I turn Dad over onto his back. His eyes are closed. I put my ear to his chest. He's still breathing, only it's shallow.

Too shallow.

How? Why? *When?*

"Dad, please." My eyes sting. "Wake up."

I hear Faisal's voice behind me. He's on the phone with someone.

After a minute, he kneels at my side and gently puts his fingers to Dad's neck, listening for his pulse.

"I just called an ambulance. They're on their way," he says when he's done. He looks at me, eyes soft, his heavy eyebrows crinkled with concern.

I grab Faisal's arm. "What happened to him?" Even as I ask, my brain frantically sifts for answers. It was obvious Dad was feeling tired all the time. He'd said he wasn't feeling well, but I'd waved it off as a summer cold. Nothing to worry about.

I'm a little worried about him, Amira had said a couple of weeks before the wedding.

Of course. Even she had noticed something was off. How did I not see it sooner? Why didn't I pay closer attention?

It was supposed to be nothing to worry about.

"I don't know. But we'll find out soon," Faisal answers calmly. His voice sounds so far away.

"What am I supposed to do? What if he—" I can't bring myself to say it. I won't say it.

I shudder, gasping for air; my rib cage feels like it's closing in on me, suffocating me.

"Breathe, Kiran." Faisal puts his hand on my shoulder. "It's going to be all right. I'm here. Your dad is here. He's still breathing. So now we need to breathe so we can help him."

I try to slow my breathing. Faisal's hand is warm and strangely soothing. Not wholly unlike Amira's.

"Okay," I say finally, but it comes out like a sob.

"I've got you." He lifts me up from beneath my arms like I weigh nothing. "The ambulance'll be here any minute. I'm going to drive you to the hospital, all right? So I need you to change into some nice warm clothes and we'll go. I'll stay right here with your dad."

I nod and move, like a mechanical windup doll, to my room to change.

And I try not to think about how I'm going to tell Amira.

"Here."

Faisal hands me a Styrofoam cup of tea.

"Thanks." I take the cup and blow on it.

He takes a seat next to me in the hospital waiting room. It's the same hospital where Dad works—Penn—so it's weird being here like this. I keep expecting to spot Dad in his white lab coat, that he'll walk over and tell me to wait a couple more minutes before we head over to Reading Terminal for lunch. We did that a lot. After Mom died.

The thing about hospitals? No one's ever happy to be in one. And being in one now is bringing up all sorts of bad memories.

It's funny. I'm grateful Faisal's here. Plus, he knew exactly what to do. Unlike me. More reason to rethink med school.

I drink slowly. It hits me then: this is the first time I've ever talked to Faisal alone.

"I bumped into the doctor in the hallway," he says, pulling me from my thoughts.

I almost spill the rest of my tea all over my lap. "What'd they say?"

"She's going to run a couple more tests, but most likely, it's stress."

"Stress," I echo.

Faisal chuckles. "I know. But stress can mess a person up. His blood pressure was really high. He must not have been sleeping well, either. He's exhausted and dehydrated."

"But . . . *stress* . . . ?" I stare ahead, my head blank. A hundred terrible scenarios had been churning through my head for the past hour, all progressively worse than the last, until finally, I kept imagining standing over Dad's grave, alone.

But it was just stress.

I slump in my chair.

"It's nothing rest won't fix. Granted, he still needs to take some time off, from everything. Between"—he swallows—"the wedding and moving and work, it's too much for anyone."

My eyes narrow. "Aren't you in the same boat? Aren't you supposed to be preparing to move to California?"

Faisal's face falls. "After everything that's happened, I'm not really sure . . ." Faisal glances over at me, and seeing my expression, he suddenly flexes a melon-shaped bicep. "But don't worry,

I'm young and healthy."

"Alhamdulillah," I say reflexively.

For a beat, Faisal says nothing.

Then the corner of his mouth curls up, and he nods in agreement, his eyes shining.

"Alhamdulillah."

We sit in silence. I'm surprised by how not weird it feels, considering everything.

If I had talked to Faisal sooner, would he have told Amira? Now I'm not so sure he would.

"I'm sorry, by the way," I mutter. "It—it wasn't personal." I regret saying it right away; it sounds so cliché, so condescending.

But it doesn't seem to bother Faisal. "Even if it was, it's okay. I understand why you'd want Amira to know the truth," he murmurs.

"So . . ." I swallow nervously. "Why *didn't* you just tell her?"

"It's complicated."

"So I've heard."

Faisal huffs through his nose, a bitter, self-deprecating sound. "You already heard most of the story from Leah, yeah?"

"Yeah."

"Except Deen said it wasn't the full story. And he's right." He breathes. "For what it's worth, I think I owe you the full story."

My pulse quickens. I want to know. The full story doesn't change anything, of course, and I have no way of knowing if it's even true. Except Faisal doesn't have anything to gain from telling me the truth now.

Nothing will change.

Deen flashes through my mind.

But maybe . . .

I clutch my cup in my lap and brace myself.

"About three-ish years ago," Faisal begins, "I was in a pretty bad place. I was in my last year of college. I'm sure Leah told you, but I was bullied for most of my life. It was mostly these two guys—one of whom was Leah's older brother. Sometimes, it'd be other people. Deen once joked it's because I had a 'punchable face.' Maybe because I was scrawny and brown or something. We went to a school that was pretty good as far as schools go, except I was one of maybe three brown kids in the entire school. So I'm sure that factored in, too. When I told Mom and Dad about it, they told me to talk to my teachers. Which I did, a hundred times. Except teachers wouldn't do anything about it. That was the problem. In the end, my parents told me to just *ignore* the bullies.

"At the end of the day, I think all my parents ever really cared about was my grades. Not that I blame them. It's that old-school Asian immigrant mentality. They struggled to come here to give us opportunities they didn't have, or they had to fight tooth and nail for. So of course they wanted me to take advantage of it.

"And Deen . . . Deen was too young to help. Even if he was older, I don't really know what he could have done."

I exhale shakily. *Three years ago.* Around the time Deen started to pull away.

"Anyway, that was middle school and most of high school. Once Leah and I started to get close, we started to lean on each other, for better or worse. Honestly, she was my only friend for a while. She hated her brother, too, so. Enemy of my enemy. Apparently her family was pretty messed up. They treated her like crap, but also demanded perfection. That's when we got introduced to focus drugs. Like Adderall."

I know this part. Except somehow it sounds worse hearing it directly from Faisal.

"Focus drugs became my life raft. I wanted to keep my grades up to make sure my parents stayed happy—though looking back on it, I really should have sat them down and talked to them. But I digress." He smiles weakly. "In the end, Adderall was just the start. And even in college, I ended up attracting the wrong crowd, except college kids are a lot more violent. The more crap that kept happening to me, the more drugs I'd take. It got so bad that one time I passed out at home in the bathroom and hit my head. Bled all over the floor. Almost gave Deen a heart attack.

"Except I didn't care. I didn't see how it was affecting me or my parents or even Deen. I was being stupid. I didn't know how to reach out to get help. Eventually my parents just gave up on me. And I think that scared the shit out of Deen. Despite it all, though, he didn't once blame me. He blamed himself."

Something in my chest unfurls, aching.

"But Deen also blamed Leah's brother. The final straw happened when I came home to visit one weekend. My parents and I had a huge fight, so I went out and bumped into Leah's brother in a parking lot. He beat me senseless. Broke my jaw. So later that night, while Deen was still in high school, he snuck over to their house and set his car on fire.

"Except it was windy that night, and he lost control of the flames. He called me, screaming. I thought he was dying. But by the time I got there, the house was almost completely burned to the ground, ambulances and police cars everywhere. Everything smelled like smoke.

"It was the wake-up call I needed. *I* drove him to that point. He just wanted to help. When I realized the police were going to arrest him, just a kid, I—"

A muscle in his jaw twitches. "Deen was class president. Perfect grades, near perfect SAT score. I couldn't let them ruin his life when it was my fault. So I told my parents and the cops I did it. It wasn't hard to convince them.

"They arrested me instead. My parents spent a lot of money covering it up, paid a big-time lawyer to get the judge to lower the charge." Faisal's expression grows dark. "It kind of made me pretty disillusioned with lawyers. Which"—he shrugs—"I guess was a *good* thing, since I wasn't able to go to law school after that."

"For obvious reasons, Deen and I have kept it a secret, and I don't like talking about it. Especially because if the truth gets out, it could mess up Deen's future. I've been on pretty thin ice with my parents since then, too, so. Understandably. But. Now that the wedding's over, I hope he'll find himself. We both could use some soul searching. My hope is that the wedding . . . that *that* was the wake-up call *Deen* needed."

My heart's no longer jackhammering because it's been caught and stifled in a wild tangle of feelings.

I wasn't prepared for this, at all. In just a few minutes, Faisal went from Personal Enemy Number One to . . .

I don't even know what.

And Deen . . .

I can't believe he went through all of this alone.

I wish I'd known.

I don't regret stopping the wedding. But right now, I feel like shit. This whole time, I thought I was fighting on the side of truth, when really I was just forcing Faisal to expose his own trauma to his parents—and an entire justice system, frankly—who'd completely failed him.

"So you're not moving to California?" I ask again. "Sounds like getting away from your parents might be a good thing."

Faisal shakes his head. "My parents were going to cover the cost of the move. Between you and me, I barely have enough money on my own right now. And they weren't happy about pouring so much money into a wedding that never happened." He laughs lightheartedly, but there's a film of sadness over it.

"Oh." I look down at my cup. I was holding it so tight, there's a seam down the middle of it.

Faisal rubs the back of his neck sheepishly. "You know, when Deen said that thing, about you two dating before . . . I think I can see it. You're both actually really similar. Both fiercely protective of your families, to a fault. Stubborn. Prideful, even."

I snort. "Sounds about right."

"Only, you're definitely way more straightforward."

"And Deen's a total desi fuckboy?"

Faisal throws his head back and laughs. "Yeah. But I'm pretty sure that's a mask he puts up."

"Yeah. Maybe you're right."

Faisal stands up and stretches his arms behind his back.

"Honestly, I don't know how to be a good brother," he tells me. "Or anything, really. All in all, I've been a complete and utter ass."

He looks at me. "But Deen . . . he can be a bit of a moron sometimes. It's part of the genetic Malik package, I'm afraid. And I know he might have come across as a dick in his efforts to look out for me. But if there's one thing you can trust me on, it's that he's one of the good ones."

Something about the way he says it makes my cheeks burn a little. I fight the urge to look at my phone.

I clear my throat. "Hey, if—if my dad gets better—"

"*When*," Faisal corrects me. "Inshallah."

"Right. When my dad gets better . . ." I swallow. "Maybe there's something we could do. About getting you to California. If you want."

"That's kind, but . . . no, thank you. I'll find a way. I want to find a way." He clenches a fist. "And I will. If I can't even do that, then I really don't have any business being with Amira."

I suddenly remember what Dad said about love. That love is messy. That love is *work*.

"Does that mean you're still going to try?" I ask. "Being with her, I mean."

Faisal grins. It looks so much like Deen's that it knocks the air out of my chest.

"Well, wouldn't you, if you could?"

I don't know why, but I'm hit with a familiar, stinging pressure behind my eyes.

"Yes," I reply. "I definitely would."

CHAPTER 36

DEEN

Friday, August 27

THERE'S SOMETHING WONDERFULLY CHARMING ABOUT three-step plans. Kiran had the right idea.

And today, I'm working on steps one and two.

"Come in." Professor Pryce's voice comes from inside his office.

I sidle in. "Hi," I say cheerfully. I don't wait for him to give me permission and take a seat at the chair in front of his desk.

Professor Pryce sets down the paper he was reading. "Deen. To what do I owe this pleasure, especially when the summer term is over," he asks jovially, though the expression on his face finishes the sentence for him: *Especially when the summer term is over, and I have literally no reason or desire to see your face ever again?*

Which, fair enough.

I lean back in the chair. "I just want to say that I look forward to taking Intermediate Poli-Sci with you next semester."

Professor Pryce's eyes narrow behind his K-pop idol wire-frame glasses. "It's interesting that you say that, Deen, because unfortunately, you would have had to get a 2.3 or above in this class to move on to the next level. But with all your absences and incompletes, I have to give you a 2.0."

"Is that factoring in my final exam?"

Professor Pryce sighs and rubs the bridge of his nose. "Honestly? You somehow managed a 3.6 on the final. But that's not enough to bring up your final grade."

I had a feeling that would be the case. But still. I have to try.

I lick my lips. "That's what I wanted to talk to you about, actually. What if—and stick with me now—*what if* you made an exception?"

Professor Pryce practically does a full-on double take, blinking hard like a freaking meme. "And *why* would I do that?"

I take a breath. "Because I want to take your class next semester. I apologize for not taking the class seriously sooner. But I'm going to now. You obviously have no reason to let me take another one of your classes, especially when you could give that slot to another student who has actually shown interest since the beginning. But it's like you said before. If I applied myself, I could go places. I'm ready to apply myself."

Professor Pryce's breath stops. He regains himself quickly. "Who are you and what have you done with Deen?" he asks, seemingly 100 percent serious.

"Someone who wants to prove that they're not wasting their potential," I respond, equally serious.

He stares at me for a while, like he's trying to read me. Or determine if I'm actually a robot clone.

Finally, he steeples his fingers on his desk and closes his eyes, like it pains him to say it. "I want you to write me a three-page paper on exactly what you hope to gain by taking Intermediate Poli-Sci with me. Email it to me tomorrow. Show me you're truly serious. Then we'll talk."

I grin, widely. It's a small win. But it's a win.

I'll take it.

"Yes. Yes! I'm so serious. Positively serious." I clap my hands together and stand up. "Consider it done."

"Okay, well." Professor Pryce picks up the paper he was reading. "We'll see."

I back away, beaming. "Seriously. Thanks, Professor. You won't regret it."

"Close the door behind you."

"Got it, Professor Pryce." I throw him a pair of finger guns. "My man."

And I close the door.

I'm lugging my backpack and two giant Bluetooth speakers (formerly Faisal's) down Fifth Avenue to my next destination and my biceps are burning. But I persevere, breathless and sweaty in places no human should ever be sweaty, until I reach the familiar red-brick building.

Rubin Hall.

I shoulder my way through the gold spinning doors and make my way up the stairs. Finally, I reach room 303.

With a groan, I set the speakers and my backpack down on

the floor, give myself a few minutes to catch my breath, and whip out my phone from my pocket. A couple of taps later, I'm on my Spotify playlist.

My heart flutters nervously as I wipe my palms down my pants. Technically, I'm supposed to be holding one of the speakers over my head, like in the movies, but I'm pretty sure if I tried that now, my biceps would give in and the speaker would squash me like a bug.

I close my eyes. Hell, even dancing with Kiran at the wedding didn't make me this nervous. Maybe because she was with me, but here, I'm alone.

All this time you've been talking and giving me excuses, but not once have you even said you're sorry, Vinny's words echo through my head.

Well, Vinny, how's this for a sorry?

I press play.

The song starts, upbeat and bubbly, and soon, the bass line kicks in, vibrating through the hallway, making the floor shake beneath me. The vocalist sings, her voice a significantly higher pitch than mine, but that doesn't matter.

I clear my throat. And when she sings the chorus, I sing with her:

Love me, love me, say that you love me;
Fool me, fool me, go on and fool me;

I'm completely off tune and my voice keeps cracking trying to keep up with the singer's soprano and I feel as ridiculous as

I probably look, but it's New York and weirder things have happened. Plus, as the song goes on, I remember how much I actually like the song. Can't go wrong with the classics.

Around me, doors open and I feel the stares, both curious and annoyed. I glance over my shoulder; someone's recording me on their phone.

I'm almost halfway through the song when Vinny's door opens.

We make eye contact and I look away, trying not to think about the fact that this is absolutely humiliating, even if that's the point.

It's okay if you feel ridiculous. Dance is about letting yourself be—I don't know—vulnerable.

I put my hands on my hips and do an exaggerated sway. I don't even know what I'm doing at this point—it's not exactly a Kiran-choregraphed dance—but I'm rolling with it. I point at Vinny, lip-synching to the rest of the song.

The corner of Vinny's mouth twitches.

Someone lets out a whistle while another person laughs loudly behind us; I half expect it to be Kiran. The thought makes me laugh, too.

I end the song with a twirl and take a bow.

The entire hallway erupts with laughter and clapping.

I turn around and bow once more. "Thank you, thank you. I'll be here never again."

The excitement and curiosity of my little audience finally dies down and everyone retreats to their rooms. Everyone but Vinny.

I turn off the song and put away my phone. "God, I'm sweaty." I waft my arms a little. "I tried doing it outside the building, but then a cop looked at me like he was going to deport me back to hell."

"Hell, huh?" says Vinny.

I nod emphatically. "Right where I belong."

"Perhaps." Vinny folds his arms across his chest.

"Oh, I got something for you." I dig through my backpack and pull out a small box tied with blue ribbon I snagged from the Duane Reade down the street.

Vinny eyes it suspiciously before taking it from my hands. He opens it and his eyes go wide.

"You—you got me chicken tenders?" His voice cracks. "From the cafeteria?"

"I asked them to make me a fresh batch."

Vinny stares at them, his mouth pressed in a thin line. I don't know if I'm imagining it, but I think his eyes water.

"What you said before . . . you were right," I say. "I am a tool. Only a tool would do you dirty like that."

Vinny's expression remains unchanged, so I continue. "I got blindsided by my own . . . selfishness. I didn't see who or what was in front of me, and I'm sorry. I should have done more to help you with Amy."

Vinny wipes his nose with his sleeve. "Idiot."

I stare at my shoes.

"No. You're an idiot because you should know it's not just about Amy," he says. "I wanted you to have my back, man. That's all I've ever wanted."

I lift my head. "Of *course* I have your back. I suck at showing it,

I'll admit, but—I do." I take a step forward. "Whatever you want, you got. I owe you," I add, mumbling.

Vinny laughs at that and slaps my back. "You don't owe me a thing. Nothing but love, D-Money."

I smile.

Vinny closes his box of chicken tenders. "But let me kick your ass in pool and we'll call it even."

"Right now?"

"Right now."

I let out a shaky, relieved sigh. And I drape an arm around Vinny's shoulder.

"You got it, Vin."

CHAPTER 37

KIRAN

Friday, August 27

"DAD, YOU HAVE TO RELAX for at least five minutes," I argue.

After an overnight stay at the hospital with an IV drip and some TLC, he was well enough to get discharged. Faisal helped me get him back home first thing in the morning, and Dad proceeded to take a very long, very well-deserved nap.

Which is why keeping him in bed is proving impossible now.

"I've rested enough," he retorts, gently hitting my hand away. "The movers are coming tomorrow."

I try not to think about it. But it's hard when the house is practically empty, walls barren and all our stuff in boxes.

"Which is exactly why you need to rest. If you're flying to Houston tomorrow, you're going to need to be at one hundred percent." And I need him to rest so I can get to work; I'm supposed to be moving to campus dorms this weekend, and I still have last minute supplies I need to grab.

Dad grumbles. But he sits back against the headboard.

I pat his blanket. "I'm going to finish packing kitchen stuff. Call me if you need me?"

Dad says nothing; instead, he reaches for a book off his bedside table and begins to read.

I close the door behind me and sigh.

Amira pops her head out from the hallway bathroom and looks at me, concerned.

She'd meant to come later this evening to help with any last-minute packing but took a morning train in after I told her about Dad.

Of course, I told her about Faisal, too. Amira didn't really say anything about it, at first; she just looked . . . pensive.

"I should thank him," she said finally, her voice almost a whisper.

"I don't think he did it for your thanks," I replied honestly. Faisal isn't the kind of guy to have ulterior motives. I think I get it now.

"Even still." Her eyes flitted to the window. "I want to."

Later, I showed her Mom's letter and we both cried seemingly for hours. But it was . . . nice. I woke up feeling lighter than ever. Surer than ever.

Except for one tiny thing. One tiny *person*.

Back to the present. Amira's sleeves are rolled up and she's wearing a bandanna to cover her hair (we're wearing matching blue ones I found in storage). She looks adorable.

"Was he fighting you?" she asks.

"You know Dad," I respond, shrugging.

"That I do." She sighs and goes back to cleaning the bathroom. "Stubborn till the end. Guess that's where you get it from."

I can hear the grin in her voice.

The doorbell rings.

"Is that finally my ice cream delivery?" I say out loud.

Amira pops her head back out and rolls her sleeves back down. "Or Faisal?"

I head for the door. "Why, are you hoping?"

"No!"

I laugh and yank open the front door.

"Hey."

Deen Malik is standing at my doorstep. He's wearing a white T-shirt and jeans, and his hair's a little rumpled, but he seems . . . different somehow. Brighter, almost, like he's wiped away a grimy filter.

I finally find my voice. "Hey." I try to steady it. "What—what are you doing here?"

He smiles sadly. "I did say I'd come see you on the other side. Too hot for a trench coat, though."

It's like the entire world suddenly tilts backward. I grab the doorway to hold steady.

"Foxx." The name comes out in a gasp. "*You're* Foxx."

I feel the surge of a million synapses, a billion memories, connecting and falling into place.

Dancer, huh. Is that really such a pipe dream?

I want to be able to change the past.

I feel like all of this stuff *is bubbling in me, set to go off at any moment.*

If we met in real life, would you trust me?

And the song at the wedding . . . of course.

"Wasn't it obvious?" Deen asks, shoving his hands in his pockets sheepishly. "I mean, not that I even knew until recently."

"I—" I bite my lip. "I wasn't sure. The thought crossed my mind, but . . ." But I couldn't believe it. Didn't *want* to believe it.

Because if I did, if it were true . . .

"I'm sorry. I wanted to tell you sooner, but I—I didn't know how. With everything that happened—" Deen rubs the back of his neck, looks away. "Just please don't stab me in the heart like Foxx told you."

I laugh, but it comes out like a hysterical squeak.

He takes a step closer. "Also, I'm sorry, not just for the wedding, but for everything I've done. The wedding was kind of . . . a much-needed slap to the face. I need to stop bottling things up. The things I said to you, they were uncalled for, and I didn't mean them. I was just trying to—"

"Protect your brother. I know," I say. "I'm sorry, too. I was doing the same thing. Trying to protect Amira. With everything that's happened to us—"

"Like losing your mom? Yeah, it's understandable. You'd need time to process it all. Maybe more time than what Amira and Faisal had."

Love isn't a feeling; it's the act of planting a seed and putting in the time and care it needs to grow.

I smile. "Yeah."

We avoid looking at each other. I don't know what this strange, warm haze is between us. I don't know what's changed in the past few days. All I do know is that this feeling is something entirely different from anything I've felt from him before—it's not the Deen I knew from the past, or the Deen who's been getting in my way these few months. It's not even Foxx.

But it feels comfortable. And hesitant. Two awkward hands brushing their fingertips against each other for the first time, feeling each other out.

Deen clears his throat. "Honestly, if I didn't have you to talk to . . . if I didn't have Kas . . . who knows, maybe I would have blown up sooner. Maybe I would have done something worse." He chuckles darkly.

"Well, I'm glad she—I—could help," I reply. "But why did you delete your account?"

"Because Foxx is a lot better about talking through his feelings than I am. And I want to learn how to do that. I've relied on him way too long. If I want to get better, then . . ." He smiles sadly. "He had to go."

Deen takes a step back. "And so do I."

His words strike me in the stomach. "Wait, what?" I blink, confused. "So soon? Are you—are you sure you don't want to come in? Talk a little more?"

Deen raises his eyebrows. But then he shakes his head. "As much as I want to, I don't think I'm ready yet." He looks at me meaningfully.

I don't really know what he means by *ready*. But I don't pry further.

"Oh." I swallow a brittle lump.

We don't say anything for a bit.

Then his mouth quirks up in a small smile. "But I do still believe that Faisal and Amira are meant to be together. When that happens, I'm sure I'll see you again. And hopefully, by then, I'll be ready, too. So that next time—next time you ever need someone, I'll be there."

It happens so fast, I'm sure I imagined it: Deen's lips brush against my cheek, and there's a gentle, warm inhale against my skin. Like a tiny flame.

He pulls away. "I have to say, I'll miss our little fights. But I'll miss our dancing more."

I roll my eyes, even though I'm certain my cheeks are totally flushed.

Deen hops down our steps, past the giant white picket SOLD sign, to his parents' car parked on the road. I watch his back, the familiar line of his shoulders.

All throughout our conversation, I've struggled to find the words. But I find them now.

"See you soon," I call after him.

Deen looks over his shoulder to meet my eyes. His face bursts into a dimpled smile, so genuine that it makes my heart clench.

"Yes," he replies warmly. "See you soon."

THREE YEARS LATER

Friday, May 3

"I CAN'T BELIEVE THE SENIORS are leaving!" whines Alina, pouting and closing her eyes to hold back her tears.

Three of our freshman members, Nura, Geeta, and Tanvi, all glare at her. We're all backstage for our annual PENNaach South Asian Dance showcase.

"Stop. You're going to make me cry." I've been a member of PENNaach since my first day on campus, when Shreya, one of the current co-presidents, spotted me at orientation.

You have that dancer . . . vibe! she practically shouted, grabbing my hands. *The, the aura! You* have *to join.*

And so I did. Not that I had much of a choice in the matter. With Shreya's long, curly black hair, she has the demeanor of an adorable, excitable poodle. I could not say no.

It's also how I met Alina, who, like me, was equally horrified that there's no dance program here at Penn. But sometimes, the two of us have been meeting up at the Arts House Dance Company for more practice.

"Good! You *should* cry! The seniors have been, like, parents to us." Alina's huge eyes suddenly grow wider. "Wait! But this means . . . *we'll* be co-prezes." She grins. "The throne will be *ours*."

I snort. "You just did a full one-eighty in a matter of seconds. Also pretty sure we still need to do elections."

"For a freaking dance club? No, no, no. *We'll* be the only two rising seniors. The choice is *obvious*."

As Alina continues with her warm-up, I peek through the curtain. Shreya is warming up the floor, commanding the spotlight with a slow, classical fusion piece, all lithe and graceful and confident. It's mesmerizing to watch. But when she reaches the end of the song, the spotlight is supposed to go dark.

And when it lights up again, we'll all be onstage with her.

I'm nervous and excited, like a hundred tiny bees are buzzing wildly in my belly. The big group performance—our final goodbye to the PENNaach seniors—is the first dance that I alone choreographed. I barely had time; I've been juggling what feels like a hundred classes and prepping for next year, when I'll start applying for PA school. But I think it's a winner.

Plus, it'll be the first time Amira gets to see one of our shows. So it *has* to be good.

"Is she out there?" Alina asks.

I scan the audience. At first, I don't see her in any of the seats, but then I spot a familiar form, standing in one of the aisles with her phone up: Amira, recording the performance on her phone, clutching it with both hands like she can barely contain herself.

I smile. "Yep."

In the seat next to her is Faisal, looking a little out of place wearing a suit jacket over his shirt. But it's just like him to try too hard.

"It's time," says Nura, waving us over to the right wing of the stage. Outside, the lights dim.

Alina and I look at each other. We both take a deep breath in through our noses, timed perfectly, and let it out through our mouths. Our little ritual we've been doing since our very first performance.

Then she gives me a thumbs-up. "Let's do it."

All of us tiptoe onto the stage with Shreya and the other seniors, cloaked in darkness, and we crouch into tightly coiled balls around them, buds in a garden of flowers. It was Dad's idea, a garden-themed dance.

When the music bursts, so do we, frantic but sharp, our footsteps perfectly in sync, thudding against the stage like one heartbeat. Our limbs whip around us and our backs arch before we fall into another formation, a giant spinning ring. I hear someone whistle loudly, someone saying my name. I can't help it; I let out a loud laugh.

Finally the song ends, and I'm basking in the familiar afterglow and the frenzied applause. I take my place next to Alina for our bow. In the audience, Amira and Faisal are standing, twin smiles on their face. Pride, warm and buzzing and alive, swells in my chest. Shreya tackles me with a hug before Alina jumps in, too, and we become a jangled mess of limbs and tangled dupattas.

I follow the girls back to one of the wings. I can't wait to get out of these clothes, to go have dinner with Amira and Faisal and hear all about their upcoming move to San Diego. Together.

Except there's someone in my way, standing by the curtain, their face obscured by shadow. Shreya and Alina step back, smiling knowingly at me.

"What . . . ?" I step ahead.

"Long time no see," says a voice. A voice that strikes right into my chest.

He steps into the light.

It's been three years since I've last seen him, and although he's a little older, his features sharper, I immediately recognize the heavy-lidded dark eyes, the tiny mole beneath the left one.

And that stupid, insufferable, beautiful grin.

Deen.

ACKNOWLEDGMENTS

I could say it was a miracle that I was able to write *It All Comes Back to You*. When I first began writing, my mother had just passed away from ALS, and all the while, I was still reeling from the loss of my brother and my father before that. I had to learn, while writing a book about family, what it meant to live without mine.

Only, calling it a miracle would be a disservice to all the people who have reminded me that the word *family* is a dynamic, ever-changing thing, and that over time, it can take on new shapes and meaning. I have lost one kind of family, yes, but I've replaced it with a hundred others—and maybe that is the miracle. Thank you to the following people for giving me the strength to keep writing:

I owe a million thank-yous to the wonderful team at HarperCollins/Quill Tree, who brought life and color to this book: Rosemary Brosnan, Jon Howard, Gweneth Morton, David DeWitt, Erin Fitzsimmons, Sean Cavanagh, Vanessa Nuttry, Shannon Cox,

Audrey Diestelkamp, Jacquelynn Burke, Patty Rosati, Mimi Rankin, Katie Dutton, Jessica White, Veronica Ambrose, Allison Weintraub, and, of course, my lovely editor, Alex Cooper. I'm so, so grateful to be working with you.

Zahra Fatimah, you brilliant, beautiful soul. Thank you for giving me what is undoubtedly, in my humble opinion, the most beautiful cover illustration I have ever seen.

Hannah Bowman, a legend, a savior—I could go on, but you would probably roll your eyes and then get back to work on the *hundred* other things you are juggling (I'm half convinced you are a primordial spirit of justice masquerading as human).

Thank you to my Muslim sisters: Farheen, Hiba, Sana, Ayla, Madiha, and so many others who have been cheering me on throughout this wild journey.

Karuna Riazi, Samira Ahmed, and Sabaa Tahir, for pulling me up. Without these trailblazers, I would be utterly lost.

Marri and Kate for the always funny (and sometimes horrifying) memes that would keep me laughing well into the night. I adore you both so very much.

Gina Chen and Em X. Liu and Zayba Shahnaz, whose early enthusiasm for the book picked me up whenever I was down (which, frankly, was a lot). Thank God I met you. And Gina—thank you for the K-Pop that fueled my frantic edits. You are my fandom Aladdin, showing me whole new worlds.

Adam Silvera and Abigail Wen, who heard about this book idea before anyone else—thank you for being the best tour buddies, guiding lights, and friends.

Eric Smith and Swapna Krishna—thank you for being another

reason I can call Philadelphia home.

My Odyssey family: Shall I compare thee to a summer's day (in New Hampshire, during a six-week, caffeine-fueled writing workshop)? RK, beautiful little sister, my partner in crime; Jeremy, a.k.a. Turtle Sensei; Josh, my favorite frenemy; Linden and Pablo, the Goth parents of my dreams; Jeanne Cavelos, ringmaster of our carnival; and the rest of the Odyssey fellows: I love you all so much.

Cara Takemoto, my favorite (metaphorical, I swear!) fire starter. Thank you for always having my back, in video games and real life.

Shaan and Alina and Mariam, to whom I owe a million halal cheesesteaks and uncomfortable hugs (sorry I'm so bad at giving them).

All the readers, booksellers, bloggers, and TikTokers who've been so supportive: I see you and I'm forever grateful.

Stephen, the worst project partner I could ever ask to be stuck with, eleven years and counting. It's almost as though you have a crush on me, and, frankly, you should be embarrassed.

And finally, Shaz. I hope somewhere, you are watching over me, laughing as I flail through this strange little life. I wouldn't even mind if you laughed. After all, it's still—and always will be—my favorite sound.